SIGNS OF THE FATHER

A DANA DEMETER MYSTERY #2

A. F. WHITEHOUSE

COVER BY
MARK BURGESS

FOR V. J.

1

On a late Saturday afternoon in November, eight-year-old CiCi played hide and seek with four new friends in her backyard on the West Side of Chicago. CiCi ran around the gravel-filled yard shared with the church rectory next door, her condensed breaths puffing out like quick little clouds.

Crouched beneath an overturned wheelbarrow with a flat tire and flaking green paint, four-year-old Emma poked her blonde head out to check if CiCi had spied her.

CiCi had. "You're out! I found you! You're out!"

When Emma squealed and popped out of her shell, a shadow from the looming church darkened her face. The winter sun began its descent.

"I'm goin' inside with my mama," Emma said.

She ran past a sandbox to the parish hall doors, one propped slightly open with a small rock, only a few steps from where CiCi found her.

CiCi thought she could hear Emma's brother and twin sisters snickering and talking in muffled whispers, hidden from view but still tantalizingly near. Where were they? She clambered down the outside steps to the basement of her home and peered into the dark stairwell.

"Anyone in here?" She yelled the question.

Her voice echoed back, reflecting emptiness. Where were they? She ran back up the steps, blowing warmth onto her icy fingers, too stubborn to wear the mittens her mother pinned to her coat sleeves. She scooted across the large churchyard, her steps crunching on the small white stones covering the area in place of grass. Pigeons huddled together on the parish roof, beaks tucked into puffed-up breasts, and maintained the silence between the house and church.

Unable to find the three still hidden somewhere in the yard, CiCi checked behind the large stone statue of an angel stationed outside the doors of the parish hall. Three kids could hide there easy enough.

Empty. She stopped to listen for their laughing and whispering but the yard was hollow with quiet. The late afternoon cycled toward evening. The clouds covered the setting sun and the wind swirled around the churchyard, carrying a deeper chill. The church bell in its tower gonged once, as if the wind forced the note.

CiCi headed into the parish hall to warm up, thinking she might find the others inside. She needed to pee but the bathroom was on the second floor, so she began to climb the long flight of stairs. The setting sun's rays coursed through a dirty transom window above the entryway and threw the shape of her shadow ahead of her. She shrugged off her coat and carried it trailing behind her, mittens bumping over each step: up, up, up. As she climbed from bottom to top, she whispered the ABC song.

At the top of the stairs CiCi turned left and walked down a long narrow hallway toward the kitchen. The bathroom was in the parish hall beyond. She wrinkled her nose at the strong smell of coffee leaching into the hallway. The faint sound of running water grew louder as she hurried toward the kitchen, the need to pee more urgent. The wooden floor creaked as it shifted under her weight. She stopped at the kitchen entrance, a round archway built over a century ago, and strained to see inside the dark room. The sound of gushing water competed with the wind whipping against the exterior of the parish building.

Outside, the street lamps blinked on in response to the setting sun. Orange light struggled through the grimy windows to illuminate water catapulting from a faucet attached to a large metal sink. The water puzzled her. She glanced at the floor beside the sink. Someone sprawled there, the top of his head lit in garish orange, the rest of him hidden in the gloom.

CiCi dropped her coat and stepped into the kitchen. A motion detector activated the overhead fluorescent lights, startling her for a moment. She knew the man by the sink who lay on his stomach. It was the janitor, Mr. Nygaard. A large gash, black with blood, darkened the side of his head. Her stomach twisted and she felt clammy, like before throwing up, her need to get to the toilet starting to hurt.

She tiptoed between the wooden table and the big fridge, stooping next to him for a closer look. The floor under his head was covered with more blood than she ever saw before, spreading out like when she painted with watercolors. She wondered if there was any blood left inside him.

"Mr. Nygaard?" She barely heard her voice over the rush of water thundering in the sink.

CiCi couldn't tell if he was breathing. She pointed her index finger and poked his shoulder. It was soft and yielded to her touch. She leaned closer to his face to see if his closed eyelids moved, like her brother's did when he dreamed. Nothing.

CiCi exhaled after seeing him close up, unaware she'd held her breath when examining his body. Inhaling deeply, she smelled something bad in the kitchen, really bad, like poop and rotten bananas and coffee, too. A large urn was upended on the floor near Mr. Nygaard's head. Dried coffee grounds dusted irregular, brown splotches on the old wooden floor.

"This is bad, real bad," CiCi said. "I gotta tell Mama."

As she spoke the word *mama*, CiCi's yearning for safety and warmth suffused her small body and she let go, wetting herself.

"Maaaaaammmmmaaaaa," she wailed, thrusting herself away from the old janitor's cold, inert body. She scrambled toward the kitchen door as fast as her stubby legs could move.

2

Saturday, 11/16, 10:00 a.m.

"DANA! UP HERE!"

Father Andrew Miklasevich waves at me from near the front of the line that snakes out of the Elite Restaurant and trails down the sidewalk. I pass people standing behind him, ignoring their glares, and cut into the line to give the old priest a hug.

He holds me at arm's length and beams, giving me a thorough once-over. I avoid his direct gaze, remembering how bloodshot my eyes looked in the bathroom mirror before I left home this morning. "Good to see you, Dana," he says. "Thank you for meeting me on such short notice, and I apologize again for the early phone call."

"Early" means nine o'clock when his phone call jerked me awake after only four hours' sleep. I wave him off and light a Kool. We'll be seated soon and I want to beat my hangover into submission with nicotine. The Pepsi I drank on the way over didn't do the trick.

I'm tall, but at six-four Father Mik's got six inches over me. I squint up at the priest and gesture at a couple of homeless men selling copies of *StreetWise* near the Elite's front door, capturing customers coming and going. "You could pass for one of these street guys if you weren't wearing your collar."

His hooded blue eyes widen and he laughs, his warm breath clouding in the frigid air. Father Mik fingers the grey-flecked outgrowth that starts high on his cheeks and provides complete camouflage down to his Adam's apple. "Yes, I could at that. My housekeeper is always after me not to grow this facial hair, but then winter starts and I feel compelled to. In my mind it somehow goes along with Advent."

I nod even though I'm clueless about what he means. The line continues its steady progress toward and into the restaurant. We're on deck near the doors. I suck at the last two inches of the cigarette, greedy for the extra hit of nicotine close to the filter, and then pitch the butt into the street.

The plate glass window spanning the front of the restaurant where we stand with the crowd is steamy with condensation, blurry colored shapes suggesting movement within. A wiggly design emerges on the pane, traced by a small fingertip pressed against the inside of the glass. A napkin swipes away the artwork, leaving a dinner-plate-sized porthole view of the occupants inside. The face of a little girl— maybe two years old—presses against the cleared window area. She grins at the outside world.

An instant stab of joy ignites in me. This could be my child. Well, not this girl's age. I miscarried only six months ago. The little one slaps the glass until two big hands lift her and haul her away. She disappears—along with my joy.

Chris Sepsakos, the owner of the Elite, steps outside at the front of the line and makes eye contact with me, touches his watch and holds up five fingers. Good. Coffee soon. I respond with a thumbs up.

Once inside, we're ushered to a window booth with red leather seats and survey the masses still shivering in line. Father Mik and I chitchat after ordering some food but my effort at being social puts an added strain on my headache. A song in Greek complains in the background underneath numerous conversations, clanking dishes and silverware, and the persistent ding of the bell summoning the wait-staff to pick up their orders.

A busboy comes by and pours coffee. I wrap my hands around the mug for warmth. "So, what's the emergency?" I ask Father Mik. "Is my soul in trouble?" My lame attempt at humor. "Or did Evie send you to strong-arm me back into attending mass?"

Father Mik is the priest at St. Nicholas Catholic church on Chicago's West Side and serves deaf people. His parents were deaf and he signs fluently, rendering all of the masses in American Sign Language. I walked out of St. Nick's at age sixteen unable to continue the polite fiction that I believed in anything transpiring at the altar.

To his credit, Father Mik doesn't react to my baiting him. I lift my cup to get the caffeine flowing but halfway there my hand starts to tremor. Gracefully—and furtively, I hope—my other hand steadies the cup and I carry it to my lips, two-handed. "Your mother is a dear, one of the faithful. But the reason I called you has nothing to do with her. I don't know if you remember Martin Nygaard? Our custodian. He was found dead a week ago upstairs in the church parish hall. I think he was murdered, although the police don't seem to think so."

The name pulls up a vague memory of a man who avoided the deaf people at the after-mass coffee hour at St. Nick's. Alone in a crowd. "Murdered? What happened?" I signal the waiter for more coffee.

"The daughter of one of our parishioners found him on the kitchen floor. I was busy downstairs preparing for the Saturday five o'clock mass. He bled to death from a gash in his head."

"And the police?"

"They think he either got dizzy or slipped, hit his head on the sharp corner of the metal sink and fell to the floor unconscious, then..." He turns his hands in an upward gesture. "I pray he didn't suffer."

The waiter brings my toast and I cover the first piece with strawberry jam. Heaven. The sugar settles my stomach. The caffeine finally kicks in and lessens the shakes but my headache remains. "Will there be an autopsy?"

"Yes, but only because the church's insurance carrier requires it. The police did not deem it foul play. The coroner told me it would take one to two weeks for a more definitive answer."

"What makes you think murder? I mean, he was old, right? Probably eighty if he was a day."

Throat clearing from Father Mik. "He was sixty-eight. Five years my junior."

I smirk at him. *"Sorry,"* I sign, my right fist planted over my heart and rotating in exaggerated circles to indicate my sarcasm.

"Still a brat, I see," he signs back.

We both laugh.

"I tried to notify his ex-wife to see if she wanted to participate in the funeral in some way but only got her voicemail. Their son," he stops to count on his fingers, "is twenty or so. He lives with his mother."

This information does nothing to erase my doubts or clarify his story of murder. The back of my neck throbs at the base, my headache increasing with a vengeance. Maybe my hangover isn't letting me understand what seems so obvious to him. I excuse myself and head for the bathroom, which is hidden in a small alcove at the end of a fully stocked bar.

When I come out of the bathroom, I notice Styrofoam cups for the to-go coffee trade at the end of the bar and stacked in front of a long line of gleaming bottles of hard liquor. I massage the base of my neck. Nearby, a Latino kid who looks about fifteen clears a table.

"Hey," I say, and tilt my head for him to come over to me. He scans the restaurant seeming to search for someone until he lands on Chris, the owner, who is busy at the register. Loaded down with hesitancy the kid approaches me, still glancing over his shoulder at Chris. I nab a white cup and step back into the little alcove. I show him five bucks and point at the bottles. "Pour me a shot."

He shakes his head and scans the restaurant again but Chris is now outside in the cold shoving a foil-wrapped sandwich at a homeless guy. The kid takes another gander at me. Something in his eyes makes me for a cop. Or is he worried about immigration? Maybe both. But he grabs the cup, moves behind the bar and tilts the nearest bottle into it. Seconds later he steps out from the bar and hands me a cup half-full of clear liquid. I try to give him the five but he shakes his head again and pushes past me while muttering something in Spanish I don't understand.

In a bathroom stall I gulp the clear liquid and flinch at the minor explosions coursing down my esophagus, spreading warmth in my stomach: ouzo. Immediately I feel better. No more throbbing neck, seasick queasiness gone, only an aura from my headache. I wash my hands and rinse my mouth before leaving the bathroom.

Back at the table I heap more jam on the second piece of toast. Several bites into it I regard Father Mik as he stirs brown sugar into his oatmeal. "From what you've told me it doesn't sound like murder, seems pretty straightforward. I'm sure older people die like this all the time, unsteady on their feet and—"

A spoonful of oatmeal dotted with raisins halts half-way to Father Mik's mouth.

"But that's not all, Dana. The day after Martin's body was discovered, one of the women from the guild noticed some very expensive things missing when she set up for Sunday morning mass. Two chalices, each worth a hundred thousand dollars, and two of the six brass candlesticks, probably worth two thousand each—gone." His spoonful of oatmeal finishes its journey.

I stop chewing and gape at him. St. Nick's is a poor parish in an even poorer neighborhood. The hundred-plus-year-old church still stands because of its historical significance in architectural circles and can't be torn down. But I know from Evie that the congregation struggles to afford even minor repairs on the old structure. Such expensive chalices and candlesticks surprise me.

"How could St. Nick's afford them?"

He waves his hand in a dismissive gesture. "Oh, we didn't purchase them. They were donated to the church in the late nineteenth century to memorialize its establishment back then. Wealthy people built St. Nick's. The neighborhood and the congregation were quite well-to-do. The chalices are exquisite remnants and reminders of the era. Each has ornate, unique designs. I'm sick about losing them."

"And you think someone murdered him to steal them?"

"That's my fear. Now, you alluded to Martin falling and I did consider that possibility. You see, his deafness was the result of drugs that were ototoxic."

I frown, sit back in the booth and cradle my coffee cup with both hands. "English, please."

"Forgive me. Years ago, before I met him, Martin had cancer and was treated with chemotherapy. Possible side effects from the chemo were hearing loss and problems with balance. In Martin's case, he suffered complete deafness and did have balance issues. I considered the possibility he lost his balance, fell, and hit his head that way."

"But the missing chalices and candlesticks are what make you think someone gave Martin a shove or in some way caused him to fall? So the thief could avoid being identified?"

Father Mik nods and pushes aside his half-eaten bowl of oatmeal. He crosses his forearms and leans onto the table. "Only Martin and I hold keys to the steel cabinets where the vestments and all the other items for mass are kept. Things often go missing otherwise. I even lock up the cheap sherry we use for communion."

I remember the nasty-tasting stuff from my childhood when I attended church. "And you reported the theft?"

"Yes, of course, first thing the next morning. But investigators didn't think the two events were connected because of the way Martin died."

"Were the cabinets broken into?"

"No. That's another thing. I keep my key to the cabinets on my personal key fob. Martin kept his in a lock box in his apartment and carried the lock box key with him—quite a meticulous man, Dana. Among his effects returned by the police yesterday I found his lock box key. When I checked his apartment, the cabinet key remained in its rightful place, locked up."

"His apartment? What good would that do? I mean, he needed the key at the church, right?"

"Oh, I see the confusion. I say apartment but Martin lived in the parish hall basement. It's a long story but he needed a place to stay after some personal problems. Then he became the church custodian and it worked out best for him to live there."

I finish my toast and the same busboy comes to deliver more coffee but I wave him off, my legs jittery from too much caffeine. He averts his eyes and asks if he can clear our dishes. I wait for him to leave. "So far I'm with the investigators on this," I say. "Martin's death and the theft don't seem connected to me, either."

Father Mik nods and lowers his gaze, clasping his hands as if in prayer. I swallow the last inch of coffee in my cup and study the old priest, sorry I can't commiserate more.

"It doesn't seem complicated, Father Mik. I'm sure you and your parishioners are concerned about both of these...uh, events. But sometimes there's no way to explain an accidental death. Or solve a theft. Shi—stuff happens." I feel foolish giving a priest, forty-three years my senior, advice about death or the nature of things in the world. Shit happens. Very helpful, Dana. He appears inconsolable.

"Yes, well, that is what I hope you can do. Find an explanation."

He appears so forlorn I relent a bit even though in my mind I am not persuaded by his story. "Let me check into this and get back to you later this next week, probably after Thanksgiving."

"I know you're busy, so I'm grateful for whatever you can manage on your own time."

I briefly consider what he says, unsure whether or not to confide that I'm on suspension from my job as a detective, so in reality I have plenty of time to devote to his cause.

"It's no problem. I'm on a short leave of absence from the department," I say, purposely leaving the reason vague..I get the names and contact information of the women on the altar guild at St. Nick's, then stand and pull my wallet from my backpack.

Father Mik grabs the check. "Please, allow me, Dana."

I slip on my jacket and hoist my backpack over one shoulder. Father Mik buttons up his black wool overcoat that appears shabby from too many Chicago winters.

"Last Sunday when I spoke with your mother she made no mention regarding your leave of absence. I pray it's nothing serious?"

The deaf grapevine is always hard at work. Evie loves to tell her world about my business, tripping a memory of my first embarrassing awareness of this when I turned twelve and started my period. Unbeknownst to me, Evie told all her friends. Before church the following Sunday her female posse surrounded me and vied with each other to give me the best advice about what pads to use, how to quell cramps, and wasn't it wonderful that I could now have children. At twelve.

Eighteen years later my life is still on display for my mother, only now the topics include my husband and my job—which is why I tell Evie nothing. "Yeah, well. It's nothing too dramatic. A minor disagreement between me and my lieutenant. I'm on suspension while I attend some counseling." I touch his arm. "My parents don't know and I'd appreciate it if you kept it between us, Father Mik. No reason to worry them."

"Of course, of course. I understand." His smile is warm and I return it. We hug. "And if you have some free time for the next few weeks, would you call my office?" Father Mik asks. "I'm sure Angeline will be eager to book you for interpreting work, especially this close to the holidays."

"Sure."

Even though I'm on suspension with pay, the extra money I can earn as an interpreter through the Deaf Catholic Office will help with the mortgage—for a house neither my husband Jimmy nor I live in—and the rent on my studio apartment, where I do live.

We head for the cash register at the front of the restaurant and join the line there. Father Mik fidgets with his cash and the bill, looking everywhere but at me. Anyone with even a minute understanding of body language could register his discomfort.

Irritated that he's withholding something I shift closer to force his attention on me. "What?" My earlier ouzo assist has dissipated.

"Evie did mention some concern about you and your husband. If there's anything I can do to help..."

Damn Evie anyway. Fury at my mother replaces rational thought. My life is her reality show. I can picture how she complains to her deaf friends: *my fat hearing daughter can't hold on to her husband.* I liberate a cigarette from my pack of Kools. Merely holding it mutes my anger enough to be civil to Father Mik.

"Jimmy and I are going through a rough time right now. He's in L.A. for a training course. We're trying to sort things out." Although it would be a lot easier to sort things out if we were in the same damn state.

"We're not done remodeling our house," I continue, enunciating my words in the hope I sound less angry than I am. If I can hold onto the house maybe I can hold onto my marriage. But there's the small matter of an empty nursery, which I wasn't able to fill. "I'm renting a studio for now because of the remodeling."

"You know the church community is a wonderful place for support, Dana. Why don't you join us for Thanksgiving mass and then stay for the annual dinner?"

Why, you old S.O.B. Evie *did* send you to shoehorn me back into church. I wince at calling Father Mik such a rude epithet in my thoughts, momentarily caught in my old childhood fear that the priest can read my mind.

"I might be eating dinner with friends," I lie, "but thanks. I'll be in touch about the chalices."

Instead of another farewell hug—our typical parting—I leave him looking unhappy and head back to the bathroom.

The scared-looking busboy, the one I cadged the snort of ouzo from, walks toward me carrying a black bin full of dirty dishes. I remove the five bucks from my jeans and move to stuff it in the pocket of his maroon smock. He tries to back away but bumps into a table, which allows my arm to complete its arc and deposit the bill. I pat his pocket.

"Keep it."

He ignores my glare and slides past me toward the kitchen.

3

—————

Monday, 11/18, 1:00 p.m.

LATE NOVEMBER in Chicago means temperatures in the mid-thirties made all the colder by rain trying hard to be snow. I huddle in my Corolla and massage my temples while smoking the last Kool in the pack, waiting for the car to warm up, waiting for me to wake up. I slept late. I glance at my car dash clock: 1:00 p.m.

The missing chalices bug me. The place to start is with the altar guild woman who discovered them gone. Fiona? Fauna? I search my notepad for the notes I took at breakfast with Father Mik.

Flora. Flora Maitland. She was at the church when the little girl found Martin Nygaard. No phone. Who doesn't own a cell phone nowadays? Her address is on the West Side near St. Nick's. With the car now warm and the nicotine in my blood flowing to the right places, I stop first at Louie's Liquor Palace for more cigarettes and a twelve-pack that I stow in the trunk.

I unravel the cellophane from a new pack of Kools and thump it on the dashboard a few times to eliminate any air lingering in the tobacco. I light up and pull into traffic heading to Flora's place but halfway there make a detour to visit Pete Christakos, a detective friend who works in Robbery and Stolen Goods. No use reinventing the wheel. He might already have the information on the missing chalices and candlesticks, but I'm not recalling whether Father Mik reported the theft to RSG or simply told the detective who responded to Martin Nygaard's death.

The corridor leading to Pete's office smells like fresh paint and the stale charred stink of cigarettes even though every building in Chicago is supposed to be smoke-free. Try getting cops to obey *that* law. The hallway opens into a large, windowless room and Pete sits at the far end, his feet up on a messy desk and computer keyboard in his lap. He finally notices me and waves before I'm halfway to him.

"Hi, Pete." I lean in and peck the old man on the cheek, get a whiff of woodsy aftershave.

"How's it going, kid, now you're a lady of leisure?"

Shit. Everybody knows. "Going okay." I seesaw my hand at him. "Still having trouble remembering I'm a citizen now. But it's only been a few weeks."

He frowns at my response as if he doesn't even want to think about being a citizen instead of a cop. He glances at a framed black and white photo on his desk of a woman in her wedding dress, circa nineteen-seventies.

"I knew since I was ten I wanted to be a cop. But my mother always wanted me to be a priest. Greek Orthodox. Always after me about the danger on the streets. One day I told her cops gotta believe in God a lot more than priests. She put a lid on it after that." He chuckles. "So, what's happening with your suspension?"

I don't want to talk about the reason for my suspension, knowing cops are worse gossips than teenaged girls. A headache insinuates itself behind my eyes. I pinch the bridge of my nose and squeeze my eyes shut for a second.

"Shit, kid. I'm sorry. I put my foot in it, didn't I?"

"No, it's okay, Pete. I don't feel well today. Had a lousy night's sleep, that's all."

He studies my face for a moment. "You are kind of yellow and puffy. But these fluorescent lights'll make anyone look like Frankenstein." He laughs.

Do I look that bad? Maybe I need to start wearing some makeup. "I need your help, Pete." I explain about the theft.

"Why doesn't the priest leave it up to his area RSG guys to work the case? I mean, you're good, Dana, but why's he bypassing them?"

"He did report it," I lie, "but surprise, they're not very motivated." The reputation of Robbery and Stolen Goods, even within CPD, is lousy. I explain further about Father Mik's belief that Martin Nygaard's death was murder even though the police haven't ruled it so. "He wants me to investigate because of the deaf connection, too. Look, I'm not going to compromise anything for the locals—"

He cuts in. "Deaf connection?"

"You didn't know my parents are deaf? So were Father Mik's. He heads up the Deaf Catholic Office and serves a large deaf congregation at St. Nick's. My mom goes to church there. He trusts me."

Pete smiles at me, then gestures at the faded photo of the woman in the wedding dress. "I get the language thing. I grew up speaking Greek at home, did a lot of translating for my mother."

"Exactly. And I don't know the West Side guys. I know you. So that's why I'm here."

"Okay. What do you need from me, kid?"

I plop into the chair next to his desk and pull out my pack of Kools, raising my eyebrows at him. He resumes an upright position, feet on the floor, and scans the room—for his CO, I'm guessing—then pulls an ashtray from a desk drawer. We both light up.

"I'm not going to interfere with the official investigation," I say. "I'm only trying to get a feel for the theft to see if there's any connection to the death. Frankly, I think the old janitor died from natural causes and it's not connected to the missing chalices. Where would someone sell church-related items that were stolen?"

"Just about anywhere these days." He picks up the keyboard from his lap and waggles it. "Ever hear of eBay?"

My willingness to investigate the theft evaporates with his gesture. If St. Nick's chalices and candlesticks were sold on eBay it will be impossible to track them down. Well, maybe not impossible but a hell of a lot more work than I'm willing to invest on a volunteer basis. "Exactly why I'm in Homicide," I say. I tap cigarette ash into the ceramic ashtray glazed pea-green, which looks like a little kid fashioned it in an art class. "Assume it's a local thing and the person doesn't use the Internet."

"If it's an amateur, mostly pawn shops. But you're still dealing with the Web, kid. Robbery and Stolen Goods has a page on CPD's site. Victims can list their stuff there, then pawnshops compare their items. It's best if there's pictures or videos of the stolen stuff, then we put it up on the site. You'd be surprised how many we nail that way."

"I don't know if an amateur did it but the chalices are worth a hundred K each."

Pete whistles. "You know, there aren't many but some shops specialize in religious items. Then there's these companies that buy and sell antique religious stuff, artifacts, for the yuppies rehabbing the old tenements. Had a case of a church's stained-glass windows stolen right out of their casings." Smoke from his cigarette trails in crazy patterns as he gestures with his hand.

I shake my head, surprised I'm still bothered by the fact that nothing in the city is ever safe or sacred or respected. "Jeez."

"I know, I know. So, it's unsolved for over a year. No leads, nothing. One day, the church's priest drives to an old lady's house to give her communion and whammo, there are his stained-glass windows in her rehabbed condo." He nods at the memory, inhales deeply from his cigarette and snorts out two thick streams of smoke from his nostrils.

"I don't know about these chalices decorating anyone's condo, Pete. I think they were stolen for the money." I take a last drag of my cigarette and stub it out in the tray.

"Then your best bet's the pawn shops. You got pictures?"

"Didn't think of that. I'm sure Father Mik does, probably for the insurance. I'll get them for you but in the meantime let's list the chalices and the candlesticks on the website."

"Sure, kid. But first lemme check if West Side already did." He hangs his cigarette in the corner of his mouth and squints at the computer's monitor. After a bit of hunt-and-peck typing Pete shakes his head and mutters an epithet about lazy cops. The St. Nick's items aren't listed.

A couple of cops enter the room at the far end and Pete quickly folds the remainder of his cigarette on top of mine, mashing it down with his finger to snuff the ember, and stashes it in his drawer. He becomes all business and types my description into his computer and after a brief moment it appears on the CPD website—a minor miracle. I smile at him and lightly applaud. "Impressive for an old man. You put me to shame."

He grins at me. "Got to grow with the times." The grin becomes a leer. "Now, the most important question is what do I get for my trouble?"

I put on a serious face and stroke my chin as if contemplating a major decision. "This rates either a hand job or some homemade chocolate chip cookies. The choice is yours. Of course, if you choose the former, I'll call your wife and tell her you're propositioning younger women."

He chuckles and I smile at him again, feeling comfort in the familiar lewd banter and relief at working with a competent cop. I suddenly register a good feeling about finding the missing items for Father Mik. I stand and peer down at him. "I'll bring the cookies over with the pics, Pete. Thanks."

He stands just as I bend down to give him a quick peck on the cheek. Our heads collide and both of us recoil. I grimace, apologize. "Forget it. I'm fine. Gotta hit me a lot harder to do some damage to this thick skull. Good to see you, Dana. Don't be a stranger."

I leave the building and get in my car, certain with Pete's help he'll get the job done, and head over to the apartment of the altar guild woman who discovered the missing chalices. Flora Maitland.

I park on the street when I arrive at her building, a twelve-story-high ugly rectangle that dates back to somewhere in the fifties, its once-modern exterior of blue, pink and white tiles awash with grime and graffiti. I literally pass through the outer door because there's no glass in the empty metal frame, and enter the main lobby.

All the mailboxes lining one wall are broken, their small metal doors hanging open or missing altogether. I wade toward them through piles of junk mail and paper ads littering the floor. The wall above the mailboxes is punctuated with a line of holes, as if someone with a hammer walked along and methodically meted out the destruction. Flora Maitland's box reads *Apartment 623*. A sign notifies me the door-bells do not work.

I push through the main lobby's inner door, which in a better neigh-borhood would be locked to protect the occupants from unwelcome intruders. Here there's a gaping hole where the doorknob used to be.

The inner lobby reveals an elevator, the opening covered with slabs of particle board and painted with a large X in fluorescent lime green. I remember reading about two men who lived here waiting for this elevator. Possibly in deep conversation—certainly not noticing anything amiss when the elevator dinged and the doors opened— they crossed the threshold and fell to their deaths. The elevator car hung useless in the shaft several floors above. I see the landlord is right on top of fixing things.

I quickly run out of breath climbing the stairs in the dimly lit stairwell and curse myself yet again for being fat and smoking a pack a day. Several minutes later I reach the sixth floor and take a long breather before leaving the stairwell to enter the hallway. As I head down the corridor I realize I haven't passed one other person in this building since my arrival, which makes me wish I had my gun. I pat my pocket for the Mace I always carry and feel slight comfort. My service weapon, a Glock 19 9mm, sits in a safe along with my badge, Lieutenant Kozlowski's final word on my suspension.

The apartments I pass on my way to 623 are occupied, though. I hear music, television shows, a man and woman arguing, and almost everyone seems to own a barking dog. As I get nearer Flora's apartment the hallway serves up the smell of pine cleaner with the underlying stench of urine, but also a hint of something sweet like fried bacon.

The bare bulb over Flora Maitland's doorway is burned out. I knock and wait but no one answers. The gap between the bottom of her door and the floor emits only dim, natural light. From this side, the apartment feels empty and I try the knob. Locked. I call out Flora's name and pound the door harder but it's useless, so I jog back down the unsavory hallway to the stairwell and hurry outside, unable to shake feeling vulnerable in the gloomy building.

Once on the road I replay my brief foray into police work with Pete Christakos, which stirs up a lingering resentment at my suspension as a homicide detective two weeks ago. A bullshit suspension based on a bullshit policy: zero tolerance of drugs and alcohol on the police force.

My lieutenant detected a little bit of booze in my system left over from some drinking I did at home and off-duty. The "choice" he gave me? Get evaluated for substance abuse or face termination. Even the union sided with the brass, told me I wouldn't win a grievance case.

So I chose the forced evaluation, which has resulted in my required attendance at an Intensive Outpatient Program. I want to save the job I love. With my husband Jimmy keeping me off balance about our future together, my job is all I have left at this point.

I head for the North Side and a favored taco place to chow down and chill for a couple of hours. My first IOP session starts in a few hours.

4

Monday, 11/18, 6:00 p.m.

GOD, I hate groups. Spare me the gooey feelings of camaraderie and understanding they're supposed to foster. Tonight, we're here to learn about the six-week Intensive Outpatient Program, or IOP, and then participate in our first brainwashing session together. I pick up my folder with a name tag paper-clipped to it, sit outside the obvious circle of chairs set up in the middle of the room, and thumb through several inches of articles and forms within.

People start to arrive. Some, also carrying folders, creep into the room and perch on the edge of their chairs. Others, not carrying folders, barge in talking loud shit and pulling chairs free of the circle to form their own helter-skelter islands. At the six o'clock starting time no one in the room seems like they're in charge. Five minutes pass and I decide to go back outside to smoke while waiting.

When I get to the door a young woman barely five feet tall sweeps into the room and ushers me back in. Her name tag reads *Jenny*.

"I'm here, I'm here," Jenny says. "Sorry I'm late, everyone." She walks up to the broken circle of chairs and stands for a minute, surveying the room. Some people ignore her and continue talking, others sit quiet and look oddly alone. A loud whistle cuts through the chatter. Heads swivel toward Jenny. She lowers her fingers from her lips. "Chairs back where you found 'em. Let's go." Her gestures remind me of a traffic cop on a busy street.

No nonsense here, I see. I return to the chair I sat in before our leader arrived. I'm still outside the circle, now reconfigured and most of its chairs occupied by the other attendees. Jenny, standing in the middle of the circle, says she's the group facilitator. As she turns to grab the closest empty chair she spies me, an outlier, not part of the group.

"IOP?" she asks.

"Excuse me?"

"Are you in the Intensive Outpatient Program from six to nine?" Exasperated tone of voice.

"Yes," I say. She's easy to rile. I wait.

"Join us in the circle." She gestures in a hurry-up motion.

"I'm fine right here." I can see the wheels turn: argue with me or let it go for now? She takes in the other people complying with her request and decides to ignore me.

"Okay. First, for the newcomers starting tonight. Normally you'd have a separate orientation group to get you up to speed about IOP and to answer your questions. The staff person who handles that is sick, so we're combining orientation with this group." Jen seems to be taking attendance while she talks, glancing at her clipboard and then at individual patients, the ones without the folders. "Let's open our packets," she says. "Oh, first, put your name tags on and let's go around the circle and introduce ourselves. I'll start."

Those with name tags detach them from the backings. Most slap them on their chests but I notice one girl—probably in her late teens —sticks it on her sleeve near the shoulder, a patch signifying membership in the Army of Recovery. From where I sit, I can tell she decorated her name tag with hearts drawn in thick black marker around her name. Ariel.

Jenny stares at me and raises her eyebrows when I don't comply with her second request. My name tag is still paper-clipped to my folder. She gives the slightest shake of the head and turns back to the group. "I'm Jenny and I facilitate the education groups here at IOP. Tonight, I'll give you an overview of the program, sort of what we expect of you and what you can expect of us in the next six weeks. Then you'll see a short video about substance abuse treatment and why it's effective. We'll end with your questions at this point about the program."

Ariel raises her hand.

"Yes," Jenny stretches her neck sideways to read the tag, "Ariel?"

"Can we smoke in here?" Ariel waves her Salems. Several other members sit up, interested in the answer.

"No. This entire building is smoke-free. Illinois law for quite a while."

A distinct rumble from the group. Jenny shows us her palm in a *halt* sign. "Okay, okay. Try not to mutiny." She cracks a smile at the group. No one returns the favor. "Two ten-minute breaks are built into the program, after the first and second hour, so seven and eight."

My phone shows we're still more than a half-hour away from the first break. Ariel glances at her phone, too, then executes an exaggerated eye roll and stuffs the pack of Salems down the front of her shirt.

The people in the circle proceed to introduce themselves by name. Jenny doesn't include me. "Ariel, why don't you start with telling the group why you're here," Jenny says.

A few people rubberneck at me, unsure of why Jenny's forgotten me out here in the cheap seats. "Uh, Jenny?" One of two white men in the group raises his hand. He's a ringer for my husband Jimmy but sounds like he's from somewhere south of I-80.

"Louis."

"Lou. Listen, Jen, there's another member who didn't introduce herself." He points to me. Now everyone in the circle stares.

"What would you like her to do, Louis?"

"It's Lou. I think she should join the group, like, get in the circle."

"Can you tell her that?" Jen, practicing those facilitation skills of hers.

Lou ducks his head when I look directly at him. After a minute of silence, Jen addresses the rest of the group. "Four of you are new tonight. The rest of the group has been attending for at least two weeks. Do any of you 'old-timers'," she draws quotes around this, "want to help Louis out?"

"Lou," repeats Lou.

A young black guy wearing the largest diamond stud earrings I've ever seen raises his hand.

"Good, Hades. Go," says Jen.

He stares at me and doesn't blink. "What's your name?"

"Dana."

"That's a nice name you got. I'm Hades. Come on, Dana, pull up your chair, be part of the group." He nods at Jenny and she nods back.

The group continues to stare at me and while I don't want to be part of the circle, I have to admit I am uncomfortable with the attention. My stomach churns. I scoot my chair close behind Ariel's but still outside the circle. This must be good enough for Jen because she continues with her itinerary. She asks the members to briefly explain why they're attending IOP. Most are here because someone in their family—husband, wife, parents—laid down the law: treatment or you're out of here. One guy who could be a double for W. C. Fields, red bulbous nose and all, is here because of a DUI. He's court-ordered. I'm the only one trying to save my job. Jen doesn't ask me, though. Lou interrupts again.

"Uh, Jen? Dana hasn't told us why she's here."

"That's right, Louis. Why don't you ask her?"

Come on, Lou. You can do it. It's unnerving how much he looks like Jimmy. Jimmy with a hick accent. Lou doesn't correct Jen about his name this time, doesn't make a sound. Hades takes over again but now without raising his hand.

"Yo, Dana, Dana with the nice name. Why you here with us in IOP? Your old man throw you out for drinking or did the cops, you know, catch you with something a little more illegal?" Hades glances around the circle at the other members, a cheerful grin on his face when his banter is met with a titter of laughter and side comments.

"My job," I answer. Something about the way I say it doesn't invite Hades to ask for elaboration. Four nights a week of this, Mondays through Thursdays, three hours each night. Six weeks long. And they expect us to do this without drinking?

We're also supposed to attend at least two twelve-step meetings every week. Jen suggests we do this during the weekends. She points out forms in our folders to take to the meetings and get signed to show we attended. W.C. Fields asks how someone can sign the form if the meetings are anonymous. Ariel laughs. I cringe at the thought of going to A.A. and worry someone I know will see me there.

At the break, seven of the eight of us rush outside without coats and smoke as fast as we can, shivering in the cold. W.C. lights two cigarettes simultaneously so he won't waste time lighting the second one when he finishes the first.

Back inside, we watch a video during the second hour, one I've seen somewhere before, maybe on The Learning Channel. I can't remember. I do remember the statistic that about seventy percent of people in treatment for the first time end up going back to drinking and using drugs. And Jen thinks this means treatment is effective? I picture the twelve-pack in my trunk.

Instead of a second break at eight—I'm already on my feet, cigarette clutched in one hand, lighter in the other—Jen asks if there are any questions. If not, we're free to go home early. Needless to say, there aren't any questions. She reminds us that Thursday this week is Thanksgiving and we won't meet that night. The group heads for the door and I follow but Jen intercepts me before I can escape.

"Can I talk with you a minute," she pointedly eyeballs my name tag still attached to my folder, "Dana?"

Busted.

"Sure, Jen." I return and this time join the circle.

Jen takes the seat directly opposite me, puts down her clipboard, and crosses her legs and arms. She gazes at me but says nothing.

I can wait her out all night, familiar and comfortable with silence, a common interrogation technique I've used my entire career as a detective.

But I don't have to wait long. About one minute later she uncrosses her legs. "I'm not going to beg you to be part of this group," she says. "We're all grownups here. I ask you to join the circle and you don't. I ask you to wear your name tag and you don't. That's your choice. You get out of it what you put into it." With that, she stands up and leaves the room.

I win.

5

Tuesday, 11/19, 10:00 a.m.

THE NEXT MORNING, after a large cup of black coffee and three cigarettes for breakfast, I park in front of St. Nick's. I slide into a spot right outside the hulking sandstone structure and, clutching my jacket against the cold, head to the rectory next to the church. Father Mik must be watching from inside because the front door opens before I finish climbing the steps.

"Dana! Thank you for stopping by. Come in, come in." Father Mik takes my elbow and steers me into a small living room where a fire flashes and snaps in the hearth. He takes my coat while I warm my hands, discovering I've lost my gloves somewhere between my studio and here. "Can I offer you something hot to drink, maybe a home-made mocha? The coffee's made and I can stir in some cocoa mix."

"Only my favorite thing to drink," I say, maybe a little too heartily, desperate for sugar and more caffeine; the sugar to combat my hangover and the caffeine to stand in for the late night I spent drinking most of the 12-pack after IOP.

"Perfect. Let's repair to the kitchen to talk. It's warmer in there anyway. This old house is drafty in spots," he waves his hand around the room, "and snug in others, like the kitchen. A mystery."

His long legs quickly lead him away and I follow down a long hall-way, passing a wooden staircase whose spindles reveal unique hand-carvings of a variety of seraphim. We arrive at a light yellow, boxy kitchen in the back of the house. Daisies repeat thematically in the café curtains, in the paper bordering the top of the walls, and in the hand towels and hot pads hanging on magnetic hooks stuck to the refrigerator. The kitchen sparkles so much it hurts my eyes. I push away thoughts of my own dingy kitchenette, nowhere near this picture of domestic calm, and take a place at the table circa 1950 while Father Mik fixes our drinks. Morning sun streams through the southern-facing windows. I feel warm and comforted, the room as snug as Father Mik predicted.

"I'm glad for the pictures of the chalices and candlesticks," I say. "We might get lucky with posting them on the Department's website, see if any pawn shops can ID them." I quickly explain Pete Christakos's suggestion.

Father Mik deposits the mocha in front of me. "The insurance company photographed the chalices for their purposes, although I don't retain any copies on file. They told me it would take thirty days to send me copies." He frowned.

"You'd think it would be quicker than that—a simple attachment to an email. Thirty days?"

"We are at the mercy of corporations, I'm afraid. But," Father Mik smiles and holds up his index finger, "here's what I did find." He sits as he slides a manila folder over to me from the head of the table.

Inside are two pieces of paper and one photo. The papers are standard eight-and-a-half by eleven sheets, each page folded in half, and because they are brown and brittle with age, both are encased in plastic covers. They're church bulletins from the inaugural service for St. Nick's. The front of each bulletin shows the same ink drawing of the church, large and imposing. Father Mik takes the one I'm holding, turns it over, and does the same with the other program.

"These are drawings of the two chalices, which were donated for the church dedication. They're done in pen and ink so it's not obvious from the picture, but one is gold and the other silver. Each is unique and designed by a man who studied under Tiffany, you know, the fellow who created those wonderful lamps. They are also encrusted with gems. Back then they cost about twenty thousand dollars to render, but recently the appraisal came to a hundred thousand each."

Their value still astounds me. Father Mik reads my expression accurately and continues. "Some of the value is related to the sheer fact they're over a hundred years old, but also the quality of silver and gold used and of course the fine workmanship involved. Even though they're insured I'm heartbroken at the loss of history these chalices represent. These pieces are priceless."

Remaining in the folder is a photograph of the church's altar. I pick it up and show Father Mik. "Are these the missing candlesticks?"

"Yes. They're made of solid brass, not nearly as valuable compared to the chalices, but they are antiques. There are six of them, each worth about two thousand dollars. For some reason only two were stolen. That may be the reason I didn't notice their absence."

"Do you know how much they weigh?"

"Probably about twenty pounds each. They appear heavier, I know."

"Meaning they could be carried off the altar easily."

"Certainly. The altar guild ladies routinely take them down to polish them and of course Martin would lock them up in the cabinet when they weren't being used."

"After Mr. Nygaard was discovered in the kitchen, who locked up that night? Flora Maitland?"

Father Mik runs his large hand through his military-style buzz cut and squints at the floor. "You know, I keep playing that night over and over in my head but I can't remember because of the commotion with the police and then the coroner. Flora had four of her five children with her, as well. She was very upset at seeing Martin dead."

"She let her children see the body?" No Mother of the Year award for this woman.

"No, no—I mean, her children were here playing in the churchyard, which doubled her stress while setting up for mass. After Martin was found dead and the police arrived, they wanted to question both of us but I insisted on holding our scheduled mass first." Father Mik crossed his arms and shook his head at the memory.

Trying to understand the timing of the theft, I ask Father Mik if he used the priceless chalices during the mass. "No, not that evening. I keep them locked up and only use them for special services."

"Okay. So did Flora lock up after the police were through with the questioning?"

"I tried to keep her calm in order to cooperate with the authorities. They made us wait until the body was on its way to the medical examiner. I wasn't thinking about things, you see, I was thinking about people. Like Flora and her children, the congregation, and our mass that evening. There was also Martin's ex-wife, and I wasn't sure whether I should try contacting her. Overwhelming."

No doubt. "So, you don't remember locking up?"

Father Mik shook his head. "Not the cabinet where the chalices were stored. It was late after the police left. I was most concerned with getting Flora and her children home. I brought them there and stayed until her oldest son came home sometime after midnight."

"And Flora discovered the missing chalices and candlesticks the next morning? I'm surprised she went back to St. Nick's after such a traumatic evening." I slip out of my jacket, overheated from the warm kitchen and hot drink.

"She didn't have much choice. St. Nick's is her placement for the work skills program and it's strict—no absences or she's dismissed. The result would be no assistance from the state. So, Sunday morning she came in to set up for mass. I helped her because as you point out, she appeared traumatized indeed." I consider the possibility of Flora stealing the valuables and pawning them. She's certainly motivated: five children to support and no job skills.

"Before I gave Flora the key to unlock the cabinets, she found them already open and of course, the chalices gone. So, obviously, neither one of us locked up the night before. But you know, Dana, the parish hall door leading to the outside locks automatically. Which means even though the cabinets remained open during the night, the building was still locked up tight. No one could get in."

"And that's why you think the theft happened earlier, why Mr. Nygaard was murdered."

"Yes."

"No other forced entry?"

"No."

I jot down the information in my notepad to try and make sense of it, sketch a timeline, fill in names. I still think the theft and death are separate occurrences but keep this to myself until I sort it out later. I slip on my jacket and ask Father Mik to show me Martin Nygaard's rooms in the church basement, wanting to view the lockbox there and get more of a feel for the old janitor, who so far seems an enigma.

"I went by Flora's yesterday to talk with her about what happened but she wasn't there," I say, as Father Mik leads me across the rectory's backyard and into the parish hall attached to St. Nick's.

"Oh?" We head downstairs to the basement but before I ask him more about Flora I glance at the timeline in my notepad and realize I started with the assumption that Martin Nygaard died on Saturday.

"Father Mik, when was the last time you, or Flora, or anyone, saw Mr. Nygaard alive?" I follow him down a hallway with a beige tiled floor, past the bathrooms that are across from the rooms used for Sunday School. Father Mik stops and turns toward me.

"The police wanted to know that, too. A small committee that plans the Thanksgiving dinner met Friday morning, the day before Martin was discovered. The coffee pot Martin was washing when he...fell, came from their meeting."

"What time did they meet?"

"They began at ten in the morning and adjourned at noon."

"And they were the last people to see him alive?"

Father Mik nods. "I assume so, yes. I attended meetings at the Arch-diocese downtown Friday and Saturday, full days both. On the way back, I picked up Flora and her children about three o'clock to bring her to the church to set up for our Saturday, five-thirty mass. I hadn't seen Martin since Thursday."

I flip my notepad to a fresh page and start a new timeline, jot down the names of the committee members. "So, Mr. Nygaard cleaned out that coffeepot sometime between noon Friday and late Saturday afternoon. And no one else entered the parish hall during that time, after the committee left, until you and Flora arrived to set up for Saturday evening mass?"

"Yes. Well, again, that's my assumption." Then he pauses, his bushy eyebrows drawn together. "Nothing else was scheduled. And I can't vouch for anyone else coming into the parish hall while Flora set up for mass." All the more reason I need to talk with her.

Father Mik points to a door at the end of the hall. "Down here, Dana." We walk a bit farther and stop in front of a door marked *Private*. From his pocket Father Mik withdraws a small key fob in the shape of a cross that bears two keys and unlocks the door. We enter and he flips a light switch on the wall. The first of two rooms, a sitting room of sorts, holds a bookcase stuffed with paperbacks, a small TV, one chair, plus the lockbox Father Mik mentioned at the Elite last Saturday during our breakfast. He motions for me to approach the box and directs my attention to the key fob by holding it aloft.

"These are Martin's keys, which he never relinquished from his possession. When the altar guild ladies needed to unlock the vestment cabinets upstairs, he would do it." Father Mik then unlocks the box with the second key on the fob, opens the small gray door, and points to the keys arranged inside. Eight keys hang on separate hooks, handwritten labels identifying each key's purpose.

"Here's the key for the upstairs cabinet. And I have the other one if, for some reason, Martin wasn't available." He closes and locks the box. "As I said before, these keys," he lifts the key fob to my eye level, "were on him when he was found upstairs." Father Mik grimaces.

I touch his arm. "Which is why I think his death and the stolen stuff are two separate incidents. I mean, if someone killed him in order to steal the chalices," I start to tick off an absurd list on my fingers, "they wouldn't take this key fob, come down here, open the lockbox to get the key to the cabinets, go upstairs to open the cabinets, steal the chalices, come back down and return the cabinet key to the lock box and then return the key fob to the body. Doesn't happen."

Father Mik's only response is a morose shoulder-shrug.

The second room is even smaller than the anteroom, holding only a twin bed, a bedside table with a plastic reading lamp, and a foot-locker squeezed into the corner. "These two storage rooms were all I could offer Martin when I first met him." Father Mik sits on the bed and looks around the room, his gaze landing on a framed black and white photo next to the lamp on the bedside table. He picks it up and hands it to me.

In the photo a woman holds a sleeping infant and peers into the camera, her arms positioning the baby so its solemn face is the object of attention. The woman is not smiling, her expression muted, but I sense a projection of pride at her display. Or maybe that's only my interpretation. The photo stands out as the sole personal item in the room where Martin Nygaard had lived alone. I hand back the photo. "I take it this is his ex-wife? Is she the "personal problem" that brought him here?"

Father Mik nods as he replaces the photo on the side table and then stands. "When Martin lost his hearing as a result of the cancer drugs—"

"Oto—oto—" I snap my fingers.

Father Mik smiles and nods. "Ototoxic. Yes, that's right. He became very depressed and tried to commit suicide. This happened twice. After the second time his wife wouldn't allow Martin back into their home. When Martin was hospitalized at Chicago Read, they asked me to visit him because he was Catholic, which of course I did over a period of several weeks.

"Once he was discharged, he had no place to go. He was fired from his job as a salesman after his second suicide attempt. We needed a custodian and he needed a job and a place to stay. I thought it a sign of grace that our mutual needs could be solved." We head back to the hallway. When we pass the men's bathroom I stop and knock on the door, then open it a crack and flash the light switch on and off a couple of times as an alert in case someone deaf inside is taking a leak. When there's no response, I peek inside.

"This is only a toilet. Where did he shower?"

"Fortunately, the rectory houses two full bathrooms, one on each floor. I ceded the first floor facilities to Martin, which he was able to access through the back door of the rectory." We continue on up the stairs and stop at the sacristy.

"There's something else about Mr. Nygaard I never understood as a kid, Father Mik. I mean, he was deaf, right? Not just hard-of-hearing, but completely deaf." In my mind's eye appears a man who stayed apart, alone. "I picture him always standing in the corner of the parish hall away from everyone else at coffee hour."

"You are an observant person, Dana." Father Mik strokes his beard and seems thoughtful. "And quite correct. Martin felt embarrassed, ashamed, and worthless after what happened to him. All because of something over which he had absolutely no control."

"But there had to be more to it. Why didn't he learn to sign? How did you communicate with him?"

Father Mik looks sheepish. "In the beginning I would write things out but that was laborious. I then began using a portable TTY to type my end of the conversation and then cellular phones made our lives easier. I would text, and of course Martin could still talk."

"Sure. But didn't he want to learn how to sign?"

"I am afraid that my eagerness to help Martin really turned out to be a hindrance. I did not take into consideration how ashamed he felt about being deaf." Father Mik's voice quavers. "I thought I could encourage him to assimilate into our deaf congregation—remember, he was a practicing Catholic—and I tried to push signing on him as a viable means of communication."

I zip up my jacket. "What happened?"

"He became further depressed, which is also when I found out he had stopped taking his anti-depressant medication. Fortunately, we were able to get him medical help and he resumed his medication. But it was my mother, God rest her soul, who pointed out what is now obvious to me."

I vaguely recall Father Mik's deaf parents—both gone now—who sat in the front row of St. Nick's during mass.

Father Mik signs to me: *"MN is hearing, not big D deaf, not like us."*

He makes the sign for 'hearing' using his index finger laid across his chin and rotating in a repeated outward motion. At the same time Father Mik repeats the sign for 'hearing' with his other hand but positions it on his forehead. The implication? Martin Nygaard grew up as a hearing person and even though he had become physically deaf, his whole disposition and outlook stayed the same as when he could hear.

"Oh. I see. How old was he when he became deaf?"

"Mid-forties. And while it is possible to pick up ASL later in life, my mother was right. I think Martin felt he would never be like those who are truly capital D deaf."

"Mmm," I say, non-committal. Coming from an all-deaf family, I have witnessed the indignities my parents and sibs suffered when hearing people openly mocked their signing. It doesn't take the ability to hear hateful, ignorant comments and slights to know how cruel hearing people can be.

My snarky thought: was Martin Nygaard originally one of those cruel hearing people? Only to find himself a member of the very group he assailed?

"So, what you keenly observed as a youngster, Dana, was a man who was isolated, in his body and in a crowd." Father Mik closes his hands over his face for a beat and then lowers them into a brief prayer position. We walk to the parish doors leading out to the backyard.

"Do you remember if the police report mentions a time of death?"

"Yes. Somewhere between twelve and twenty-four hours of his being found."

"So that means from sometime after the committee meeting finished at noon on Friday until about four o'clock on Saturday," I say, remembering when Father Mik, Flora and her kids arrived at the church to prepare for five-thirty mass. Father Mik confirms this. I jot it down.

"The little girl who found him, she lives on the other side of the rectory?"

"CiCi, yes."

Father Mik opens the parish door and we step outside, the day as grey and cold as the immense stone angel adjacent to the entrance where we stop. He gestures at the swing set, slide and sandbox dotting the yard.

"She and her brothers often use the rectory yard because we have a small playground set up. On Sundays the children like to burn off their energy after being in Sunday school and church, and the parents get a welcome break during the after-mass coffee."

"I'd like to talk to Cici, find out if there's anything she can remember that might help." I slip my notepad in my back pocket.

"Mrs. Menendez is CiCi's mother. Would you like me to introduce you to her?"

"Not necessary, but thanks. I'll be in touch when I have something."

"Thank you, Dana. I hope you'll reconsider coming to our dinner this Thursday."

Father Mik's expression is kind and I know he means well, but I can't shake my discomfort at again feeling roped into attending church via the annual Thanksgiving dinner. I tell him I'll think about it and head for the house next door.

6

Tuesday, 11/19, Noon

INVESTIGATE what happened to the missing chalices. Simple. But now I clutch a list of deaf parishioners to interview about their last interactions with Martin Nygaard. And I still need to talk with the quixotic Flora Maitland. Then I realize I'll be able to kill these proverbial birds with one stone if I actually do attend St. Nick's this Thursday for Thanksgiving service. Exactly what I don't want to do. I can picture the delight on Father Mik's face when I show up. Oh, and Evie's, too.

It also occurs to me to contact Felice Abandonato, my partner in Homicide. Even though I'm on suspension I'd like to run the whole episode by him and get his take on it. I add him to my mental list and remind myself to ask for the police report, little Cici's interview still on my mind. When I left Father Mik and made my way over to the house next to the rectory, Mrs. Menendez wasn't exactly welcoming. She kept me on her back porch when I inquired about CiCi.

"What is it you want?" Mrs. Menendez demanded. "The police were here and talked to her already." Her voice quavers but I pick up an angry vibe as the cause, not fear.

"I understand," I say, doing my best to be gentle and non-threatening. I gesture at the parish hall. "I'd like to talk to her a little bit about what she saw."

Mrs. Menendez takes a step toward me and thrusts her index finger upward, but she's so short she ends up wagging her finger under my chin. "No! I don't want anyone to talk to her anymore about it. She has bad dreams! She's only a little girl."

"I understand. I'm sorry she has bad dreams. But she might be able to help us find out how Mr. Nygaard died, and—"

"No. Besides, she's in school right now."

I check my phone. Eleven. "Of course, I see. Can I come back later?"

Cici's mother plants both fists on her hips and tilts her head to size me up from a different angle, as if to better transmit her point. "She's a little girl," she repeats. Her hands come off her hips and she crosses her arms. "You will leave her alone now." Before I can plead any further, Mrs. Menendez slips back into her house and a muffled clank sounds as she slides a dead bolt into place.

I drive back to my studio, first passing through Rogers Park to check on the place Jimmy and I called home not that long ago. I double-park, put on my flashers, and gaze at the white, two-story A-frame, which boasts a generous front porch. Friendly Japanese maples flank the front stairs. Right after New Year's we started a renovation to provide an addition for the child Jimmy and I anticipated, but when I miscarried in April everything started to unravel.

Jimmy left for L.A. in July for a three-month training. Now it's November and he's not back. A large blue plastic tarp covers the gouge on the right side of the house and one edge flaps disconsolately in the wind. When Jimmy returned, we were both supposed to stay in my studio until the work on the house was done. I halted the remodeling work until further notice. My uncertainty about my husband along with my suspension from work have both conspired to keep me from moving forward with the expensive addition.

The photo on Martin Nygaard's side table appears unbidden in my mind; the woman and the baby, their happiness and love captured in a brief moment. But from what Father Mik imparted, those feelings didn't last long and what followed was a lot of grief. In spite of the melancholy I'm feeling, I smile at my home. Some houses simply have a happy semblance. I disengage the flashers and drop the Corolla into gear but then linger a moment longer.

How is it two people who love each other cannot stay together?

A question I have not been able to answer.

I gaze once more at our home before driving off and remember Jimmy promised to come home if I got help. But like the woman in the photograph, our life here seems far away.

WITH LESS THAN an hour before IOP, I stow the twelve-pack of beer in my fridge for later and open another pack of Kools. At my desk I consolidate my notes and make additions to what Father Mik told me when my cell announces a text. Evie.

Hi r u home?

My anger at my mother flares for gossiping about me to Father Mik. Thank God I procrastinated in setting up my video phone. Evie won't see the emotion I'm feeling. I take a deep breath to calm down.

Hi mom. Yes, home. How r u?

Fine. you interest for to come to dinner thanksgiving?

Nope, no interest, none. Not if you're going to pump me for more tidbits about my life that you can spread around to the entire deaf community in Chicago. *Yes, fine, can come. What time?*

Church finish home 4:00

OK. What time church start?

10:00 you go? Evie's rising hopes are visible with her question: her daughter might come back to the ecclesiastical fold. But in the back of my mind I know I must attend in order to interview all of the people on my list about Martin Nygaard. No reason Evie needs to know this, though.

Maybe, not sure. See u Thurs. at dinner. I can bring some beer.

A pause before a return text. *not need beer*

For dad. See u soon. I disconnect and turn off my phone before she can respond.

I'VE NEVER SOUGHT out therapy, either individual or group, and after my experience last night with Jen in the education group, my avoidance is well-founded.

Tonight in IOP we have individual therapy. Mine is with Marvin, an African-American man who I calculate is somewhere in his late forties. He tries to engage me in conversation about myself, but I'm reticent to talk about even the most mundane topics: favorite foods, books, movies, my family. All there for mining. We're in the second half of my one-on-one appointment, which I've learned happens once a week, like the education group yesterday, and group therapy tomorrow night. Thursday nights are reserved for something he calls "bridge group." When Marvin doesn't bother to explain further about what we'll do there, I wonder idly if it means the card game.

"Look, Dana, let's be straight with each other, okay?"

Sure, Marvin. Go right ahead.

"Me sitting here trying to engage you in a conversation only works if you talk too." There's thirty minutes left in this sixty-minute session and I crave a smoke break but know he won't give it to me. And while I get some pleasure from watching Marvin squirm trying to fill my silence, my boredom peaks.

"Okay, Marvin, here's what I want to say. I don't want to be here. No, make that I shouldn't be here. My suspension is a load of crap. I didn't drink on the job. A lot of the other cops I work with *do* drink on the job, and I've seen plenty of them. Not. Me."

Marvin leans forward and smiles. I guess he thinks we're relating now. "Okay, good, Dana." He fingers open a manila folder on his desk and peeks inside. "So, if you didn't drink on the job what's with failing the Breathalyzer test?"

My internal screen plays a clear vision of holding the small test kit in my hand, blowing into it, and then watching the damning numbers register. What I can't recall is the story I told my lieutenant about why those numbers still registered the morning after I drank the previous night. I need the story to match what I tell Marvin. "Look. I felt sick the night before and drank some sherry, you know, it settles your stomach. When Koz tested me the next morning, a little stayed in my system."

Marvin leans back in his swivel chair and laces his hands behind his bald head. "Mm-hmm. Your blood alcohol level measured point oh-seven. Just below the legal limit for civilians. But do I understand it right, cops can't show any BAL—"

"Zero," I interrupt, aggravated with his reminder. "Chicago Police Department calls it zero tolerance. No substance, legal or illegal, measurable in the body while on the job."

Marvin regards me, his face serious, his tone mild. "How late did you drink that sherry?" His question confuses me. I expect a "how much," not a "how late" inquiry. "Come on, Dana, it's not a hard question. This only happened three weeks ago."

The longest three weeks of my recent life, suspended from my job for a really questionable charge. "I don't know. Late. Midnight?"

"And you got tested," he refers to the folder again, "at ten the next morning. Tell me, how much sherry did you need to settle your stomach?" He draws quotes around the last phrase.

Here's the question I've been expecting. I look him in the eye, intent on projecting honesty. "I drank two glasses."

"Two glasses? Hope you're not thinking I'm going to believe you drank two bitty glasses of sherry and that's why you still blew a measurable BAL." He straightens in his seat, runs his hand over his head devoid of any hair, and sighs.

"I don't care what you—"

Marvin interrupts. "Because you know, or you will after you sit through some of our workshops, your liver churns through about an ounce of alcohol an hour. Takes longer if you're a small woman, which you aren't. So, my guess is you were drinking a lot more than two glasses of sherry if you came up positive ten hours later. Or else you were drinking from a thirty-two ounce glass."

I cringe at his attempt at humor. "If you already figured that out, then what're you asking me for?" I cross my legs and arms. I hope my body language is obvious to my counselor.

"A real basic idea in treatment is getting honest, Dana. With me, with the group, with yourself. Starts with acknowledging how much and how often you drink. I see how angry you are about being here, being suspended from work. That's a place to start. That's a consequence. There's no one definition for an alcoholic—"

I start to protest and he cuts me off again.

"Relax. I'm not calling you an alcoholic. Shoot, people get so bent out of shape about that word. What I'm trying to say is that drinking too much or too often usually has consequences."

I must look puzzled at this statement because Marvin pauses for a long moment.

"Here, try this on for size: a person is in trouble with alcohol or drugs when it affects any major part of his or her life. Those would be work, family and health." He ticks off these three starting with his baby finger, which sports a long, manicured nail.

This I understand. My heart beats harder and faster in my chest until it seems almost audible. I feel like a ballplayer caught in a rundown. All three areas Marvin mentions do fit: suspended from my job, estranged from my husband, overweight and addicted to cigarettes. Consequences. The added possibility my miscarriage resulted from drinking arises for consideration, an idea suggested by my doctor in a recent physical exam. I reject it within seconds and instead take out a Kool, signaling to Marvin I'm ready to leave.

Marvin gives me the once-over and seems to decide not to push me any further. He pulls out a piece of paper from my folder and slides it across to me.

"Here's your homework until our next session. It's a worksheet I want you to fill out. Write down what areas of your life are affected by your drinking. There's two hours left tonight, so take a break, then you can do your homework either before or after watching the video set up in the library. I'll see you tomorrow—group therapy."

I leave without saying goodbye.

7

_____

Wednesday, 11/20, 5:30 a.m.

PRIOR TO SUNRISE there are plenty of empty places to park in the hospital lot. I lounge for a minute before shutting off the engine and take the last drag on my cigarette, which tastes harsh. I wash down three ibuprofen tablets with the remains of a large coffee from Dunkin' Donuts and get ready to go inside. The air is cold and damp. My breath is visible in the light from huge halogen lamps in the parking lot as I make the short walk to the entrance, which does nothing for my hangover but does wake me up.

When I arrive at the pre-op desk to check in at six a.m., the patient I'm interpreting for—a deaf woman—and her husband are already waiting for me. The nurse takes us to pre-op and gives the patient the gown and head covering she'll wear for her gall bladder surgery.

The doctor comes by to explain the surgery, which I interpret, and asks the woman to sign some forms, which she does. They wheel her off to surgery at seven and I spend the next hour interpreting for the worried husband, who asks a million questions of an incredibly accommodating nurse.

With about two hours free before I'm needed in post-op, I'm about to leave and search for coffee but the husband wants me to stay and chat with him in the waiting room. In these situations, I've noticed that younger deaf people prefer to commune with their cell phones or tablets and ignore the interpreter, while older deaf still want and expect me to sit and socialize with them. But I want to get away, desperate for coffee. Another reason to keep my professional distance from the husband is that he possibly knows Evie or JJ, my parents.

I beg off and go search for the cafeteria; maybe some toast would go well with the coffee, although I'm pretty queasy from drinking after IOP last night. A niggling thought appears. In a post-Marvin video at IOP, filled with people talking about their drinking, their habits, how they came to know they were alcoholic and the like, one woman's story stood out for me. She was about my age.

What cinched the alkie label for her was the realization that she drank even when she needed to stay sober for something important, like taking care of her kids. What hit closer to home was her admission she drank late into the night even though she had responsibilities early the next morning.

I shake off the comparison, though. Yes, I did drink late last night, got about four hours sleep. But this morning I still managed to get my ass out of bed, in gear, and arrive at this job on time—unlike the woman in the video. Not the same. Not at all.

In the cafeteria I contemplate some Twinkies instead of toast. My cell phone chirps. It's an unknown number. I drop the yellow cakes onto my tray, next to a large container of coffee, and lift it one-handed as I answer the phone and head for the cashier. "Demeter."

"Not too early for you?"

For a split second I can't place the voice. My heart skips a beat when I realize Jimmy's on the other end. Unknown number. He changed it and didn't tell me. "Hey. No, not too. I'm on a break from an interpreting job. How are you?" I really want to know where, not how, but I feel oddly formal talking with him.

"Okay. Listen, I know it's the day before Thanksgiving and everything, but I'm back and—"

"What? When'd you get back?" He's been in L.A. for four months and now shows up unannounced?

"Late last night. Hey, I'd like to—"

"Why didn't you tell me you were coming?"

"I did." Pissed. As if *I* got it wrong. "I told you three weeks ago when we talked that I'd be back by Thanksgiving."

I experience a fleeting sense of confusion, then anger. When we last talked he said he was coming home for Christmas. I'm sure of it. Neither one of us says anything for a minute. During the silence I deposit my tray onto a table but my hand shakes, causing the coffee to slosh over the Twinkies package.

"Shit, I can't believe that happened."

"I can. You were drunk when we talked—"

"Jesus, Jimmy! Not that. I spilled my—oh, never mind. I'm sure you said you were coming back at Christmas, okay?" He did, I know it. He's trying to keep me off balance.

"I'm not going to argue with you, D. I'm here, at the house. How long you working? Can we meet after?"

I sit down at the table and pull the Twinkies package out of the spilled coffee, mopping up what I can with a napkin the size of a sticky note. My head throbs from a lack of caffeine and nicotine and an overabundance of stress. Jimmy wants to meet today?

"I'm booked here until noon. Any time after that, okay." I sound a hell of a lot more confident than I feel.

"Good. Make it lunch at Brau Haus. I'm dying for a brat with sauerkraut." He disconnects before I can respond.

LINCOLN AVENUE still holds no open parking spaces when I swing by Brau Haus for the second time. I head southeast on the diagonal street for two blocks and slide into a spot. At the parking box I'm unsure how much time to buy, hoping for and yet worrying about a long lunch. I hit the max button for two hours and push away the worry, then walk toward the restaurant.

When the faded wooden sign comes into view, a tiny joy springs up inside me along with the same nervousness I felt when we went to Brau Haus on our first date. Twelve years later the place hasn't changed much. A few customers lean against the century-old wooden bar decorated with a brass foot rail, which spans the entire left side of the room. The remaining space is dotted with square tables. The high ceiling is covered with pieces of hammered copper now green with age. Over the sound system Elvis sings about a blue Christmas.

I scan the room for Jimmy, unsure if I'm early or late since he didn't specify a time, but don't see him. Then a waitress moves away from a table near the rear and there he is, back to the wall and facing the door. God, he's tan. He exudes health. But wearing only a windbreaker in this weather? I hurry over, trying on a smile I don't feel.

Jimmy stands when I approach the table but doesn't come around to greet me, so I go to him. He accepts my kiss but turns his head slightly so my lips land on his cheek. It hurts as much as a punch.

"So," he says. "Thanks for meeting me. I miss this stuff in L.A.—god, it's so good to be back with real people, you know?"

Sitting across from him, I nod, but I don't really know because I've never been to L.A. or California, period. I'd never leave Chicago—my parents, really—and if I did, it wouldn't be for L.A.

"Warm weather year-round makes people soft," I say. "Give me the Midwest anytime. People are hearty enough to shovel a foot of snow dumped overnight and still get to work on time the next morning."

Before he can respond, we both turn at the sound of a bunch of guys entering the bar, their voices loud, bantering, laughing and making crude jokes. The group heads our way and scrapes two tables together only a few strides from us.

The waitress returns with a draft for Jimmy and takes my order. When she leaves to retrieve a Beck's for me his gaze follows her, doing a complete scan from top to bottom and lingering at ass-level. I glance at my jeans and jacket and realize I'm not exactly a candidate for the feminine finals, in fact, my duds seem pretty butch compared to hers. She returns and bends over to deposit the bottle in front of me, flashing cleavage packed into a form-fitting maroon sweater, then leaves. He watches her retreat again. I scowl at him. "You can put your tongue back in your mouth now."

"Sorry." He's smiling but sounds sheepish. Good. Still, I soften being with him again. Four months apart. Too much time and too much worrying for me.

"You look good, Jimmy."

"Thanks, D." No corresponding compliment comes my way and I feel even more self-conscious about my appearance. He downs half his draft. I drink straight from the bottle.

I want to ask why he stayed in L.A. an extra month after his three-month training on gangs, but my question falters. "You got back—?"

"Yesterday, like I said. Flew in late. Had some things to square away with the brass today, before Thanksgiving. You know."

I nod for the second time but again don't know what he means, certain my face must register what I'm feeling. He clears his throat in a way I do know, a message we're embarking on a serious conversation.

Before he can begin the waitress is back with our food. Jimmy waves off another draft and asks for a Coke. I order another Beck's and get raised eyebrows from him, which I ignore. She moves on to the group of guys and takes their food orders. They have become rowdier and more obnoxious after downing a couple of pitchers of beer.

The bar begins to fill with the lunch crowd. The jukebox plays a rap song with a percussive, penetrating beat, which goes through me and amps my jitters. Jimmy concentrates on finishing his brat but I push away my plate after eating a small portion of the hot German potato salad and drink instead. The beer settles my stomach. He gestures at my plate and I give him the go-ahead sign to take it. I marvel at his appetite. And not an ounce of fat on him.

One of the guys in the group picks up an empty pitcher and walks over to the bar where our waitress is serving other customers. He's tall and slender but has large hands and powerful forearms, like he lifts weights or performs physical labor of some sort. His blue eyes and white-blond hair slicked with gel remind me of a surfer, his strut says he's insufferable because he knows he's cute. He bangs the pitcher on the bar and gestures for her to fill it. She takes it and nods back toward his table indicating she'll bring it to him.

When she delivers the beer to their table she asks for payment. The surfer stands, swaying slightly, and starts digging into his pants pocket. It's obvious when the light comes on in his pea brain. He broadcasts his next idea to the waitress and his buddies.

"It's in here." He pats the front of his pants, provocatively low, and leers at the other guys around the table before addressing her again. "Why don't you give me a hand pulling it out?" The other guys hoot and clap at their friend's come-on.

Jimmy notices, too. He drops a plastic container still half full of coleslaw onto his plate and wipes his hands on his jeans as he stands, pushing his chair back until it hits the wall. The waitress ignores Surfer Dude's insinuation, snatches up the pitcher she just deposited, and walks back toward the bar.

Surfer Dude is next to her in a flash. He latches a hand onto her right arm, squeezing until she sags on that side and relinquishes the beer. Jimmy's behind the guy in the next instant. He knocks the pitcher away, the beer spraying in an arc over several tables. He grabs the guy's right wrist and twists it up behind him, high and tight. I follow his lead and get in the jerk's face. Remarkably, the guy's left hand is still clamped onto the waitress's arm.

I shout in his face. "Police! Let her go! Now!"

His bloodshot eyes widen as he jerks his head back. My adrenaline revs from confronting this doofus. He drops his hold on the young woman and she scurries behind the bar. Jimmy stiff-arms the guy back to his seat and shoves him down.

The entire room is silent except for Burl Ives belting out "A Holly Jolly Christmas."

"Here's the deal." Jimmy's low growl cuts through the music. "You never come back here and I don't arrest you for harassment and being drunk and disorderly."

He lays a look on the group that clears the chairs in ten seconds. Surfer Dude pulls some bills from his pants pocket—the one he invited the waitress to help him with—and throws it on the table. He scoots out the door backwards, never taking his eyes off Jimmy.

Back at our table there's a fresh draft and another bottle of Beck's along with our tab marked "on the house," and signed *Rosalia*. The noise level is getting back to normal. Smiling, I raise my bottle at the waitress and she mouths *thank you* across the room. Jimmy pushes the fresh beer to the middle of the table and instead sucks on an ice cube from his Coke.

"Shit, that's like old times. Rousting some assholes," I say, giddy from the action.

Jimmy grins at me and I know he feels the same way. Abruptly, his grin drops and his face changes—serious but anxious at the same time. He pushes up the sleeves of his sweater, like he's getting ready to do some dirty work. "I want to move to L.A., Dane."

That's Jimmy. No foreplay.

"Let's see, you left in July for a three-month training. Thanksgiving's tomorrow." I count in a mocking way on my hand and hold up four fingers, look at them, front and back. "Seems like you already have."

He hunkers down, stretching his forearms out on the table and bringing his head close to mine. "Don't," he says. "Don't put this on me. The training was legit. I stayed because I couldn't stand seeing you sad anymore, D." He eyeballs me with a slight turn of the head but quickly returns his gaze to his folded hands.

"Sad? Christ, Jimmy. You lose a favorite ring? You're sad. A good friend moves away? You're sad. I lost our baby. I'm fucking devastated." Instead of meeting my gaze or reaching out to touch me, he trains his eyes on his folded hands where his fingertips grip tight at the knuckles. I push my chair away from the table and head for the bathroom, blindsided by Jimmy's news, my tears unstoppable.

Jimmy is still seated at the table when I return and says nothing when I sit and finish the bottle of Beck's. He crosses his arms over his chest. "So that's your answer? Check out with booze?"

I deposit the bottle on the table harder than I mean to, making our empty plates jump. Try being quiet while upset—impossible. "I'm not the one running away, Jimmy. I stayed here, damn it. I can't grieve this any faster. Not for you, not for my parents, not for my job." My voice registers high scorching anger and people at nearby tables stop talking, their heads turning toward us.

I'm beyond tears now and feel mean but I don't care. The booze gives me license to act. I stand, pick up his abandoned draft beer and chug the entire glass, wanting to rile him. It works. Jimmy jumps up and rams his arms into his ridiculous windbreaker. "Come on, Dane. Let's go." Like he's rousting *me* now.

A woman at the table next to us makes a fearful noise and when I glance over, she scoots her chair away from me and nearer to the man with her. He drapes his arm around her and pulls her close, then has the temerity to grin at me. Great. Now we're a floor show for the quieted room.

I gesture at Jimmy's jacket. "It's thirty fucking degrees outside, Gennaro."

He grabs my arm and holds my coat up as if he's going to stuff me into it. "I'm taking you home, D." I jerk my arm out of his grasp, swipe my coat back and throw it on.

"Taking me home? Where's that, Jimmy? You left our home and I'm not there anymore." I glare at the guy enjoying our show as I stalk past him and out to the parking lot. Jimmy ends up following me out of the bar and tailing me in his car back to my studio. I hope he worries every inch of the way about me driving under the influence.

8

Wednesday, 11/20, 4:30 p.m.

THE EARLY MORNING job combined with a beer lunch on an empty
stomach both conspire to knock me out for a nap. Two hours later I
wake up ravenous but my kitchen cabinets and small fridge yawn
with emptiness, so I make a grease run at a McDonald's drive-
through on the way to IOP. I arrive at group early, the only one in the
room fifteen minutes before the six o'clock starting time.

The ring of chairs is once again set up in the middle of the room.
Because I feel deflated from fighting with Jimmy, I have no strength
left to rebel against joining the circle. I fume again. He told me
Christmas, damn it, *not* Thanksgiving. It's a shitty way to keep me off
balance, unsure of myself. Like changing his phone number but not
telling me. And by showing up unexpectedly I bet he thought I'd
jump all over him in gratitude instead of asking him why the hell he
didn't come back in October when he was supposed to.

But replaying our conversation in my mind I realize we got interrupted by the guy hassling the waitress and I never did get an answer for why he stayed the extra month in L.A. Except that he doesn't want to see me "sad," which I'm sure is his codeword for drunk. But if he doesn't want to see me "sad" because I'm grieving my miscarriage, then he's a shitty husband. For better or for worse was the promise.

The members of the group straggle in and fill up the circle except for two chairs. No counselors—again. I recognize some of the group members from Monday. Some chat easily, a few remain quiet like me.

Jen sweeps into the room. "Okay, people. I'm here. Sorry I'm late. Oh. No Marvin? Let me round him up." She pages him from a phone on the wall and we wait for a few minutes until he arrives, apologizing. It's six-fifteen. I crave a cigarette.

Group therapy: not educational, not individual, but everyone together sharing personal problems. I hate it. First a "check-in." Marvin polls us individually, asking us to give a one-word feeling to describe our mood and then choose a number on a scale from one to ten to show the intensity of that feeling. I'm glad I'm the last one to answer because I need the time to come up with something, anything, which will sound plausible. "Tired. Ten," I say.

"Tired's not an emotion, Dana," Jen pipes up. "It's a state of being." She glances at Marvin and he nods at me.

"Try again, Dana," he says.

The other group members turn to me. I feel pressured to perform. Even though I think I did answer the question I'm pissed I need to conform further to Jen's rule. "Pissed." I gesture toward my comrades. "How come we all seem to be able to get here on time but you two are always late?" Then, remembering I'm supposed to rate my feeling, I hold up both hands with my fingers splayed out. "Ten."

Members in the group nod and a few chuckle. Hades gives me a thumbs-up. Marvin and Jen regard each other, some kind of silent communication happens, and then Jen speaks. "You're getting here on time and that's good. Marvin and I are very busy but want you to know we will be here, even if that means we're a little late sometimes. Try not to focus too much on what others are or aren't doing, Dana. Try to keep your side of the street clean." Jen smiles at me and turns to Marvin with a go-ahead nod.

"Good," Marvin says. "Now, last week I suggested the topic for us to discuss because no one could think of anything. But at the end of group I asked everyone to come prepared tonight with at least one topic you want to talk about. Like something that bothers you or makes you happy or that you find challenging, and so on. Remember?" He scans the group. The guy I think looks like W.C. Fields avoids Marvin's eyes and stares at the floor. Ariel shrugs at me. Louis fidgets. Finally, Hades raises his hand. "Hades, good. Go."

"Yeah, okay. I got a couple things. First, I got to say I feel pretty good, you know, in my body. I'm off blow and pills for two weeks now but I'm still kind of nervous, edgy. Can't sleep too good."

"Okay, thanks, Hades. Group, what do you want to say to what he brings up?" A Latino guy on my right raises his hand. "Izzy?"

"Yeah. My wife and me fight all the time, you know, and I'm here because I drink. I never did any drugs and I don't like them. Drugs are dangerous and they kill people. I teach my fifth graders to stay away from them." Luz, a Latina about my age, sits next to Izzy and hangs on his every word, nodding her head like crazy at his pronouncements.

"Remember what we're learning in education group, Izzy." Jen says. "Alcohol is a drug same as pills, cocaine, or marijuana." She sounds like she's talking to a little kid.

"But those things are illegal, Miss. Nobody ever got arrested for drinking," Izzy says. Luz grins at his brilliance.

"Plenty of people get busted for drinking," I say, before I even realize I hold an opinion. "You ever hear of drunk and disorderly?"

Izzy crosses his arms and looks sideways at me. "Well, what I mean is you can buy alcohol at the store, it's legal. Those other drugs are illegal, you can go to jail."

I don't respond.

"Man," says Hades, "you not talking about what I'm talking about. I said I'm feeling nervous without using and that's hard. Don't care if it's illegal. And hell, you can too get arrested for drinking!" Hades looks at W.C. Fields and points. "William there been arrested twice for DUI." William's gaze stays firmly on his feet.

"Yes, okay," Marvin says. "Good, Hades. Good, Izzy. You're talking about your drug of choice and some consequences of using," he nods at William. "And consequences of not using," then nods at Hades. "Let's get a read on individual preferences. Main drug of choice cocaine? Raise your hand." Hades' hand goes up. Ariel pokes her arm up halfway.

"Marvin? I'm pretty much crack," Ariel says. "Is that included? I mean, I think of cocaine, I think of fluffy piles of blow." Ariel laughs when Hades holds out his hand and she slaps it.

"Good question, Ariel. Anyone in the group know the answer, maybe from your education group with Jen?" Nobody knows or nobody cares to answer, so Jen reviews some basic chemistry for us, allowing how crack is part of the cocaine family. So, Hades and Ariel are our resident drug addicts and the rest of the group drinks.

"Cinderella?" Marvin gestures to an African-American woman on my left who uses a heavy hand with her pancake make-up, her face an unnatural shade of dark copper. Unfortunately for her, the cosmetics only enhance the heavy bags under her eyes and sagging chin-folds cascading down her neck. "You haven't said anything yet tonight. What do you think about Hades' topic?"

"Cindy," she says. "I like Cindy." Cinderella glances at Marvin and then around at the group. Her face shows no affect and her lips barely move when she speaks. "I can't sleep neither," she says. "The doctor, he told me a glass of wine help me sleep but Jen says I can't drink anymore in this program." Deep brown circles below her eyes and her slow way of talking make me think she's telling the truth about her lack of sleep.

"Okay, good. Thank you, Cinder—uh, Cindy. Anyone else have difficulty sleeping now that you're not using?" Marvin says.

I think about my four-beer lunch and two-hour nap but I'm not inclined to share this with the group. A few other hands go up in response to his question and Marvin discusses some "natural" methods to relax.

I zone out while he's talking, thinking instead about Thanksgiving and going to St. Nick's tomorrow. I plan to get there before the church service starts so I can talk with the altar guild women and at last meet Flora Maitland. I also want to find Ben Warshawski, head of the committee that drank the coffee from the fateful urn Martin Nygaard washed. I assume Ben and the other committee members will be at the annual Thanksgiving get-together, since they planned it.

I dither with myself about trying to interview CiCi, the little girl who found the janitor. I don't want to further traumatize her and doubt I'll get past her gate-keeper mother. Easier to call Felice Abandonato, my estranged partner in Homicide, run everything past him, get his take on it, and ask for a copy of the girl's interview with the police.

We break for a cigarette. The second half of group drags on mercilessly while each member details the consequences of their drinking or drugging. "Dana?" Marvin gives me what I interpret as an encouraging smile. I think of the blank homework sheet he gave me yesterday where I'm supposed to write about how my drinking affects my family, work, and health. It's still blank.

I again feel the same pressure to perform and then lecture myself about how stupid it is to feel pressured because this is only a group of people trying to—do what? Stop drinking? Solve their problems? I don't even know. And I'm mad at the group's ability to make me feel anxious, mad because I don't want to answer Marvin. "I don't know, Marvin." I'm hoping he'll skip over me but his gaze doesn't move.

"What is it you don't know, Dana?"

"The answer to your question."

Marvin defers to the group to "help" me. My pal Hades once again decides to explain things. "See, it's like this. You're here for some reason. I think you said your job before." He looks to Ariel for confirmation. "Didn't she?"

Ariel nods.

"Yeah, your job. Means you probably absent too much 'cause you hung over or some shit like that. Boss gives you the big talk, tells you to get you some treatment or don't come back? That about right?" He grins at Marvin and bobs his head.

I can feel Ariel staring at me from across the circle. Suddenly she points at me, her voice squeaky with surprise.

"Wait a minute, she's a cop!" Ariel stands up like she's ready to bolt from the room. "She said drunk and disorderly before. That's cop talk. Fuck! She can't arrest me can she, Marvin? Or Hades? Fuck!"

Marvin invites her to take a seat—no one's going to arrest anyone. "Dana, why don't you tell the group your situation, why you're here?"

Here it is. So, what do I say? It's a big misunderstanding and I only agreed to go through with this because I don't want to lose my job, the most important thing in my life other than my husband. The group looks at me expectantly but I'm at a loss for words. How do I explain the suspension? I can't. I don't even understand it myself.

Cindy pats my shoulder and murmurs something so low I can't hear it but I can tell from her tone of voice it's meant to convey pity or sympathy. "I might be moving to L.A. My husband's thinking about transferring there and of course I'd go with him. We're both in Homicide right now but he wants to join a special gangs unit. He just got back from a training course out there." My words come out in a rush. I can't believe the whopping lie I'm telling these people. There's no way I'd ever move to California.

"Damn! I love L.A. Beautiful women. The ocean. You get warm weather all year long—nothing like Chicago," Izzy says, and actually shivers when he recounts our current weather. Luz nods enthusiastically.

"L.A.'s cool," says Ariel, now distracted from her initial freakout about me. "Lots of parties. My girlfriend went out there and stayed high for a month on other people's—"

Jen interrupts the group reverie. "Two things, Dana. First, you didn't answer Marvin's question about why you're in IOP. Second, you ever hear of a geographical cure?"

She doesn't give me time to answer the second question. Instead, she launches into the definition: people who try to avoid a problem by moving to another location, deluded in their thinking that life in a different town or state or country will somehow solve things.

"The only flaw in the geographical cure idea for an alcoholic or drug addict is wherever you go, there you are. If drinking is a problem for you in Chicago, you'll encounter the same difficulty with it in L.A." Jen tries to catch my eye but I avoid her.

"Yeah, but at least you can drink on the beach," Ariel says, laughing, and the group begins to chatter.

9

Thursday, 11/21, 10:30 a.m.

A COLD START to Thanksgiving morning, the sun making me squint as I drive south on Western Avenue. Neighborhoods colored with brightly painted storefronts, taquerias, and bars serving *cerveza fria* slide past my windshield. Traffic is light. Farther south there's a gradual decline where the buildings are rundown or empty with gaping storefronts. The taverns recur on every block, mean and uninviting—where metal bars cover the windows and doors—places I would never frequent if I wanted a drink.

Panhandlers and people who are homeless compete for empty doorways in order to escape the wind and my thoughts are unkind; these are the real alcoholics, people who have lost everything in search of the blessed high. Not me at all.

I turn west on Washington. Even in the bright sun the street and sidewalks are dark and gray, any color bled out. Grit skitters across my windshield. In front of a twenty-four hour liquor store a few old Black men sit in a circle on broken-down kitchen chairs and pass around a brown bag. Block after depressing block of shabby tenements, their windows opaque with steamy condensation, populate Chicago's West Side where Father Mik's church stands out as an oasis.

I park behind St. Nick's in a lot by the alley, which is surrounded by a chain-link fence so decrepit even a six-year-old could breach it. I remove a garbage bag of empty beer cans from my trunk and quickly stow it in one of the trashcans lining the back of the parish hall. I cross the yard, the crushed-stone gravel crunching under my shoes, and enter the parish hall door next to where the larger-than-life stone angel stands guard. Inside, the fragrant scent of roast turkey permeates the air, people bustle around, and kids run up and down the long staircase to the second floor.

In the main hall upstairs, men set up long folding tables end-to-end and top them with orange plastic tablecloths. Hearing and deaf kids mark individual place settings with white plastic forks and knives. Clay cornucopia candleholders—making their annual appearance since before my time—adorn the tables every few feet.

Not finding the women I want to interview I return downstairs and run into Sarah Gilbert, head of the altar guild and a good friend of my parents. Next to her is a woman I don't recognize. Sarah's left arm is in a cast up to her shoulder and in a clumsy way she uses it to gesticulate at the metal cabinets Father Mik showed me on Tuesday.

"Hi, Sarah. How's your wrist?" I give her a quick hug and she hugs me back. The red curly hair on top of her head skims my chin.

"It's improving. At least now I don't need to wear the sling—I hated it!" Sarah signs quickly and clearly with her unencumbered hand. *"I'm surprised you're here. Evie didn't tell me you were coming today."*

My mother must be slipping. I assumed she would somehow figure out my attendance today and broadcast it. Then again, something mundane like my coming to church isn't as juicy as my private life. I manage to avoid Sarah's invitation to badmouth Evie. *"I want to talk with you when you're free for a minute."* I glance at the other woman while I sign to Sarah. She obviously isn't deaf or at least doesn't understand American Sign Language because I'm not using my voice and she hasn't watched our conversation from the start.

"No, not right now. I'm helping Flower," she nods at the other woman, *"get the altar ready for mass."*

"Her name is Flower?" I scrunch my face into a question and touch a rounded, O-shaped hand to each side of my nose for the floral sign.

"That's a name sign we made up for her. Really, it's F-L-O-R-A." Sarah uses her fingers to spell out the woman's actual name. *"I forget her last name, M-A-something—"* Her fingers flutter and trail off, the visual equivalent of blah, blah, blah.

I take up the fingerspelling with *"M-A-I-T-L-A-N-D?"* and Sarah points at my hand, her head tilting in affirmation.

"She's hearing. Doesn't know ASL," Sarah signs.

I face the young woman, who stands about five feet tall, and use my voice and sign at the same time so both women can understand me. "Hi, my name's Dana Demeter." I fingerspell my name as I say it. "My mom's deaf and goes to church here. And I used to, a million years ago." I laugh, trying to engage Flora.

Both of her hands fidget with the end of her long, pale-blonde braid trailing over her left shoulder. "Hi. I'm Flora Maitland." The short sentence seems to cost her some effort. Contrasted with Sarah's peppy signing this woman's Southern twang comes off tired and flat.

Sarah signs that the mass starts in fifteen minutes and they need to finish setting up. Still speaking while I sign, I ask Flora to join my meeting with the other altar guild women after church. She agrees. I duck outside to smoke and settle on the parish hall steps next to the hulking stone angel. The yard seems smaller than when I played here years ago with my twin brother David and younger sister Daphne, who are both deaf. I survey the area, noting the swing set and sandbox—possibly the same ones we played on—still occupy the same places in the yard, more weathered from time and exposure.

One Sunday when David chased me around this gravel-filled lot he almost caught me but I faked him out by stopping dead cold. He slammed right into me. He fell backwards and hit the gravel hard enough to drive some of the sharp stones into his scalp and draw blood. Outraged, he jumped up and lunged at me. The split second before he made contact, I realized we weren't eye-level anymore: I was looking up at him. Incredible sadness stung me in that moment. I knew my twin and I would grow apart, his slight height advantage already starting the process, and this separation would continue as we aged. I was hearing and he was deaf. I could communicate in ASL as fluently as my deaf family, which was a plus, but I could never *be* capital D deaf like them; therein, the sadness.

David gave me a deserved shove right into a pile of dog shit, which stained my Sunday dress. Evie—furious—made us kneel on the wooden floor in our pew for the entire mass. No plush kneeler cushions for wayward children. The memory of Evie's punishment makes me smile as I stub out my cigarette and throw it behind the stone angel because I'm too lazy to dispose of it properly.

Back inside, the organ notes of the opening hymn signal the start of the church service. The smell of coffee draws me upstairs to the kitchen, which is adjacent to the room where the tables are set for the dinner. I try to stay out of the way of the six church ladies who are in the final phase of assembling the Thanksgiving repast, and sidle up to the metal credenza that holds an industrial-sized coffeemaker. But before I dispense a cup, the old wooden floor next to the sink captures my attention. It's marred by a dark brown stain the size of a manhole cover. Martin Nygaard, the old church custodian, died here.

At the metal sink I trace my finger around the outside corner where its two edges meet; sharp, and in Martin Nygaard's case, deadly. A scene plays out in my mind. The old man is dizzy and falls, his head hits this sharp corner and he drops to the floor, bleeding to death.

My initial reaction to Father Mik's story still holds: No way this is related to the theft. I suppose it's possible the thief came upstairs searching for more objects to steal and surprised Martin, then shoved him into the sink hard enough to kill him. But that conjecture feels forced. Besides, if someone downstairs heard Mr. Nygaard upstairs, my bet is they'd bail, not climb umpteen stairs to investigate the noise. And the chalices and candlesticks were a significant haul so there was no need to hang around looking for more. And because the kitchen is on the second floor, far from the storage cabinets down-stairs, someone in the kitchen wouldn't hear a person stealing the chalices—it's too far away. Besides, Martin was deaf.

I tap a cup of coffee from the urn. My hand trembles slightly when I raise the cup to my lips and I slosh a bit on the floor. Shit. I grab a paper towel and bend down to wipe up the spill. A corner of some-thing white peeks out from under the credenza. Curious, I pull out a sheet of heavy bond paper. There's a poem printed on it with the title *I Never Knew You but I Miss You All the Same.*

As I scan the words something itches at me and I realize the blood-stain on the floor forms a backdrop and contrast to the white paper I hold. One of the church ladies finds me an unused clear plastic gallon bag and I slip the poem into it. The chance is slight but if the person who dropped this paper is somehow related to Martin Nygaard's death I don't want to compromise possible evidence.

I take the poem and my coffee and settle at one of the empty tables in the room next door, which in an hour will teem with deaf and hearing families chowing down. I read through the poem's twelve lines twice but can't really make any sense of it. It seems like a love poem but there's another quality to it, something lost and forlorn. The last lines of verses one and two are the same as the title but the final line in verse three substitutes the word *love* for the word *miss.* I place the poem in my backpack and sip coffee while the women in the kitchen begin to load food onto the serving tables.

Two men enter the room carrying folding chairs, which they open and set up at a table across the room from me. They chat with each other, signing in a public way, and I casually eavesdrop because I can; if they wanted to keep the conversation private, they would turn their backs to block my prying eyes. They talk about being out of work, which is no surprise. A lot of deaf people are unemployed or work at jobs below their skill levels.

One guy who's bald says he's going to apply for the janitor job now that Martin Nygaard's dead. This gets my attention. Although I still think the theft and the janitor's death aren't connected here is a possible motive for murder. I make a mental note of the man's features, then sling my backpack over one arm and take my coffee downstairs and outside to smoke again until church is finished. I smoke quickly in the cold, then duck back inside to wait by the parish hall doors. A crush of people streams through the hallway leading from the church into the parish hall and on upstairs to the waiting feast. Sarah makes her way over to me with two teenage girls in tow and introduces them to me as sisters who are deaf and students at Whitney Young High School; Nina, a senior, and Tina, a junior.

"The three of us are the altar guild," Sarah signs. *"We take turns. One other woman too, J-E-A-N-N-I-E, but she moved away three months ago. Now Flower joined but she's new and we're still teaching her. It's hard. She doesn't sign and she's hearing."* The girls nod in agreement.

"There's something wrong with her, too. She's not very smart," Tina signs.

"And she's got so many kids," exclaims Nina. She signs *children* with exaggerated repetition, her arms pumping up and down, to impress upon me the hordes that are Flora Maitland's offspring. *"We want a fourth person on the guild so we can each work for a month, then take off two months. Easier that way."* More head nodding. I scrutinize the thinning crowd and ask the trio where Flora is now.

Sarah raises one eyebrow. *"She and her kids were going to stay for dinner but I saw her leave church after communion."*

Flora Maitland's elusiveness increases my suspicion about her stealing the relics. I make a quick plan to return to her apartment and talk with her after finishing at St. Nick's. *"Okay. I need to ask you a few questions about the chalices and the cabinets."* All three of them begin signing at the same time. *"Time Out! Let me ask a question, then you can take turns answering,"* I sign, as I extend my L-shaped hand and aim it at each of them, a slight twist of the wrist showing who's first, then second, then third. I raise my eyebrows as I sign so they know I expect a response to what I propose.

In unison, they sign: *"Fine."*

I chuckle at the irony. Sarah apologizes and begins to reprimand the girls. I wave her off. But after a few minutes it's clear the three of them aren't suspects and they don't have any new information. Their ritual for opening the cabinets never varied: Martin Nygaard unlocked the cabinets when they needed to get in and he locked up afterwards. He wouldn't let them use the key. *"Not even for one second,"* Sarah signs.

"You know Mr. Nygaard, he's so...so perfect in his ways." Nina makes the sign for *perfect* with the tips of her index fingers and thumbs touching each other crisply, her face a sneer projecting a negative comment on this perfection. I picture Martin Nygaard's rooms in the church basement, neat to the point of anonymity, and wonder if his compulsiveness caused his loneliness. Or was it a result?

"Right, right," Tina agrees, moving her hands forward a bit so her extended index finger, inherent in the sign, actually points at Nina.

"Martin didn't want Father Mik to think he couldn't do his job," Sarah adds. *"He was such a hard worker."* A kinder, gentler reading.

"Did Father Mik ever give any of you his key?" I ask. A trio of negative head-shakes.

Sarah, Tina, Nina, and I climb the long staircase to where the Thanksgiving dinner is in full swing, the three of them heading for the kitchen while I get in line behind Father Mik. He's holding a paper plate and a napkin with a gold turkey stamped on it.

"Everything's just wonderful, Father Mik," I sign, then gesture at the room, warm with festive decorations and the savory smell of turkey and dressing. *"This hasn't changed in more years than I can remember."*

Father Mik stuffs his napkin in his jacket pocket and clamps his paper plate under his arm in order to sign unencumbered. *"Dana, hello!"* He smiles and surveys the crowd, love emanating from his lined face. *"I'm always pleased and humbled by our Thanksgiving celebration. The deaf people here feel at home and their fellowship is deep and connected."* I agree with him about St. Nick's. The families here are relaxed and accepted in a place where they can freely use their language. There aren't any ignorant hearing people gawking at the fluid hands slicing through the air, or worse, mocking deaf people openly by crudely mimicking American Sign Language. Throughout my childhood I soaked up plenty of slights and derision aimed at my parents and siblings because they were deaf.

"We missed you at mass but I'm glad you're here," Father Mik signs. I feel uneasy once again at his implied invitation, which I interpret as trying to get my ass in the pew on Sundays. He hands me his plate and steps back to let me go in front of him. I hand it back and make excuses about going to Evie's later for dinner but stay with him while we move up to where servers are portioning out slices of turkey, dressing, and mashed potatoes. The sight and smell of the food make me wish I hadn't been so hasty in refusing dinner.

"I wanted to tell you I talked with the altar guild women," I gesture at the kitchen where the three are ferrying more food to the serving tables, *"but found nothing new. But another question occurred to me about who'll be taking over Martin Nygaard's job."*

Father Mik subtly points out the man I'd noticed earlier setting up the chairs and signs close to his body so only I can see it. *"That's Frank*

Safer. He applied for the job. He's had his problems in the past but I'm trying to help him get his feet on the ground."

It isn't hard to read Father Mik's coded language. I stop signing and use only my voice. "What did he do time for?"

We've reached the food serving station and a hearing teenager loads Father Mik's paper plate with turkey, stuffing, and mashed potatoes. As Father Mik protests about the amount of food the next server ladles an unhealthy stream of gravy over the whole plate. He holds onto the plate with both hands or risks dropping the whole mess, and uses only his voice. "Assault with a deadly weapon." A deaf woman server admonishes Father Mik for being too thin and stacks two dinner rolls on top of his loaded-down plate. He mouths *thank you* to her and I follow him to one of the tables where we sit a bit apart from the others, careful to keep our conversation low.

Father Mik breaks off a corner of one of the dinner rolls and chews for a moment. He's loath to not sign while in the midst of his deaf congregation—the equivalent of thumbing his nose at them—but he's even more concerned about anyone intercepting and reading his signs about Frank Safer's criminal background. "Frank got into a fight with another man at the deaf club, kept hitting him over the head with a beer bottle until it broke. The man suffered extensive brain damage. Frank did four years and then was freed two years ago." Father Mik shakes his head. "He needs a job. His ex-wife is suing him for back child support, which he couldn't pay while incarcerated." Father Mik cuts into some dark meat, spears it with the practically useless plastic fork, and smiles at the taste.

"Ample motive for stealing and possibly murder," I say.

He puts down his plastic fork and knife and looks like he's lost his appetite. "Dana, you don't think..." He trails off. There's defeat in his sagging face. He wants to believe the best about people and tries to concentrate on the good but somehow mundane evil continues to intrude. I pat his hand and try to reassure him.

"I don't know anything for sure yet. I still need to talk to Ben Warshawsky and then I'll do some checking on Frank Safer. But most pressing, I need to catch up with Flora Maitland. I think she's avoiding me. She agreed to talk after mass but then snuck out halfway through." I check my phone for the time. "I can swing by her place now before going over to my parents' house."

Father Mik glances at his uneaten plate of food and then at me. "Would you be willing to take her some leftovers? It's strange she left. Her situation is dire. The woman has five children and depends solely on food stamps—I thought for certain she'd eat with us."

We go into the kitchen and Father Mik loads up a large shopping bag with carryout containers of Thanksgiving dinner food. The credenza in the kitchen reminds me of my discovery earlier. I show Father Mik the poem encased in the plastic bag. He scans it and frowns. "Rather melancholy, isn't it?" He holds the paper at arm's length and squints a bit while he reads the first stanza aloud.

> *"I have a feeling you're larger than any one name,*
> *Love is harder than anything I knew back then,*
> *Watching your shadow play over and over again,*
> *I never knew you but I miss you all the same."*

Goosebumps erupt along my arms. "Wow, Father Mik. The way you read that sounds almost like Shakespeare."

He chuckles and hands the poem back to me. "I fancied myself an amateur poet long before I became a priest. I specialized in love poems. A lot of unrequited feelings back then. What do you make of it?"

"Not sure." I glance at the bloodstain by the sink and consider the room where I found the paper. "Do you want to give it to the cops investigating Mr. Nygaard's death?" I offer the sealed poem.

He shakes his head. "I don't regard it as relevant, do you? The police made it abundantly clear they think no foul play occurred, that Martin's death was purely an accident. I will not be satisfied with that explanation until after the autopsy, but the police are done with it." I return the puzzling poem to my backpack and help Father Mik gather food for Flora Maitland and her children. "I appreciate your help, with this," he hands me the shopping bag, "and with everything." He still seems sad.

"I haven't done much yet." I'm acutely aware of the truth of my statement. "I'll call you sometime this weekend, okay?" Gently, I prod him toward the buffet line. "Why don't you try again? Go eat something." I seek out Ben Warshawsky but he adds nothing new either. The Thanksgiving dinner committee met in the parish hall at ten on Friday morning. Martin Nygaard made coffee for their meeting and when it adjourned, the committee members all left at the same time because they were going out to lunch together. He saw no one else at the parish hall that morning.

"But you know about Frank Safer, right?" Ben asks.

My deaf gossip antennae tingle from the way he poses his question. I worry Ben watched my conversation with Father Mik but then remember we didn't sign when Safer's criminal past came up. I place the shopping bag on the floor, make my face as neutral as possible, and gesture with my hands—palms up, fingers splayed and slightly curled—which in this case roughly translates as *"What about him?"*

Even though we're at the back of the parish hall and away from the crush of the crowd, Ben grabs the shopping bag and ushers me by my elbow into the hallway so no one can observe our conversation. *"He's been in jail. Twice."* He cocks his eye at me expectantly as if this is enough for me to go arrest Safer on the spot.

I glance at the ceiling, rehearsing the most diplomatic phrasing I can muster. I tell Ben I know Safer has a criminal background, although I don't mention that Father Mik told me about only one incarceration.

"Can you tell me anything about Frank Safer and Martin Nygaard?" While Ben Warshawsky strokes his salt-and-pepper beard in contemplation of my question, I consider what motivates him to badmouth Frank Safer. As far as I know through my number one deaf news source—Evie—the two men aren't in conflict with each other.

"Well, he went to ISD, didn't finish." Ben offers this bit of insight with the knowing air of someone who not only went to college but also graduate school, a feat unusual twenty years ago when Ben finished his master's at NTID, the National Technical Institute for the Deaf.

"He didn't graduate from high school, so what?" I sign. *"Deaf people drop out same as hearing people."* Of course, I also read in Ben's statement an implied disdain for the Illinois School for the Deaf. The K-12 residential school carries a stigma among some deaf high achievers who label ISD as a last resort for deaf kids who don't "make it" in their home schools. An unfortunate and mostly inaccurate accounting because ISD provides an inclusive signing environment, a haven for many deaf kids whose parents and families don't sign.

Now Ben gets to what appears to be bothering him. *"He needs the janitor job,"* he says, reiterating Father Mik's assertion about the ex-wife, and adding that Safer's girlfriend won't agree to marriage until he has steady work. *"Maybe he pushed Martin down, or tripped him,"* he says. Ben's hands describe a vicious shove at an imaginary Martin, his right hand then becoming a body falling in slow motion until it forms a fist—Martin's head—making hard contact with the kitchen sink. He ends with a graphic display of blood spilled everywhere, a gruesome, dramatic touch for my benefit. The man rivals Evie in terms of speculation and penchant for nitty-gritty detail.

"His name is in my notes." I pull out my notepad to show Ben so he knows I'm not discounting his input. No sense in giving the gossip purveyors more dirt to spread about me. *"Thanks for your time."* We exchange signed wishes for a *Happy Thanksgiving*, purely fake but necessary social amenities, and I grab the bag of food for Flora and her kids and head for the stairs.

10

Thanksgiving, 11/21, 3:00 p.m.

BACK IN FLORA'S grimy apartment building I wait at her door and listen to the sound of kids running around inside. I knock but no one answers. I pound louder and call Flora's name, then faintly hear a kid yell, "Mama! Someone's at the door." After a long wait the door opens a crack. Flora Maitland's watery grey eyes peer out over the safety chain. "Hi, Flora. Remember me? Dana—from church today?"

She nods her head and stares, not moving. Okay, no social skills here. "Hey, I'm sorry to bother you on Thanksgiving but Father Mik thought you and the kids were going to stay for dinner. When you didn't, he put this together for you." I lift the shopping bag of food and hope my smile is warm. The woman doesn't move to open the door until a little girl clutching at her leg says, "Mama, I'm hungry."

"Hold a minute," Flora says, closing the door and unlocking the chain to let me in. Two other girls, identical twins, join us at the door and trail after Flora as she carries the bag of food down a hallway to my right to what I guess is the kitchen. I close the front door and stay behind. To my left, normally a living room, six single mattresses line up next to each other on the floor, three covered with faded sheets, the other three bare except for a shared, torn bedspread. A small TV tops a crate and faces the mattresses. There is no other furniture.

Sunshine struggles to permeate what resembles plexiglass windows along the wall where the mattresses line up. A headless doll lies naked on the floor, its belly pointing toward the ceiling. Two doors, one along the wall opposite the windows and one along the far wall facing me, are closed. The whole place smells like dirty laundry and the underlying, unmistakable odor of shit. It's cold. Flora comes back without the girls. "Thank you for the food. My food stamps ain't come yet and we're low." She bows her head.

Flora uses the old term for food assistance from the state. "No problem. Why didn't you stay for the dinner? It was free."

Flora stares at her toes but doesn't say anything. She moves past me into the large room with the mattresses and lowers herself onto the end of one, gesturing at me to take a place next to her. "I don't got much furniture. Kids sleep in here and my bed's in the other room," she says, glancing to the left toward the closed door at the end of the room. Her washed-out complexion flushes pink.

I plop down on the mattress next to her. The odor of dirty clothes gets stronger. God, she's so embarrassed about this place. I feel the need to put her at ease. "Actually, I sleep on the floor too, on a futon. Good for your back. So, you're new to St. Nick's?"

She avoids my eyes but nods. "Uh-huh. Really, it's a job for me." She doesn't elaborate.

"Going to church is a job? I don't get your meaning." I say this to get her talking even though I remember what Father Mik told me about St. Nick's being Flora's pre-placement for work training.

"Oh! No, no, I ain't Catholic." She pronounces it *catlick*. "They're making me get off the welfare. It's a law or something sayin' you can't be on more'n two years, then you got to get a job. I ain't never worked a job so Father Mik pays me to fix up the altar, you know, practice working. After that, he thinks I'll be ready for a regular job." She kneads her fingers and appears unconvinced of any such possibility.

"Father Mik's a good man," I say. She nods her agreement. "Flora, I came over here to bring the food but I also want to ask you a few questions about what happened with Mr. Nygaard."

Her eyebrows squeeze together and her already gaunt face tightens. She turns away. "I don't want to talk about that." Shaky voice. It doesn't take a genius to understand her reluctance but I'm unsure whether it's tied to reliving the trauma of seeing a dead body or if she's actually hiding something.

"I'm checking into this for Father Mik because he thinks the police didn't get the whole story about what happened."

Her head bobs up at me, startled. "You a private eye or something? Like on TV?"

"Something like that. Would you help Father Mik by talking to me?"

"I guess." Her lack of enthusiasm matches her worn-out demeanor.

"Good. Two Saturdays ago, you were at St. Nick's to set up for the evening mass." She nods. "Who unlocked the cabinets for you?" Flora's pale-lashed eyes close for a long moment as if she's visualizing what happened.

"He...I asked him to do it because Mr. Nygaard wasn't...around." Her voice falters and she starts to cry. I dig out a tissue from my jacket and hand it to her.

"Take your time, Flora. I know this is upsetting. Did Father Mik unlock the cabinets for you?"

She sniffles, nods, and dries her eyes. "I started to take the stuff out for the mass. Father Mik showed me which clothes he wanted to wear and told me to, you know, set up everything."

"And you only took out the vestments, you didn't take out the chalices or the candlesticks?"

She nods. "Yeah. There's a lot to do to set up the altar but he likes his clothes set out first so he can get ready while I set up the other'n."

"While you were setting up for mass did anyone else come in?"

"Other than my kids, you mean?"

I kick myself mentally for forgetting to ask about the kids first and take out my notepad and a pen. "Let's start over. Tell me everyone you saw at the parish hall on Saturday."

"Let's see. Father Mik, me, and my kids. Jump, he's my oldest boy, wasn't there—out running around somewhere. But Porter, my next oldest boy, the twins, Moira and Mia, and the baby, Emma, come with me. They played hide-and-seek with that little Mexican girl next door, you know, the one what found Mr. Nygaard." At the mention of his name, she starts to tear up again.

I pat her arm. "It's okay, you're doing great. This is very helpful information." Which is a total lie because other than her kids' names, I already know all this. But she seems so fragile I feel the need to prop her up or she won't be able to finish. "I know your kids were with you but playing while you set up the altar. Were they inside or outside?"

"Oh, you know kids, they like to roam, inside and out. That door to the parish locks if it's closed, so I put a rock there to keep it open. I didn't want 'em bothering me if they wanted in to pee or something."

Wonderful. This means anyone could've come in while she set up the altar and she could have easily missed it. "Did anyone else come into the parish hall on Saturday while you were there?"

Flora pulls her long braid over her shoulder and fiddles with the rubber band encircling the frayed ends of her blonde hair. "No, only them kids running in and out."

I make a note. "When the little girl CiCi found Mr. Nygaard were you finished setting up the altar for mass?"

Flora shakes her head. "No. I took out Father Mik's clothes and then started putting those wafers in the little box on the altar, so I'm in the church when I hear her screamin' for her mama. I go see about the commotion and she come running down them steps in the parish hall. But she pushed on past me and out the door, didn't stop." Flora shudders and crosses her arms in front of her, grips her elbows. "I was scared something happened to one of my kids so I run up the stairs to find out and that's when I saw...him." No crying this time, but her face is somber and white. "You know the rest of it." She flips her long braid over her shoulder.

I do. The cops come, the ME comes, everything's bright lights and unending interrogation until finally the body gets hauled off to the morgue and the cops get tired of bullying you with questions you can't answer and let you go home. "I'm almost done, Flora, but there's one more thing I need to understand a little better." It seems impossible but the young woman's face pales further. She draws her legs up to her chest and circles them with her arms, resting her chin on her knees. Her expression is pensive but dull.

"Saturday night, did you put the vestments away in the cabinets?"

"Yes ma'am, I did." Her twang seems stronger with the affirmation. "Father Mik and the police, they stayed upstairs. I put away the clothes and the little box with the wafers in it. But Father Mik had the key. I didn't lock them."

"Did you notice the chalices or candlesticks at that time?"

"No ma'am, but I wasn't thinking about them things. The police come and took me upstairs and talked to me a long time. They could've been or not, I'm sure I don't know. I was so tired and upset I could only think about getting me and my kids home." At the mention of being tired, she turns her head so her cheek rests on her knees.

"And then Father Mik drove you home."

"Yeah."

I flip my pad shut and rise. Flora stays huddled on the mattress. A little girl comes into the room and stands next to her. Flora drops her knees into a cross-legged position and the little girl plops into her lap. She's so small, even her petite mother dwarfs her.

"This is my youngest, Emma. Say hi to the lady, Emma." Emma stares at me and then ducks her head under Flora's embrace. Her summer T-shirt and shorts hang on her frame and expose bony arms and legs. She peeks out at me, shy. Same wan expression as Flora's. Blonde flyaway hair frames her face and sharp cheekbones pronounce hunger. These two are an unwitting poster for poverty in America.

"Hey, Emma. She's your spitting image, Flora." Flora's arms tighten around the little girl. I can hear the twins laughing in the kitchen. My empty studio and our vacated house rise, unbidden, in my thoughts. Even in this bleak apartment I'm certain Flora's children cut through her loneliness. A tug of jealousy jerks through me seeing mother hug daughter. How good it must feel to love and protect a small child.

The twins' laughter echoes down the hallway to us. "Would you mind if I talked to your kids about last week, just a couple of questions? Maybe they know something that could be important."

Flora's arms tighten around Emma, who squirms in response.

I try to reassure her. "I mean, right here with you. Nothing formal." Flora loosens her grasp on Emma and sends her to the kitchen to summon the twins. The three girls arrive together, the twins holding hands and giggling, while Emma straggles behind.

"You girls sit down," Flora says. "This is Miss Dana and she wants to talk to you, so you listen to her." She turns to me. "One on the left is Moira and the other is Mia." The twins plop down on the floor in front of me, no more laughing after Flora's stern order.

"Hi." I address first Moira and then Mia, and I'm a little unnerved by the two identical faces gazing back at me. They even wear their pale blonde hair in the same style: a ponytail pulled up high in back. Impossible to tell them apart. Then both girls grin and I'm given an easy identifying marker—one of Moira's front teeth is missing.

Emma comes to where Flora and I are parked on the mattresses and situates herself between us, then leans against me. "Okay girls," I begin. "Remember two weeks ago on Saturday when your mom helped Father Mik get ready for church? You," I point to each of the twins, "and Emma," I turn my pointing finger at the little girl and lightly poke her in the tummy, and she laughs. "And your brother, um, um..." I snap my fingers like I can't recall his name.

"Porter!" all three chime in together.

"Right, right. Porter." I pull out my notepad and flip to the page with notes about the incident. "You were playing hide and seek with CiCi."

Mia holds up her hand. "Miss Dana?" Before I can answer, Moira slaps her arm. "You're not in school, stupid."

"You're mean." Emma scolds Moira. "Mama, Mia's not stupid."

Flora leans forward and pulls roughly on Moira's arm. Pain registers on the girl's face. "Say sorry right now or go stay in my room."

Moira yanks her arm away and rubs it, scowling at the floor.

"Say it," Flora repeats. Instead, Moira jumps up and runs to the door at the opposite end of the room. She pushes it open, goes inside and slams the door. How did this get out of hand so quickly?

Emma stands and faces Flora. "Mama, I'm hungry."

"Let me get her something," Flora says to me. "You go ahead and talk to Mia." She and Emma leave the room.

"Okay, Mia," I say. "Ask me your question."

"CiCi was at church today. She said that man was dead." Mia's inflection stretches the last word into three syllables.

"That's right. He had an accident and hurt his head pretty bad. When you were playing with CiCi two Saturdays ago, do you remember other grown-up people there?" Mia appears to be giving my question ample consideration. Finally, she shakes her head. "So only you, CiCi, Moira, Emma, and Jump played outside, right?"

"No!" She almost shouts her answer. "Not Jump, Porter! But he didn't wanna play with us. He mostly played in the sandbox."

My little test proves Emma right: Mia is not stupid. I ask her a few more questions but uncover nothing helpful. I struggle to get to my feet from the mattress. Mia joins me at the closed door of Flora's bedroom. I knock softly. "Moira? Can I come in?" A few beats later Moira opens the door. She huffs at us, crossing her arms in front of her body, then backs up and leans against Flora's bed. Except for some clothes stacked at the end of it, the only other remarkable item in the room is a plastic package of disposable diapers—the pull-up kind parents use for potty training. I assume these are for Emma. "You want to come out and talk with me, Moira? Or should we talk in here?" Without looking at me she shakes her head and turns her body sideways. Okay. No talking, period.

I hear Flora and Emma come down the hallway. Mia and I leave the bedroom and meet them at the apartment entrance but Mia continues down the hall to the kitchen. "When do you think your Link Card will come?" I ask.

Flora seems confused for a minute.

"Food stamps."

"Oh, that. Well, maybe tomorrow or Saturday. It's hard with these kids." She looks worried.

"I'm sure five kids are a handful." I don't know how to help her.

"Mama." Emma tugs on Flora's shirt. "*Mama.*" Insistent. Flora responds and Emma beckons her to bend down. She puts her mouth to Flora's ear, covers it with her thin hand and whispers something.

"That's our secret, baby." Flora straightens up to face me. "I don't know what I'm gonna do if them stamps don't show up."

"If your stamps are late you can go to the welfare office and get some emergency help to tide you over, or you could go to a food pantry."

Flora sighs. "It's so much work. These kids wear me out with worry and I don't know what kind of job I'm gonna find. I got no phone. The welfare office is two bus trips away and I ain't got the money for it. Anyway, I don't even know where a food pantry is." Her voice comes out in a sad, repetitive monotone.

"Did you ask Father Mik to help you with those things?"

"I ain't really Catholic or nothing."

I don't get how the two are related but don't press the issue. "If you want, I can put in a call to the welfare office tomorrow to find out what's holding up the food stamps." A quick search on my phone confirms that Public Aid is open the Friday after Thanksgiving. I don't really want to do the work for her but I feel sorry for her kids, especially little Emma. During my childhood my parents considered how every dollar got spent, but I never wondered or worried where my next meal would come from. It must be frightening.

Flora shakes her head at my offer but then stops, as if reconsidering. Mia returns to where we congregate at the door, chewing on a dinner roll from the donated food. "I hate to put you out..." Flora begins.

"It's no problem. I'll call tomorrow and then come back after that." My cell phone search delivers the address of a food pantry on the near North Side. I jot it down on my notepad, tear out the page, and give it to her.

"They're open nine to five, every day of the year." I dig ten bucks out of my pocket. "Here's bus fare."

Flora takes the money and starts tearing up again. I'm embarrassed my small act of kindness yields such an emotional response. When I open the door, Mia says goodbye and waves at me with the hand holding the dinner roll. Emma clutches her mother's leg with one arm and leans into her. I crouch down to her level.

"'Bye, Emma. See you soon," I say. She regards me with a solemn expression and then nods.

I say good-bye to Flora and hurry out of this stink-hole of a building.

11

Thanksgiving, 11/21, 5:00 p.m.

OUTSIDE FLORA'S building the wind picks up, whipping errant leaves into a small dust devil on the sidewalk. I drive east to get on I-94 and ponder Flora's passivity. She and her kids are barely alive, eking out an existence at the hands of whatever Fate throws their way. Food stamps late? Sit and wait until they arrive. No bus fare? Stay in your apartment and don't seek help from a friendly source only a few blocks away.

I can't figure out if Flora's scared, stupid, or just plain lazy. Hell, I wonder if she'll even use the ten bucks I gave her for bus fare and go to the food pantry. I'm angry and puzzled at the woman's behavior but at the same time feel compelled to help her.

Night has taken over the city and because of the holiday the expressway is free of the usual traffic so I arrive at my parents' bungalow on the South Side in twenty minutes. I retrieve two six-packs from the trunk of my car and go around back to enter the house through the kitchen. The back door is wide open and inside Evie struggles to lift a roasting pan holding a large, steaming turkey from the oven. I hurry inside and shovel the beer onto the table. I grab some potholders to retrieve the turkey from her and hoist the heavy pan onto the top of the stove.

Evie signs in quick, short bursts. *"Wow! Glad you came in. I might've dropped it!"* Her cheeks are flushed from the tussle with the turkey and the warmth of the kitchen. I tower over my mother, who looks up at me as she tucks a loose strand of white hair behind her ear and then turns to close the oven door. At sixty-two years old Evie's not overweight but does embody a solid plumpness some women assume when they age. She misses nothing, though. Her bright blue eyes spy the two six-packs on the table. She faces me. *"Two? Too much. JJ will drink one can, no more. Who's drinking the rest?"* She narrows her eyes at me. I meet her stern gaze. We both know the answer.

I extract one can, ignoring her question, and put the rest of the beer in the fridge. I pop the top and purposely drink down half the can. When I eye her to gauge her reaction, I notice the back door still gapes open. Only I can hear the smack of my beer can on the tabletop when I slam it down and stride to the open back door. I sweep my arm to indicate the door—top to bottom—an overly florid and sarcastic gesture to alert her I'm displeased and angry. *"I tell you and tell you and tell you. Keep it locked when you're home!"* It's an old scold.

"I feel safe." It's an old answer. But this old answer has become suspect. Evie shrugs her shoulders when she signs *safe*, which shades the meaning to show she's not really feeling safe at all.

I lose it. *"Safe?"* I advance on her and enlarge my signing space to express my anger. *"Jesus! Your head isn't even healed from that woman attacking you two weeks ago."* A home invader entered my parents' home and hit Evie on the head hard enough to knock her out and to require stitches. The case is unsolved and odd because nothing was stolen from the house. Why come inside, attack Evie, and then leave empty-handed. But I thought the obvious takeaway from the incident was that Evie shouldn't leave the back door unlocked. Wrong me.

I step to the door, slam it shut, and throw the deadbolt into place. *"Lock the goddamn door!"* Evie touches the wound on the back of her head, abruptly plops down on a kitchen chair, and bursts into tears.

Shit. Why am I such an asshole? I rush to her and kneel beside the chair to encircle her with my arms. She folds into me, her hands covering her face, sobbing. "I'm sorry, Evie, I'm sorry!" I say this over and over using only my voice, not signing my apology, because I don't want to let go of her. We stay huddled this way for a few minutes until she cries herself out, then slowly pulls away from me. I grab a napkin from the plastic holder on the table and hand it to her. While she dries her eyes and blows her nose, I apologize so she can understand me. *"I'm sorry I'm so crabby about the back door."* I mime throwing home the deadbolt with a flourish to make fun of myself, which elicits a smile from her. But then I become serious and contain my signs so they are tight and staccato, emphasizing each one. *"I love you, Mom. I'm really afraid someone will hurt you again."*

My memory serves up the image of Evie lying unconscious on her bedroom floor where I found her a couple of weeks ago. Now I burst into tears and Evie embraces me. Fine couple, us. Once my crying subsides, I promise I won't yell at her about the back door and she promises she'll keep the door locked when she's home. Truce.

Evie declines my offer to help with dinner. Before she shoos me out of the kitchen, I loosen another can of beer from the fridge and grab my open one. I find JJ in the darkened living room ensconced in his corduroy lounger, feet up, watching the Bears. Not wanting to startle him, I jostle the back of the lounger before continuing on around to his line of sight. The TV screen lights his face and his smile is broad and warm, and not simply because I tossed him a can of beer. I can feel my father's uncomplicated love in his gaze, my position as first-born child on firm ground.

He pushes down on the footrest to bring the lounger upright while I plop down on the couch across from him. On the side table next to me I flip on the lamp so we can talk. JJ opens his beer and nestles it between his knees, then tells me my two siblings won't be home for Thanksgiving. My twin, David, a computer geek in New York, and Daphne, a Deaf Services Coordinator for a social service agency in Minneapolis, will both be in Chicago for Christmas.

"I wish they were here," I sign to JJ, letting him infer that I mean home for Thanksgiving when I really mean here permanently, to deal with stuff like Evie being attacked. Or to deal with our mother's stubbornness. Life is so much easier when it's the three of us versus the two of them. Not the first time I grouse to myself about my sibs leaving home as quickly as they could. Why don't they feel the same responsibility toward our parents that I do? *"How is Evie's dizziness? Better?"*

JJ peeks around the side of his chair into the kitchen to discern whether or not Evie can observe our conversation and then he seesaws his hand at me in response. *"She hangs onto a lot of things when she walks around the house. She never did that before. I don't know if she's dizzy or feels weak. She gets mad when I ask her."* I ascertain that Evie's stitches come out on Tuesday and tell JJ I'll accompany them to the appointment so I can find out exactly what's going on with my mother, besides her insistence on having things her own way.

Discussing Evie's injury spurs JJ to ask if the police have made any headway identifying the woman who attacked Evie, leaving her unconscious, a gash on her head. There's nothing to report on that front. I tell him we're working on it even though in truth it's highly doubtful we'll find any hard leads. In addition to nothing being stolen during the break-in, no unidentified fingerprints were found.

With the football game almost over and the Bears in a comfortable lead against Detroit, JJ and I put out the plates and silver while Evie loads the table with enough food for eighteen people. My guilt kicks into high gear as I dig into sage and sausage stuffing. A picture of tiny Emma blooms in my mind. Flora and her kids, one step away from being homeless, garner my attention. Though the woman's passivity about her plight confounds me, I have promised to help her tomorrow with a phone call. My hunger takes over and I push away thoughts of the Maitland clan, intent on relaxing.

Evie serves coffee with dessert, her homemade apple pie everyone in the family prefers to pumpkin. I decline both and crack open my third beer, which earns me a glare from my mother. To distract her, I tell my parents about little Emma in her thin t-shirt and shorts. *"Did you save any of our clothes from when we were kids?"* I ask Evie.

She shakes her head. *"I donated those years ago to rummage sales at St. Nick's. Some of my friends have grandchildren,"* she holds the last sign in mid-air and gives me her signature significant look, *"and I can ask them to donate old clothes."*

"Thanks. And you can knock it off about the grandchildren. It's not my fault Jimmy wants to stay in L.A." Even though he's back in town I'm not about to give Evie gossip for her grapevine.

My mother gives my father a long gaze that says, *See? I told you how defensive she is.* Evie tries again. *"You could talk to him, make him come back. If you lost some weight, it would help. Jimmy never liked fat women."* Here she plumps her cheeks out and exaggerates the sign, her hands wide at her sides to describe a tubby waistline. *"He told me he liked curves."* Her thumbs trace a curvaceous female outline in the air. It's easy to tell which of my mother's descriptions belongs to me. And what the hell kind of conversation were they having when he told her such a thing? Evie might be making this up just to rile me or maybe to drive home her point about non-existent grandchildren.

I avoid telling them anything about Jimmy being home because I'm so unsure about where the two of us are headed, especially in light of our lunch at Brau Haus. *"I still love Jimmy,"* I sign, *"but he decided to stay in L.A. His decision, his decision."* Repeating this fact, while staring at the empty space where I've placed Jimmy as we talk about him, reinforces the idea for my parents. Then I draw my gaze away from the absent Jimmy and lock eyes with Evie and then JJ. *"Not my deci-sion."* I shake my head to throw extra emphasis on this statement. *"We're still married and I don't know what he plans to do. We're not talking much."* I sign *finish* with both hands in a cranky manner to underline that the topic is closed for further discussion. I go into the kitchen and retrieve another beer from the fridge.

When I return, JJ asks me what I have found out about Martin Nygaard's death. *"How did you know about that?"* I sign.

"I talked to Sarah and Ben at church. They both told me you asked them questions about it. Are you and F-A assigned to the case?"

F-A is my partner, Felice Abandonato, his name sign configured from his initials and signed over the heart, which is the same space for the sign *police*. Clearly the deaf grapevine is keeping my parents apprised of my activities. But I hesitate at how to answer his question about whether Abandonato and I are working Martin Nygaard's case. My parents don't know I'm suspended or the reason for it, mostly because I don't want them to worry, but also because Evie's criticism about my personal failings is the last thing I need right now. They're both under the illusion that I currently work full-time as a homicide detective. And it's going to stay that way.

"There is no case," I sign. *"Father Mik told me the police think Mr. Nygaard died from a fall—not murder."* I explain more in depth about the police's theory and provide my avid audience of two a detailed description of the events transpiring in the parish hall. When I reach the part about the probable accident, Martin Nygaard slipping and hitting his head on the sharp corner of the metal sink, Evie jumps in.

"True, true. I showed Father Mik that sink dangerous," Evie signs. She mimes her experience of running into the deadly metal corner and ends with rubbing her hand along the side of her waist. *"It hurt. A lot."* JJ nods at her, taking in the story. I'm doubtful anything like what Evie's describing really happened. It's my mother's way of trying to be part of whatever current catastrophe reigns among her deaf friends.

When Evie takes her seat, I tell my parents why Father Mik asked me to investigate further. Evie pays rapt attention to every bit of information about the missing chalices and candlesticks—storing away details in her personal stash—to tell her friends at the next deaf gabfest. But for this I don't mind. It's even possible Evie and JJ might incidentally uncover a bit of pertinent information that could steer me in some kind of direction. *"Such an odd man,"* Evie signs. *"Really, he never got used to being deaf."* Evie points at JJ. *"He reminded me of you."*

My father's face shows surprise and a bit of hurt. This ought to be interesting, Evie comparing JJ to a recluse. Sometimes she doesn't know when to quit. *"I'm like Martin Nygaard? How?"* JJ asks.

Evie reads JJ's understandable indignation and tries to soothe him with an appeasing gesture, holding her hands out in front of her and patting the air in a repetitive motion. *"No, no, don't misunderstand me. I think you're mostly deaf in the way you behave with other deaf. But you and Martin are the same because you startle when someone comes up behind you. If Dana comes up behind me and taps me on the shoulder, it doesn't make me jump. I expect it. It's like you're still hearing, that way."*

JJ ponders this without responding and I, too, consider what Evie says. Born deaf and raised in an all-deaf family, she is a true one-hundred percent capital D deaf person and her behaviors, like the one she's pointing out to JJ, were instilled from birth. My father, on the other hand, became profoundly deaf at three from a high fever, and his mother never accepted his deafness or allowed him to sign. She spent an inordinate amount of her time—and his—making him practice speaking. In the meantime, the hearing kids in the neighborhood who otherwise might have been his friends, played football, chased dogs, and pursued play. JJ grew up isolated at home and at school surrounded by well-meaning but misguided hearing people.

As if reading my mind about his upbringing JJ responds defensively to Evie. *"My mother didn't know anything about deaf people. She never accepted that I started signing when I met you."* Evie's eyes dance at this familiar story, proud of her part in "turning" JJ deaf.

"You look a lot like my mother," JJ signs to me. *"But you're so different from her. You're hearing, yes, but you sign same as deaf and you understand us."* Evie nods at this. I can't escape a chronic uncomfortable feeling that because I'm hearing, there's a tiny bit of envy in JJ's comment. Or maybe it's simply because he wishes he could still hear. Even though he has been deaf sixty-two of his sixty-five years it is possible that, like Martin Nygaard, he still doesn't feel like he fits in with other deaf. Losing his hearing at three years old had to be a frightening and disorienting experience for a little boy. One he would not forget.

I'm aggravated with Evie for tweaking JJ about this but what flashes through my mind are Martin Nygaard's solitary rooms in the basement of St. Nick's. It's easy to understand how his isolation could foster intense sadness and the recurring depression Father Mik described to me.

Evie jumps in. *"She really hated ASL. She slapped JJ's hand when he signed—"*

"'I love you' to her when she was dying." I finish the sentence with her.

It's an old story about Grandmother Demeter. JJ shakes his head but I'm uncertain if it's at Evie for dredging up this sad memory or if it's about his mother never accepting his deafness. To take the focus off JJ I steer the conversation back to an earlier thought I had about my parents knowing so many people in the deaf community and bring up Frank Safer's name.

Evie immediately makes a face, showing her dislike. *"He's dangerous. He beat up an old woman, jail fifteen years, then he got drunk and used a beer bottle to—"* She stands, transforming herself into Frank Safer holding a beer bottle by the neck and attacking his victim. Then, with the same speed, she mutates into the man receiving the blows, showing us how badly the attack hurt him. *"Jail four more years."*

Frank Safer is bald. Evie displays Safer's name sign using his initials "F-S." Starting on top of her head her hand shows an 'F' and then slips backward in a smooth motion as the 'F' morphs into an 'S'.

Other deaf who know of him may not remember his exact name but would recognize the name sign because of the physical connection. *"He's dangerous."* She embellishes this last sign with a repeating protracted swoop that adds emphasis to her judgment. I sign an affirmation to her statement only to show I'm paying attention because I wonder if she has the facts about Safer right.

JJ thumps the table to get my attention. He holds up his palm at Evie to stop her and averts his eyes so he won't take in what she continues to sign. It's effective. She lowers her hands. I shift in my seat to face JJ. *"Yes, F-S did those things. But now he's different, not dangerous."* JJ mocks Evie's estimation of Frank Safer by executing a perfect impression of the exaggerated way she signed *dangerous* but shakes his head at the same time to negate the meaning. He wags his finger at her. *"F-S free two years now, no jail, goes to church."*

JJ's assessment when combined with Evie's makes me think that the truth about Frank Safer is probably somewhere in between the two extremes. I make a mental note to ask Abandonato for Safer's priors.

I finish the last can of the six-pack after I clear the table and wash the dishes. JJ assembles leftovers from dinner and packs a large shopping bag for me to take back to my studio. I give him a big hug of thanks. I stow the remaining six-pack on top of the food and my parents walk me out to my car to say good-bye.

"You okay to drive?" Worry wrinkles JJ's forehead.

"I'm fine. Don't worry. I ate a lot at dinner. It'll absorb the beer."

I dimly realize I'm signing this in a slow, deliberate manner, making sure my signs are clear. I put the food in the back seat of my car. As I give JJ a hug I glance at Evie. Her facial expression could wither a dozen roses: *My daughter's fat, a failure at her marriage, and now she drinks and drives.*

I resist the urge to say anything I'll regret but before we hug I remind her of her promise to keep the back door locked. She nods but her hug is decidedly cool and I'm sure I'll be the headline topic in the next gossip session with her deaf friends.

I slide into the driver's seat and lean over to give one more wave good-bye when Evie flaps her hand at me to get my attention. I respond with both hands, palms up, fingers curved: *"What?"*

She slings one sharp sign, *"Seatbelt!"* and then shows me her back and heads inside.

I raise my eyebrows at JJ and then shake my head, hoping to transmit my disgruntlement with Evie treating me like I'm twelve. But I do buckle up and JJ responds with a worried face and an admonition to drive safely when I wave good-bye and pull away.

12

Thanksgiving, 11/21, 10:00 p.m.

TRAFFIC IS light on the side streets leading to the Dan Ryan expressway and it doesn't get much heavier once I head north. The turkey and beer I consumed combine to make me feel sleepy, so I stay in the slow lane and keep it at fifty. My only quarrel with driving in the far right lane on this expressway is the frequency of other drivers entering and merging from limited on-ramps, also on the right, which occur at regular intervals.

Reviewing tonight's dinner conversation, I'm amused all over again at my mother comparing JJ's startle reflex to Martin Nygaard's. Sometimes she's oblivious to other people's feelings, especially of those close to her. A short bout of self-pity follows when I remember her goading me about Jimmy but I let it go. What was it Marvin said? Something about what you dwell on, expands. I guess that can be either positive or negative. I *am* pissed she thinks she can tell me how much I can drink, though. But right now I feel mellow and cut her some slack about the booze. A drunk driver killed her only brother when he was a teenager, so it's understandable Evie is touchy on the subject. But boy, she really demonizes alcohol.

The point she made about Martin Nygaard still reacting like a hearing person gives me pause when I consider the old janitor's manner of death. It makes perfect sense. If someone approached him from behind while he washed the coffee pot at the sink, he wouldn't know, couldn't hear it, he'd startle and—

A blaring horn from a huge car roaring down the on-ramp to my right jerks me to attention. Instead of allowing me to pass first before merging, the SUV accelerates and hurtles in front of me just before the entrance lane disappears. The driver flips me off and zooms across three lanes of traffic.

"Same to you, asshole!" He's doing at least eighty. Where the hell are the State cops?

When my heart rate returns to normal, a thread of a thought I had at dinner surfaces, something about Flora and her kids being so poor, something about six being too many? Too many what? Kids? Hell, she has five kids and that's too many. But I'm tired and fuzzy and can't make sense of it, so tuck it away for further consideration tomorrow. The day's events jumble in my mind and I recall talking with Father Mik about Frank Safer, remember I want to ask my partner to run a check on the ex-con. I pull my cell phone out of my jacket and momentarily glance down to scroll to his name in my directory.

A few seconds later I look up and the back of a black compact fills my windshield. A burst of exhaust from its tailpipe shows the driver is trying to accelerate enough to clear my front fender but the compact's four-cylinder engine doesn't provide enough oomph. I punch my brake pedal with both feet but our cars are too close and I plow right into the rear of the Hyundai. It skids to the right. My right front tire blows and spins me almost completely backwards. I end up facing the on-ramp at 43rd Street. Traffic in my lane swerves around me and the Hyundai, horns blaring.

Almost immediately a white Camry enters the ramp I face and heads straight at me. I watch helplessly while the headlights advance and blind me, my seatbelt cinching me tight. The Camry swerves at the last minute but still rocks me with a glancing blow and comes to a stop inches from the Hyundai. Both cars rest near a retaining wall buttressing the highway. Steam shoots from under my smashed hood. I'm dazed and my air bag hasn't engaged.

When I check myself over nothing seems broken although both impacts have thoroughly jolted me. My seatbelt still plasters me in place. The driver of the Hyundai emerges and stalks over to the Camry, cell phone to her ear. She starts screaming at the driver. I can't tell who's in the Camry but the Screamer doesn't seem to get a response so she pokes at her phone and speaks to someone, then returns to her car and leans against it.

I unhitch my seatbelt, take a deep breath to clear my head, and check my ribs. Sore. When I try to exit, my door won't budge. The passenger side door is also crimped shut. I slowly lower the back of my seat until it lies almost flush with the rear seat and then gingerly climb into the back, cursing my extra weight. I step into the cold night. Bad move. The Screamer is in my face, ranting. "What the hell is wrong with you? Don't you yield? You couldn't move over a lane, for God's sake? Shit!" She points at the cement wall where her dented Hyundai lolls. "Look at my new car!" She begins to cry, her mascara painting lines down her cheeks.

"I never saw you! Hey—let's move before any more traffic comes down this ramp." I start to steer her to a safer spot but she yanks her arm away and hurries back to her car.

I approach the white Camry. The dome light illuminates a boy in the driver's seat who seems too young to hold a valid license. He stares through the windshield, dazed. His right hand is clamped over his forehead while his left hand wipes blood from his face. Cracked glass is etched in a circle on his side of the windshield, no seat belt on him.

I knock on the passenger-side window and call to him. "Hey! You okay?" The door opens easily and I'm hit with a strong whiff of booze. He gives me a heavy-lidded stare, a glazed expression of non-comprehension. His orange tie-dyed t-shirt reads *Born to Party*.

"My parents are going to kill me," he says, eyelids fluttering. His hands fall to his lap and he pitches over sideways on the passenger seat toward me, out cold.

"Shit!" I pat my pockets for my phone but no luck. I yell to the Screamer. "Hey! What's your name?!" The bitch ignores me. "Hey! This kid's hurt—call 911!" The orange streetlights illuminate her glare at me but she begins poking at her phone. I trot back to my car for whatever kind of first aid I can find and only come up with some disposable hand wipes and a roll of paper towels. Better than nothing. I punch on my hazard lights to warn approaching traffic because our cars partially block the right lane.

I get back to the kid and squat in front of the open passenger door to get a better view of his wound. He's bleeding heavily from a large gash near the top of his head where his hairline and forehead meet. Pieces of pebbled glass are in his hair. I blot the blood running across his forehead and dripping onto the leather upholstery, carefully swab around the gash, then fold a paper towel lengthwise and press it firmly to his wound. The Screamer approaches and watches my ministrations, hugging her arms around her. "Did you call?"

"Yeah. They said three minutes." Petulant. She's quiet for a moment, taking in the bloody scene. "Geez, he's so young."

A patrol car arrives at the top of the ramp above us and blocks the street entrance to the expressway. Another patrol approaches from the south and pulls up behind my car and positions his car at an angle to completely block the right lane, his lights flashing.

A cop struggles from the driver's seat and stands while trying to hitch up his duty belt but his gut the size of a large beach ball hinders any progress. He gives up and lets his gear sag. He pulls out his ticket pad and approaches us. "So, ladies, let's start at the beginning. Names?"

The Screamer snuggles right next to him, leaves maybe an inch of space between their bodies. "Officer, I was coming down the—"

He's not having any of it. The cop thrusts his arm out and points away from his body to indicate a proper spot a couple of feet away. "Lady, do what I tell you. Name! Then I wanna have your license, proof of registration and insurance. In that order. Got it?" She edges away from him. "Margaret Turner," she says. "I—" She lifts her hands and gapes at them, realizes they are empty. She points to her car. "My purse—" He flicks his hand allowing her to retrieve it.

The cop turns his attention to where I squat attending to the boy. I take a big breath and draw myself up. "And what's going on with—" He stops and raises his eyebrows, then his mouth twists into a small pursed circle and he whistles. "Well, well, well. If it ain't Dana Demeter, ex-detective and well-known booze hound." He tilts his hand back and forth, miming drinking.

I flinch at the reproach and check the cop's face in the orange light from the street lamp. He obviously knows me. A quick glance at his shirt shows no name tag to help me out. I point at the kid. "He's passed out, probably from drinking, and connected pretty hard with the windshield. Ambulance is on the way." As if on cue an ambulance screams toward us on the opposite side of the expressway, exits and races across the overpass, and is allowed down the ramp. "And we're going to need IDOT to tow these cars."

"Still acting like you're in charge, eh Demeter? You're a civvie now. Hole up in your car until I'm ready to talk to you, got it?" His lips press together, a mean smirk. Before I can talk with him any further to suss out how he knows me, the Hyundai driver rushes up to him with her wallet open, cards at the ready.

I return to survey my Corolla. The right front bumper and fender are crumpled inward over the blown tire, and a puddle of anti-freeze on the cement glows neon green in the reflection of the ambulance's revolving red-and-white lights. The passenger side is caved in, front and back doors caught in the Camry's sideswipe. I'm lucky he didn't hit me head-on but dismayed at the extent of the damage. I enter the driver's side rear door, awkwardly climb over the seat again, and sit in excruciating pain, my chest and ribs on fire. I raise the seat to a semi-reclining position, take shallow breaths and hope the pain will subside. It doesn't. This is going to be a long night.

The starter whines when I crank it once, twice, but on the third try it quits with a defining clunk. Out of commission. I root around in the glove compartment for the insurance and registration cards the cop wants, then make the clumsy journey into the rear seat. My backpack is on the floor and I manage to extract my license from it. The bag of food JJ packed rests on the seat tilted over on its side. Only the six-pack has jarred loose and lies on the floor, my cell phone next to it. I right the shopping bag and position it on the floor to hide the beer, grab my cell and stow it in my jacket. Moving the bag hurts my ribs even more and my body stiffens up as the the adrenaline surge from the accident wears off. I close my eyes for a moment. What seems like a few minutes later, my shoulder is jostled.

"Demeter! Come on, wake up!" Cold air sweeps the hair off my forehead. The cop stands at the opened back door of my car. His belly crowds the doorway and gets in my face. Pain shoots down my side as I use my hands on his significant gut to shove him backwards. "Hey!" He stumbles a bit but clears the doorway.

"Lighten up, asshole. You're not rousting winos on the West Side here." I massage my ribs and stay seated but manage to swing my legs to the side so my feet rest on the pavement. The motion makes me dizzy and I lean my head against the driver's headrest, eyes closed.

"Funny thing about that, Demeter, 'cause you smell exactly like 'em. How many you down tonight?"

"A couple of beers with dinner." My gut flutters.

"I'm sure." I open my eyes and he wiggles his fingers in front of my face. "I.D. Come on, come on." His expression broadcasts distaste, like he's inhaling the egg-stink from the refineries of Gary, Indiana. I hand over what's expected and he copies everything down. "Okay. Twenty-five or less." He tosses my cards back in my lap.

I tell him what I remember and hope it agrees with the other driver's story.

"You didn't yield while she merged." An accusation, not a question.

"Couldn't. Another car passed me on the left at the same time and I couldn't get over. She sped up, tried to outrace me." My anger kicks in at the woman's gall. "Fucking four-cylinder piece of shit." I gesture at the ramp. "I ended up here and then the kid bounced off me. My car's totaled." My voice sounds nowhere near as aggravated as I feel.

The cop hands me an accident report form. "Here. Your insurance companies can fight about it. Tickets all around: failure to yield. Out of the car, Demeter, field sobriety test. Let's go."

I take the form from him and pretend to study it in the weak glow of the car's dome light. I'm nauseated and beaten up from the dual impacts. Fear sends a warning and my heartbeat speeds up. I pull myself out of the car and stand to face this tub of lard, my ribs screaming. Another concerted search for his name tag. Nothing. "You know, you seem to know me but I don't think I've ever met you." Keeping it friendly, hoping being civil will make him respond in kind.

He smiles. I try a smile back, again hoping for some camaraderie. His finger punches a hole in my shoulder and ends that dream. "Come on now, you know me. My brother-in-law's in deep shit 'cause of you."

Then I do recognize him but can't pull up his name. Alberto Carrera's brother-in-law. Fuck me. I step back and tilt my head trying to find the stars in the night sky but the city lights obliterate them. I take a deep breath but can't think fast enough to smooth things over with Tubbo in order to get out of this jam. I go with the truth. "Carrera's in deep shit 'cause he's a crooked cop. Tried to shake down a murderer for money and then let him go."

"Says you."

"Yeah, me. Oh—and all the evidence." I say this with all the sarcasm I can muster but because I'm in a great deal of pain from the one-two punch of the accident, I give up without more of a fight. "Carrera will get his day in court. Look, I'm screwed either way here. You know I can't pass the blow test. And as you so delicately pointed out, I'm on suspension for drinking."

"You shoulda thought of that before you got behind the wheel drunk, Demeter. Come on, let's go." He motions to me with his hand and I follow. At his squad car he opens the trunk and rummages around, finds the Breathalyzer test kit and slams the trunk shut.

The sight of that test kit is becoming way too familiar. I grasp at the only thing I can think of. "Is there some way we can work this out?"

"You gotta be kidding me! You think I'm gonna let you slide? Right after you cop to a DUI?" The back door of the squad is open. I place my hand gingerly over my right side and motion to him I need to sit. He nods and hands me the kit. I lower myself onto the back seat of the squad, facing out, my feet on the ground.

For the second time in less than a month I'm forced to take a Breathalyzer test for something that is not my fault. The unfairness of it jabs at me, deeper this time than last. I glance at Fatso and he gestures for me to hurry up, so I take a deep breath, blow it out completely, my ribs protesting, then inhale again and blow into the tube. The red numbers on the kit zip quickly to point-one-nine. Shit. I hold out the kit. "You sure we can't work this out?"

An Emergency Medical Technician interrupts to let us know he's taking the teenager to Stroger Hospital and then hurries back to the ambulance. After the ambulance leaves, siren blaring, Tubby pivots back toward me and lifts his beefy hand. For a second I think he's going to hit me. Instead, he grasps the top of the squad's open door and leans on it, his weight slightly lowering the side of the car. He grabs the kit and tosses it into the squad and then steps so close to me his belly touches my forehead. I'm directly facing his crotch. I lean back from his gross intimidation and bow my head, eyeball my feet.

"Take a taxi home and never, ever drink and drive again," he says. "You do, I'll personally haul your ass into court and ask the judge to put you away." He pulls out a business card and writes on it, attaches it to my ticket, and drops it in my lap. "I'll be in touch." He spits on the ground right next to my foot. "Get the hell outta my sight."

When he moves off toward the Hyundai driver, my stomach unclenches. While he talks with her, I use both hands to push myself up and shuffle in slow motion to my car. Inside, the flashlight on my phone provides enough light for me to read the card attached to my ticket. Luigi "Lu" Fabrizio. Alberto Carrera's brother-in-law. I can't wait to tell Nuts about this. The printed phone number is crossed out and another number written in. I fold it up with the ticket and stuff them in my backpack. The sound of a car door slams shut and Fabrizio's patrol squad disappears into Thanksgiving night traffic.

Two of IDOT's yellow dinosaur tow trucks arrive and grumble to a stop. One driver tends to hooking up the boy's Camry while the driver from the other truck swings into place in front of my car, quickly puts warning flares in the lane several yards beyond his truck and approaches me. He gestures at my car. "Drivable?"

"Nope."

"Mechanic?"

"Yep." I search my phone and give him my mechanic's address and number. "Any chance I can hitch a ride there with you? My guy isn't far from where I live—I'd appreciate the ride. I'm pretty banged up." I hold my hands over my sore ribs.

"Naw. Sorry, lady. We're not allowed. Rules. But if you want to call someone to pick you up you can stay in my cab 'til they get here. At least it's warm." He smiles at me and I consider who to call. It's ten-thirty at night. "Listen," he says. "I'm gonna go talk to that other lady, check if she needs a tow." He nods at the idling truck. "Go on and get in my cab." He saunters over to the Hyundai.

I push myself upright from the back of my Corolla. My entire body stings and aches and turning my neck is torture. I struggle into my backpack, then reach into the car, pick up the bag of food, and nestle the six-pack on top. I take some mincing steps toward the IDOT truck but stop for a moment when I spy a white Beemer arrive and park at the top of the ramp still blocked off by the squad car. A tall guy gets out and gestures at the Hyundai as he chats with the cop, and then begins to walk down the ramp to the woman I assume is his wife.

The woman is talking to the tow-truck driver and doesn't notice the tall guy until he gets close. She jumps out of her car and rushes to him. They embrace. She points at me and starts blubbering but I can't make out what she's saying. He pats her on the back, dismisses the tow truck driver, and ushers her up the ramp to the Beemer. A young man—their son, I assume—gets out of the Beemer and helps the woman inside, then comes down the ramp with his father. The son goes to the Hyundai while the older man approaches me. "Hi. Uh, you the Corolla?" he asks.

"Yeah."

"Listen. I'd like to exchange insurance information with you so we can get on our way. My wife is kind of upset and I'd like to get her home." He runs his hand through perfectly coiffed hair.

"Sure." We trade information.

He returns to his son in the Hyundai. "Go straight home," the older man instructs the kid and gives the roof a reassuring thump. The kid maneuvers the car onto the expressway and takes off. His father climbs the on-ramp for the last time and heads toward the Beemer. I open the door to the tow truck and hoist the bag of food and the beer onto the seat, followed by my backpack. My body is stiff with cold and pain and I crawl into the truck's cab like a geriatric mountain climber. A minute later the tow-truck driver swings into the cab, backs up to my Corolla, and exits to hook it up.

I clutch my cell phone and stew about the little family vignette I just witnessed, and feel the stinging loneliness of my life. The woman exhibits obvious security, a dependable husband and son. A bright, tiny sliver of envy cuts at me. Then anger at Jimmy trumps the envy. While a tow-truck driver hooks up my destroyed car, I sit here with a six-pack and a bag of turkey leftovers. Alone. On Thanksgiving. I pull out my pack of Kools from my jacket pocket only to find it crushed from the damn seatbelt. Of the three left inside, one is bent in half, so I snap it in two and smoke the top half without the filter. Nicotine laced with menthol surges into my bloodstream and I calm down.

I ditch the butt out the window and extract a beer from the remaining six-pack. The tow guy seems to struggle with hooking up my car and hops in and out of the cab several times to re-position the truck. I'm at least fifteen miles from home. A taxi from here will cost more cash than I've got and both my credit cards are maxed out. I finally settle on calling Felice Abandonato, hoping he'll be up or even tooling around chasing down leads on some case.

"Abandonato." His voice is crisp and wide-awake.

"It's Dana. Got a problem and I need your help."

"What's wrong?"

"Any chance you can pick me up? I'm at 43rd Street on the Ryan—my car's totaled."

"You okay? What happened?"

"I'm mostly shaken up. It's nothing serious but I'm sore as hell. My car got hit twice and the seatbelt worked really, really well."

"I'm in Lincoln Park. Give me fifteen minutes." No good-bye.

My phone says it's almost eleven. Total exhaustion from the full day finally catches up with me. I crack open the beer and chug the entire twelve ounces, intent on dimming some of my physical pain with the best painkiller I know. My eyes are closed when the driver-side door opens again and the tow guy jumps in and stays this time. He switches on the dome light and holds out his hand.

"I'm Roosevelt but people call me Butter." We shake hands.

"I'm Dana. People call me Dana."

He's kind enough to laugh at my lame joke and then gestures at the cell phone on my lap. "You got a ride coming?"

"Yeah. A friend's on his way from Lincoln Park—fifteen minutes." Butter's a skinny African-American guy, grey stubble circling his shiny dome. He ups the heat and tunes the radio to a station playing soft jazz. "Thanks for letting me stay with you 'til he gets here."

"Sure thing. I'm on all night. And I wouldn't leave nobody on 43rd Street at night." He pauses. "Not even an ugly mother with a gun."

We both laugh. "Want a beer?" I open the bag and start to pull out a can for him but his hand on my arm stops me.

"No thanks. Don't touch the stuff anymore."

"It's only beer."

"Does it got alcohol in it?" He pronounces it *akahol*.

"Well yeah, of course. What's your point?"

"No point, Miss Dana. Every time I drink it don't agree with me."

"What, like you're allergic or something?"

"Like every time I drink, I fall down. Drunk." He gives me an earnest look but he's smiling.

More for me, then. I stifle my irritated response and stack my empty in the bag. Butter turns up the volume. A man's voice—all smoke and aged scotch—recaps the recently played pieces. "Who is that?" I ask.

"Dick Buckley. May the man rest in peace. He know more about jazz than...than...well, anybody. And—"

"Wait—rest in peace? How's this guy doing a radio show if he's dead?"

"This here's a re-run of his old show. Love the man, love him. Love working nights so I can listen to his show. Music does it for me, you know?" Again, the earnest look. I shake my head. "I used to smoke, get high," he says. "Lived life like a wine-head for a lot of my younger years. Jazz takes me places higher than any of that ever did. See?"

I shake my head again. It's hard to explain exactly why I don't like jazz, especially when he seems so sold on it. "I don't get jazz—it seems too unformed or something. You can't sing along with it. And when I finally recognize the tune, it takes off for parts unknown."

"It ain't for everybody, Miss. Like drinking. Some can handle it, some can't." His expression is something I can only interpret to mean me. Then he leans back against the headrest and drums his fingers lightly on the steering wheel in time with a peppy tune. I'm about to ask him what the hell he means but Abandonato pulls up and honks. "There's your ride, Miss. Easy does it."

Irked at the guy, I say nothing and decamp. Even with the recent beer circulating in my blood the climb down from the truck cab sends shock waves through my chest and stomach. I hold still for a long moment and take short, shallow breaths to try to quell the pain.

Abandonato gets out of his car and holds out his arms for the grocery bag. For a second I don't want to surrender it, afraid he might eyeball the six-pack. I casually cinch the curled top of the paper bag a bit tighter, hand it over, and he places it in his trunk. Butter blasts his horn a couple of farewell belches and pulls away with my sad little Corolla trailing behind.

"Hey, Nuts." I slide into the passenger seat and greet my partner using a nickname coined by the guys in Homicide—a shortened version of 'donuts,' which Felice hates and never eats. When he doesn't respond, I glance at him. His hands are tight on the steering wheel. He's not smiling.

"God, I can smell it on you. Are you crazy? Drinking and driving while you're on suspension—for *drinking*?" He slams the transmission into Drive and pulls into traffic. I feel my face flush but bite back the retort I want to fucking hurl at him.

"Oh. So now you're judge and jury before you even hear me out?" I consciously straighten up in my seat. He glances at me, his mouth set in a tight line, but says nothing. I take this as a nod to continue. "I ate with Evie and JJ and drank two beers with dinner. That's it. Two." This time my stomach doesn't flutter with the lie.

"I was driving home. Sober." I draw out this last word for emphasis. "Some North Shore woman who probably never drove on the Ryan before tries to out-race me while she merges. She clips me, sends me one-eighty so I end up facing the on-ramp. Then this kid comes down the ramp and almost hits me head-on, but swerves and clips me on the other side. None of it my fault, Nuts. None." We pass dark buildings hunkered down alongside the expressway.

"Listen. I don't care who's at fault, okay? Two beers, ten beers, you shouldn't be behind the wheel. Period."

"Message received." I want to mollify him, so I capitulate. Time to take the focus off me. "Why so grouchy?"

"I pulled a double shift today—lots of cops on holiday leave with their families. I'm doing it again tomorrow. Tired."

Felice is regimented, no doubt there. It makes him a great cop and a lethal detective: he follows rules, writes and hands in reports on time, and collects, sorts and interprets information about homicides in a way that gives him the best solve rate in the department. It makes him a sub-three-hour marathoner. He trains, eats and sleeps according to schedule and doesn't vary from it.

It also makes him a real pain in the ass.

"Sorry." I'm not sure why I'm apologizing. "I didn't know who else to call. I gave my last ten bucks to this woman who needed it and—oh, never mind." My body screams at me and I rest my head back and close my eyes.

"Okay, okay. But you know the stats—even two beers can impair your reaction time. Did the cops come? Or did you only swap insurance info?"

"Both. Did you know Carrera has a brother-in-law who's a cop?" I sink lower in my seat and flinch when the seatbelt tightens over my injured ribs.

Felice groans. "No shit?" He pats my knee and I warm to his sympathy.

"Yeah. Name's Lu Fabrizio. Gave me a Failure to Yield but let me slide, otherwise." *Is that true?* He did Breathalyze me. I close my eyes again, picture the small card with his name and hand-written phone number, the threat behind his innocuous *I'll be in touch*. I'm bloated, my face is greasy, and I'm shaky and deflated because the initial surge of adrenaline released during the accident has now dissipated.

I doze until I feel a rush of cold air when Felice opens the door on my side of the car, grocery bag in his arms. Home. I feel like I can sleep twelve hours straight. I swing my legs out so I'm sitting sideways on the seat and then struggle upright in stages until I face him and hold out my arms for the bag. "Here, I'll take that. Thanks for the lift. You're a good man."

He shakes his head.

"What?"

His index finger slips into the top of the bag and pulls it back to reveal the beer. A steely-eyed glare. "How's treatment going?" He shakes his head again in a dismissive motion.

I grab the grocery bag, ignoring the pain shooting from my ribs, and head for my building. But I stop half-way there and spin around to face him. "What the hell do you want from me, Abandonato?" Loud.

He peers at the night sky and then closes the gap between us in a quick jog until he pulls up, his face six inches from mine. "I want us back together as partners. I want you to do everything in your power to make that happen." His voice is guttural. He points to the bag. "This? This is bullshit."

Before I can say anything he rips a tear in the grocery bag, grabs the beer and methodically opens one can after another, pouring the contents onto the grass. I'm so stunned I can only watch until he's finished and the empties lay scattered at my feet. Abandonato wheels away from me and jogs back to his car, gets in, and punches the accelerator hard enough to make his tires squeal, an obvious effort to get as far away from me as fast as possible.

The empty cans on the grass form a ragged half-circle at my feet. A full moon projects enough light for me to stomp them flat and stuff them back in the bag. My chest and ribs scream as a reminder to take my time lifting the bag from the ground. All I want at this point is a few more beers to quell the pain. Or several ibuprofen. Or both.

Mindful of the pain as I fumble to keep the food from spilling out of the bag, I creep to the entrance of my building where I find Sandor, the building manager who lives on site, holding the door open for me. I push past him without a glance as I pass into the lobby, convinced I appear as horrible as I feel.

"Hello, Miss. You are being okay? Mrs. Sandor heard noise and is waking Sandor to go outside and see." He closes the entrance door.

I stop and face him. He's in pajamas and wearing a woman's pink bathrobe too large for his small frame. He closes the gap between us, his moccasins scuffing the ceramic tiles.

"I—I'm sorry, Sandor. My friend and I had an argument, a fight, we were pretty loud and—"

What first looks like puzzlement on his face quickly morphs into the same tight-lipped visage as Abandonato's, and for the same reason: Sandor smells booze on me. And he does not approve. My anger at my partner spills over onto this harmless little man. I bend down and get in his face and purposely blow my breath on him. "Why don't you go back to your apartment and tell your wife to mind her own fucking business—the show is over out here."

He recoils from my brief diatribe and scoots to unlock the inner door for me. I feel the cheap sense of triumph that occurs when I lash out at someone without thinking. But self-loathing for my immature behavior extinguishes my brief foray into superiority. I push away self-recriminations as I sail through the door, ignoring this innocent bystander, and climb the three flights to my studio.

While throwing out the flattened cans and refrigerating JJ's care package I consider Abandonato's exhortation about wanting us back the way we were. I, too, want the same thing.

Marvin's homework sheet, which I haven't perused since he gave it to me, flutters in my memory: how does drinking affect three main areas of my life—work, family, health? I know how I would answer in light of Abandonato's little drama played out on the front lawn. And now I can add Sandor to the list of those I abuse.

My last thought when I crawl into bed is that I didn't ask Nuts to do a background check on Frank Safer. Now I doubt he'll want to.

13

F riday, 11/22, 11:00 a.m.

JJ ARRIVED at my studio earlier this morning, supposedly to help me assemble some book shelves but I know worry on my father's face. He wanted to be sure I got home safely last night. I told him I had car trouble on the way back and that Abandonato gave me a ride home. JJ wanted more details, so I told him it stalled out and wouldn't start again. Not the whole truth but not a lie, either.

Until my car is out of the shop JJ is loaning me Evie's car. She failed her most recent driver's test and can't drive until she gets the glasses she obviously needs. But she won't get the glasses because she refuses to consider there's anything wrong with her vision. Refusal to admit she has a problem or weakness is a lifelong attitude of my mother's. Not one I admire.

I drop JJ off back home and thank him profusely for the car. He waves me off, even bristling a bit at my question of how he convinced Evie to let me have her car. *"Both cars are in my name. I bought them."* His role as the sole breadwinner in our family is a source of great pride for my father. I show him props with a huge smile and sign *wonderful* with enthusiasm.

On my drive over to Flora Maitland's apartment the radio allows as how this Black Friday is no different than those in the past; Americans continue to live up to their deserved reputation as conspicuous consumers.

The radio reporter continues with breathless updates on the availability of parking spaces at the various malls around the suburbs. O Come, All Ye Faithful. I feel particularly peeved at the thought of tons of money being wasted on pointless gifts when there are people literally starving in Chicago. Of course, I'm picturing Flora and her kids, but there are thousands in similar circumstances in this city. I snap off the radio.

At a stoplight I pull out my list of things to do and add a phone call to Abandonato about Frank Safer, unsure if he'll even talk to me after our dust-up last night. The light turns green and I continue to scan the buildings I pass hoping for a Walgreens so I can stop for ibuprofen. I've had my share of injuries in the line of duty but none compares with how much I hurt from last night's car accident. I imagine how someone with severe arthritis or chronic pain must feel. A few beers would ease my physical agony but I mentally kick myself for thinking about drinking at eleven o'clock in the morning, especially when I'm attending my first A.A. meeting tonight.

At Flora's building I park and gingerly heft the shopping bag of food JJ packed for me last night, avoiding heavy contact with my bruised body. From my own kitchen I have included a box of instant oatmeal bought in a two-for-one sale. Easy to make. Even Flora can muster enough energy to boil water.

Because I don't want to enter this building again with only Mace for protection, my personal Glock is zipped up in my jacket pocket. My service weapon, also a Glock, is locked up in my lieutenant's office, along with my badge, while I'm on suspension. I slide my cell phone into the other pocket.

Inside the building lobby three young girls jump rope—I recognize Double Dutch from my schoolyard days—while two little boys chase a ball around, giggling and tripping over each other when they try to capture it. The ball skitters toward me while I make my way to the stairwell so I stop, give it a slight boot with my foot and send it back toward the boys, who scream with delight.

This bombed-out lobby is a pathetic playground but at least it offers more protection for these kids than playing outside, drive-by shootings being what they are in Chicago. I encounter only one other person on my slow way up the stairs to 623 but he's passed out at the third-floor landing, vomit and alcohol the overriding stink emanating from his body.

Flora lets me in, exclaiming over another bag of food, telling me *you shouldn't have* but smiling the whole time.

I should have.

Emma plants herself firmly on Flora's left leg, half hiding behind it but smiling at me in a shy way. This time I follow them down the long hallway to the kitchen. I take a seat at a card table replete with a long crack down the middle and Emma climbs into a chair on the opposite side. She studies me with great concentration.

Flora boils a pan of water for instant coffee while putting away the food. At last, she sits at the table with us and we sip the coffee for a short while without talking. The apartment felt cold when I entered but in here the stove burners blaze and heat pours out of the yawning oven door. I shrug off my jacket. Flora wears a shapeless shift. Emma is clad in the same shorts and t-shirt from yesterday, her feet bare.

"I brought over my cell phone for you to call Public Aid yourself instead of calling for you. Lot easier that way." This is my way of not saying what I really want to yell at the woman: *stop being so passive and do something!* I hand her my cell phone.

"Oh, okay, sure." Flora puts the phone on the card table, leaves the room for a few minutes, then returns with a sheet of paper that's been folded several times. Smoothing out the sheet, she reads a phone number out loud from it and then scans my cell with no comprehension. She hands it back to me, her face flushed. "I ain't never used one a these."

Emma slides out of her chair and comes over next to me and watches while I punch in the numbers for Public Aid Flora reads from the piece of paper. Emma holds up her tiny index finger, her face an unspoken bid for permission.

"Sure, go ahead. Push number six." Emma pokes at the six and when her effort is rewarded with a beep, she grins at me. I grin back and then hand the phone to her to give to Flora, who talks with Public Aid. Emma looks up at me, again with a studious gaze and serious eyes. The little girl intrigues me, her attitude belying her young age.

"Where are your sisters, Emma?"

"They're in mama's room playing dress-up."

"Don't you want to play with them?"

Emma shakes her head but says nothing. From the table she retrieves the piece of paper with the Public Aid info and returns to her seat. She methodically smooths out the paper and carefully refolds it into an airplane.

She makes sure I'm watching and with a slight fling of her fingers sends the plane across to me. It nosedives onto the table. I chuckle, pick it up, and after straightening out the bent nose send it on a return flight. Emma's face lights up. She snatches the plane in mid-air with a deft touch.

Flora indicates she's on hold and will be for a while so I beckon to Emma to bring the plane with her. We go to the long hallway.

"You stay here and I'll go to the other end. We can fly the plane back and forth to each other better that way, okay?"

She nods and waits for me to get to the other end, then sails the plane to me in a perfect arc. I catch it and sail it back but even this small effort reawakens my body ache from the accident last night. Got to score some ibuprofen when I'm done here.

The flight elicits a giggle from the little girl and she sends it back to me. I'm elated knowing our game makes her laugh. She's just the same as the kids in the lobby, caught up in the moment and happy playing a simple game. I sail the plane to Emma but it overshoots her and ends up in the kitchen. Emma's hand covers her mouth, her eyes wide.

"I'll race ya," I say and start a slow jog down the hallway, my body telling me this isn't the smartest move. Emma squeals but waits until I almost reach her, then darts into the kitchen and scrambles under the table to retrieve the plane.

Flora hands me the phone. "Here," she says. "I'm done, but I don't know how to, you know, hang up." She motions with the cell phone and I laugh when I take it. Emma crawls from under the table, reaches for the phone, and asks if she can push the button.

"Sure." I squat down and hand her the phone, showing her which button to push, then stow the phone in my jacket hanging on the chair.

"They said I gotta go over to a resource center, get a new Link card. It's not too far from here. One bus." Flora sounds tired.

"That's great, Flora. Still got the money for the bus fare?"

Her face projects something between hurt and pride and she gestures for me to follow her to the front of the apartment. We walk down the long hallway to the mattresses where her purse rests. She unclasps the top and pulls out the ten I gave her yesterday. She'll be able to get over there today and get the card, be set for December. I feel oddly happy at helping this woman even though I think she's a lame excuse for a mother.

I gesture at her summer dress. "Aren't you cold in here? Feels like the heat's off."

Flora glances down at her dress and smooths the skirt with both hands. "I tell the manager every time he comes to get the rent but nothing changes. Me and the kids come up here in May from Texas and we don't got no winter clothes yet."

I make a mental note to check with Evie about the donated clothes she mentioned yesterday. The cold room reminds me my jacket is still in the kitchen. And so is Emma. Along with my Glock. I hustle down the hallway calling the little girl's name. Emma crouches under the table and I'm relieved she's only holding the paper airplane.

My jacket is heavy and I pat my pocket to confirm the gun is still there, zipped up and secure. I'm so quick to criticize Flora for being a neglectful mother and here I've left a four-year-old in the same room with a loaded handgun. I crouch down to be eye-level with her. "I'm going home now, Emma. Come say good-bye to me?"

Emma looks up with her solemn expression and nods. For a moment I flash on the little girl living with me, taking care of her, being her mother. I mentally slap myself for the thought and shake off the fantasy but my joy from our game together is extinguished. Emma jumps up from the floor and holds up the paper airplane. "Here," she says. "You take it to your house. Then you can come back and play with me again."

I take the plane, touched. "Thank you, Emma. I will." Emma takes my hand and accompanies me to the front room where Flora stands. I wag my finger in mock anger at Flora. "You get that Link card." I point at Emma. "And feed these kids!" I scoot out the door wanting to get away from their long faces.

On my way down the stairwell I stop at the third-floor landing. The drunk guy is still there, still passed out, still smells of puke and booze. That ain't me. Never has been. Never will be. I hold up Emma's paper airplane, which almost glows in the gloom, then fold it in half and slip it into the back pocket of my jeans as I hurry away from the stink.

Evie's car offers solitary respite from my overwrought feelings about Emma. I crack open a window, light up a cigarette and close my eyes, trying to calm down before getting back on the road. A few minutes later I hear shouting. In front of Flora's building two boys, one twice as big as the other, are slapping and punching each other. A bicycle with a large canvas bag across the handlebars lies on the ground.

"You gonna give me your bike? Right?" the older boy says as he holds the other kid in a headlock. The younger boy can only grunt until he pulls free and spits a wad of phlegm at the older boy.

"You shit head fuckin' asshole!"

The aggressor turns back. In one leap he covers the three steps he has taken toward the bike and tackles the small kid, punching him in the head and stomach, anywhere he can make contact. The younger boy starts screaming.

"Hey! Hey!" I take a half-step out of my car and flick my cigarette into the street. The punching stops and they both stand and look at me but then the older one pulls the younger one in a tight embrace from behind. He says something in the boy's ear.

The smaller boy's body language changes and he slumps in the strait-jacket hold, his body going limp. When the older boy lets him go, the little boy collapses on the sidewalk. Before I can make my way over to them the older boy grabs a wallet from the other kid's pocket, ditches the canvas bag from the bike and rides off down the street.

I hustle to the little boy. "You okay?" I ask. The younger boy, furious, wipes his nose with a swipe of his arm. I offer him my hand to help him up but he ignores me and struggles to stand, clearly hurting from the fight. I gesture in the direction the other boy went. "Who is that kid?"

"He's a fuckin' shit head." He stares at the street where the other kid has disappeared with the bike.

"You know him?"

He looks at me like I'm the slowest one in the class. "Yeah. I *know* him." He spits again and picks up the canvas bag. I start to tell him who I am, thinking maybe I can help him get his bike back but he interrupts. "You ain't my mother." He slings the empty bag—emblazoned with the name of a newspaper delivery service—over his slight shoulder and limps into the building.

I trudge back to my car. His words sting. I'm well aware that in the last hour I have failed twice to exhibit any mothering ability.

On the drive back to the North Side I buy some ibuprofen and a bottle of water, chasing three tablets with most of the twenty ounces in one long drink right there in the store. My hunger kicks in at last. Earlier, when JJ came over, my body-ache and hangover didn't allow me to ingest anything other than coffee. McDonald's takes care of my grumbling stomach and I draw hard on a large chocolate shake while I drive back home.

At my apartment, Jimmy emerges from the building entrance but doesn't see me and walks in the opposite direction from where I park. I hesitate calling out to him, remembering how badly our meeting at Brau Haus ended. Even though I'm sure he's still angry with me, especially about drinking, the sight of his retreating figure tears at me and I want to rush to him. "Hey!" I yell, as I exit my car. He turns around. His arm thrusts in a quick small wave and he jogs back to meet me.

"Been trying to get a hold of you—didn't you get my messages?"

"What? No. Hold on." I pat my jacket pockets, feel the Glock, but don't find my cell phone. I dig around in my backpack. Nothing. I hand my backpack to Jimmy and search the car floor, picturing my phone slipping out of my jacket pocket on the drive home. Again, nothing. It's either at Flora's or I left it at the store when I bought the ibuprofen. I glance at Jimmy and he looks impatient. I explain the missing phone. "Come on upstairs." I lead the way.

Once inside I start some coffee brewing and try to straighten up the place a bit, self-conscious about the continued mess even though I moved in a few weeks ago. There on my desk is the traffic ticket from last night along with Fabrizio's card. While Jimmy uses the bathroom I quickly pile some papers on top of the ticket.

I borrow Jimmy's cell to call Felice about doing a background check on Frank Safer but he doesn't answer and I end up leaving a terse message. I don't allude to how he left me last night, standing in the middle of the lawn surrounded by beer cans he emptied in a furious tantrum, because I don't want to chance Jimmy overhearing what happened.

I also call my cell in the hope someone will answer and give me a clue to its whereabouts. While I'm on the phone Jimmy wanders around the room peering out the windows, inspecting the newly assembled bookshelves, viewing the photos stuck to my refrigerator with plastic alphabet magnets. His face tells me nothing about what he thinks of the studio. No one answers my cell and I disconnect.

"I look like a punk in this one," he says, tapping the photo of the two of us on graduation day from the police academy. He slips it out from under the magnet for closer inspection. "But god you're cute, Dane." He gazes at the photo for another beat and brings it to the sofa where I hand him a cup of black coffee and lower my aching body next to him. I rubberneck a look at the pic he holds. He's right. In the photo I'm twenty and damn cute.

Jimmy blows on his coffee to cool it before taking several sips. "I hear your car stalled out," he says.

I'm puzzled for a second, but recover. "From JJ?"

He nods. "I couldn't get hold of you so I called your parents on the relay. Didn't you tell them I was in town? He was surprised."

I start to reiterate my aggravation with him for keeping me off-balance with his appearance right before Thanksgiving when I'm positive he told me he'd be home at Christmas.

He waves his hand to cut me off, as if this is not his concern. I stifle my irritation with him and am left with a niggle of self-doubt about my recollection of our previous conversation.

"JJ told me he loaned you Evie's car. What happened with yours?"

"Not sure. When I drove back from their house last night it stalled out at a stoplight and wouldn't start. I got it towed to Cargiver's. Nuts gave me a ride home." The story sounds even more plausible in the retelling since I tried it out on JJ this morning. We drink our coffee while I update him about my suspension from Homicide and about starting the Intensive Outpatient Program this past Monday.

Jimmy hands me his empty cup and declines more. I get up and try to avoid grimacing at the complaint from my ribs—the ibuprofen doing little to reduce the sharp pain—and put the cups in the sink.

"So how come they let you drink?" Jimmy asks.

I'm confused by his question for a moment, then realize he must mean drinking at Brau Haus when we got together two days ago. I don't want to revisit our painful argument from that day because I'm relieved Jimmy is here and actually talking to me, don't want my anger to scare him away. I also don't want to be reminded of my miscarriage. I return to him and sit on the edge of the couch. Outside the window, I view the tops of the trees that line the street, their black branches stripped of leaves and forming a jumbled, fragmented pattern. A grey sky has overtaken the earlier sunlight.

"The truth is I promised Koz I'd attend IOP so I could save my job, but I never promised him I'd quit drinking altogether."

Silence.

I sit back into the couch and look Jimmy in the eye. "You know the suspension is a load of crap, right? I never drank on the job."

Jimmy breaks our eye contact, puts our photo aside, and focuses on folding his hands in his lap. "And what about us, D?"

He asks this question so quietly I almost miss it. My blank homework assignment from Marvin raises its ugly head again and I think I understand what my husband wants to know. I reach out and lay both my hands over his. "I'm sorry I got out of hand at Brau Haus—it won't happen again. I'm in IOP for six weeks. Can you hang around for me to finish?"

He listens and nods but doesn't ask any questions, then gets up and goes to the coffee maker but stops and comes back to the couch wearing an expression I can only infer as dispirited. "So, I spent yesterday at the house. I'm staying there while I pack up what I want to take back. Anything left you can sell or donate to Salvation Army."

Just like that.

I search his face trying to understand how we got to this point, unsure whether he's including me in his move or trying to tell me something else. "I can't go to L.A., Jimmy, I'd hate it. I can't leave my parents. And what about our house?"

I'm surprised my overriding feeling is confusion, not anger or sadness at how far apart we are. Confused and numb. I get up and open a new pack of cigarettes, and he makes a face at me when I settle down on the couch and light up. He goes to a window and cracks it open, then takes a chair to the side and upwind of me.

"We gotta sell it," he says. He snaps his fingers and pulls his wallet out of his back pocket, opens it. "Here's my half for the mortgage payment this month."

I take the check from him and place it prominently on the side table next to the couch, a visual reminder to pay my bills and get them in the mail by tomorrow morning.

"I know the market's rough right now," Jimmy says, "but I can't afford paying for two places."

He's right, because I can't afford two places either. But I tear up when I picture the blue plastic tarp that covers the unfinished addition that waits for our baby who never came home.

"Aw shit, Dane. Come on, don't." He comes to sit next to me and envelopes me in a hug while I cry. He plucks the burning cigarette from my fingers and stubs it out and we stay like this for a long time, holding each other. When he lets me go, I ask him when he's leaving for L.A.

"A week from today. Listen, I know you said you don't want to move to L.A., but think about it. It's a great place to start over. You can leave the sadness and drinking here. Everybody's really in shape there, too. LAPD has its own fitness center. Give it a chance, D."

Maybe he's right. I'm relieved he wants me to join him, relieved this isn't the end. His hope is contagious and inside I feel a slight swell of it. Then Jimmy's fluffy description of the good life we can enjoy in L.A. echoes too loudly Jen's description of a geographical cure. I hug my sweater tightly around me. The thought of another Chicago winter compared to living in warm California is a strong motivator. I push away Jen's talking head but two other people intrude.

"What about Evie and JJ? I can't leave them here alone."

"News flash. Your parents are in their sixties and can take care of themselves. David and Daphne understand that."

"But that's exactly what I mean. My brother and sister both moved away so I'm the only family here for my parents."

Jimmy has known my family since high school and after all this time I thought he understood how much my deaf parents depend on me. He says nothing but checks out the photo of the two of us again before rising to re-affix it to the refrigerator with the letter 'O.' He returns to the sofa and kneels down on the floor, face level with me, taking my hands in his.

"Dana, I love you. We've got problems, I know. But we can work them out if you come to L.A. Please? Let's try again. At least think about it?"

He's being so nice to me I almost hate him. Why can't he be a prick and make this easier? My own perversity makes me smile. He smiles back. "What?"

"Why can't you be a son of a bitch and dump your fat wife?" I start laughing. He leans into me, holds my face between his two warm hands, and kisses me in the soft, sweet way I have missed these last four months. I rise and begin to pull him over to the futon but he hesitates.

"What?" I ask.

He pinches his nose with thumb and index finger, the universal sign for *stinky*.

"I'm on it." I head for the bathroom to brush my teeth and grab a quick shower.

14

F riday, 11/22, 5:00 p.m.

JIMMY LEAVES around five to meet some buddies from the force for dinner and a night of beer and darts. I read over the information about the A.A. meeting I'm attending at eight this evening. It's in the basement of a YMCA about three miles away and the meeting directory describes an "open speaker meeting," whatever that means. I'm a little put off by the hidden meanings or lack of definitions I keep encountering, like IOP's 'bridge group.'

But then I read more of the pamphlet and find out open meetings are for anyone to attend, alcoholics and family, anyone interested. I'm almost giddy with relief at this news. I can be someone attending simply to find out about A.A., maybe for a friend or a family member.

I'm happier still that Jimmy came over and we reunited. I'm pumped about L.A. I can even talk to Evie and JJ about moving out there with us so it won't feel like I'm abandoning them. JJ would agree to it in a second, I know. Evie will be the harder one to convince. But it's the confirmation of Jimmy's love that makes me feel positive again after many months of negativity, which started with my miscarriage and continues because of my present job suspension. I celebrate the good feeling with a beer while I watch the evening news.

At seven-fifteen, when I stand up to toss out the five empty cans and get ready for the meeting, I feel woozy and leave the cans on the counter. I've been drinking on an empty stomach. I think about picking up takeout on the way to the meeting but then recall Lu Fabrizio's admonition—and Abandonato's—about drinking and driving. I hate when they're right. I'll have to cab it over to the Y. First though, I scrub my teeth and gargle with mouthwash before leaving.

There's no time for a fast food fix by the time I hoof it over to Clark Street to wave down a taxi. Chips and a pop from the corner convenience store make do and I arrive at the meeting five minutes before it begins.

The large basement holds one hundred folding chairs set up ten-by-ten, and two banquet-sized tables line the back of the room, one offering coffee and cookies, the other covered with pamphlets, books and assorted bumper stickers. Almost every seat is taken.

Next to a podium at the front of the room a man and woman talk to each other, the man glancing at his watch and then at the door propped open nearby. Outside, near the door, another man stands smoking a cigarette. I find a seat near the back of the overly-warm room and settle in, grateful for the handful of cookies I snatched and the cup of coffee, both of which should help alleviate my buzz. It's an open meeting but I'm still nervous I'll run into someone I know.

I try to figure out a story about why I'm here. Maybe researching A.A.? In my job as a cop someone might need a referral. But that sounds too fishy and I stick with a simpler idea: My friend drinks too much. I'm here to get some information for her. Him.

The man at the podium rings a bell and the room slowly quiets down. He waits until it is silent. "Welcome to the Friday night Open

Speakers' Meeting of Alcoholics Anonymous. My name's Jeremiah and I'm an alcoholic."

"HI, JEREMIAH!" The whole room responds with a roar. It startles the shit out of me and I slosh coffee on my jeans. The woman next to me hands me a napkin and a look of sympathy.

"Hi, everyone," Jeremiah says. "The format of our meeting is two speakers, one from A.A. and one from Al-Anon. We'll take a short break in between for those of you who are still slaves to nicotine." Chuckling ripples through the audience. "We'll end promptly at nine. Can we start this meeting with a quiet time, please?"

Many in the room bow their heads. I don't, and instead survey the variety of people in attendance. I'm surprised the room is filled with a cross section of Chicagoans you'd pass on an average street on an average day.

"Not to embarrass you but is there anyone new to A.A. attending tonight?"

I freeze. It feels like those in the audience looking around are staring right at me. I feign indifference and match their casual glances to the left and right. A few hands go up. Jeremiah points to one person and asks for her first name.

"My name's Louise."

"HI, LOUISE!" the crowd roars again.

A few people call out "welcome" and "good to see you" as the audience applauds. Jeremiah takes us through a few more new attendees but I keep my novice status to myself. We also meet a few who are attending this particular meeting for the first time, some who actually identify themselves as alcoholic, including the woman next to me. Introductions finished, Jeremiah instructs us to complete another bit of socializing. "Shake hands with someone you don't know."

The woman next to me offers her hand. "As you heard, I'm Dorothy."

"Dana." We shake hands. I study her from the corner of my eye as the first speaker is introduced. Dorothy resembles the librarian I had in grade school: sixtyish, chubby, with horn-rimmed glasses and an up-do with more hair falling down than staying put.

"So, is this a good meeting? You've been here before," she says. I realize too late she surmises this because I didn't raise my hand as a newcomer or a first-timer at this meeting. Crap. Now what do I do? Before I can answer, Jeremiah starts introducing the first speaker so I nod at Dorothy and then turn my attention to the podium.

"...always enjoy what he has to say. Please help me welcome Jack." The room breaks out in polite applause and a guy in the front row holding a cup of coffee gets up and strolls to the lectern. I'm surprised by his youthful face and check out his ring finger. No band.

"Hi, I'm Jack and I'm an alcoholic." He beams at the crowd when they respond to the greeting, again in megaphone volume. "I want to thank Jeremiah for asking me to speak tonight. Lately I've been on a dry drunk and really need to tell my story again, just so I don't forget where I came from. Okay, I'm supposed to tell you what it was like, what happened, and what it's like now." He stops and takes a sip of coffee, then places his cup on the table next to the podium.

"Easy. It was hell. In short order, I started drinking senior year in high school and never looked back. The first time I drank I went into a blackout, so I thought that was normal and what people experienced when they got drunk. I drank my way through college—Yale—and managed to graduate, although my grade point average was exactly that, average. My parents were very disappointed. They were both college professors and thought I'd make a better showing. I won a National Merit Scholarship in high school, so it's obvious they had high hopes for me."

Dorothy nudges me and when I look at her, she raises her eyebrows. Not sure of her meaning, I give a non-committal hum and turn my attention back to the speaker.

"Anyway, I married right out of college, ten years ago. My wife and I met at a bar during finals and she could really keep up with me drinking-wise. I knew I'd found the girl of my dreams."

I laugh along with the crowd.

"I'm a computer analyst and my wife taught in elementary school. We made our home in suburbia—Schaumburg—and had a good life for the first few years. We planned for children and our son made his debut seven years ago, so we were happy. And we drank. A lot. We drank to celebrate, like with our son, and we drank on sad occasions, like when my father died. Mostly we drank for no reason. It's Wednesday night, let's hoist a few."

Most people do imbibe on special occasions. I do. This afternoon I drank to celebrate reconnecting with Jimmy, so it's pretty normal. And I still made it here, not passed out in some gutter.

"It upset my parents when I drank, because they were teetotalers," Jack continues. "I recently discovered both of my grandfathers were alcoholics and died from this disease. That's why my parents were horrified by the way my wife and I drank."

This reminds me of Evie's aversion to alcohol—her teenaged brother killed by a drunk driver. I get it.

"Okay, what happened." Jack says. "Six years ago, right after our son's first birthday, I got a phone call at work from the police. They asked me my name, address, my wife's name, if I had a baby boy."

Before he completes his statement my stomach clenches. I know what's coming. I've made those phone calls.

"When he asked about my son, somehow I knew. My wife was drinking, got in the car with our baby and had an accident. But it was worse than simply an accident. She crossed the median line and had a head-on collision with a truck. My wife and son died at the scene."

A murmur filters through the audience while Jack swirls his white Styrofoam cup and finishes his coffee. My recent accident wasn't anything like his. I didn't hit her, she hit me. Jack turns away from us for a moment and runs a trembling hand through his hair a few times. When he returns his attention to us his face appears older.

"I had to identify both of them and that about finished me. I wanted to die right there, be with them. I started drinking that night and stayed drunk through the wake, the funeral, the burial. I mired in booze for six months. My boss laid me off, told me to get into a program. I ran out of money, the bank took our home and I moved back with my mother, collected unemployment."

Jack stops, pulls out a handkerchief and swipes at his eyes, then blows his nose with a loud honk. Instead of returning the handkerchief to his pocket he holds it with both hands and makes small, twisting motions. "My mom tried to help me but I shut her out. I was in so much pain I didn't want to see anybody or do anything but wallow in it, which meant drinking every day until I passed out. Then I'd get up and do it all over again the next day."

His voice takes on a distant, echoing quality and I can't discern his words anymore. I'm driving in my car, wracked with hot spasms coming hard and fast, down low, where the baby is. I hunch over the steering wheel and peer through the windshield to check if I'm near the hospital yet but the pain dims my vision. I feel a gush drop from me and spread warmth through my clothes and onto my inner thighs —somehow, I know I'm sitting in blood.

The room breaks out in laughter and I'm back in the bright lights of the A.A. meeting at the YMCA. I chuckle too, only so I appear to know what they're laughing at. "I couldn't quite hear him," I say to Dorothy. "What did he say?"

She leans close to my ear. "He got twelfth-stepped by the guy who sold him his booze." I chuckle lightly, more pretending. Again with the secret code words. What the hell is "twelfth-stepped?"

"It's true. I ran a tab at Binyon's and paid Joe every month when my check came in—he was cool with that. But the last month of my drinking I really pounded it down and had no scratch to pay him. Joe asked me if he could take me out for a cup of coffee. Now understand, coffee was the last thing I wanted—more like oblivion. But I thought if I sucked up to my booze connection, my source, he'd let me slide on my tab. Typical drunk, always scamming. Right?"

More laughter and nodding from the crowd but I cringe because the lies I've been telling recently don't make me want to laugh.

"We had coffee and he told me his story, how he got sober. To this day I can't really remember anything he told me except for the very first thing out of his mouth. 'You don't have to do this anymore.' For some reason that got my attention. Really, I had no other plans except keep drinking until I died.

"That happened six years ago. Joe told me if I wanted to get sober to go home, sleep it off, take a shower, and he'd come by at seven-thirty and we'd go to a meeting together. If I wasn't outside waiting for him he'd know I wasn't interested.

"Again, for some reason—and today in retrospect I see my higher power working in my life—I did what he told me and we went to that meeting together. Joe became my sponsor and I'm happy to say I owe him my life. And not one drink since then, a day at a time." In the front row, Jeremiah raises his arm and waves at Jack.

"I'm getting the high sign," Jack says, "so I'll end with this thought: there's nothing so bad that a drink won't make it worse. Thanks, and I'll keep coming back." The audience applauds. After Jeremiah shakes Jack's hand he announces a short break. Half the group exits the door where I noticed the guy smoking earlier. I go out to smoke but keep to myself because the raucous banter of the crowd feels intrusive and annoying. If this was anywhere but an A.A. meeting I'd swear these people were buzzed.

Back inside we listen to a woman speaker during the second half but she's pretty boring talking about Al-Anon and how she has a happy life even though her husband still drinks. It's obvious Jimmy isn't going to sign on to that.

Uncomfortable in the folding metal chair, I tune her out for the most part and fidget, wanting to leave, but I need to get the IOP form signed after the meeting so I stick it out. I'm cranky from hunger, lack of sleep, and could use a few more beers because the physical pain from the accident is back in spades since my afternoon buzz wore off.

Jimmy's idea of moving to L.A. occupies my thoughts. I picture us living near the ocean, maybe a condo, and I'll exercise every day in the sunshine and lose these extra forty pounds, get back to my svelte self. I'll probably work as a beat cop for a year or two before anything opens up in Homicide. But that's okay, as long as we're together. He said he wants to try again. Maybe, just maybe, I'll be ready by then.

Mercifully, the woman finishes after fifteen minutes and Jeremiah comes back to the podium. "I forgot to pass the basket before our last speaker. Our Seventh Tradition states that A.A. is self-supporting through our own contributions, so please give what you can." Two men pass medium-sized plastic bins back and forth across the rows and people drop folding money as well as change into them. Christ, it's like being in church. I don't donate and pass it on to Dorothy.

"We finish this meeting by saying the Serenity Prayer. For those who care to join us, please form a circle."

This keeps getting worse. I panic because I don't know the words. Everyone stands and I follow and join hands, Dorothy taking mine, which makes me extremely uncomfortable. It's like IOP. I don't want to participate but feel like I've been manipulated into it. The group recites the prayer and in short order I drop the hands of the people on each side of me.

"Nice to meet you, Dana," Dorothy says, donning her coat.

I fake a smile. "Same here. Well, good night."

I head toward where Jeremiah stands in front. He's talking with Jack so I wait, paper in hand. On the wall behind him are framed posters with various lame sayings: One Day at a Time; Keep Coming Back; Easy Does It. That last one rings a distant bell although my memory can't pull up where I heard it. Sobriety by cliché, how does that keep people from drinking? Jack notices the sheet I hold and motions for me to interrupt their conversation.

"Uh, thanks. I need this signed, I guess by you?" I ask Jeremiah.

"Yep, that's right." He writes on the paper and then returns it.

Jack sticks out his hand to me. "Thanks for coming. This is a good meeting, lots of good sobriety here."

When I shake his hand something like an electrical charge runs through me and I pull back. "I—I liked your story." I'm immediately horrified at my words. Why say that about such an incredibly sad story? "I mean, I understand because..." I'm unsure how to finish. How do I tell him about my miscarriage, something so personal?

Jack doesn't say anything, simply waits.

"I'm a cop," I say, falling back on firmer ground. "Been at a lot of those accidents." God, now what do I say? Your wife should've known better than to drink and drive, especially with a baby in the car. Yes, I'm sure he doesn't know that, Dana, very helpful. I fumble with the meeting log paper and fold it. "I'm sorry for your loss," I finally offer. He shakes my hand again but no corresponding buzz this time. These people are so damn social. I keep my fake smile in place, tuck the paper into the back pocket of my jeans and hurry to the exit.

I remember too late that I cabbed it over here and forgot to ask for a return ride. And I still haven't found my missing phone. A few people are leaving the meeting and talking outside but most are still inside socializing. I pace at the curb and hope a taxi will come by trolling for a fare though there isn't much traffic. If I weren't in such crap shape I'd just hoof it the three miles home.

Dorothy walks by keys in hand. "Someone picking you up?"

"Uh, no." I explain about the cab, my phone.

"Where do you live?"

When I tell her she inclines her head toward what I assume is the direction of her car. "Come on, I'll give you a ride. You're on my way."

The temperature has dropped and the cold increases my physical pain. The beer buzz from earlier is gone and I feel morose. I don't want to wait out here any longer so a ride sounds great and I fall in step with her. On the drive north she chatters about the speakers, glad she went to the meeting because she'd been working at home all day and felt squirrelly. God, these people can talk. I pinch the bridge of my nose and close my eyes.

"You okay?" she asks.

"A little tired. Been a long day."

"So do you go to other meetings around here?"

I'm stumped. I can't fake an answer to this direct question. If I say yes, she'll ask me what meetings, and if I say no, she'll ask me where I do go. Either way she'll know I'm lying. "Shit, Dorothy. I—this is my first meeting."

Her body stiffens a bit at my answer. "Oh. Well, good. I'm glad you came tonight. It's always good for me to meet newcomers. Jack's right, you know." She stops at a red light and turns to face me. "You don't have to drink anymore."

I shake my head. "Really? I got depressed listening to his story."

"You were drinking tonight, weren't you? I can smell it." The light turns green and she accelerates.

I really need to invest in some kind of breath mint or better mouth-wash or something. Chew parsley, maybe? Seems like whenever I drink someone's always picking up the smell on me. "You mind if I smoke?" I pull out a pack of Kools and light up without waiting for her answer but I do crack the window a bit.

"I remember my first meeting," Dorothy says. "Scared to death. I thought I'd see someone who knew me and then tell everyone I'm an alcoholic." While I'm interested in the coincidence of her experience matching my fear about tonight, I'm loath to ask her to tell me more. I don't need to wait long though, because she does anyway.

"I went to quite a few meetings in the beginning. I drank every night and going to a lot of meetings really helped with that. Then when I was about six months sober, I ran into someone I knew."

I hate to admit it but I'm listening to this woman's story.

"This guy I went to high school with. He recognized me but I didn't recognize him until he told me his name. Of course, the funniest thing was after we talked, I sat down for the meeting and suddenly it hit me—he came to the meeting because he was an alcoholic, too!"

Okay, I get it. I'm an idiot because I'm worried there'll be someone who knows me. Everyone's in the same boat. Nobody's tattling. It's anonymous, Dana.

"Talk about being self-centered." She laughs.

I direct her to turn on Clark Street and we arrive at my studio a few blocks away. She double-parks and turns on the dome light. "I'd like to give you my phone number, Dana. Please call me if you feel like talking or if you need a ride to a meeting." She searches her purse.

At this point I'm so tired from the whole evening I say nothing and just wait until she finds a business card, turns it over, and scribbles her cell phone number on it.

"But if you call me, do it *before* you take a drink."

Well, at least that makes sense. If I'm drunk, why would I want to talk to you? "Thanks for the ride, Dorothy." I take the card and slip it into my pocket.

Once upstairs I unearth the card, propping it up against the lamp on my desk, and stare at the small rectangle of white cardboard. How is this supposed to keep me sober? And what do I do now? I'm sore as hell and I want to drink away the pain, there's beer in the fridge, nobody knows, and nobody can stop me.

15

Saturday, 11/23, 9:00 a.m.

A HOT SHOWER, two cups of black coffee with a cigarette, and a small pep talk gets me moving as I clean up the cans of beer I drank prior to and after the A.A. meeting yesterday. I didn't really want to drink once I got home last night but flashing on my miscarriage during Jack's story overwhelmed my emotional reservoir. After Dorothy's ride home I swallowed three ibuprofen for my aching mid-section and chugged two beers before I hit the sack.

Now, after a solid nine hours of sleep my ribs aren't torturing me and I actually feel like I can do some chores. Dirty laundry heaped on the floor in the corner near my futon begs to be washed. I have no laundry basket, which forces me to carry my clothes down three flights to the basement and then back up again to my studio.

I check pockets for any forgotten change or tissues. A pair of pants I've worn the last few days yields the IOP form showing A.A. meetings attended: one. I tape it to the wall away from the mess of papers on my desk. We're supposed to attend at least two a week. Fat chance.

In another pocket I find the paper airplane Emma and I tossed back and forth in our little game. I perk up the wings and set it on my desk next to Dorothy's card, a happy reminder of Emma. I empty my backpack to ferry my clothes to and from the basement and find the odd poem from St. Nick's. After another quick read of the content I'm still puzzled, especially by the second verse.

> *A few small pictures won't show me who you really are,*
> *I press them gently to my hopeful heart and say,*
> *The world is wide and I will search for you near and far,*
> *I never knew you but I miss you all the same.*

I read it aloud and try to mimic Father Mik's dignified rendering but fall pathetically short. The poem, still intact in the baggie, gets scotch-taped next to my A.A. attendance form. These small additions to the area around my compact desk, tucked into the corner near the windows, help make my studio appear comfortably lived-in.

While one load runs in the washer I return to my desk and review my list of things to do, bills to pay. Update Father Mik. Hopefully talk to Nuts about Frank Safer. When I used Jimmy's phone to text Nuts a message yesterday, I didn't bust Jimmy's chops about not telling me his new phone number, but I did jot it down and stick it in my wallet.

I search my car again for my phone but with no success and I'm irked all over again at losing it. Logically, I've either left it at Flora's or maybe dropped it at Walgreens. I'm hopeful I'll find it at Flora's when I deliver the clothes Evie collected from her friends.

I dig out the traffic ticket hidden in the paper piled on my desk and read the summons with the odd sensation that the accident happened a while ago even though it occurred only night before last. No word yet from Fabrizio but I'm sure the other shoe will drop sometime soon. I pay the hundred-buck ticket, then write checks for the remaining end-of-the-month bills. When I finish, there's only a little over five hundred dollars remaining in my checking account.

I head south to my parents' bungalow. As I park, JJ appears from the rear of their home and struggles to place an extension ladder against the side of the house. I hurry out of the car to help him.

I point at the ladder. *"What's this for?"*

"Need to clear out the gutters once more before really cold weather." He gestures at the ancient silver maple tree in the front yard, which tends to be the last in the neighborhood to let go of its leaves.

I gaze at the two-story house, the gutters surrounding the roof, and cringe at the distance between the first rung of the extended ladder and its precarious resting place at the top. Ordinarily I could help JJ with this chore. But even though I'm better, my body is still rebelling from the accident and there's no way I can climb that ladder, which irritates me.

To make matters worse, JJ is wearing his house slippers. I want to admonish him for his faulty footgear but then take a different tack. *"You shouldn't do this alone. It's dangerous. Let me call Jimmy and ask him to come help you."* JJ holds up both hands and flutters them back and forth—deaf applause. His obvious delight that Jimmy has returned reminds me how much he loves his son-in-law. I know Evie does, too, but there's a strong connection between the two men. Jimmy's father died when he was only ten and his mother never remarried. JJ always refers to Jimmy as his son, something my husband blushes at and I know pleases him.

"Yes. Surprised me," I try to smile as I sign this, not wanting my still-simmering resentment about Jimmy's timing to spoil JJ's pleasure at his son-in-law's return. I point at JJ's feet to argue with him about wearing slippers for this work.

"My other shoes over there," he gestures at the garage, *"for change, not wear these."* He mimes climbing the ladder in his slippers and falling

off, but he wags his finger at me to negate the scenario. His sub-text: *I've done this before, you know.* My worried expression gives him pause though, and he agrees to the offer of help from Jimmy.

I go inside to use Evie's cell phone and realize this would be a perfect time to talk with my parents about moving to L.A. All of us. Jimmy could persuade Evie and JJ, just like he did me, telling them stories about California, the weather, how much easier it is to live there. And there would be a lot of deaf people in a city that size. That fragile bump of hope reappears.

"Gennaro."

My antenna rises, finely attuned to Jimmy's moods. He's pissed.

"Hey. How's it going?" I say.

"We need to talk." Tense. No explanation.

"Okay, sure." Mentally I scramble through any number of things he might be pissed about but through the living room window I spy JJ shivering by the ladder and put those thoughts on hold. "Listen. I'm at my parents' house and the old man's trying to clear out the gutters on his own. Scares the shit out of me. Any chance you can swing by and give him a hand? We can talk after."

Jimmy doesn't answer for a long moment and then agrees, telling me he'll be by in half an hour. He disconnects without a goodbye. My previous excitement turns to unease at Jimmy's coldness.

I beckon JJ inside and tell him the new plan. Evie shows me the clothes she's collected for Flora. I bundle everything in a box and stow it in the Escort's trunk, thanking Evie for loaning me her car while mine's in the shop. We're in the kitchen drinking coffee when Jimmy arrives. Both Evie and JJ give Jimmy big hugs and a warm welcome but I can tell from his expression he's putting on a show of friendliness he doesn't feel. He barely acknowledges me but goes outside with JJ and they begin circling the house with the ladder.

Not one to miss anything and ever sensitive to facial expression, Evie notices the snub. *"You two argue, fight?"* She mimics a fair imitation of Jimmy's facial expression.

"No. Well, yes, but we made up. I don't know what he's mad about now." I go outside to help with the cleanup but mostly to get away from Evie's prying. I grab a lawn waste bag and a rake, gathering and depositing the clumps of wet, decomposing muck Jimmy scours from the gutters and heaves to the ground. JJ steadies the ladder. I retrieve the hose and give it to JJ to hand to Jimmy and go turn on the water. He finishes the final rinse and gives me the hose to store in the basement while he returns the ladder to the garage.

When we enter the kitchen there are snacks and drinks laid out on the table for us. Evie beams at Jimmy and gestures for him to eat.

"Tell your mom I'm not hungry. I'm going to the can."

He walks out of the room and heads for the second floor. I sign *bathroom* to Evie so she knows where Jimmy's going and then grab a plate of cheese and crackers, some chips and a Pepsi. At the table, my parents gape while they watch me eat. *"No breakfast,"* I explain. Then I bring up the idea of a possible move to L.A.

"Los Angeles?" Evie signs. *"Why do you want to move there?"*

I explain about Jimmy working for LAPD but before I even finish Evie scoffs at the idea. *"West Coast is full of goofy people,"* she signs, naming a few movie stars unfaithful to their spouses, which doesn't meet with her approval. *"Besides, they're lazy."*

I give Evie my best puzzled expression. How has she concluded this?

"You know. Warm all year, no snow, no bad weather. Makes them lazy."

In my mind this is another non-reason, something from my mother's book of The Right Way to Act. And Evie hasn't even catalogued actual horrific problems in California. Like drought and wildfires. I begin to doubt how any of this is going to work.

JJ picks up on Evie's theme but he gives the same information a positive spin. *"True. Live in Chicago, shovel snow, rake leaves."* He lists more of his usual chores including today's gutter maintenance, then cocks his arms in a mock body-builder's pose. We all laugh but I'm aware convincing my parents to move will be harder than I thought.

Jimmy takes a long time in the bathroom and I'm finished eating by the time he returns. Still somber. My gut starts to tremble when I view his expression but I'm also angry at his ability to put me on guard like this. How has this happened? Only yesterday we made love and talked about moving to L.A. Evie tries to fix him a plate but he shakes his head at her. He points at me. "We need to talk. Outside."

"Okaayyy." I'm trying for sarcasm but his tone amps the tap dancing in my gut. I explain quickly to my parents and tell them we'll be back in a minute. Whether this is true or not, I don't know.

The back door hasn't even closed before Jimmy starts. He halts on the porch, hands on hips, head thrust forward. "Did you think I wouldn't find out? Is that it?"

I step back from him and mimic his stance, not threatened by his attack. "What the hell are you talking about? You come over here pissed off and now you jump on me! Give me a clue here, Gennaro."

"Car trouble? You told me you had car trouble on Thanksgiving night. Nuts told me what kind of trouble you were in. Shit, Dana! You're fucking lucky you didn't kill someone!"

My stomach rolls over and I'm furious at Abandonato. Then at Jimmy. Then at being caught in a lie. Before I can come up with any kind of retort Jimmy rages on.

"You know what? I don't even give a shit about that anymore—you drive drunk, you pay the price. This has been going on too long. You lied to me, right to my face. This isn't about losing the baby or anything else, Dane. You're a drunk! Fucking unbelievable."

He steps off the porch and thrusts himself into one of the Adirondack chairs Evie has set up in a circle near the back door. I follow and perch on the armrest of a chair across from him. My mother chooses this moment appear with a bag of garbage which, oh-so-coincidentally, takes her past us on the way to the alley. I roll my eyes at her, knowing she's been watching us from the window to glean what she can from a combination of lip-reading and body language. She trots to the cans, deposits the bag, and comes back to where Jimmy broods.

I jump up and flap my hand at her to get her attention. *"Evie! Go inside and mind your own business!"* My signs are large and jerky with anger. Instead of heeding me she bends down to Jimmy, gives him a solicitous pat on the back and shows him a sympathetic face. My husband, who in our ten years of marriage has mastered maybe five signs, abruptly stands and mimes a scene for my mother. He points at me, weaves like a drunk, grabs a steering wheel out of thin air and pretends to drive and get into an accident.

Evie understands perfectly. She turns to me. *"I knew it! You drive home drunk and cause accident! And you lie to JJ about your car!"* My mother is so upset her voice becomes audible during her rant even though the words come out squeaky and unintelligible.

JJ hesitates at the kitchen door as Evie bawls me out. My father's defeated expression acknowledges the truth of Evie's diatribe. His clear disappointment that I caused an accident because of drinking takes the fight out of me and I collapse onto the lawn chair.

Evie stomps into the house, gets her car keys and retrieves the box of clothes I put in the trunk earlier. She plunks it down at my feet and points toward the street where her car is parked. *"You can't use my car anymore! You drink too much!"* With that pronouncement she marches into the house. JJ follows her.

Jimmy studies his folded hands.

"Jimmy, can't we—"

"Save it." His eyes are lowered and a deep frown creases his forehead. "I can't do this anymore. I'm going back to L.A. tomorrow." Finally, he looks up to make sure I get the next message. "Alone. Get help, D."

I watch him leave, numb at what happened. Only six months since I lost our baby and he's ready to call it quits. I wish I had thrown that in his face but it's too late. As I sit and chain smoke, worrying about money and how I'm going to manage without a car for the next week, Marvin's annoying word *consequences* keeps jabbing at me.

JJ comes out a short time later to keep me company. After a while he offers me a ride home. When we get in his car the enormity of Jimmy's returning to L.A. alone hits me and I break down crying. My father gives me an awkward hug across the stick shift of his Beetle, which ratchets up the pain in my ribs—an unfriendly reminder of another consequence.

I pour out my fears about Jimmy leaving me, trying to manage alone financially, even the minor frustration over losing my cell phone. The one thing I don't mention and still keep from my parents is my suspension for drinking and being ordered to attend IOP. JJ tries to help by loaning me his car until mine is out of the shop.

And of course, he makes me promise I won't drink and drive.

16

Saturday, 11/23, Noon

I HEAD NORTH on Western Avenue to Flora's place on the West Side and chain-smoke the entire trip, cold air rushing through my open window. The chill helps me focus on driving JJ's car, a Beetle stick-shift, which I haven't done for years since my father taught me to drive. The smoking tamps down my anxiety about Jimmy. The box of donated clothes Evie unceremoniously dumped at my feet sits next to me on the passenger seat. Flora and her kids in their skimpy summer clothes should be happy to get some warmer duds.

Once that's done, I'll get some food, talk to Father Mik about what I've found, pick up some booze and head home. I'm too exhausted from what has happened with Jimmy to do further work today.

I lug Evie's donation up the six floors to Flora's apartment, stopping at each landing to catch my breath. A box of Dunkin' Donuts I picked up on the way slides back and forth on top of the box of clothes. The corridor leading to her door is much brighter than my last visit, and now that the burned-out bulbs have been replaced it's much easier to read the gang graffiti shouting from the walls. At apartment 623 I knock and call out Flora's name. No one answers. I can hear muffled conversation coming from inside, though. Then a boy's loud voice.

"Yeah? And how come we never looked for my daddy?"

A softer voice—I assume Flora's even though I can't make out the words—responds. The boy again. "How come all a them's daddy is so important you wanna chase him up here in this cold place? We been here six months and you ain't found him! I bet he ain't even here. He told you a lie and you're so stupid you believed him! I'm gonna find my daddy and go live with him!"

I drop what I'm carrying and pound on the door, calling Flora's name louder. The door opens a few inches hindered by a chain lock. Flora peers out, blinks a few times, then closes the door and scrapes the chain to unlock it. When the door re-opens an adolescent boy pushes past Flora so fast that he bumps into me but recovers quickly and runs down the hallway to disappear into the stairwell. I recognize him as the older boy who beat up the younger kid yesterday. So that's Jump. And the younger kid must be her other son. Peter? No. Porter.

Flora waves me in. The apartment is still cold. I dump the box of clothes in front of the living room closet door. Directly across from me and sitting on the mattresses are the twins, Mia and Moira, one braiding the other's hair. Flora seems flustered at my arrival but doesn't say anything about the argument she must know I heard.

"I brought you some clothes my mom collected for the church rummage sale. These might be warmer than what you're wearing."

"Look, Mama! Doughnuts!" The twins approach the box of clothes, pointing and touching the pink-and-white box on top.

"You girls get away from there! They ain't yours!"

"I brought them for everyone, Flora. A little treat." I try to smile at her but my heart's not in it. Jimmy's diatribe weighs on me and this woman's sad circumstances are pathetic.

"Oh," she says. "Okay, then. And thanks." She nods at the girls to pick up the doughnuts. They grab the box and run down the hallway to the kitchen.

I gesture at the box next to the closet. "There are clothes for boys and girls in here but I'm not sure about sizes. Why don't you take what you want and I'll drop off what's left at St. Nick's." Flora nods and sets to work sorting through the clothes, making two piles on the floor. She pulls a boy's maroon sweater from the pile and hooks it on the closet doorknob.

The door to Flora's bedroom opens up and Emma appears, sucking her thumb with one hand and rubbing her eye with the other. I walk over and squat down beside her. "Hi, Emma. Did we wake you up?" Her white-blonde hair billows out in gravity-defying angles. Her pale grey eyes meet mine and she nods. "Hey, now you're awake, want to come to the kitchen for doughnuts?"

"Yes." Her voice sounds thin and tired. Her little hand is cold in mine.

"Your hands are popsicles!" I slip off my jacket and put it around her, zip it up. Emma views herself in the mirror on the closet door. The jacket becomes a full-length coat on her small frame.

"I look like I don't got any arms," she says, twisting and turning so the jacket's arms flap uselessly on each side.

I catch her gaze in the mirror and we both giggle. She maneuvers her arms into the sleeves and we walk down the long hallway toward the kitchen. Halfway there she stops and without a word holds up her arms to me. I swing her up and prop her on my hip, easy and familiar, like hoisting a small bag of groceries.

In the kitchen I try to set Emma down on one of the folding chairs at the card table but she clings to me so tightly I sit and settle her on my lap. Grey light—the only light in the dim room—emanates from a dirty window next to the stove where heat escapes from the open oven door. Any warmth the oven provides dissipates quickly. At the table, Mia and Moira stare at the box of doughnuts as if they're guarding a precious gift. It seems they're waiting for further instructions. I call out to Flora still in the front room sorting clothes.

"Okay for the girls to eat some doughnuts?"

When her assent drifts back to us, both girls grab at the box and wrestle with it. Before I can say anything, one side rips and doughnuts tumble onto the table. Both girls stop the tussle and turn toward me for my reaction. Emma picks up a jelly doughnut that has rolled to a stop near us and takes a bite. The two older girls put their hands to their mouths as if Emma's action is even worse than their tug of war. I grab a chocolate donut and gesture for them to go ahead and take what they want.

Flora comes in and makes instant coffee for the two of us and gives the girls water. After Mia and Moira each scarf down a second doughnut Flora tells them to go try on the clothes she has sorted out. Giggling, the girls sweep out of the kitchen and run down the hallway pushing at each other. A minute later I hear the bedroom door open and close repeatedly, the final time with a slam.

"I'm sorry them girls is so wound up. They can't play outside unless me or their brothers are with 'em. Porter's out doing odd jobs. I'm not sure where Jump's—well, you saw. I ain't been able to get going yet this morning." Flora stands, pulls her long, lank hair into a high ponytail and wraps a rubber band around it, and then refills the pan with more water and sets it on the stove to boil for another round of instant coffee. I experience a recurring feeling about Flora: she's in over her head so deep she'll never find her way out.

"Jump's your oldest?"

"Yeah. He's thirteen and more'n a handful. Now he's angry about his daddy who I ain't seen since before that boy's birth."

I don't say anything, not wanting to know more about this woman's beleaguered life. Emma works slowly on her jelly doughnut, gnawing her way to the middle where the cherry goo waits. When she comes up for air to chew, her tight clutch on the pastry makes the jam bulb out and hang precariously at the edge of her bite mark. I swipe my index finger at the blob of jam and catch it in time. Emma watches me plop it in my mouth. She offers me a bite of her doughnut.

"You eat it, Emma, I'm fat enough." I puff out my cheeks and make a goofy face at the little girl. She leans back in my lap and pokes her tiny finger at my inflated cheek and I let the air out in a whoosh. She giggles, squeezing her eyes shut against my breath. A chain around her neck holds what I assume is the key to the apartment along with a skeleton key. I pluck at the chain. "Is this your necklace?"

Emma's small hand closes over the two keys and she shakes her head, her eyes aimed at her feet. "Porter let me wear it."

Flora deposits my coffee on the table and leans against the stove to sip hers. "We come up here to find these kids' daddy, you know." She says this with a firm voice as if I've challenged her on the point. I don't even remember what we were talking about before my interlude with Emma. The confusion I feel must register on my face. "Well, a course, Jump's daddy ain't their daddy." A vague gesture takes in Emma. Not sure about the twins or Porter.

"Me and Grady was only fifteen when I got his baby. But he didn't stay and hopped a train for Houston, wanted to ride the rodeo. He don't even know he got a son. We was two stupid kids and that's that."

Without meaning to, my mind performs some quick math. Jump at thirteen means Flora is either twenty-seven or twenty-eight. With five kids. Christ. While the loss of my baby is difficult to manage, I can't begin to think what my life might be like with five children. Not something I want, even at thirty. Against my better judgment I ask Flora where this other father is.

"Harris left us a year ago, said he had a job at the Wrigley gum factory in Chicago. I never did hear from him. We lived with my Texas cousin in her trailer but it got too crowded with the kids and all, so she gave me money for us to come up here, search for Harris." Emma squirms, fits herself into the crook of my arm. "And do you know," Flora continues, "there wasn't no job here. That gum factory went out of business a long time ago. He lied to get away from me and the kids."

And your response is to sit on your sorry ass full of self-pity instead of finding a way to take care of your kids. Emma jams her thumb into her mouth all the way up to where it meets her palm, closes her eyes, and drifts off.

"What's Jump so mad about?" I ask, unable to stop myself. Flora moves to the chair across from me and sits.

"I told him he's gotta pull his weight around here, help me more, like Porter do. Collect cans, deliver papers, wash cars. All that kind of thing. He got mad and said he wanted to go live with his daddy."

I feel sick inside at the role reversal with her boys Flora lays out for me. Bad enough these kids tolerate a mother who drags them from some small town in Texas to a city the size of Chicago, from the warmth to the cold—they need to be the breadwinners, too? I don't want to learn any more about her lousy parenting right now.

Emma sleeps through our conversation and my arm is numb from holding her in one position. I gingerly shift her to recline in my other arm. "Flora, I lost my cell phone yesterday, sometime between my time here and when I got home. Did you find it?" Flora looks around the kitchen as if she'll spy it and then shakes her head.

Shit.

I get ready to leave the cold apartment. I wake Emma and stand her up next to me, loath to strip my jacket from her. When I do, goose bumps erupt along her thin arms, so I take her hand and we hurry to the front room where Flora has formed distinct piles of clothes. A small gathering of long pants, a couple of long-sleeved sweaters, and a fleece jacket are clearly Emma's slight size.

"These are for you, okay? What do you want to wear right now? Pick what you like." The little girl considers each piece of clothing with the judiciousness of a professional buyer, finally settling on a pair of blue jeans, a pink sweater, and the grey fleece. She holds them in a bear hug and hurries to her mother's bedroom to change. When she reappears, she walks toward me but her concentration is on the fleece jacket's zipper, which doesn't seem to be cooperating.

Emma stops in front of me and wordlessly releases the confounding fastener. I stoop in front of her and grasp both parts of the zipper, showing her how to insert one side into the other, then pull it up to her chin. The collar of the jacket becomes a turtleneck with the zipper completely up. Emma resembles a tiny model, her white-blonde hair flowing over the fleece. The clothes fit her and her cheeks are even a bit rosy, as if she's finally warm.

I take her over to the mirror on the closet door and she admires herself, front and back, and then runs down the hallway to the kitchen and Flora. "Mama! Mama!" Excited.

I hear the two of them talking in the kitchen and once again imagine taking Emma home and caring for her—properly—not like the sorry excuse she has for a mother, who hasn't managed to stay with either of the men who have fathered her children.

I open the door and step outside of the apartment. My fantasy disappears in an instant when I remember Jimmy is leaving for L.A. tomorrow. Without me.

Pot meet kettle.

17

S aturday, 11/23, 1:30 p.m.

I CHECK at the Walgreens where I might have lost my cell but nothing has been turned in so I buy a cheap, pre-paid phone to cover me while holding out hope mine will turn up soon. I sit in my car in the drugstore parking lot and add a few names and numbers to the burner phone's directory, including my missing cell's number so I can call the voicemail and retrieve messages. One from Felice about Frank Safer has registered.

"Your boy got arrested at eighteen for B and E, armed robbery. Tied up an old woman in her home and threatened her with a knife. Stole her cash and jewelry. Stayed a little bit too long, didn't hear the squad car pull up when neighbors reported the old woman screaming."

Yep, Frank's deaf, but I don't like the sneer in my partner's voice when he notes this fact, his implication not subtle that Frank is also stupid.

Felice continues. "Got fifteen years in Joliet and did every day, too. Not model prisoner material. Nothing much else for about ten years until he nailed the guy with the bottle. Four years for that and got out two years ago. Nothing since." He leaves a Skokie address for Safer, who lives with his sister, and then disconnects without any mention of how we parted on Thanksgiving night.

I listen to the message again and take notes. I'm furious at Nuts for narcing on me to Jimmy but at the same time find myself absurdly grateful for the information on Safer. I didn't think he'd do me any favors after finding the beer I brought home Thanksgiving night. I resist the urge to call him back because I'm afraid I won't be able to contain my anger at him for tattling, then change my mind.

"Abandonato." Clipped, tense.

"Got your message."

"You get a new phone? Your name didn't come up."

I explain about the burner phone and he's somewhat sympathetic about my lost phone. "You got a minute to talk about Safer?" I manage to sound nonchalant.

"Maybe five."

Additional irritation flits through me. "I won't keep you, then. I didn't know about the first B and E. *Two* violent priors make me real interested in this guy. And I could use your input on some things." I run down the information about the parish hall door being propped open with a rock the entire day, allowing anyone access; about the Thanksgiving dinner committee meeting Friday morning but no one noticing anything; about the odd poem I found in the kitchen. "I was almost convinced it was just an old man unsteady on his feet taking a fall," I say. "But Safer seems a credible suspect: violent background, needs a job, responds in a physical way. What do you think?"

"Let me know if you get anything from talking to him. This is low priority to us, really. It's closed."

Abandonato sounds bored. He doesn't want to engage, tell me what he thinks. His words are a clear reminder to me I'm on suspension and no longer part of the active investigation team. In the past we would've tossed theories back and forth, challenged and encouraged each other, and enjoyed the process. Now I feel disregarded.

I tighten my grip on the cell. "Sure. No problem. Don't be a stranger." I disconnect without saying thanks or goodbye. The phone rings immediately and the screen displays Abandonato's name. I almost reject the call but then accept it, ready to get into it with him.

"Demeter, pull that crap again and I won't only be a stranger, I'll be a former friend."

"Some friend. Fuck you, Nuts. Why did you tell Jimmy—"

"He asked, straight up, if I knew you were drinking. I told him about Thanksgiving. Wasn't going to lie to him."

And he wouldn't, not Abandonato. Most of the time I admire that about him. Most of the time.

"And I wasn't going to mention it, *friend*, but I did you a favor. That little girl? CiCi? Her mother called me to complain about you. Said you wanted to drag her daughter through the whole mess again. You're lucky she called me. I talked her out of reporting you to Koz."

I suck in my breath at this news. "Oh crap, Nuts." My anger at him about Jimmy deflates in a gust. "I...I don't know what to say."

"I'd say we're even. Call me if there's anything legit I need to pursue."

"Sure, of course." I realize he's about to hang up. "Wait. Can you summarize CiCi's interview? Or send it to me?"

"There's nothing there. The old guy was already dead when she found him. Don't waste your time." He clicks off without a goodbye.

I hit a 7-Eleven for some chips and a sandwich and consume them in my car, then sip a large cup of coffee. After Flora's, I didn't want to do anything but go home and retreat to my bed. *Oh, and drink,* my little voice reminds me. If only to forget about Jimmy for a while.

But my exchange with Abandonato lifts my spirits. He did me a solid convincing CiCi's mother to abandon the idea of reporting me to Koz. Proof that he's sincere about wanting us back together. And although he's clearly still upset with me, I allow myself the brief fantasy we're partners again working on this case, which spurs me to follow up on Frank Safer. At least he's a possible lead in The Case Going Nowhere.

Traffic is light on the Kennedy Expressway and merges with the Edens for a quick trip to Skokie. But my effort turns out to be worthless. I'm stymied in terms of pinning anything on Frank Safer. The day before Martin Nygaard died, Safer flew to New York for the funeral of a relative, shows me a boarding pass to prove it, and his sister vouches for him. *"I'm straight, two years. Don't want to be arrested again,"* he signs, his manner is earnest but his face radiates fear. *"My girlfriend wants to get married but she tells me job first, then wedding."*

He morphs into performing an impression of his girlfriend ragging on him to work and not be a deadbeat, which elicits a smile from me. I recall Ben Warshawsky's gossip about Frank Safer and mentally award him one point for a tiny bit of accuracy.

But Safer isn't done. *"Growing up, I was angry all the time—you know, deaf boy, hearing people not fair, parents stupid, never learned to sign. Old story. But in prison Father Mik visited me many times, showed me how to pray. I changed and feel better, not angry all the time. Want a good life, a wife, maybe children."* He ducks his bald head, now covered in sweat, and breaks eye contact with me.

"Soon I'm fifty, so maybe no kids," saying this more to himself than to me. Then he looks me in the eye. *"But no more jail!"* His emphasis on this point is clear and believable. I wish him luck with applying for Martin Nygaard's job and he shakes my hand, turning it into a modified hug, the universal greeting and farewell of many deaf.

I leave and drive east toward the lake intending to take Sheridan Road home but when I reach the curve at the cemetery separating Evanston and Chicago, I head into a side street and park. I pull out my cell and call the Deaf Catholic Office.

"Hey, Angie. It's Dana Demeter. Long time. How're you?"

"Well, look here who the cat drug in!" Her voice booms through the small earpiece on the cell. "Where you been? Could've used you on about a thousand jobs since yesterday, you know."

My mood lightens at her warm voice and friendly banter. "And I could use a few of those jobs to earn some extra cash. Can we talk schedules after I speak with Father Mik?"

"Sure, sure. He's right here, hold on."

"Dana. How are you?" Father Mik says.

"Got some info for you, Father." I run down my recent trips to Flora's. "What's with her, anyway? Flora's got no food or furniture in her place and three skinny girls bordering on malnourishment but she doesn't ask anyone for help. She even balked at taking the food you packed for her." My anger at the mulish woman resurfaces.

"It is hard to understand," Father Mik says. "Yet in my outreach work I often find people whose pride won't let them accept what they call charity. Especially if they feel they haven't earned it in some way."

"But she's on welfare and she doesn't earn that. I don't know, Father Mik, there's something off about her."

"It's probably fear, Dana. A lifetime of poverty and caring for five children on her own can do that, can paralyze a person. And the state won't let her collect welfare much longer. If I can document she's consistent and punctual at her church work, the state will allow her to participate in a skills training program, which may help her find real work. That's the theory, anyway."

I picture the wan, listless woman in the empty apartment that smells vaguely of shit and dirty laundry and shake my head. "You have a lot more faith in people than I do."

He chuckles. "Well, that *is* why I'm in this business."

I relate everything Flora told me about the cabinets and the missing items, the committee members meeting, the propped-open parish hall door. Finally, I recap my visit to Frank Safer. "I'm becoming convinced Martin Nygaard's death truly happened as an accident. I think the theft was a separate incident. I'll follow up with Pete Christakos on Monday about the website and the pawnshops."

"You've done so much already, Dana. I appreciate your perseverance. There's some new information you might need. The police won't perform an autopsy because they found nothing indicating a crime. They released Martin's body."

I experience momentary exasperation at Abandonato for not telling me this earlier but then remember Father Mik already told me a week ago when he first asked for my help—my foggy memory at fault. "The insurance company is requiring one though, right?"

"That is correct. It is the only way they will pay out the death benefit. Martin's ex-wife and son are his beneficiaries and it turns out he carried quite a bit of life insurance. The autopsy will be done privately this Monday and the family will support the expense. The wake follows on Wednesday and then the funeral on Thursday."

"How much is the policy worth?"

"Half a million dollars."

I pull out my notepad and jot down this startling bit of info. In my mind Martin Nygaard had lived hand-to-mouth and squeaked by on his meager pay from St. Nick's, which wouldn't include enough money to even buy life insurance. I ask where the ex- and son live.

"In Indiana, near the border. They'll attend the wake and funeral." I add the names Edna and Buddy Nygaard to my list as Father Mik anticipates my next question.

"He and his ex-wife have been estranged for years, Dana. They divorced when the boy was little, somewhere between one and two. I doubt they were even in contact by phone."

My memory serves up Martin Nygaard's basement apartment and the picture of the woman holding the baby. Even if, as Father Mik notes, there had been no contact, it's clear that for the old janitor his ex-wife and son appeared front and center—every day. I thank Father Mik and disconnect, determined once again to find out what happened to this man at the end of his solitary life.

The phone rings thirty seconds later. "Demeter. Uh, hello?" I'm trying to break the habit of answering the phone like a cop and use 'hello' instead, but then the phone rings and I'm like a trained dog who hears the command to bark. Angie's deep chuckle fills my ear.

"Glad I caught you, girl. I told the old man to let me talk to you after he finished but he hung up anyway. What am I going to do with him? Think I should call the retirement home and reserve a room?" I hear Father Mik laughing in the background.

"Well, he is seventy-three, you know. Might be time."

"Mm-hmm. You and me both be lucky to get to his age, sweetheart. Now, here's the thing. Mr. Nygaard's going to be waked next Wednesday and here it is Saturday already and we need an interpreter. So, talk to me. You available? It's from four to eight. Just one interpreter. Most of it is standing around, being available for the hearing family if they need you. There'll be a short prayer service at the end, twenty minutes tops."

I hesitate for a second and consider if I should attend the wake to observe the crowd when Angie cuts into my thoughts.

"Now, if you can't handle the whole four hours we could split it so you do half and someone else does the other half. That work better for you?"

I picture the meager balance in my checkbook after paying bills this morning. "Angie, I'm one broke cop. I'd be a fool to turn you down. I'll do the whole four hours. Thanks for thinking of me."

"Hey, you're the one helping me out, let's get that straight." She gives me the details of the job. "And dress formally, Dana. All my customers been complaining lately about you gals dressing way too casual." She sets me up with several more jobs in the coming week and we say goodbye. I toss my replacement cell phone onto the passenger seat, start the engine and get ready to pull out but then kill the ignition, stuff the cell in my back pocket and exit my car.

Large chunks of rock line this area where Lake Michigan touches the shore along Evanston. Sheridan Road continues, curving away from Evanston and toward the North Side of Chicago. I take the sidewalk to the jumbled boulders designed to keep the lake at bay and climb a bit until I find one flat enough to rest on. I lower myself and sit cross-legged facing the lake, my back to the street. In the late afternoon dusk the water's calm, flat surface reflects the sky's deep granite.

This morning's argument with Jimmy dominates my thoughts while I gaze across the massive expanse of water to the horizon. He's most mad at me for lying to him about the accident. Correction: the cause of the accident. I can at least be honest about that. Okay, it's easy to understand he doesn't like me drinking, or as he puts it, sad. The two do seem to go together for me.

Behind me a car whizzes by on Sheridan Road, gears grinding, engine revving at a high pitch. A few seconds later another car zooms by, its siren punctuating my quiet respite. Hundred-buck ticket, easy. I have felt the rush of flooring the gas in a squad car to catch some rich guy doing sixty in a thirty zone. Always fun when someone tries talk his way out of a summons.

Abandonato also doesn't like me drinking and driving—not hard to understand. Witness Jack's story from last night. Nuts might be afraid I'll get killed. Or kill someone else. I'm heartened that he got me the info on Frank Safer and convinced Cici's mother not to call Koz—it's a start to repairing our relationship and I'll have to do more there.

But as it now stands, Jimmy is lost to me. I don't know any way to bring him around or back to us. Besides my parents, my husband and my work partner are the two most important people in my life. Right now, I can't face losing Jimmy or my job as a detective. But I am sure I can stop drinking—I quit for seven days in a row just a few weeks ago, right after Koz Breathalyzed me and ordered me to start this whole IOP thing, although I can't recall why I picked up a drink after the seven days dry.

I count backwards to the last time I drank—not hard to remember because it happened only yesterday after Jimmy and I reunited, right before I went to the A.A. meeting. Oh, and after. But not a drop to drink today. With so much on the line—and to show Jimmy I'm serious this time—I promise myself I will continue this kind of self-restraint, which I'm sure I can manage until I finish IOP. What comes after I finish IOP is anybody's guess.

In my back pocket the sudden buzzing of my cell against my ass startles me out of my rumination. I don't recognize the number. "Yeah? Hello?" I'm brusque as I answer, fully expecting it to be a friend of the person who last had the number of this burner phone.

"Demeter? That you?" A man's rough voice.

"Yeah. Who're you?"

"Fabrizio—you remember. Carrera's brother-in-law."

I bought this phone less than two hours ago. "How'd you get this number?"

"Your partner. Or should I say, your ex-partner? Abandonato was happy to help a fellow cop."

I'm sure—especially because he's angry at this cop. I'm uneasy about getting an answer to my next question. "What do you want, Fabrizio?"

A mean chuckle. "Me? We'll get there, Demeter. There's the small matter of a DUI report on you that's supposed to be submitted with all my end-of-the month reports. I'm holding it aside until you and me set up a little confab. Tomorrow."

He gives me the address of an apartment building in Rogers Park, not too far from where I sit right now. "Tell me what you want," I repeat.

"Three o'clock, Demeter. Don't be late."

18

S unday, 11/24, 2:30 p.m.

I CIRCLE around the block in Rogers Park for a third time, unable to find a parking place near the address Fabrizio gave me. The neighborhood is dominated by apartment buildings in need of better maintenance, with a few rundown homes scattered here and there.

Ironically, wealthy owners of some of Chicago's most expensive real estate lining the lakeshore reside only a few blocks away but at a great remove from the people on this street, who I imagine live paycheck-to-paycheck.

The fourth time around I get lucky. An old beater pulls away from the curb trailing a black cloud of burning oil from its tailpipe. I park and crack my window open to smoke, a whiff of the acrid oil wafting in as I observe the neighborhood, wait for three o'clock, and contemplate what Fabrizio has in store for me. If he wanted a straight-up payment for losing my report we wouldn't need to meet, he'd simply blackmail me over the phone. And I would pay. My job can't be measured in dollars. But meeting him in person makes me wary.

I exit my car, toss the spent butt into the street and walk to Fabrizio's place, a six-unit apartment building in the middle of the block. The lobby shouts student occupancy: flyers pasted on the wall announce club meetings, a coffee house, "WOMYN" taking back the night.

The tag next to the doorbell for number three-eleven is blank. Maybe he's new here and hasn't had a chance to fashion a label with his name. I push the doorbell button but there's no intercom system. Not much security. The lobby's inner door emits a low buzz. I pull it open and begin to climb three flights. Higher above me a door opens. "That you, Demeter?"

"Yeah, yeah." I round the second landing and lean over the railing to trace the voice's origin. Fabrizio's fat face leers at me from the top floor. "Give me a minute." I stop and wait for my breathing to slow down a bit. I'm close to hyperventilating, from cigarettes certainly, but mostly from nervous energy. I reach the top landing and Fabrizio grins at me, all chummy.

"Right on time," he says, tapping his bare wrist. His wedding ring is wedged solid between folds of fat on his pudgy finger.

"Let's get this over with." I smell booze when I pass him and enter the apartment. He comes in behind me and closes the door, throws the deadbolt and scrapes the security chain in place. "Grab a seat, Demeter." Mr. Solicitous.

"I'm not here for a Sunday afternoon visit, Fabrizio. Get to the point. What do you want from me?"

"I'm gonna have a beer. You want one?" His smarmy insinuation makes my skin crawl.

"No."

He disappears through a swinging door, which I assume leads to the kitchen. The living room surroundings are anonymous, like an unused office cubicle. A hideous orange couch with an ottoman lines one wall and faces a large-screen TV on the opposite wall. Side tables cap each end of the couch and hold lamps that don't match. The walls are painted baby blue. Not a winner in a Better Homes and Gardens interior design competition.

It's obvious this place isn't home but some kind of way station for whatever bullshit Fabrizio's up to. He returns carrying a Foster's Lager can—the large size that holds twice the amount of a regular can of beer. It fits easily into his paw, though. He gestures with the can. "Sit, sit, Demeter. We got lots to talk about." He crosses over to the orange monster and plops down but I stay standing.

"I'm fine here. But you seem comfy, Fabrizio." And he does. He's wearing low-rider jeans, which I suspect is more for his bulbous gut than any nod to fashion. A faded long-sleeved T-shirt touting the 2005 White Sox World Series winners is equally baggy on him. And his feet are bare. I gesture at the almost empty room. "You know, you and your wife gotta work on decorating this place. Needs some homey touches." For some reason he startles at this, then leans back and takes a long drink.

"So, we got what? Six days 'til the end of the month," he says. "Like I said, my reports from November are all written and in the computer. And that includes your little escapade on the Dan Ryan just waiting for me to push the send button. But you and me gotta come to an agreement about something first." He takes another swig of beer, pats the couch indicating I'm supposed to sit down next to him.

Instead, I motion with my right hand for him to hurry up and tell me his demand. "Stop dicking around, Fabrizio. Give."

He takes another drink and belches, puts the can down on the side table and stands, then walks right up to me and leaves only inches between us. We're the same height but he's got fifty pounds on me, easy. I look him in the eye and don't flinch. You can't show fear or back down with guys like him—it's exactly what gives them a hard-on. I tilt my head slightly and smirk. "Well?"

He hooks his leg around the back of my knees and jerks it forward faster than I can react. My legs buckle. I end up in a prayer position in front of him. His meaty paws clamp down on my shoulders and hold me immobile. My heart races but I force myself to seem outwardly calm. "What is this? You want me to sit on the couch? I'll sit on the couch." I force a small laugh to show him I'm making a joke.

"Hands on your head, face down on the floor. Spread 'em."

"Christ, Fabrizio, what the hell—"

"Do it!"

I dart a glance at the locked door—deadbolt and security chain in place—and mentally kick myself for not unlocking it during the few seconds he was in the kitchen. "Then get your fucking hands off me."

He lets up on my right side. I raise that arm, place my hand on my head, then the weight on my left shoulder eases and I place that hand on my head. Getting face down on the floor is more complicated without the use of my hands but I finally manage it.

"Spread 'em," he says.

I try again, hoping I can talk him out of whatever the hell it is he's doing. "You don't need to—"

"Shut up."

Fabrizio starts at my shoulders and I endure a full-body frisk, his hands rough, especially when he travels up my inner thighs. He cups my ass with both hands and chuckles. "Okay. Get up. Keep your hands on your head and get up on your knees."

He wanted to check if I was carrying. But I'm only half right. Once again moving with more speed than I can believe for a guy his size, especially a guy who's drinking, he cuffs my hands behind me. My heart hammers in my chest, my breath is quick and shallow—I can't hide it. "Don't do this, Lu. Don't."

"Shhh. This won't hurt if you try and go along with me here." He goes to the end table and chugs from the giant can of beer. He comes back and faces me, sways a bit, then lifts his baggy shirt, gropes for his zipper and pulls it down. His super-size jeans drop to the floor. He's naked underneath. I draw breath to scream but he reaches behind his back, pulls a gun from a waist holster, and racks a round.

I stop. Hot tears of frustration and panic prick my eyes. My mind races through a bunch of ways to escape this lunatic but nothing coherent forms. I duck my head to the left, away from his engorged cock sticking upright in my face. He holds the gun at his side but doesn't make a move.

"Here's the thing, Lu." I do my best to sound humble and scraping. "I'm not well. I just had a miscarriage. I'm not all together, if you know what I mean. I got a serious infection down there, some kind of crotch rot. I'm taking drugs for it. Really." I don't move my head but instead strain my eyes sideways and up to get a glimpse of his face.

He laughs—a big, booming sound. His sickening sweet beer breath wafts down around me. Fabrizio takes a step to his right so once again his cock is in my face. I close my eyes. "Oh, you're good, Demeter." His heavy hand ruffles my hair like I'm a little kid. "A good lie has some truth in it, right? But you got me wrong, I ain't a animal. This ain't no rape. You get to keep all your clothes on. All you gotta do is suck on me 'til I come. Easy-peasy. And don't get any cute ideas about using your teeth to hurt me, get it?"

That's exactly what I *am* envisioning: take him into my mouth, he gets distracted focusing on how good his cock feels when I suck on him, and then wham! Bite it off with one good chomp. I'm not sure I can manage acting on this fantasy but the scenario plays out in my mind in an instant. I open my eyes. He lifts the gun and waves it lazily at the ceiling. Fabrizio's drunk. He'll blow my head off without hesitation if I attempt my vision of dental surgery.

"Fine," I say, resigned to what's coming. "I want a drink first. I'm pretty dry." It's the truth. My tongue practically sticks to the roof of my mouth when I talk. I steel myself to blow this jerk and try to be grateful he isn't going to rape me. Christ. I wish I'd listened to my gut about this and kept our meeting in a public place.

Fabrizio steps out of his jeans puddled around his ankles, goes to the kitchen and brings back another giant Foster's Lager. He pops the top and takes a long drink, then holds the can at my mouth. Shit, so much for my promise to not drink today. Absurdly, I tell myself it's not really drinking because my hands are cuffed and he's literally forcing it down my throat. Just as I open my mouth, the sound of a key in the door lock halts Fabrizio's movement. His gun hand rises and points at the door as it opens. The security chain halts the door's progress and on the other side comes a man's startled voice.

"What the fuck?"

Fabrizio tosses his gun onto the couch, puts the beer on the floor next to me and pulls on his pants as he motions for me to be quiet. He hurries over to the door and peeks through the open crack. "Cryin' out loud, Manny!" he says. "Today ain't your day!"

"Moron! It's all pushed up a day 'cause of Thanksgiving!" Manny mumbles something else and they start arguing.

"Hey!" I yell to be heard over their voices. "Hey! Manny! Help! I'm Dana Demeter. I'm a cop—Homicide. D-E-M-E-T-E-R. Help me! Fabrizio's got me in cuffs against my will!" I start screaming loud and long and try to stand but only succeed in falling over on my side.

Fabrizio kicks the door shut and strides to the couch. He grabs the gun. I cringe when he raises his arm and lunges at me, terrified he's going to shoot. Instead, he whacks me on the side of the head, hard. I'm stunned silent. He returns to the door and opens it a crack, tells

Manny to come back in fifteen minutes. Fabrizio returns to hover over me and hooks one large hand under my armpit, pulling me to my feet, my hands still cuffed behind me. The side of my head throbs and my ear rings where he belted me.

"Here's what you're gonna do for me, Demeter. I got forty-five thou I need cleaned. Take the cash, open five three-month CDs at five different banks in your name. Nine thou in each. Bring me the deposit slips. We'll wait the three months for the money to settle down and then you're gonna close the accounts and give it all back to me."

From a shelf on one of the end tables Fabrizio retrieves a backpack about the size of a large lunchbox. He brings it to me. I show him my back and wiggle my fingers so he'll unlock the cuffs, silently thanking the powers-that-be Manny interrupted Fabrizio's sexual assault. But he doesn't unlock my cuffs yet. He comes around to face me, gun in one hand, backpack in the other. "You agree to do this, I'll lose the report. But one misstep, anything, and your lieutenant gets the word and you're done bein' a cop."

There's no way out, not right now anyway. I agree to what he's asking, anything to get out of this jam. Fabrizio frees my wrists but my hands are completely numb from the cuffs so he helps me strap on the backpack holding forty-five thousand dollars. "And don't get any funny ideas about my dough. Bring those deposit slips to me tomorrow, here, or your DUI goes to your lieutenant."

"*Your* dough?" I ooze sarcasm and feel feisty now the cuffs are off. "Forty-five grand is a nice piece of change. Where'd you really get it?"

He takes a minute to answer, as if he's deciding whether or not to tell me. Then he laughs in my face. "Like Dear Abby used to say, Demeter: MYOB."

It's easy to guess the money is dirty, maybe marked, which is why he wants to be sure it isn't traced back to him. There's no allegiance to honesty when it comes to the oldest form of collusion between cops and criminals; if money's involved, there's only greed. I shake my head but say nothing. I approach the door to leave and suddenly understand what this place is. I stride right back to Fabrizio and get in his face. "Listen, asshole. I'm not coming back here to your fuck pad. We meet in public, lots of people, lots of witnesses."

He laughs. "Like my brother-in-law says about you Demeter, you're pushy, always actin' like you're in charge. We meet where I say we meet. Fuck you very much." He grabs my upper arm and frog-marches me to the entrance, scrapes off the security chain and opens the door, then shoves me out.

I hustle down the three flights fueled by the adrenaline pumping through me. When I get to the lobby there's a skinny white guy about my height leaning against the wall next to the mailboxes. He's alone.

"You Manny?"

He nods. "You the one doin' all the yellin'?"

"Yeah." I don't know whether to thank him, warn him to stay away from Fabrizio, or simply get the hell out of here. I finally settle on, "Fabrizio's an asshole."

A lazy smile. "You got no argument from me, honey."

I hook my right thumb onto the backpack strap at my shoulder and feel foolish for even talking to Manny. If he and Fabrizio are fuck-pad buddies then Manny's not exactly an upstanding cop either.

Police corruption takes a multitude of forms and theirs is chump change compared to the totality of the less-than-honest cops in the system. Besides, forty-five grand nestles on *my* back, money I agreed to launder for lard-ass upstairs. Father Mik would remind me of my hypocrisy with something about criticizing a speck in another's eye while ignoring the log in mine.

I slouch out the door and down the street where an African-American woman sits on the curb next to my car. Her head swivels in my direction. "Got a square?" she asks.

I approach and squat next to her, my heart still recovering from the massive jolt of Fabrizio's attack, and pull out my pack of Kools. She makes a face at the brand but takes one anyway. I extend a light to her, then light up mine and take a deep drag. The menthol and nicotine combined soothe my hammering heart.

I tilt my head toward Fabrizio's building. "You with Manny?"

She nods, pulls on her cigarette and French inhales, the smoke billowing from her mouth and traveling upward in a compact trail into her nostrils, then out through her mouth again.

It doesn't take me long to size this woman up. Too much makeup, which includes a smattering of purple glitter across her nose and dark-skinned cheeks, skimpy clothes in spite of temps hovering in the low forties, and the inevitable stilettos. Even though I think I know the answer to my next question, I want confirmation of what I suspect. "Why you with him?"

She throws me a sideways glance and goes back to resting the side of her head on her left fist. Her shoulder-length hair is black but a stark swath of blonde cuts through it from front to back.

"You a cop?" she asks.

"You know I am. Not trying to get you into trouble, only looking for some leverage here."

She doesn't answer. Then, "I do Manny a favor, he do me a favor."

My gaze follows her as she stands and flicks her cigarette butt into the middle of the street.

"Lu, too?"

She doesn't answer in words. Instead, she makes a humming sound and walks toward the apartment.

AT HOME I dump the backpack on my desk and assess it while I chain-smoke three cigarettes. My hands shake as I light each fresh cigarette from the ember of the previous butt.

I stub out the third one and make some coffee, then return to my desk and open the backpack. Four strapped bundles of hundred-dollar bills, a hundred per, tumble onto my desk. Another bundle held together with a rubber band is thinner and I assume it's another 5K, rounding out the forty-five thousand.

My very first thought? Steal the money and fuck Fabrizio over. Who's he gonna call to complain about me stealing his dirty money? Money he's blackmailing me to launder for him? Internal Affairs would love it. But of course, that would only end up with Koz finding out about my DUI and I would no longer be a cop.

Other ideas come and go but I realize I need to talk about this with someone I trust. I refuse to launder this asshole's money—especially given the way he "asked" me. I flash on Fabrizio standing in front of me, gun in hand, telling me to suck him off.

"Easy-peasy my ass," I say. "Fucking asshole."

I gently touch the side of my head where he clouted me and pull my hand back from the pain. First, ibuprofen; then, because my small freezer has no ice and holds only a solitary frozen chicken breast in a plastic baggie, I wrap it in a paper towel and hold it to my head.

I grab my cell and my finger hovers over Jimmy's name, the urge strong to talk to him about this mess. His flight to L.A. left today but I don't know what time. Besides, considering the way we parted I doubt he'd even talk to me. If he did take my call and I told him Fabrizio was blackmailing me about drinking and driving, Jimmy would have no sympathy, only an I Told You So. If anything, I need to keep him from ever finding out about Fabrizio's scheme.

Other than Abandonato, the only other people I trust to confide in are my sister and my twin brother. I consider Daphne but dismiss the idea—she's twenty-four and lives in Minnesota, is single, and pretty naive. Her closest scrape with the law was bouncing a check as a teenager.

David might be more helpful, my twin has always had my back, but his moral code is such that he reduces everything to black and white. Which is why he likes working with computers—either it's right or it's wrong; no gray areas. If I tell him the reason Fabrizio is black-mailing me there would be no sympathy, only him telling me I should've taken my medicine and copped to the DUI, regardless of the loss of my job. So, he's off the list, too.

I take the coward's way out and call Abandonato. Even though he and Jimmy are equally pissed at me about my drinking, I do think he'll be more sympathetic about my situation. But I get voicemail—or else he's not picking up because he now recognizes my new number. I leave a terse message to call me back.

"It's important."

19

Monday, 11/25, 9:00 a.m.

I'M six feet away from Pete Christakos's desk and he still hasn't noticed my approach, doesn't show that hyper-vigilance most cops seem to come by naturally. "Hey, Pete!"

He glances up in my direction and I heave a small white bakery box at him. He catches it nimbly, like a first baseman making a routine out. "For me?"

"Yeah. A gift."

He holds the box to his ear and shakes it.

"It's a necktie," I deadpan. Frustrated at his prolonged fumbling with the box's string bow I grab scissors from a neighboring desk and cut through the snag. "I know I promised you homemade cookies last time but this is what you get. A nice Italian lady made them. Enjoy."

"Man, there's nothing like these little beauties." He closes his eyes, sticks his nose in the box and inhales, which alerts two cops sharing an adjacent desk.

I pat the air with both hands, an appeasing motion. "Keep it down. The other vultures are starting to circle."

Pete hugs the small box tight to his chest and addresses the two cops who now assume menacing stances on each side of Pete's chair. "You two can just forget about it. These are mine and mine alone."

One guy groans and retreats, the other guy gets back to his desk and launches a wadded-up piece of paper at Pete's head but misses. I sit in the visitor's chair next to Pete's desk, undo the lid on my large Styrofoam cup of coffee and sip.

From the box Pete plucks a small cookie shaped like a shell, its edge dipped in chocolate, tosses it in the air and catches it in his mouth. He pumps his fist and chews, swallows, and grins at me, then repeats this performance. "What've you got for me on the chalices, Pete? Any hits from the website?"

"We got real lucky on this one, kid." He spews cookie crumbs. "Those pictures you gave me helped a load. A shop not far from here took in the chalices. Described them to a T. I told him to hang onto 'em, that you'd come by for the ID. My guess is he's got your candlesticks too, but he's got a lot of those so you gotta eyeball them."

He launches another cookie. Chocolate sprinkles fly. "If your ID's positive, let me know who hocked 'em and we can bring him in. Unless the priest wants to press charges at the West Side RSG."

I thank him and jot down the address of the pawnshop. It's on the West Side, roughly between St. Nick's and Flora's apartment.

"Glad my favor with the website worked out." He's reminding me of his cooperation. Maybe my cookies don't show enough gratitude.

"Here's the thing about this robbery, Pete." I review how I'm checking into Martin Nygaard's death and how the theft might be tied in. "Nuts worked on it for about a minute and then told me it's closed."

Pete winks at me, knowing Abandonato's by-the-book reputation; sometimes admired, sometimes not. "Understood. I'll bring the guy in and then sweet-talk Abandonato into loosening up a little."

I filch a small, round cookie dusted with confectioner's sugar and eat it whole while I consider his offer. Pete leans in toward me. "Even if the case is closed, we both know *Abandonato* won't pass up questioning the guy. You know, just in case." He emphasizes my partner's name, a broad hint I should forget about trying to question the suspect myself.

"Yeah, that's good," I say. But Pete doesn't know he's doing me another, different favor. Since my friction-filled conversation with Nuts on Saturday I'm loath to ask him directly for further help, and worry he'd refuse if I did ask. Nuts will do this for Pete, though.

Then there's the matter of Fabrizio assaulting me yesterday afternoon and blackmailing me in order to launder the forty-five grand. Nuts hasn't returned my urgent call. Prior to our falling out he would've called me back as soon as he got the message. I could confide in Pete. He's been around forever and I'm sure isn't a stranger to cops jacking up other cops. But the shame of the DUI keeps me constrained.

"I'm going over to the pawnshop right now," I say, "see what he's got. I'll call you."

Pete doesn't answer. We both stand and he gives me a sidearm hug, then tilts his head to peer at the side of my face. "Christ, Dana. What the hell happened here?" He reaches out to touch my face and I flinch.

I don't wear makeup and have nothing to cover the deep purple bruise from my ear down to my chin, a gift from Fabrizio's clout yesterday. I hesitate. Pete's a good guy, one of the honest ones, and I count him as a friend. I'm aware if I don't tell him something believable, gossip might get around that Jimmy smacked me.

I stroke my cheek with a light touch and grimace. "I know. It's pretty sore. Let's just say there was a disagreement between me and a really, really bad guy."

Pete nods. "Give as good as you got?"

I smirk. "A lot worse, actually. He won't know what's coming." Once I figure out what that is.

"Good, good. When you back on duty, kid? Any news?"

I'm stumped again at how to answer him. Returning to my detective job depends on successfully completing IOP treatment, and at five more weeks to go it's way too early to predict how it will turn out. "I'm feeling good, Petey. Keeping my nose clean." And that's true. For two days now. Saturday I went home from the lake, ate dinner, and watched an old movie on cable. Oh, and took a six-pack lurking in my fridge and gifted it to the college guys who live below me.

In a burst of energy on Sunday I finished unpacking from my move, cleaned my studio, and laid in a week's worth of groceries. All before my journey to Fabrizio's fuck pad. But he didn't get a chance to pour Foster's Lager down my throat in that apartment and I didn't drink when I got home.

"I'll let you know when I'm back, okay?"

"Sure, sure. Keep in touch."

I PARK across the street from the Second Chance Pawnshop, a sign in the window announces *B rite back*. I chain smoke while I wait, anxious to find out who pawned the items and whether there is a connection to Martin Nygaard's death. I briefly reconsider Flora as a possible candidate but dismiss the idea. Stealing and pawning would take too much organization and planning—she can barely get to the food pantry. Still, desperate people do desperate things. And, in my experience, stupid things.

A pudgy man, a cigar clenched in his teeth, strolls up to the pawn-shop and unlocks the door. One last pull on my cigarette before I jump out of the car and jog over to him. "Hey! Got a minute?"

Shorty turns and takes his time giving me a full body once-over. The guy's sixty if he's a day. He pockets the key, puffs on the stogie, and revisits my five-foot-ten inches from his five-foot-two inches until his eyes reach mine. "What can I do for you, doll face?" Somehow, he shifts the cigar from one side of his mouth to the other without using his hands.

I touch the tender side of my face, self-conscious of how it looks although this guy doesn't seem to have noticed, or if he has, he's not bothered by it. "My *name's* Dana Demeter. I'd like to talk to you about some stolen chalices you took in for pawn. Got a minute?" I gesture at the McDonald's bag he's clenching in his left hand.

"What're you, a cop?" He chuckles, checks if I'm laughing with him.

I oblige with an amused smile. "Used to be, more like private now. Listen, I'm working with Pete Christakos of the Chicago Police Department on these chalices. He talked to you, right? They're from a church not far from here. I'm supposed to ID them, get the name of the guy who hocked them."

He stops chuckling and puffs furiously on the cigar, then pitches the overwrought butt into the gutter. Squinting up at me he sighs, unlocks the door, and holds it open for me. I brush past his protruding belly certain he's ogling my ass when I walk through.

The room inside is the size of a Chinese carryout storefront, devoid of any furniture except for a small table next to the front window, which holds a tray of dark purple African violets in various stages of budding, flowering, and shedding.

"Okay, doll. You wait here while I go get us some chairs."

He leaves the bag on a ledge in front of a window shuttered with a rolling metal gate, where I assume customers transact business. A minute later he's setting up two chairs at the table with the African violets. "You don't mind I eat while we talk, do you, sweetheart? I been up since four this morning and I'm starved!"

Instead of waiting for my response he empties the bag of four hamburgers, a large box of fries and an apple pie and spreads out the fast food in a small semi-circle. He gestures at me with a hamburger.

"Want one?"

"No, thanks."

"More for me!" In a practiced move he strips three of the burgers from their buns and piles them onto the one that remains, then takes a huge bite.

I pull out Father Mik's pictures of the chalices and push them across the table. "Pete Christakos tells me you described these to him. Are they the ones?"

He glances at the two drawings and returns his attention to the fries, pushing them into his mouth in groups of three. His diamond pinky ring glitters with the movement.

"Yeah. Guy came in here coupla weeks ago with 'em, wanted a loan, said they were in his family for years but now he's scratching for cash and wants to pawn 'em. Gonna buy them back when he gets his Christmas bonus." He makes quick work of the disappearing stacked burger. I envy his appetite. He starts to talk again and I hold up my index finger to pause him, pull out my note pad and a pen, then nod a go-ahead.

"Told him they'd be here 'til the end of December. If he bought 'em back I'd get a nice little holding fee. Otherwise, I'm free to sell them. Happens a lot. People don't come back. Anyway, I know a good thing when I see it. Guy only wanted t'ree hundred. Those cups got real gems, gold and silver, the real deal." I jot down this information.

He taps his temple. "I don't think the guy knew that, wasn't too bright." He bites into the apple pie, makes a face. "Cold. Damn! I love these things when they're so hot they burn the roof of your mouth. This? Like glue." He shoves it into the bag.

I nod, trying for something like sympathy. "Maybe you could microwave it. Listen, Mister—uh, I never did get your name."

"Sorry, doll face. It's Fellowes, Billy Fellowes. Call me Billy." He wipes the grease from his hands onto his pants. We shake hands. He holds on for a beat too long and tickles my palm with his index finger. I remove my hand with a quick jerk.

"Hey!"

He shrugs. His grin is all teenage boy.

"Okay Billy, here's the bad news. Those chalices need to go back to the church. They don't belong to the guy who hocked them—he's in deep shit. You're out the three hundred unless you can get it back from him. You got his information?"

He frowns at me and crosses his arms over his paunch. "Nothing but hypes and poor people trying to get by around here." He pulls a piece of paper from his pocket and unfolds it. After studying it for a long moment and frowning some more, he hands it to me.

"That ain't the guy," he says.

The sheet is a photocopy of an Illinois driver's license belonging to a man named Cyril Brack. I give Billy my best *then why the hell are you giving me this?* face and toss the paper onto the table.

"I mean, that's the card he gave me, but it ain't him." He leans back, hands behind his head, elbows out.

"Maybe you were too busy drooling over the chalices, how much they were worth."

"Hey, I followed the law. I copied his card."

From a drawer in the table he withdraws a small ashtray and a black cigar easily a foot long. He cranks his Zippo and puffs continuously until the end glows orange. I hold up my index finger again to make him wait and pull out a Kool, which he lights for me. We smoke in silence.

"Yeah, you followed the law." I lean forward and add some grit to my voice. "But now we've got nothing because," I tap the paper, "*this* guy isn't *the* guy. Guess you were too busy counting your money to inspect the license picture to make sure it matched." I inhale deeply and sink back in my chair, dispirited at another dead end.

Billy is unperturbed. "Hey, you think I'll get a reward for finding the cups?"

I shake my head. Billy's got one thing on the brain. His gaze drifts to my breasts. Make that two things.

But the shabby pawnshop gives me pause. He can't be making much of a living in this neighborhood—the chalices might represent a tidy retirement package to this guy, so I reconsider his request.

"I don't know. I guess it's worth asking. Let me talk to the priest, tell him you're out the three hundred."

"Oh, I'm not worried about the Benjamins. I'll get those back easy. But I thought a reward for helping out the police, you know, might..."

I straighten up and stub out my cigarette.

"Get them back? I thought you didn't know the guy."

"Maybe 'know' is a little strong, sis. Don't know his name or nothing. He's a regular around here, you know, delivering the paper, driving the truck. Like this morning. I'm up at four, can't sleep, putzin' around my apartment. I got a nice little place upstairs." He has the nerve to wink at me and points up at the ceiling.

"You're at least sixty and I'm married." I twirl my left hand at him, amazed and thoroughly depressed this guy's hitting on me.

"I'm fifty-two and you ain't got no ring on, honey."

I take a gander at my left hand for a split second and remember I shed my wedding ring yesterday, not wanting to wear it again until I know for sure what Jimmy intends. I motion for him to continue.

"So, the paper comes at five-thirty, I make coffee and read what's happening in the world. It's like I told you, the guy's got a job. That's why he coulda bought 'em back with his Christmas bonus."

I take down this information. Adrenaline pumps through me as my body registers the excitement of chasing a strong lead. Billy can't come up with a name for the suspect but describes a skinny white guy in his early twenties.

"We'll trace him through his job at the paper," I say. "Here's my card and the name of the priest who'll pick up the chalices. He'll identify the candlesticks."

Billy squints at the card and then at me. "And?"

"And?" And what? For a moment I don't know what he means. Oh, right. Billy and money. "And I'll talk to someone about a...reward."

"Hey, t'anks for that. You're okay. Gotta make a living somehow. Am I right or am I right?"

He sucks on the stogie and blows three perfect smoke rings in a row.

20

Monday, 11/25, Noon

I GRAB lunch after interviewing Billy Fellowes and then call Father Mik from my car to give him the good news. He does want to press charges against the thief and also agrees to talk to the church finance council about a reward for Billy. Next, I trace the driver's name through the newspaper's delivery office and call Pete Christakos.

"Yeah, Pete. The guy's name is Manfred Schwab. You can call him Moochy, according to his manager. On vacation, won't be back until the end of the week. Friday. Nope, he didn't know where. I asked his boss to send you Moochy's picture so you can put out a warrant."

Driving to Flora's apartment I try to contain my frustration at the stall with this important find. I relive my excitement at Billy fingering Moochy, the only link left for me to possibly figure out how Martin Nygaard died. Knowing I'll be with Emma in a few minutes takes the edge off my aggravation. I'm happy simply at the thought of her.

Even though it's only noon Flora's apartment building looms forbidding and flat against a dark grey sky. Lights from inside various apartments spark the façade and make the day seem all the darker. From my trunk I retrieve a large box sitting next to the backpack holding the 45K. Later today I'll comply with Fabrizio's strong-arm tactic and deposit the ill-gotten money. Abandonato hasn't called me back yet. I push the thought away with the hope I'll hear from him soon.

I make my way up the stairwell to the sixth floor and pass several women on two different landings. One group seems to be going to a potluck gathering, each woman carrying a dish, the other group helps a very old woman with a laundry basket. At number 623 I stop, stuff the box under my arm, and knock. Inside, footsteps pad on the floor near the door. On a hunch I knock again. "Is that you, Emma?"

A small voice says, "Yes."

"Is your mommy home, honey?"

Hesitation. "No."

"Is anyone there with you?"

Long hesitation. "No."

"Emma, it's Dana. I brought the doughnuts Saturday. Remember me?"

No answer. "I got a surprise for you, Emma. Would you like to see it?"

"Porter says don't open the door for *anyone*." Her exaggeration of the last word comes out louder than the rest of the sentence.

"And Porter's right about that. Okay. Well, I'll leave your present out here and when your mama comes home she'll give it to you." The door stays shut. I put the box on the floor in front of the apartment door and start back toward the stairwell. Halfway there I hear the click of a lock and whirl around as the apartment door opens. Emma, clad only in underpants, hugs the edge of the door and stares at the box. I hurry back, pick up the box and bustle the little girl inside.

Even with my coat on I can tell the apartment's cold. The radiator in the quasi-living room is tepid to my touch. I kneel down next to Emma. "Where are your clothes, Emma? It's too cold in here, even with clothes on!"

"Mama took the clothes and went to wash them."

"She left you here alone?"

She shakes her head. "Porter 'upposed to watch me but he left."

"You're very brave to stay here by yourself, Emma."

I'm dumbfounded Flora left the little girl without anything warm to wear and seriously consider reporting her for child neglect. I scout around the apartment for something to clothe Emma. In Flora's bedroom there is no blanket on the bed and the mattress is stripped bare. Otherwise, the room is empty with the exception of the package of pull-up diapers I saw last time I was here. I glance over my shoulder into the living room. "Emma, come here."

The little girl comes to me and I point to the diapers. "Aren't you supposed to wear those?"

Emma glances down at her underpants and then up at me, shakes her head. "I know how to go potty," she says.

"Oh, okay. Sorry."

She drapes herself along my leg and leans into me. I bend and put my arm around her slight shoulders and lead her into the living room. We sit on the bare mattresses, the box I brought nestled between us. I touch the box and then point to her. "This is for you."

The little girl places her palm on the box and gazes up at me, her grey eyes serious.

"Go ahead, you can open it."

She struggles a bit but finally pries off the top. The down coat billows out from its prison. Emma stares at me, her eyes wide. "It's pink."

"Yep, it's pink. And it has," I draw the coat out, "a hood with fur around it. It'll keep you warm and toasty." It's fake fur, but still. She runs her hand along the edge of the hood, like she's petting a cat. I help her into it, extra glad I bought a coat that reaches to her knees instead of a shorter jacket. I show her how to zip it up and she practices a few times, gets the hang of it, then goes to the closet door mirror and stares. Up goes the hood and she stares some more.

Watching her gives me a feeling of satisfaction, of something more than only making a little kid happy, more like a feeling of fullness, a feeling of protection toward her. Emma swishes her way back to me, her arms swinging wide to make the coat zing.

"Here. I also brought you this." I pull out a pack of bubble gum from my backpack and hand it to her. She solemnly takes it and puts it in her coat pocket.

"Are you hungry?"

She nods.

"Let's go into the kitchen and I'll scare something up for you."

Emma goes back to the mirror and I head down the hall to the back room. The kitchen isn't warm today, the oven is off and its door shut. Enough cold air leaks through the window frame to push at the decrepit window shade. I don't find much for Emma in the kitchen. There's milk and peanut butter in the fridge but no bread to make a sandwich. The cupboard yields one box of Froot Loops about half full. I wash a bowl in the sink and hunt down a spoon. "Emma! Come get your cereal."

I hear Emma say something and then she's running down the hall into the kitchen, scrambling into the seat at the place setting where I put her food. A minute later the front door opens and then slams shut. The boy I now know is Porter saunters into the kitchen carrying a large black plastic bag bulging with what appears to be empty pop cans.

"Who're you?" he asks. But it's obvious he recognizes me from when I interrupted Jump whaling on him.

"I'm Dana, a friend of your mom's."

"She brung us doughnuts before," Emma says, "but not today."

I laugh. "Maybe next time, Emma. And you're Porter, right?"

He nods, places the bag in the corner and comes to the table, watching Emma eat. I offer to get him some cereal but he shrugs me off.

"Can I wear the keys, Porter?" Emma says.

"Nope. You already wore 'em, once. That's enough." He fingers the keys on a chain around his neck.

I check my phone. s only 1:30. "What time do you get out of school?"

Porter studies me, appearing older and wiser than his probable ten years. He sticks his finger in his ear and roots around while answering my question. "Don't go to school. Too busy." I remember Flora's description of Porter doing odd jobs to bring in money. The realization that this little kid spends most of his time doing what the adult in his life should be doing makes me sad, but anger quickly follows. Before I can respond to him, I hear the front door open.

Emma jumps off her chair and flies down the hallway. "Mama, mama! Look! Look what Miss Dana give me!"

"Hi, baby. Oh, you got a pretty pink coat."

I leave Porter in the kitchen. Flora's carrying a basket of jumbled clothes and dumps them near the living room closet. "Hi, Flora. I hope you don't mind me getting this coat for Emma." The little girl latches onto my leg and raises her face up at me.

"Mind? No, no, I don't mind. You're very generous to us. I hate I can't get these kids what they need." She slips off a lightweight jacket and goes to hang it on the closet doorknob, then changes her mind.

"Yeah, it's still cold in here. Any luck with the building manager?"

"No. He ain't been by yet to collect the rent but I'm gonna ask him." The beaten and hopeless expression on her face tells me she doesn't intend to talk to the manager about the heat. Porter comes into the room with the large bag of cans slung over his shoulder. "Here's my little man. How'd you do so far, honey?"

Porter puts down the bag, pulls a wad of cash from his pocket and hands it to her. "You need more." His voice isn't worried, it's angry.

"Just wait a minute." Flora lowers herself onto one of the bare mattresses and counts the money.

"Fuckin' Jump," Porter says in a much louder voice.

Flora continues counting. "It *is* short," Flora says, "but we'll give it to Mr. Sharf when he gets here. Maybe I can explain it to him."

"I had enough but Jump stole it."

"I know, baby. It ain't your fault. Don't worry." Flora gets up from the mattress and goes to Porter, gives him a pat on the head. He leans into her for a brief moment but pulls away when he notices I witness it.

"I'm gonna go cash these in," Porter tells Flora.

"You be careful out there, honey. Don't talk to no strangers."

I don't know why I continue to be amazed at the lousy parenting this woman provides her kids but this puts me over the top. "Flora! He can't be out there alone, especially in this neighborhood."

"Porter ain't afraid. Tell Miss Dana, honey."

Porter starts to say something but I cut him off. "Doesn't matter. It's got to stop—now. He's what, ten? He's a little kid and can't be out making money for you. And isn't he supposed to be in school?" I give her my best glare. Her response is a puzzled face, like I'm speaking a foreign language.

"It's fuckin' Jump's fault," Porter says. He swings the bag over his shoulder and throws open the front door, then stops, turns back to me. "And I ain't a little kid. I make plenty of money for my mama." He tosses a sneer my way and hustles out the door.

Flora shuts the door. "It's only for a little while, then Porter'll be back in school. Same as the twins." She smiles, like this is normal life. She picks up the laundry basket and plops down on one of the mattresses near where Emma plays on the floor with the bubble gum I gave her. "Father Mik told me I'd be ready for that training program real soon, maybe two weeks more." She digs around in the basket of clothes.

I struggle with the fact that Flora is close to qualifying for her training program, which will lead to a job and more stability for the family. I don't want to screw that up by reporting her to DCFS. The child protective services agency would get a load of this situation and take the kids away from Flora.

What are my responsibilities here? As a cop, I'm mandated to report observed or suspected child abuse. I wouldn't characterize Porter's situation as abuse but certainly neglect, big-time. A ten-year-old kid not in school and out scrounging up rent money for his mother? Yup. Father Mik is her supervisor, of sorts. He must know what's going on here. Mostly though, because I'm suspended and not required to do anything about Flora, I take the easy way out and leave it alone.

I approach Emma where she plays. She's arranged six pieces of the bubblegum in a circle on the floor and holds one piece in each hand. "I'm playing Duck, Duck, Goose. Watch." She shows me how the gum in each hand represents one person chasing the other around the circle until one plops down, leaving the other one out. She unwraps the omitted piece and pops it in her mouth.

Flora picks through the laundry in the basket, pulling out some clothes and tossing them on one of the mattresses, then carries what's left into her bedroom. I follow her into the room, then shut the door. "Flora, when I got here I found Emma alone in the apartment."

She stops sorting the clothes and settles on the bed. "Porter was watching her for me."

I push the basket to the middle of the bed to make room and sit next to her. "He wasn't around when I got here."

Confusion on her face. "But he was here."

I'm struck again by Flora's stupidity but I can't help but wonder if she's playing me a little bit, too. "He came home just before you got back. But that's not my point. Emma's what, four? She can't be left alone. It's dangerous. And it's against the law, you know?"

Flora shakes her head at me as if I'm the one who doesn't understand. "Not dangerous. Emma's a lot smarter than her age. She wouldn't do nothin' scary like play with matches or drink bleach."

"I can't argue with you about this right now. I have to go. Emma's smart, you're right. But what would she do if the building caught on fire? Or if someone convinced her to open the door, like I did? Think about it. If it happens again, I'm going to report you. That means the state could take your kids away and you could go to jail." Flora says nothing. I leave the room. IOP starts at six and I've still got to deposit Fabrizio's money and deliver the receipts to him.

Flora comes out of the bedroom to meet me at the front door. "Emma loves her coat." She calls over to the little girl. "Don't you, honey?"

Emma nods, her face solemn while her hands shuffle the bubble gum on the floor. Near her, I notice three wrappers and I wonder how she crammed it all in her mouth.

I start to say goodbye but Flora interrupts. "Jump's gone."

"What? What do you mean, gone?"

"Saturday, when you were here? You know, he left outta here, mad? He ain't come back since then. Sometimes he stays out late but he ain't never been gone overnight. Now it's two nights."

"Did you report it to the police?" A stupid question for Mother of the Year. Of course she didn't. She confirms this with a shake of her head. I rub my hands over my face and try to get my aggravation under control. "Flora, you've got to report this. He's under seventeen, right?"

"He's only thirteen," she says.

"The police will search for him, then. Come on. Let's call." I dig out my cell and call the closest station house, then hold the phone out to her. She starts to protest but I grab her hand and slap the phone into it. What I don't tell her is how quickly a missing child becomes a murdered child—and he's been gone two days?

I settle on one of the mattresses next to the clothes Flora laid out. I assume they're for Porter, since Jump is gone. While Flora talks I watch Emma play, kicking myself for ever getting involved with this woman and her children. When Flora's finished, she tells me she has to go in person to fill out paperwork on Jump. I check the time on my cell. "Okay. I'll take you over to the station but come on, we've gotta get going." Then I realize the twins will be coming back from school while we're gone. Flora tells me they won't be home until four-thirty because they're in an after-school club.

Our little caravan leaves the apartment. Emma is dressed in long pants and a sweater, and preens in her pink coat as Flora locks the door. Midway down the hall a short, wiry man talks to a woman standing in the doorway of her apartment.

Flora halts in her tracks. "That's Mr. Sharf." Her voice wobbles, hushed, scared. Even though she whispers, Sharf turns at the mention of his name. I urge Flora down the hallway toward the stairwell but as we near the building manager, the woman he's talking with closes her door. He crosses his arms in front of his chest, moves to the middle of the hallway, and blocks our progress. Sharf gives me the once-over and seems to dismiss me. He addresses Flora in a tone that manages to be flat and threatening at the same time.

"You're two days late. I need your rent right now." Flora digs in her purse for the money Porter gave her. I put my hand out to stop this and step in front of her and Emma, using every inch of my height to loom over Sharf. "You the building manager?"

He takes me in from toe to head, craning his neck upward, and squints. "Do I know you?"

"No. But the landlord-tenant ordinance should be familiar. Until Ms. Maitland's apartment is heated to 68 degrees from eight-thirty in the morning 'til ten-thirty at night," I lean my face into his, "the way the *law* says it's supposed to, she's not giving you one penny for rent."

"You can't do—"

I hold up my index finger. "And I'll be checking with Ms. Maitland about the heat. It's a five hundred buck fine each day the owner doesn't comply."

That shuts him up. Sharf pulls a cell phone from the back pocket of his pants and begins poking at the screen. I lift Emma up and she clings to me.

"Come on, Flora." I push past the small man and continue down the hall but then stop and face him again.

"And you tell the owner he's got one week to get busy fixing that elevator, too. I'm one phone call away from reporting him to the Department of Buildings."

21

Monday, 11/25, 2:30 p.m.

ON THE DRIVE to the station house, Emma and Flora in tow, my cell rings. I pull the car over to the curb and my stomach tightens when I check the screen—Abandonato. "Hey. Thanks for calling back."

"You said it was important."

Otherwise you wouldn't call me back? "Right. Listen, I'm in my car with someone and can't talk. Can I call you back in fifteen?" He agrees and I disconnect. Abandonato sounded unconcerned and even a bit cold. I begin to doubt reaching out to him about Fabrizio.

I drop off Flora and Emma at the local police station. She wants me to come in with her and I almost do but my urge to talk to Nuts overrides her need. Besides, if I keep holding this woman's hand she'll never, ever fend for herself. "This is something you can do yourself. I don't need to be there. Just go in and talk to the person at the front desk, tell them about Jump." I make a slight shooing motion with my hands. Flora looks scared but manages to leave the car with Emma trailing behind. I'm irked she doesn't hold the little girl's hand.

Nuts answers on the first ring. "So," I say, unsure how to start. "Remember when you picked me up after my accident? And Carrera's brother-in-law Breathalyzed me and it registered—" I hesitate, trying in vain to remember how many beers I told Nuts I drank that night but all I can dredge up is that I lied to him, whatever the number. "It registered on the meter." I take a deep breath and blow it out. Abandonato says nothing and I'm heartened, although I do worry he still might throw Thanksgiving night back in my face. "I thought Fabrizio would let me slide but he's holding it over me, says I've got to launder some money for him. If I don't, he'll send the DUI report to Koz."

Abandonato grunts on the other end. Long pause. "Christ, Demeter. How do you do it?"

"Do what? I need your help here—this asshole tried to rape me, Nuts." I kick myself for letting this slip out, using the attack to garner his sympathy—it's not like me to default to a weak woman stance. "Anyway," I force a breezy quality into my voice, "I got lucky and someone intervened." A blur of Manny's face surfaces. I flip down the sun visor. Reflected in the mirror is the purple bruise lining the side of my face. The pain is stark when I touch it and my body erupts in goose bumps and an involuntary shudder, as if manifesting the fear I stifled during Fabrizio's assault. This does take the focus away from my aching ribs though, which I guess is a kind of silver lining.

Abandonato says something. I haven't heard it and ask him to repeat it. "I said, did you get to the ER?"

"What? No." Isn't he listening? "No. He only got as far as smacking me around." I run my hands in a rough rub over my arms. Maybe Abandonato isn't the right person for this, after all.

"How did you get yourself in a position to—"

"Just stop, okay? That's not what I need your help with. How the hell am I going to deal with Fabrizio's money?"

"How much?"

"45K."

Nuts blows out a long breath. "You're SOL either way. You can't launder the money—it's illegal, for chrissakes. But if you don't, Koz'll find out you're drinking and that ends our partnership for good." Abandonato's voice is scratchy and indistinct, like he's distracted by something. I tighten my grip on the cell phone and press it hard to my ear. My stomach clenches. Why is he repeating what I just told him about my dilemma instead of offering some ideas or solutions? "It's bad enough you're gone for six weeks, keeping us apart, making me team with some idiots who couldn't solve a murder if it happened right in front of them."

I'm floored he's making this about him and refusing to even discuss how I should handle it; a clear rejection. I flip the visor back in place and erase all helplessness from my voice. "You owe me, Nuts. Jimmy's gone because you couldn't keep your fucking mouth shut about me. You don't get to pry into my marriage because of—"

"Cut the shit. You're in up to your neck because of what *you* did, not me."

I suck in my breath but he's still not done.

"Don't lie to me. *Ever*. Right now, the only thing I want to know is when you're coming back. Got it?" Before I can answer, he's gone.

Acid roils in my stomach and then visits the back of my throat, leaving a greasy burning reminder of the fast food I ate for lunch. I dig past Fabrizio's money I transferred to my backpack, unearth a roll of antacids and chew two, then toss in a third for good measure.

My anger at Abandonato's dismissal spills over into impatience with Flora, so I enter the station to find out what's holding her up. She huddles with Emma on a bench in front of the desk sergeant. I join them and grab the clipboard Flora holds. "So, what did you finish?"

Flora taps the paper and sighs. "They're wantin' a lot of information."

I read over what she recorded about Jump but it's not much: name, birthdate, physical description. I hand it back and encourage her to finish so we can go.

"Is this for that Amber thing on TV?" she asks.

The desk sergeant raises his head at overhearing this question. "You got an abduction?" he says to me.

I raise my eyebrows at Flora, asking the same question.

"What is that, 'xactly?" she asks.

"Do you think someone took Jump, stole him off the street?" I say.

Flora snorts in response. "That boy done run away, nobody took him. And if somebody did, then it's Jump's fault."

The cop at the desk must sense my aggravation with Flora because he takes over explaining to her that it makes a difference in how he'll proceed. "If someone abducted your son then we put out the Amber Alert. But we have to know that's what happened to him. Means you or someone had to witness it," he says.

Flora shakes her head. "He wanted to find his daddy, that's all."

"And he's sixteen or under?" the cop says.

Flora nods.

"Any disabilities?"

At Flora's puzzled expression, he rephrases his question to explain that if her son is sixteen or older but with a physical problem—like diabetes—that puts him at risk or makes it easier for someone to kidnap him, then an Amber Alert can be ordered.

Mother of the Year responds. "He's thirteen. Only thing wrong with that boy is he don't listen."

"That's not what he means, Flora." I roll my eyes at the sergeant and indicate Jump doesn't have any disabilities, and then gesture at Flora to hurry finishing the form. She takes her time writing but finally stands and delivers it to the cop at the desk.

"You left your phone number blank," he says, handing it back to her.

I collect Emma, approach the desk and give my name and phone number as a contact. So much for getting this woman to fend for herself.

AFTER I RETURN Flora and Emma to their apartment, I commit my first illegal act in ten years as a cop and open CDs in five separate banks for nine thousand dollars each, stick the receipts in an envelope, and write asshole's name on it.

At Fabrizio's apartment on the North Side, I ring the bell several times but there's no answer. I push a couple of other doorbells and finally someone buzzes me in, allowing me to climb three floors to his fuck pad where I slide the envelope under the door.

When I hurry back down the stairs only one thought dominates: In the next three months—the life of the CDs—I have to figure out how to extricate myself from this mess and screw Fabrizio over.

22

Monday, 11/25, 6:00 p.m.

JEN'S ready to give us the talk about How Addiction Affects the Family when Marvin interrupts to collect our A.A. meeting attendance logs. He takes mine, scans it and gives his head a slight shake, but when he reviews Hades' sheet, they both grin and bump fists. He proceeds around the circle and collects sheets from the rest of the members. Next to me Hades hisses to get my attention. "How many you got, Dana?"

I glance at Marvin to make sure he doesn't see me and then show Hades my middle finger. He laughs.

"You got only one?" he says. "Talk to me at break, tell you how to increase your meetings." After last Friday there's no way I'm going to go to more meetings.

"Okay, group," says Marvin. "I also need to let you know we'll be taking a break in one hour and right after that we're going to do a drop, so be ready for it." He leaves the room.

Confused at Marvin's announcement I elbow Hades.

He arches his eyebrows at me. "You never heard of a urine drop? Piss in a cup and show the folks what you been putting in your body."

I try for nonchalance even though I'm furious because I feel blind-sided by the surprise, which I'm sure is the point. "Yeah, I know what a urine drop is." My voice oozes more sarcasm than the words can hold. "But why the secrecy? They didn't say word one about this during the orientation."

"Oh, it's there," Hades assures me. "In that folder, you know, the written stuff they give us, yeah."

I try to remember what I did with the folder from the first night of IOP, which started last...Monday? With so much happening since then it's hard to believe only a week has passed. Yesterday morning, during a burst of domesticity, I piled a bunch of paperwork on my desk to sort through with an eye toward throwing out any junk. Folder's probably in there. I better read it. Who knows what other surprises are in store for me?

The urine drop worries me, though. After two failed Breathalyzer tests I don't want another failure. My last drink happened after the A.A. meeting on Friday. Only three days ago? I try to recall the formula Marvin told me for the liver metabolizing alcohol but can't bring it to mind because it's hard to concentrate while Jen yammers on about dynamics in alcoholic families.

But I didn't drink Saturday or Sunday and I'm clean today, too. Still, the urine drop has me spooked: I don't know if it's a more sensitive test than the Breathalyzer or how far back it can detect my drinking.

Break rolls around and everyone lines up in front of Marvin to get a plastic cup with a light blue cap and wrapped with a white sticker showing our names. Marvin gives me a cup along with a meaningful look of concern as he touches the side of his face. I pretend I don't understand his gesture about my Fabrizio-induced bruise and move along. Even though I haven't had a drink since last Friday, or maybe because I need one, I break out in a sweat and my heart hammers in my chest.

I leave the room but instead of heading to the bathroom with the other women in the group, I grab my jacket and continue down the elevator and out the front door. In the parking lot I scrape off the cup's sticker as best I can, making sure my name is obliterated, and toss it in a trashcan next to my car. I begin the drive to Louie's to pick up some beer but then Jen's voice in my head reminds me: "One hallmark of an alcoholic is drinking alone." Damned if I'm going to let Jen have the last word. Instead, I head south on Lincoln to Brau Haus.

WHEN I RETURN from the john to my stool at the bar there's a Coke waiting for me instead of the draft beer I ordered with my food. Even though it's Monday night, Brau Haus is rocking with a large group of twenty-somethings celebrating what seems to be three participants' birthdays.

Try as I may, I can't recall the name of the young, pretty Latina who waited on Jimmy and me when we were here earlier last week. She's the only one working, trying to manage the large party and at the same time keep us bar solos happy. I start to push away the Coke but then reconsider because I'm thirsty and drink half of it down. I can always order a draft when she gets a minute.

The bartender disappears into the kitchen and returns a few minutes later, my brat with sauerkraut steaming on the plate. A side order of German potato salad heaped next to it glistens from the overhead light. She delivers the plate in front of me, sets me up with silverware. "It's good to see you again," she says. "Is your husband coming later?"

Her question is innocent and reasonable. My reaction is anything but. "Nope. He left town yesterday and doesn't want anything to do with me. Says I drink too much."

Shit.

My smile is half-hearted. I'm sheepish because I had no intention of saying something this personal. What a cliché—telling a bartender my problems. And after skipping the urine drop and walking out of IOP, Jimmy seems like the least of the problems I now face.

I grab the Coke and drain the remainder and slap the glass down, ready to order a draft beer. The young bartender—I still can't dredge up her name—drapes her hand over the bottom half of the glass and encloses my fingertips in her warm grasp. I don't draw away my hand. We stare at each other for a long moment.

"So. You want another Coke?" she asks.

Her eyes, as she peers intently at me, track my gaze back and forth. I'm about to jump down her throat because she's trying to control my drinking, the same as everyone else. Then a strange pride takes hold at the thought I could have *three days* without drinking, almost halfway to my seven-day personal best from a few weeks ago.

Earlier tonight I didn't want Marvin to find out I drank, afraid of what the urine drop would disclose. I again count back to the last time any booze passed my lips; Friday, before and after the A.A. meeting. If Marvin springs another drop on us tomorrow, Tuesday, I'm sure I'll pass it. But only if I don't drink right now.

I gently push the glass toward her and she releases her clasp on my hand.

"Sure." Over her shoulder I read a chalked message on the wall board: *Rosalia is Your Bartender Tonight.* "Another Coke would be good, Rosie."

The tangy smell of the sauerkraut hits me and I dig in.

23

Tuesday, 11/26, 8:00 a.m.

SOME KIND of noise pulls me out of a dream. I rise to my knees on my futon, which is positioned below the southern facing windows of my studio, and lean against the windowsill. The sky is the color of old pewter. Darker clouds push up behind the bare treetops and the hundreds of rooftops that roll away from my view. There's nothing obvious outside to indicate what woke me.

I lie down again to try to get back to sleep. At Brau Haus last night my anger persisted at Marvin over the surprise urine drop. I guzzled Coke after Coke, trying to prove to myself that I could resist booze. Once I returned home, the caffeine kept me awake until three when I finally fell asleep. But I didn't drink. My cell phone whines on the desk. The thought hits that it might be Jimmy so I jump out of bed. "Demeter."

"Good morning, my name is Lynn Patner. I'm a real estate agent with Morton Realty. Perhaps you've heard of us?" Without waiting for my answer she forges ahead. "I represent a couple transferring to Chicago who are house-hunting. They'd like to purchase new but won't be able to with their budget."

When I hear her inhale to continue her monologue, I interrupt. "And why in the world would I care about this?" While trying to figure out if she's a telemarketer of some sort, I glance at my phone. At eight in the morning?

"One of my numerous contacts in the field told me you're in the middle of building an addition to your home. Rogers Park is a well-established area, exactly what my clients are in the market for. It would be perfect—"

"And again, why are you telling me?"

"Ms. Demeter, I'm trying to ascertain if you're interested in selling your home."

I hit my desk chair with a thud. "Did Jimmy put you up to this?"

"I'm not sure who—"

"Gennaro. Jimmy Gennaro. My husband. Did he call you and tell you to put our house on the market?" I'm awake now, my heart pounding in my chest. I scratch around on my desk for a cigarette, find one, fire it up. "Listen, Ms. uh..." I've forgotten her name already.

"Patner."

"Patner. You woke me up and I'm not ready to deal with this crap. Don't do anything with our house. I'm part owner. Got that? I'll get back to you if we're going to sell." I disconnect and toss the phone on my desk but then grab it back. I call Jimmy's number. It rings six times and I almost hang up when a sleepy voice picks up on the seventh ring. A sleepy, sexy, female voice. I'm speechless for a beat. "Let me speak to Jimmy." My stomach clenches.

"Gennaro." His deep, three-syllable utterance at once breaks my heart and makes me go ballistic, picturing him in bed with the woman who answered the phone.

"There's only one thing I want to know. Were you already sleeping with this bitch when you came home?"

"Why are you calling so early? Is something wrong?"

"Jesus—that's your response? I catch you fucking around on me and you're mad I woke you up?" I stub out my cigarette with short, stabbing thrusts.

"Is that why you called? Checking up on me?" Pissed. Like he's been wronged.

"Now I get why you stayed in L.A. for another month."

"Hold on," he says. Jimmy's phone clatters on something hard and then he and the bitch have a muttered conversation, though I can't make out the words. A door slams and Jimmy comes back on the line. "What do you want, D?"

"I want to know what you were going to do with your girlfriend if I *did* move to L.A. with you." I stand and mark the distance between my futon and the front door: three steps there, three steps back. It's a short trip and ups my anxiety but I can't sit still.

"Leave her out of this." Big sigh. "Listen, here's my side. You're not trying at all, Dana. You're drinking while you're in treatment, for god's sake. That can't be protocol. It sure isn't what you agreed to. And you drink and drive, then lie to me about it. I'm done with your bullshit."

Absurdly, because he's right about me on all counts, I can only come back with the reason I called in the first place. "I got a phone call from the realtor you hired to sell our house. It's a hell of a way to tell me, Jimmy." Tears start leaking from the corner of my eyes but I try to keep my voice steady; he won't get the satisfaction of hearing me cry.

"What? I didn't tell anyone to sell our house—that's bullshit." His denial sounds sincere. "I mean, it's being renovated, right? Would someone buy it like that?" He seems to try on the idea like a new jacket in an unaccustomed style. I can tell from his voice he's considering it.

"I don't know, Jimmy. I didn't get any details."

"Call 'em back, get more info and let me know. We should jump on this, we really should."

The last bit of hope I hold since our clash at my parents' house—that somehow I can make it right with him even though it seems hopeless —vanishes. I'm left with only his willingness to give up on the house, give up on our marriage, and give up on me. I slump into my desk chair and put my hand over the mouthpiece to mute my sobs.

"I don't have the money to cover my place out here and the mortgage," he says, "and I know you don't either. The house is an albatross. We gotta cut it loose. The sooner the better." His consideration of the idea morphs into capitulation so fast my sobs become acid.

"So that's it? Sorry, Dane. Let's end our marriage because the weather's better in L.A. Oh, and the women are easier, too. What a fucking joke you make of our life together. Don't worry, Jimmy. I'll deal with the house."

I disconnect and slam the cheap phone on the table hard enough to dislodge the battery from the back. It falls on the floor. I leave it there.

Extracting the last cigarette from the crushed package on my desk I light up and stare at the papers taped to my wall while I replay the conversation with Jimmy, over and over. After a while I realize I'm reading and re-reading the odd poem I found in St. Nick's kitchen. I read the final verse out loud.

> *"I have to find or follow you, seek what is unknown,*
> *And leave the wonder to another who cries alone,*

> *The time has come for me to hop a bus or train,*
> *I never knew you but I love you all the same."*

Even though I know Jimmy has nothing to do with the poem, my imagination serves up my husband chasing this unknown woman, while I'm the one who cries alone.

I yank the poem down. The tape holding it in place rips some paint from the wall. I unzip the gallon baggie, grab the paper out and crush it into a tight ball, then heave it at the trash with all my strength. I miss.

After a while, as I reattach the battery to my phone, I realize Jimmy lied to me. He had to be the one to set this up with the Patner woman because there's no way she would have the number for my burner phone. I steam for a minute but then think back to buying the cheap phone on Saturday. It was *after* Jimmy and I fought at my parents' house. I never gave him the number. Which leaves Nuts as the culprit; he wouldn't hesitate to give Jimmy my number. The same way he didn't hesitate to tell Jimmy I was drinking on Thanksgiving night.

So Jimmy did have it and did give it to the realtor.

I scoot my chair close to the desk and rest my head on my folded arms like a little kid during a school-time nap. I'm exhausted. I lied to Nuts. I lied to Jimmy. Now they're paying me back.

Later, I call the Patner woman and arrange for the house-hunting couple to view our vacant home on Sunday, the urge overwhelming to quickly sell our home and divest myself of the remaining baggage of our marriage.

24

Tuesday, 11/26, Noon

DR. RAPPAPORT LEANS over the back of Evie's head and parts her white hair with his fingers, searching for the six sutures Evie received in the hospital emergency room two weeks ago after being attacked at home. My mother sits on the examining table, the doctor on one side and JJ on the other.

The interpreter hired for the appointment stands next to Dr. R— which is what Evie calls him because his last name is too long for her to remember or spell with any accuracy—so my parents can easily see both of them. As the fifth person in this crowded examining room, I stand with my back against the door and point my smart phone toward them for my sister Daphne, who's watching the vignette on FaceTime. It won't kill her to take some time out of her day for our parents.

"Ah, here we go," Dr. R says.

Even though he's talking more to himself than to any of us in the room the interpreter still signs his words so both my mother and father see what's being said.

"Take them out." Evie's signs are given voice by the interpreter. "They itch."

Dr. R pats my mother's shoulder and goes to a drawer at the sink to extract a small pair of scissors, snipping them playfully in front of Evie's nose before going to work on her scalp. She graces him with a chuckle.

While Dr. R removes the black thread, my phone vibrates on mute with an incoming phone call—Abandonato. I swipe the notification to send it to voicemail, not wanting to interrupt my FaceTime call, though I'm curious why he's contacting me.

"How are you feeling otherwise?" the doctor asks. "Any dizziness? Are you tired? Any trouble walking?" I continue to record for Daphne while the interpreter does a credible job of breaking down the doctor's barrage of questions into bite-sized chunks so Evie can answer them one at a time. The problem comes with my mother's answers: Everything's fine, I feel fine, no dizziness, no problem walking.

The doctor is halfway out the door when JJ appeals to me to say something about the whoppers Evie has just told. "Hold on a sec, doc," I say. I quickly tell my sister I'll call her later to let her know how the appointment turned out. We disconnect and then I ask the interpreter to interpret for me.

Doctor R closes the door and returns to again stand next to the interpreter, facing Evie and JJ. I cross my arms and lean back against the door. "On Thanksgiving, my father said my mother had dizzy spells and held onto things when she walked around the house. Ordinarily she doesn't need to do that." I watch Evie take in what I say via the interpreter and brace myself for her reaction, then glance at JJ with a quick apology for throwing him under the Evie Bus.

"No, no," Evie replies, the interpreter's voice capturing my mother's irritation. "That's over a week ago, no dizziness now. I'm fine." She says this while pointedly holding JJ's gaze and I read the silent admonition she radiates. JJ shakes his head, resigned.

The doctor withdraws a penlight from the breast pocket of his coat and peers into Evie's pupils, instructs her to follow his moving index finger with her eyes, watches her walk across the room and back. "She seems fine," he says to JJ. My parents watch the interpreter, then Evie claps her hands once and retrieves her purse. "You keep an eye on her and if she has any problems, let me know." The doctor shakes hands with JJ and exits with the interpreter.

"You two worry too much," Evie signs, eyeing JJ and then me.

"You tell the doctor if you're dizzy, not pretend everything's fine. Don't lie." I lean on this last sign with emphasis—the visual equivalence of raising my voice—saying what I know JJ is thinking but won't put out there. And for once Evie doesn't spit out a snappy comeback for me, which makes me think JJ is right—she still experiences some after-effects of the attack. Instead, my mother slings her purse over her shoulder and heads for the door.

My father catches me making a crabby face at Evie's back after she passes me. JJ places the edge of one palm against the flat of his other palm and repeats a forward and backward sliding motion. *"It's alright, it's okay."* His unwillingness to pick a fight with Evie, even when he's right, reminds me of his innate kindness and pokes at me the possibility that had I treated my husband in the same way, he might not have left. I push away the self-recrimination when I remember the bitch on the phone this morning, the one in my husband's bed.

After saying goodbye to my parents, I head to my car and retrieve the message from Nuts.

"Thought more about what you told me about Fabrizio and the money. Went to Internal Affairs to make a report about him laundering money." Abandonato's voice is fairly neutral. He doesn't sound as angry as the last time we talked. I'm surprised he changed his mind about helping me, which says he's still committed to our partnership. My earlier irritation with him about giving Jimmy my phone number lessens; after all, just giving out my number doesn't make him responsible for what Jimmy did with it.

"Unfortunately, IA won't take a hearsay report. They want hard evidence, so if you have any proof about who he stole from or witnesses, anything, then you'd have to deliver it."

Shit. Even if I did have proof, which I don't, I'm also worried that I've already committed a crime by depositing the money.

"One more thing that's problematic. IA won't allow anonymous accusations either. That's because of the possibility the person making the charge could be trying to frame the other person. It boils down to this: you have to present evidence and you have to identify yourself as making the accusation. Let me know what you decide." He clicks off.

So of course, I can't go to IA. Fabrizio's blackmailing me to do his bidding and in return, he won't send my DUI to Koz. If I out him for money laundering, I might as well hand in my resignation.

25

T uesday, 11/26, 6:00 p.m.

"IT FELT like you were checking up on me." As I answer Marvin's question, I keep my eyes focused on my folded hands instead of on him. He leans forward in his chair and wheels it a bit closer to my chair, which is next to his desk.

"Well, yeah. You're right, Dana. Urine drops are pretty much that. Let me explain something. There are some basic things in IOP we expect you," he nods at me, "to follow. One is, we expect you won't drink or use. To help you with that, we do unannounced testing." I hate this shit. Marvin gives me his full-on gaze but I avoid eye contact with him. "Because you left yesterday without doing a drop you'll be marked like the test result came back positive."

This gets my attention. I squint at him. "How the hell is that fair?"

Marvin holds up his hands, palms toward the ceiling. "Not the point. If you've got nothing to hide then the drop won't be a problem. But avoiding it is admitting you're afraid of what it'll show." He's infuriatingly friendly about the whole thing. "Get it?"

I do. I hate this shit even more. And although today is my fourth day without a drink, I'm still not sure if the urine drop would've confirmed my dry status or registered a measureable blood alcohol level. And I'm not about to ask him for the facts because I don't want him to know I did drink since starting IOP.

"We also expect you to attend A.A. meetings on the weekends, more during the week if you can. You're not working right now so that shouldn't be a problem." Marvin pulls a sheet of paper out of a folder on his desk that displays my last name and first initial. He slides the sheet over to me. On it is the A.A. meeting's name I wrote on the first line, the date, and Jeremiah's signature in florid blue Sharpie. "You've gone to one meeting? Or do you have other logs?"

"No. Friday night. That's it." I slide the sheet back to him. I expect to get reamed for not racking up more meetings but Marvin's voice is kind. He returns the form to my folder and leans back in his chair. He tilts his head up and looks at the ceiling as if musing.

"Meetings are important for ongoing sobriety, really. More important than anything we're doing for you here. Because drug testing alone won't keep anyone straight, Dana. Think about it. How you gonna stay straight and sober after you get out of treatment?"

After I get out? I can't even stay sober while I'm in.

"Tell me what you got out of the meeting."

"Those people talk a lot."

Marvin laughs. "Too much socializing for you? How'd you like the lead, you know, the speaker?"

"I liked the first guy okay, I guess. Jack. Sad story. I didn't pay attention to the second one." I pull a cigarette out of the pack in my pocket and hold it between my fingers.

"Fair enough. Your thinking will clear up when the body gets rid of the booze. Easier to concentrate on things."

"And that reminds me of something I don't get. The guy, Jack, said he got twelfth-stepped. What is that, some kind of ritual of theirs?"

"No. You've heard of Twelve-Step programs, right? That's what A.A. is. You follow the twelve steps for recovery from alcoholism. The last one, step twelve, encourages members to do this thing they call, 'carry the message' to someone who is still actively drinking but wants to stop. Basically, the person who is in A.A. tells the drinking person his —or her—story. Like Jack did in the meeting you were at."

"Oh. That's pretty simple."

"That's a good question, a good sign, Dana. Shows you retained some of what you heard." Marvin gives me a fresh A.A. meeting log and encourages me to get to as many meetings as I can, which should be simple because after all this is Chicago and there are thousands of meetings. I put the form in my backpack but make no verbal commitment, especially because it is not a requirement for staying in IOP. He sifts through my thin folder. "So last week I gave you some homework, remember? Write about how your life's been affected by your drinking. Got that with you?"

The unfinished sheet of paper languishes on my desk at home. "Sorry. Forgot."

"Forgot? Or didn't do it?" He says this without sarcasm or anger. I'm again surprised he doesn't judge me and wonder if I appear as sheepish as I feel.

"Busted. I've been pretty busy with a case—"

"Really? I thought you were on suspension."

"This is more like consulting work, private."

"Okay." He sorts through some files in his desk drawer and pulls out a sheet. "I have another one. Let's go through it together and you can tell it to me. How about that?"

My silence is my answer. I place the cigarette on Marvin's desk.

"The point of this homework is to begin to identify how drinking impacts your life. Now I know that's pretty general and a huge area to cover, so let's narrow it down, okay? There's work, family, health. Why don't you choose one?"

My head spins with all the possible subjects for investigation in each area. None are free of taint from my drinking. My phone call with Jimmy this morning is so fresh, though, it elbows out all the other players clamoring for a place on the stage of my personal drama. "Well, my husband Jimmy and I—"

Marvin nods. "Right. You're moving to L.A."

"Uh, no." I forgot the whopping lie I told in group about L.A. "Those plans changed. He's going and I'm staying."

Marvin maintains eye contact with me. "Trial separation?"

"Something like that. I don't know." But once the words are out of my mouth, I do know. "He's leaving me, going to live in L.A."

Marvin's voice is so quiet I almost miss what he says. "That's rough."

I entwine my fingers and rest my hands on my lap, grip them tightly together. "He is so fucking unpredictable." I can barely contain my anger about Jimmy. I release my tight grip and slap the top of Marvin's desk. "Tells me on the phone—after some *bitch* answers."

Marvin says nothing, only leans back in his swivel chair, puts his hands behind his head, and watches me.

"He told me in October he'd be home at Christmas and then he shows up at my apartment a week ago with his big plans about L.A.

Swears up and down he told me he'd be back at Thanksgiving." I'm surprised I'm still so furious at Jimmy about these inconsistencies.

"Quick question," Marvin says. "Were you drinking when you had this conversation?"

I shake my head, not as an answer to Marvin's question but at the insinuation that I misunderstood Jimmy because I was drunk. "I was drinking when he told me he was coming back at Christmas but I wasn't *unconscious* for chrissakes—drinking doesn't affect my hearing."

"No, but memory can be impaired."

I acknowledge this with a brief glance and then continue, absorbed with my thought. "It's the same way I found out about this woman he's fucking—he likes to keep me off-balance. He says one thing, does another. But, oh! 'Dana got it wrong, that's not what I said.'" This sudden insight into Jimmy's game feels accurate and I'm aggravated it has taken me so long to pinpoint it. Sure as hell wish I nailed him with it when he first showed up before Thanksgiving.

I grip my hands together again for a minute before I cover my face, bow my head, and begin to cry. Marvin lets me go for a minute, then silently places a small tissue box on my lap. It takes six squares of tissues, each the size of a sticky note, to dry my eyes and blow my nose. I hand the box back to Marvin.

"Unfortunately, you're a common statistic," Marvin says.

"What?"

"I don't remember the numbers—gettin' old—but with couples where the male is the addict, the female stays with him something like eight or nine out of ten times. The statistic flips completely when the woman is the addict—only one or two men stick around."

Somehow, the stats don't surprise me. Women tolerate a whole lot of shit from men before throwing in the towel. They probably wash the towel before leaving, too.

Marvin groans and throws up his hands. "Not proud of my gender here! How long you been married?"

"Ten years."

"Any kids?"

It's a normal, common question. But it continues to prick at my pain. My miscarriage occurred in April and now it's late November. The baby would be a month old already. "No. No kids."

"So. What would you say about how your drinking impacts your marriage?"

I would say I have no marriage left but I'm not convinced it's because of my drinking. "My husband says he can't stand to see me sad. I guess he thought treatment would stop my sadness. But it's not something I can control, you know? Not much, anyway."

"You drink when you're sad."

I think about this. "I guess so." But then I remember this past week after Jimmy and I made love. I drank then, happy we were back together. "Well, not always."

"What about other times? Like when you're stressed? Being a cop is pretty high on the list of stressful jobs," Marvin says.

He doesn't know the half of it and I'm not going to spill about Fabrizio strong-arming me into breaking the law. Or mention he tried to rape me or that he banged me upside my head with his gun. I lift my hand to finger the still-sore lump but quickly shift to tucking my hair behind my ear. The bruise is covered with some concealer I bought on the way to IOP because I didn't want any questions from people. So far, Marvin hasn't mentioned anything about noticing my bruise last night. I cross my arms tight against my body. Yeah, last

Sunday was a bit traumatic, all right. When I don't bite at his invitation to spill about the stress in my job, he tries again.

"Going through a divorce is right up there, too. Stressful. For some people it could also be traumatic." Marvin the Mind-Reader.

"We got married ten years ago." I pluck my cigarette off his desk and hold it between my first and second fingers.

"So you said. It's like this, Dana. Drinking can be a symptom of a deeper issue that's bothering us, maybe we try to understand it or work it out but can't, so we avoid it or escape with booze." I don't look at Marvin but listen hard to every single word he's putting out, latching them together like a stack of Legos.

"But here's the tricky part," he says. "What often happens is people become physically hooked on alcohol. So, the strategy of using booze as a way to cope stops working. Person has to drink because the body demands it—they can't control how much booze because they don't know what'll happen anymore when they pick up."

That's true. On Friday I thought I'd drink one can of beer to "celebrate" being back with Jimmy and ended up downing five. Before an A.A. meeting, no less. Not my smoothest move. Marvin checks my folder again, searching for something. "There's nothing in here but I want to ask to be sure. You ever been diagnosed with depression? Been on medication for it?"

"No." I place the unlit cigarette in the corner of my mouth.

Marvin asks me a few more questions and does a quick screening for depression. He hands me a sticky note with the name of the program psychiatrist and recommends I go for a full diagnostic workup.

We're at the end of the session and I wave the sticky note at Marvin and make a show of putting it in my backpack for safekeeping. When he asks me if I have any plans for what's left of the evening, I let him know I'm going to Brau Haus for a late dinner and regale him with a brief story of my "success" there last night, but he doesn't show much enthusiasm for my display of willpower and repeats the bromide about staying out of slippery places if I don't want to slip.

By the time I get outside to smoke, I'm thoroughly done in. Marvin's sticky note will remain in my backpack, unused, and even though I made a cursory agreement to an assessment with the shrink, I have no intention of following through.

I know why I'm sad.

Jimmy knows why I'm sad.

It doesn't take a shrink to diagnose grief.

26

Wednesday, 11/27, 6:30 a.m.

A RUSH of cold air wakes me up. It's dark and I don't know where I am. I'm so hung over and my vision so blurry, I can't even make out the time on my phone clutched in my right hand. I jerk upright and throw off the blanket covering me and a woman's voice comes from the direction of the cold air at my back.

"Good morning." The voice is familiar but I can't place it.

I assume a sitting position and aim my phone flashlight toward the greeter. Rosie, the Brau Haus bartender, crouches down, her hands pressed against her thighs, and peers into what I can now identify as the back seat of my car. I question her assessment about the time of day though, because the only thing mimicking anything like morning is the bright yellow scarf wrapped around her neck and tucked in front. It finally registers that I slept in my car last night.

"Sleep okay?" she asks.

"Yeah, I guess so."

The young woman's face shows concern. I squint and then lower my gaze because a streetlight behind her glares as much as any sunlight. When I pull the thick blanket back over my legs, the confined space in the rear seat of my car ignites the elusive wisps of a dream. "I had the weirdest dream. I couldn't get out...no, the room, the door was locked and wouldn't open..." I run my hands over my face, a dry scrub, unable to grab hold of the fading and frightening images that I can't identify or force to reappear but leave me shaken anyway.

Rosie laughs. "Well, maybe you realized I locked your car doors last night—I wanted you to be safe out here."

"Oh. Yeah, maybe that's it." But what looms large in my mind's eye is the double-locked door to Fabrizio's fuck pad while he tries to assault me. A slight dusting of PTSD? Trapped and can't get out? Powerless to open the door? I push away the lingering image of being cuffed and kneeling in front of Fabrizio, his pants puddled at his ankles. I rub my eyes and stretch, take in the unfamiliar neighborhood through the windshield, and point to the three-flat behind her.

"Your place?"

She nods.

"Can I use your bathroom?"

"Sure. Come on." I hand her the blanket and panic for a minute at my missing backpack but she assures me it's upstairs. Once inside, she leads me through the kitchen to the bathroom. The mirror reflects exactly how lousy I feel so I avoid further inspection and wash my face, first with hot water, then rinsing with pure cold. It helps.

I spend a long time on the john trying to piece together what I did after leaving IOP last night. All I can remember is my fury at Jimmy, Abandonato, and Fabrizio. God, I don't want to engage in the What Did I Do Last Night conversation with Rosie, who waits for me in the living room, but I'm damned if I can figure out a graceful exit. The smell of coffee brewing draws me out of the bathroom.

"I didn't think you'd be hungry but maybe these will help." Rosie nods at the side table next to the couch. A large glass of orange juice and a cup of steaming black coffee wait for me along with a bottle of aspirin. I sink onto the couch and start with the juice to wash down the aspirin, then nod at her to show it's exactly what I need.

When I start on the coffee, a wave of nausea hits. I hate this kind of hangover. I feel like shit and I'm dying for a cigarette, but I know the first one will taste horrible so I put off smoking as long as possible. My body has other ideas. I put down the coffee and pat my pockets. "Mind if I smoke?"

"No, but if you're searching for your cigarettes, don't bother. You finished them last night at the bar."

"Oh. I don't suppose you—"

"Nope. Never have and never will."

Back to the coffee, which goes down better now, and this uncomfortable conversation, which doesn't. I check my phone again, glad I can now focus. It's six-thirty in the morning and I get why it seems like the middle of the night. No sun for at least another half hour.

"You want something to eat? I've got cereal or I can scramble eggs."

"No, no thanks. This is great." More nausea as I gesture with my cup.

"So, aren't you going to ask me what you're doing here?" Rosie gives me a shy smile and flips her long dark hair behind her shoulders.

I try to laugh. It comes out a croak. "The thought crossed my mind."

She leans forward in her chair and squints at me, her expression pained. "You got pretty wasted at the bar last night. And I kept serving you—that's my fault."

I smile at her. "Hey, you didn't pour it down my throat."

She begins to detail the legal responsibilities of bartenders toward patrons but I wave her off, not interested in her role in what is obviously my problem. "By the end of the night you couldn't walk straight," she clasps her hands together in her lap. "Even to go to the bathroom. I got worried crazy about you driving home."

None of her story sounds familiar. It's extremely odd to hear someone tell me how I acted when a search of my memory bank comes up empty. I nod and pretend I'm tracking what she's saying.

"To be honest, I was worried even more because I could lose my job for over-serving you. I kept trying to get you to call someone to pick you up. You know, like your husband or a friend." I can guess how that went over with me drunk but Rosie seems intent on recounting the story. "You said, 'Rosie, they can all go to hell.'"

Yes, that's exactly how I feel about my family and friends right now, drunk or sober. I glance around the neatly kept living room painted in a lively teal, the furniture clearly second-hand and shabby but comfortable, and a desk with a computer, stacks of books and a rolling file cabinet underneath, leading me to believe she's a college student. "Hey, listen. I didn't mean to dump my personal shit on you. I'm really embarrassed about last night."

My cup is empty but before I can request more coffee Rosie jumps up, takes the mug, and disappears into an adjacent room. She returns and hands me more blessed coffee that is strong but not bitter and has a hint of cinnamon. "It's okay. I'm glad I could repay you for helping me out the other day with those drunk guys."

It takes me a minute to register what she means. Then I remember the scene with the surfer dude and his buddies that Jimmy and I rousted at Brau Haus. "Right. So, I slept in my car?"

Rosie pulls my keys from her pocket and hands them to me. "When I took you to your car you were dizzy and wanted to lie down in the back, but then you passed out before I could get directions to drive you home. Since I didn't know your address I drove us here." Her voice drops and she sounds shy. "I hope you don't mind."

I recoil at the news that I passed out while in a stranger's care. But how could I mind? She probably saved me from getting another DUI, which would have been the end of everything for me. I touch her forearm. "You did me a big favor, Rosie. I owe you." We smile at each other. I blow on the surface of the hot coffee and begin to gulp it as fast as my tongue will allow, my nerves now singing for nicotine. A check of my cell tells me it's almost seven. The only thing going today is interpreting at St. Nick's for Martin Nygaard's four o'clock wake. Thank god. It'll take most of the day to get rid of this hangover.

"It's okay," she says. But her face belies her words, concern wrinkling her tawny, flawless skin.

"What?"

Fingers on one hand flutter around her cheek, then she rubs her neck, and finally ends up grasping and twirling a rope of her long hair. "It's only—I mean, who's Fabrizio? You kept calling him an, an—"

"Asshole?" I finish for her. We both laugh and she blushes.

"Yes. But you wouldn't say anything more about him last night. Are you in trouble?"

I deposit the half-finished cup of coffee and my burner cell phone on the low table in front of us and rub my eyes to stall for time. I'm acutely aware that Rosie is offering me a perfect opportunity to spill about what happened last Sunday. But since she seems to think we're even-steven in the doing favors for each other department, I don't want to be on the owing end again.

I lean back into the soft couch cushion and cross my arms. "With Fabrizio, it's kind of like last night at Brau Haus, Rosie. I put myself in a bad position and could've ended up hurt." I glance over at her. She's half-turned toward me, her right arm draped over the back of the couch and her hand rests inches from my shoulder. "But I'm lucky—like last night, too. I got a little banged up." I touch the side of my head, the lump now reduced but the bruise out of hiding because I washed the concealer off my face. "Basically, I'm fine, though. Only need to be more careful."

Rosie touches my chin and turns my head to inspect the bruise. She whispers something in Spanish and drops her hand to my shoulder for a light squeeze. "So next time at Brau Haus I'm only serving you Coke, right?" She draws out the last word but flashes a grin.

I know she's not trying to control my drinking, only teasing me, but her comment gives me pause. "You know, I thought I would only eat dinner like the night before, and drink Coke, yes. I'm not sure I even remember ordering beer." And that's the truth, right out there. Not that Rosie cares one way or the other about my drinking. But it's good for me to say it out loud. I think I just proved to myself what Marvin told me yesterday—I didn't intend to drink last night and yet got so drunk I passed out. Slipping in slippery places. We both get up, Rosie retrieves my backpack, and we exchange phone numbers along with vague plans to get together for a movie. I thank her again and leave.

I pick up a pack of Kools at a convenience store. Back in my car, I wait for a traffic signal to change, pull the cellophane from the new box, light up, and inhale deeply. As expected, the taste is harsh and leaves me dizzy but the nicotine rush starts to smooth out my hangover. Rosie lives close to St. Nick's and as I pass the church some early parishioners climb the steps to enter the building. Daily morning mass.

Two blocks later I pitch my cigarette butt out the window while waiting at another red light and notice a small figure across the street. There's a large canvas bag looped over his shoulder and flapping against his leg; Porter, Flora's second son. The light turns green. I execute a tight U-turn, pulling up alongside him, and toot my horn. He glances over at me, then away, and picks up his pace. I lower the passenger side window and call to him, asking if he needs a ride. He shakes his head and keeps walking.

Dark clouds bloom in the sky and a cold wind has erupted from the west in the half hour since leaving Rosie's apartment. Porter hurries along, hunched over, wearing only a hoodie—although for the life of me I can't understand why he hasn't raised the hood over his bare head. I figure he's at least a mile from home. It starts snowing, a thick white curtain dropping from the low-hanging clouds. I honk my horn at him again but he ignores me. I pull ahead and block the crosswalk, get out of my car and sprint over to the passenger side to open the door. When he gets near, I herd him into the car's warm interior. He doesn't resist.

The snow coating his head melts and leaves his pale blond hair darker as it mats against his scalp. He shivers. I blast the heat and head toward Flora's apartment building. "Good thing I found you in time to get you out of this storm. Were you delivering papers?"

"It's hard 'cause Jump stole my bike. I ain't got any other way to deliver 'em except walking. Jump's an asshole, making me late. Lotta people mad at me 'cause they didn't get their papers 'til after seven."

"But didn't you deliver everything? Your bag's empty."

"Don't matter. People get mad, they tell my boss and he gets mad at me. Sometimes he won't pay me if I don't do it right."

I think about that and wonder if there's anything I can do but shake off my penchant for further involvement with this family. "Why'd Jump steal your bike?"

"'Cause he's an asshole. He beat me up and stole my bike and my money. I ain't sorry he's gone and I hope he don't ever come back."

"How much money did you lose?"

Porter hesitates and shrugs. "I don't know. Maybe thirty dollars."

My recollection of the two boys fighting comes to mind and for a moment I feel bad for Porter, sorry I didn't intervene more back then. I've been so absorbed in my own shit I've forgotten to check whether Flora's police report on the missing Jump has yielded any results. But from what Porter says, Jump's still missing. I pull up in front of the weary tenement and park. Porter begins to open the passenger door but I place a heavy hand on his shoulder. "Hold up, I want to talk to you a minute. Close the door."

Porter scowls at me and for a moment I think he's going to bolt but then he pulls his door shut. I keep the motor running so the heat keeps us warm. I release my seat to the farthest-back position so that our seats are even and we can easily converse. A simple shift to my right and I face him even though he stays facing forward and surveys the street through the windshield. "I wanted to ask you about the Saturday you and your sisters were at Saint Nick's with your mom. She helped Father Mik get ready for church inside. Remember?"

His only response is a shrug, which I take to mean he's not sure. I try again. "You, Moira and Mia, Emma, and a little girl named CiCi were playing hide-and-seek. Then CiCi went inside to use the bathroom and found Mr. Nygaard upstairs. Remember?"

Porter nods. "Yeah, the dead guy."

"Right. What I want to know is if there were any other adults at the church while you were playing outside." Porter reaches for the air vent by the passenger window and his thin, tapered fingers flip it closed, open, closed, open. I reach out and cover his hand for a moment to stop his fiddling. "Leave it open—your hair's still damp." He responds with a sideways scowl. Nope, no way this kid will allow anyone to mother him. I lift my hand from his. "So? While your mom worked in the church, did—"

"'Course there were people goin' in and outta the church, lots of 'em." Porter averts his face and gazes out the passenger side window. "But I don't know them people," he says, anticipating my next question.

I hadn't really expected any hard information to come from questioning him, more like going through the motions. And knowing Flora kept the parish hall door propped open with a rock makes it impossible to discover the identity of 'them people.' I search my memory for what Porter's sister Mia told me and if it matches Porter's story. But the fog of my hangover doesn't allow her words to surface.

I shut off my car and in spite of Porter's protests, I accompany him inside. The elevator shows no sign of repair work. Clearly, my threat to report the owner for non-maintenance didn't register with Sharf. Of course, only two days have passed—I'll cut him the tiniest bit of slack and wait until next Monday. Then I make the call.

Porter and I trudge the six flights in silence and when we arrive at the apartment, he frees up the chain around his neck from under his hoodie. Two keys jangle. Porter works one key in the lock as the other one, a skeleton key, slides up and down the chain. We step inside. The apartment is empty and, as always, cold. This I will report. As soon as I'm done with Porter I'll call 311, the city's non-emergency line. And get another cup of coffee. I check the time, surprised Flora's not home at seven-forty in the morning. Porter reads me accurately before I can ask. "She's at the church with the twins and Emma. They got morning church at eight o'clock. She's gotta set up everything."

"You going to be okay here by yourself until your mom gets back?"

As happened with our former run-in he blisters me with a practiced, withering look. "'A course. I ain't a baby. I do it all the time. That's why I got my keys." He fingers the chain around his neck. He relents in a softer tone. "You can go. It's okay."

I hesitate. Maybe I should stay until Flora returns. But my head throbs, I'm thirsty and nauseated, and I only want to get home. "What's the skeleton key for?" I ask.

His hand closes over the keys and he turns away from me. "Nothin.' I like the shape is all."

But Porter's body language is a concise message that he's lying, for whatever reason, about the keys. It's the second time he has physically turned away from my questions. My memory suddenly serves up my conversation with Mia and what I couldn't recall earlier. "Porter? You said there were lots of people going in and out of the parish hall the day Mr. Nygaard died, you know, when you were playing in the yard. But I asked Mia the same thing and she said there weren't any adults there, only you kids playing."

He leans his shoulder against the wall, his back to me. "That's wrong; she played hide and seek. A lotta times she didn't see the same what I did." I consider his explanation. It could've happened that way. But something still bothers me about his evasiveness. He turns toward me. "She's six." As if this needs no further explanation.

I raise my eyebrows at the hostility in his voice. "Okay, okay. I'm just trying to find out what happened that day." I place my hand on his shoulder, once again feeling more like a mother hen than a homicide detective. "Don't let anyone in that you don't know."

Porter ducks slightly and shakes loose from my hand. "I know, I know," he says, not hiding his irritation.

My chastisement of Flora about leaving Emma alone makes an appearance and taps me on the shoulder. But Porter's not Emma. He's got a lot of street savvy, would know what to do in an emergency, wouldn't let anyone get anything over on him.

Yeah, but he's only ten. My better self stands up to my lazy self. I cast around for what to do. Bring him back to my place? But I'm hung over and want to take a shower and catch some ZZ's. Which makes me no better than Flora in neglecting the kid. Then the obvious strikes.

"Come on, we're going over to Saint Nick's so you can be with your mom and sisters. I can't leave you here alone, Porter."

"Get outta here. I ain't going to no church with you." But his pale face belies his words. The dim light from the living room windows throws shadows that emphasize his emaciated face. This kid must be starving.

I crouch down to his level and rest a light hand on his shoulder. "Listen. I only woke up a little while ago and I'm hungry. Let's go to McDonald's and get some food. Your mom will be done by the time we're through and we can get her and your sisters, and I'll give you all a ride back."

He refuses. I'm out of patience and feel like shit, don't want to play head games with him anymore. He shrugs off my hand so I straighten and zip up my jacket.

"Okay. Well, 'bye Porter."

He doesn't respond except to close the door when I step into the hallway. Behind the closed door comes the sound of the security chain scraping home.

As I head down the long, dank hallway toward the stairwell, I wonder what a skeleton key would open. What valuable possession does such a poor boy own that needs locking up?

I'm halfway down the stairwell when a door slams above me. I lean over the railing and crane my neck up to pinpoint what I hope is the source of hurried footsteps.

"Wait! I'm comin' with you," Porter yells.

27

Wednesday, 11/27, 3:00 p.m.

"IT APPEARS Martin did not experience a heart attack or stroke. The autopsy did not uncover anything physically wrong with him that would cause him to fall and hit his head. Other than his hearing loss, he was healthy for a man his age."

I listen to the phone message from Father Mik as I drive to Winston Funeral Home to interpret the wake for Martin Nygaard. I arrive at three, a full hour before the wake is due to start. The limestone building looks like an architect's take on a castle and the parking lot a moat surrounding it on all four sides. Probably an old mansion from the early 1900's converted for its current use. I'll bet it could withstand the battering of a wrecking ball.

Inside, the dark red carpet and gold-flocked wallpaper seem more suited to a whorehouse in a western movie than a funeral home. There's no one on the first floor but a silver stand at the end of the lobby lists three wakes, two from this morning and Martin Nygaard's this afternoon. A long staircase with a balustrade covered in gold leaf takes me to the second floor and Viewing Room C.

I enter the rear of a large room, rows of empty chairs set up ahead for mourners. At the front of the room a man and a woman sit before the closed casket, their backs to me. Although it's cold outside this room is stifling from an overactive furnace. The stink of mums grows stronger when I approach the couple, and because the carpet masks my steps, I clear my throat to announce my presence. The woman turns at the sound and stands.

"Hi," I say. "You must be Edna Nygaard. I'm Dana Demeter. Father Mik said you'd be here." I shake the woman's hand as my peripheral vision takes in the young man still seated. He stares out one of the large windows behind the casket without any acknowledgement I'm in the room. "I'm sorry for your loss."

"Thank you. I don't know what to make of this." She gestures at the spacious room. "Father Miklasevich arranged it but I'm not sure my ex-husband knew this many people." Her face is devoid of make-up, her expression forlorn.

"Did Father Mik let you know I'd be interpreting for you this afternoon?"

Edna Nygaard nods.

"Good. Have you ever worked with an interpreter before?"

Negative shake.

"There'll be some deaf people attending the wake because they knew Mr. Nygaard from St. Nick's. Many of them use American Sign Language—ASL—to communicate. They'll want to offer their condolences to you and your family and of course they'll use ASL."

I pointedly shift my gaze to the young man still sitting in the chair, still staring out the window. "I'll stand next to you and tell you what they're signing. Whatever you want to say, you can say directly to them and I'll sign it at the same time. Does that make sense?"

Edna Nygaard nods again, smiles at me. "Why yes, your explanation is very clear. I've never really met a deaf person, you know. Well, Martin couldn't hear, but that came from illness. He didn't use those hand signs. This will be a new experience for me and my son. Oh! Where are my manners?" She turns to the young man.

"This is my son, Buddy. He's really Martin Nygaard, Junior, but it seemed like such a formal name when he was a little boy. I didn't want other kids making fun of him in school, so I called him Buddy. A much friendlier, easier name for a boy to handle, don't you think, Dana? May I call you Dana?"

The woman's flighty chatter makes me nervous. "Sure." I regard her son and hold out my hand. "Hi, Buddy."

He gives no indication that he hears me. I study the young man for a moment before lowering my hand. He wears a suit that seems a tad too large on him, like a little kid wearing hand-me-downs from an older brother. I imagine if I tugged on his polyester tie I'd find a clip-on. A green rubber band holds his shiny black hair back in a ponytail at the nape of his neck and offers a stark contrast to his milk-white skin, apparently a complete stranger to sunshine. I pin his age at early twenties.

Edna Nygaard, who must sense my discomfort at Buddy's snub, takes me by the arm and leads me to the back of the room. "Please excuse my son. He's very upset over his father's death." She speaks in a low, confidential manner.

"Understandable," I say.

Lines crease her forehead. "No, not really. He never knew Martin. We split before Buddy turned one. But he wanted to come today, so I guess there's no harm in that." We walk downstairs together and while I hunt for the bathroom she goes outside to smoke.

When I return to the viewing room on the second floor Buddy stands alone, his back to me, with one hand on top of the casket. I can't make out what he's saying. I move closer and hear what sounds like an apology. I begin to step forward to talk with him but Edna Nygaard calls my name from behind. Startled, I turn around. Two deaf people are with her so I hurry over to interpret, making a mental note to catch up with Buddy Nygaard later.

Many of the deaf parishioners from St. Nick's—including Evie—attend the wake and most stay until the end. Father Mik leads the mourners in the Twenty-Third Psalm, the Hail Mary, and finishes with The Lord's Prayer. From what I remember about Martin Nygaard keeping to himself at the church, I assume the turnout is about the deaf parishioners participating in uninterrupted social time more than any fond remembrance of the janitor. The crowd begins to disperse but many lag behind to talk.

Someone grasps my arm from behind. "I want to thank you." I turn around to face Edna Nygaard. "I...I've never seen...well, I didn't know how beautiful ASL Sign language was...You brought tears to my eyes." And right on cue, her eyes well up. I've been interpreting my entire life and am familiar with this over-wrought sentiment from hearing people: *Oh, you were lovely. Your hands were like a Hawaiian dance. Even though I don't know signs I felt like I understood everything you did.* On and on. But Edna Nygaard's grey demeanor makes me stuff down my adverse reaction to her absurd compliment. Instead, I feel pity.

"I'd like to talk with you and Buddy about Martin but I realize this isn't the best time," I say.

"No. I'm exhausted and Buddy—" She checks around the room. "I think he's already gone. Maybe tomorrow? We're hosting a small luncheon after the funeral. Please come." I accept and thank her, then make my way downstairs.

The lobby is alive with deaf people loath to say good-bye and checking with each other about attending the post-wake reception of coffee and cookies in the lower level. I spot Evie by the exit engaging in a spirited discussion with Sarah Gilbert from the St. Nick's altar guild who is helping train Flora and is an old family friend. I stop—knowing Evie can't spot me from this angle—and watch my mother for a minute.

She's listing out her volunteer activities while Sarah nods. My uncharitable assessment is that Evie's angling for a pat on the back. Then she shows Sarah the spot on her head where the stitches came out. I make my way toward the two women and stop to button up my coat against the cold before stepping outside. I'm close enough now for Evie to see me. She turns to Sarah and, making sure I can read her signs, gives her the latest on my drinking and driving exploit.

Tired from standing during the wake for four hours, tired from being hung over, tired from obsessing about Jimmy and his girlfriend, exhaustion overwhelms me and I come down on Evie. Hard. I stride over, grab her upper arm, and hustle her outside to escape the crowd. But my hoped-for privacy doesn't materialize. The parking lot is lit up like a football stadium at night and some of the deaf rubberneck at the window to catch the action.

"Goddamn it! Why do you tell every detail of my life to all the deaf? You didn't even ask me if I got hurt in the accident! At least JJ cared enough to find out." I glare down at her.

Evie doesn't flinch. Her next gesticulation is only one sign, but she uses both hands to add flourish and emphasis. *"Finish!"* She stretches her arms high to make sure her yelling hands are right in my face.

"JJ never asked me if you could borrow my car—he took it and gave it to you. That's my car! You're not responsible! You drive drunk, get hurt, maybe hurt other people. I don't like it!"

Marvin's homework sheet pops into my mind. Areas of my life affected by my drinking? My family. My mother, to be specific. She's in good company alongside my husband, who heads the list. I feel at once both sheepish at Evie's accurate assessment of my behavior and angry because she stands up to me. Our recent truce? Cancelled. I want to lash out and hurt her.

"You don't even know how to drive that fucking car!"

I'm so embarrassed at my ridiculous response that I thrust myself away from her and run to my—JJ's—car. Forget about going to the reception. I want to distance myself from any deaf people I know, one in particular.

My phone signals a text before I get a chance to start the engine: Daphne.

'Hey Sis! You didn't call me back yesterday. What happened with mom's appointment? She okay?'

I take three deep breaths. Respond now or wait until my thoughts are more coherent about Evie?

Mom's fine, great. Gotta go—can't text and drive. xoxo D.

There's always lying.

28

Thursday, 11/28, 9:30 a.m.

THE POSTLUDE ORGAN music at Martin Nygaard's funeral service is not excessively loud but the low bass notes throb in tempo with my headache. I didn't drink last night after the wake and instead went home to bed. This morning's malaise, though, seems heightened by my lingering anger at Evie. I settle next to Edna Nygaard in the front pew, ready to interpret, as a handful of people who attended the service file past to offer condolences, but no one stops to talk to her except my father. The others—including Evie, who ignores me—seem intent on heading upstairs to the parish hall for something to eat. And the inevitable socializing.

JJ chats briefly with Edna and then signals he wants to tell me something in private, so I leave the pew and we walk a few steps away. I glance at Edna and then back at JJ, confused about the need for privacy. *"She doesn't know how to sign."*

JJ nods. *"She would wonder what we're saying. Not fair to do that."*

My father's innate kindness toward others sometimes brings me up short and, in this case, puts me to shame. I had not thought of Edna's feelings. I focus on my feet for a moment and then gesture to JJ that I understand. *"What do you want to talk about?"*

"Last night, after the wake, your mother came home upset. She—"

I cut him off. *"JJ, she's pissed off because of the car and I—"*

He cuts me off, politely, by extending both of his hands slightly in front of his body and patting the air a few times, a gesture to mollify me. He includes a negative head-shake to emphasize I'm off-base in my premature interpretation about Evie. *"Not that. She came home, felt tired and went bed. About two hours later I got ready for bed and your mother woke up, crying. She told me she had a dream about the woman who attacked her two weeks ago. She remembers the woman's face."*

This is progress. At first my mother couldn't remember anything about being attacked, probably because she was hit on the head. Then about a week later she freaked out when I sequestered Rameeka—a Black woman I was protecting—in my parents' house. The good news? Seeing Rameeka jolted Evie's memory and she recalled her attacker was also a Black woman, but not much more than that. The bad news? My trying to help Rameeka and slip one by Evie added to my transgressions on my mother's shit list.

JJ waits for my reaction, sure I'll be happy about this newest development in the unsolved case of Evie's attacker, but I still carry a grudge about last night. I pat JJ's arm. *"Good, good. I can give you phone number, police sketch artist. You and Evie go."*

"Interpreter there?"

"You must ask. They will hire one." JJ easily reads the subtext: I won't be helping out. To his credit, he doesn't chastise me about it or guilt me into doing the interpreting. He nods and tells me he's going upstairs to join the other attendees for some food. We hug.

I return to sit with Edna, who surveys the empty church. She positions her coat around her shoulders to ward off the chill, which emanates from the ancient stone walls that rise up to meet wooden arches connecting them to the ceiling. "I noticed Buddy wasn't here."

Martin Nygaard's widow seems to shrink into her coat. "He worked last night after the wake. A bar on the North Side—Cisco Kid's, I think it's called—he and three other boys play in a band. They work pretty late and go out afterwards, you know how it is. I suppose they went back to his friends' apartment and crashed...isn't that what they call it? Such violent images kids use nowadays." She shakes her head.

"Does Buddy live here?" I ask.

"No, he still lives with me in Indiana. When the band plays a—what do they call it?" Her face puckers. "A jig?"

"Gig?"

"That's it. A gig in Chicago, Buddy stays with them. If they play in Indiana, the boys stay with us."

"Still, I'm surprised he didn't come today."

"My son is taking Martin's death hard, which frankly I don't quite understand."

"You mentioned that yesterday."

"My husband and I were divorced twenty years ago. Buddy couldn't possibly remember our split. He was just a toddler." Edna Nygaard is an older woman and must've had Buddy pretty late in life. She nods her head like she knows what I'm thinking. "I didn't marry when most of my friends did. I was very shy and inhibited but excelled at my studies, especially the sciences. I wanted to participate in the space program and joined the government after graduate school."

"Impressive."

"Yes and no. I loved my work but quickly approached spinsterhood." I wince at the word and she laughs. "Well, that's what they called it. Or at least, how my parents characterized it. Because I was an only child they were disappointed I wouldn't produce grandchildren."

"But Buddy?"

Her eyes take on a sparkle when I mention his name. "On my thirty-ninth birthday some friends took me out to celebrate. Little did I know they were also setting me up. I met Martin that night. We hit it off and were married six months later." She returns from the memory and places her hand on my arm. "I wish you could've known him back then. His bright, funny personality, so outgoing. He worked in sales and had a way with people, could draw them out."

I consider the dour man of my childhood church and his dank, sparse bedroom in the parish hall basement—hard to reconcile my image with hers. "What happened?"

Edna tucks her chin-length grey hair behind her ears and straightens up, angling her shoulders back. "We were very happy. Martin earned enough to buy us a house. He was forty-five when we married. But he did things according to his own timetable. Said he never met the right woman before me and didn't want to marry until he knew. I loved that about him." She glances at the casket still situated in the aisle next to where we sit. "I got pregnant almost immediately. You understand, I gave up hope of ever marrying but by luck met Martin. Then I gave up hope about bearing children and surprise, Buddy came along."

I nod at her, hoping to hurry her story along. We're the only two left in the cold church.

"My life felt complete, Dana, complete. The day I found out my pregnancy test proved positive I waited for Martin to come home to give him the news."

Her story trips a brief personal vignette: I didn't wait for Jimmy to come home to tell him my news. I found him on stakeout and jumped into his arms.

Edna's voice intrudes. "But when I told Martin I was pregnant he got morose and angry. I tried to talk to him about it but he avoided me for days. Finally, I picked a fight to try to get him to talk, and boy did we fight. He kept saying he couldn't afford a child, which was ridiculous because we had enough money. Given my age, my only chance to have a child was blown up by the man I loved."

Father Mik appears at the door where the church and the parish hall connect. Trailing behind him is one of the altar boys carrying a candle snuffer. They ascend the steps leading up to the altar and Father Mik demonstrates how to extinguish one of the six candles still burning from the service. He gives the long-handled douter back to the young boy who, after a few failed attempts, succeeds in snuffing the five remaining lighted candles, which I note means the two that were missing are back home. Father Mik lowers his hand for a high five and the kid grins and responds with a loud slap.

"You come on Sunday and now it's your job," Father Mik signs. The boy signs that he understands, scoots down the stairs and passes us, throwing a *thumbs up* at me when I sign a quick *good job.*

Father Mik comes down to us and settles next to Edna Nygaard.

"I'm learning about Martin's early married life," I tell him.

Edna clutches Father Mik's hand. "Martin finally told me he had cancer and felt he let me down when I told him about the baby coming. He felt vulnerable, weak. We were both scared. Cancer in those days seemed like a death sentence." She falls quiet.

"So, cancer?" I'm puzzled by this. "But obviously he didn't die."

"No, no he didn't. We muddled along for a while but it was hard. I mean, we were neophytes at marriage and my pregnancy and then his cancer put a huge strain on us."

"Father Mik told me how the cancer drugs destroyed his hearing."

"Poor man." Edna Nygaard's voice quavers and she pulls some tissues from her pocket. "A difficult time for both of us, wasn't it?" she says to Father Mik.

He nods and she gestures at him to complete her story. "Dana already knows how I met Martin at Chicago Read, about his depression."

"But when he got home, he stopped taking the medication they gave him," Edna says. Anger tinges her voice and supplants the tears. "Eventually his depression returned. I became frantic thinking he might kill himself in our home."

Father Mik loosely drapes his arm around her shoulders. She leans into him. Her story brings to mind Marvin screening me for depression on Tuesday and then recommending a full psychiatric work-up, which I'm not going to do. Listening to this pathetic story confirms I am nowhere near the abject low Martin Nygaard experienced in his sad life. I would never contemplate suicide.

Edna continues. "Feeding the baby every two hours at night left me exhausted. At that point, my parents urged me to move back to Indiana so they could help me with the baby. I didn't want to leave Martin but Buddy was my first priority. And I felt like I didn't know Martin anymore." She shoves the balled-up tissue into the sleeve of her coat.

Father Mik nods. "That's when Martin came here to work. But he was quite isolated in his deafness."

Edna Nygaard pulls away from Father Mik. "So, he never accepted it?"

"No."

"After Martin got out of Read," Edna says, "he filed for divorce and sent me the papers. He wouldn't answer my letters. By then I'd been with my parents for almost a year. Buddy was thriving, I felt more optimistic. I thought it in our best interest we stay there and make a life for ourselves, so I signed the papers."

"Did Buddy ever meet Martin later?" I ask.

She shakes her head. "I had a few snapshots of Martin that Buddy hoarded but that's the extent of it. Buddy asked about his father, of course. But I told him I didn't know where his father lived." She grips my forearm again. "And I feel very guilty about that because I did know. Martin sent me money every month. When I found out Martin died, I had to own up to my deception all those years. Buddy's been giving me the silent treatment since then."

I relay Buddy's apologizing at Martin's casket. Edna wrinkles her forehead and squints in thought. "I can't imagine why my son would apologize to his father. It seems to me it should be the other way around, no?" Her eyes challenge me to disagree but then her face softens. "I'm sorry, Dana. Martin's death has unearthed some resentments I thought were gone." She closes her eyes for a moment and then retrieves a notepad from her purse. She writes something and hands me a slip of paper. "My son will be playing at this bar tonight through Saturday. Starts late—9:00 or 9:30, if you want to talk with Buddy. I'd appreciate a call about anything you may learn since he has chosen to ignore me." She excuses herself to use the bathroom.

I lock eyes with Father Mik and scrunch up my nose. "Mothers sure know how to sling the guilt."

He laughs. "And she's not even your mother."

I beg off going to the post-funeral lunch because of my persistent headache. "First let me show you what you recovered," Father Mik says, and leads me into his office. He kneels in front of a large, old-fashioned safe, spins the dials and swings open the door, revealing the two missing chalices.

"Keeping them in the safe instead of the cabinets now?" I say.

Father Mik chuckles. "Yes. And I am the only person who knows the combination." I lean down to gaze at them and even in the dark vault, they glow. They're a beautiful, if overly ornate, link to a past era of craftsmanship and refinement. "The church is indebted to you," he says. I wave him off and start to leave but step back inside and close the door.

"I need to talk to you a minute about Flora Maitland." Father Mik gestures at two easy chairs side-by-side in front of his desk. We both sit. "This past Monday I went to her apartment and found Emma all alone."

Father Mik's eyes widen.

"Flora left Porter in charge of her but he was gone when I got there. Emma's four and Porter's only ten. Are you aware Flora's doing this?"

He shakes his head. "I had no idea. I confess to not monitoring her children when she is here doing her training."

"Then on Tuesday I found Porter walking home after delivering early morning newspapers. The kid's wearing a spring jacket, it's super cold and snowing, and on top of that he's truant. He runs around all day scrounging money any way he can to help Flora."

Father Mik glances at the closed door and I realize he's concerned about someone hearing me, because in recounting Flora's neglect my voice has risen to a blare. I breathe and tone down my stridency. "In my job I'm mandated to report child neglect and abuse but I'm on suspension, so I've been letting this slide." My arms feel like bugs are crawling on them. I scratch at the creepy sensation. I have no excuse for not reporting Flora and I squirm at rationalizing this. "You've got to talk to her. She won't listen to me. Those kids are in danger."

Father Mik stands, puts his hand on my shoulder. "I understand, Dana. You're right, of course. I am afraid I became too involved in my own projects to provide little more than cursory supervision of Flora. I naturally assumed she'd secured childcare for the children when they weren't here with her. But if I had given it any thought, I'd have realized she doesn't possess the necessary resources."

Naturally. You're a man. A man who is not married. A man who has probably never considered what parenting is like for a woman with five children, a woman who can barely care for herself much less her kids. I stuff my snarky thoughts and stand to leave. Father Mik squeezes my shoulder and then releases it.

"Please don't concern yourself further, Dana. I will pick up Flora and the five children first thing in the morning and drive them to school. That way Flora and the little one," he snaps his fingers several times.

"Emma."

"Yes, Emma! After we drop off the older children at school then Flora and Emma can come here." Father Mik's thoughtfulness immediately makes me ashamed I dissed him.

I slap my forehead. "And that's another thing! Her oldest son went missing last Saturday. She told me about it two days later and hadn't called the police or done anything. Christ!" Too late, I remember to watch my language. When I apologize to Father Mik, he chuckles.

"I'll think of it as your invocation to ask our Lord to help, Dana."

We walk to the sacristy door. "I'll work on Flora's missing son."

"And I will speak with her about how I can help with the other four children. It would be the utmost irony if something happened to them at home while she's here working." Father Mik nods at the safe. "And thank you again for recovering our chalices."

"I'll feel better once we bring in the guy who actually stole them."

Father Mik nods. "My greatest hope is that he can shed light on what happened here that day."

29

Thursday, 11/28, 5:30 p.m.

I DRIVE to IOP in my almost-new Camry. Like wearing cashmere after only knowing polyester. My mechanic gave me the bad news that my Corolla's engine needed replacing. That, in addition to fixing the bodywork from being hit twice put me out more money than simply buying a used car. I'm strapped, but money from the sale of the house will come. After the funeral, I stopped at my parents' home to see if JJ could float me a loan for the car's down-payment until the house is sold. Evie threw a fit when he wrote the check but my father ignored her. With only three hundred miles on the demo, I took it for a test drive. The thrust of the V-6 engine, power everything, and the deep red exterior with cream-colored upholstery, swept away any ideas about frugal living.

I punch on the radio, search for and find some upbeat music. The program tonight at IOP is bridge group, whatever the hell that means. I realize it has been exactly a week since my accident and I grip the steering wheel a bit tighter. Even though I got so wasted on Tuesday

Rosie had to rescue me, I didn't touch a drop yesterday or today and don't plan on it tonight. I've got new wheels. And if Marvin gives us another drug test I'm pretty sure I'm okay.

Bridge group turns out to be more talking, surprise, surprise; graduates from IOP return to tell us how they're doing in the "real world." In the group therapy room a woman about my age stands at the podium with Jen. I recognize the others from our group but there are also about ten new people wearing hospital bands on their wrists. Hades settles next to me, lifts his chin in greeting.

I gesture at the strangers. "Who are..."

"They from the third floor, in-patient. Real sick people, need to be in the hospital to come off their drugs."

I take in this information and study the people wearing wristbands. Some of their faces have an ashy pallor, some have greasy complexions, and a few people seem nauseated and sit with their eyes closed. None are pictures of health. Jen calls us to attention and introduces the woman speaker. Hades and I both lean back in our chairs, arms crossed in front of our bodies.

"Hi, my name is Kendra and I'm a drug addict and alcoholic. My husband left me and the court awarded him custody of our children because of my drinking and drugging. But that didn't stop me."

God. Do they do this on purpose? I don't want to hear about her marriage problems; the pain of my own is too fresh. I turn inward and try to focus my mind on something else, anything to tune her out.

Flora's son Jump surfaces. Still missing. Four—no—five days now. Although he seems like a pretty tough kid who can hold his own, any missing child makes my skin crawl. The longer he's missing the greater the likelihood he has been abducted or murdered.

If he ran away to find his father, he would need money. He stole Porter's money and bike but how much money could the younger kid really earn from a paper route and collecting cans? Couldn't be much. If memory serves, Porter told me Jump took thirty dollars off him. Flora said Jump's father lived in Texas, which would be expensive if the kid went by plane. There's the train or bus, and those might be easier for him to access and pass through unnoticed, but thirty dollars wouldn't begin to pay his way.

And then it comes together: Jump stole the chalices. Probably gave the newspaper driver a cut of the three hundred for hocking them. That leaves plenty of money for a one-way ticket to Texas. Maybe he used Porter's bike to get downtown to the bus or train station. Or he could've sold that, too. I bet he's got my cell phone. Then I remember he wasn't there the day I lost it. Only the twins. But no, they were in the bedroom trying on the clothes I brought over. Emma.

I picture my jacket in the kitchen, my cell in the pocket. She probably took it out to play with like a toy because I had let her punch the keys. And I was so distracted worrying Emma would find my Glock in the other jacket pocket that it never occurred to me she took my phone. But somehow Jump got it from her, I'm sure of it. If only to hock it for more money. Or use it to try to find his father once he got to Texas.

I struggle to remember who Flora said she and her kids lived with in Texas but can't dredge it up. Someone related to her, I'm pretty sure. If nothing else, Jump could use my phone to call this person on his way to Texas or once he arrived there. Adrenaline pumps through me when I pull these threads together. It makes sense. And I'm quick to criticize myself because I've taken so long to figure it out. It also makes sense in connection with Martin Nygaard's death. The theft never seemed related and this theory supports the lack of connection. He somehow fell and hit his head—purely an unfortunate accident.

Kendra sounds like she's winding down her spiel when she says something that hits home. "What I really like about the tenth step is that I can continue to make things right with people I harm. Sometimes it's just a simple apology for my behavior—I don't always think about other people or their feelings, just like to barrel through my day," she says, then laughs.

I don't know anything about the "tenth step" she's referencing other than to assume it's part of the twelve steps. But front and center is my rude behavior Thanksgiving night toward Sandor, my building manager. I wonder if all it takes is an apology. Her remedy seems simplistic but I store it away for the next time I bump into him. I get ready to bolt for the first cigarette break but Marvin motions at me to come meet him. When I approach, he turns to walk out of the room and we come to a stop outside the doors. "What's up?" I ask.

"That's my question," he says, smiling.

We lock eyes. "Not sure what you mean, Marvin. I'm fine, clean, haven't touched a drop since Tuesday." Technically a lie, but he doesn't need to know that. "I haven't had a drink yesterday or today.

"Right. Good. You know IOP meets Monday through Thursday, right? I had to mark you absent yesterday. Didn't get a phone call you weren't coming."

Crap. He's right. I completely forgot about IOP last night. "I had to work and you're right, I did forget to call in about it."

"Work? Dana, the EAP tells me you're on suspension from your job while you're here." Marvin says this in a tired way—he has heard phony excuses too many times.

"Yeah, that's right. From my cop job. But I also freelance as a Sign Language interpreter. My parents are deaf. They asked me to interpret a wake for a close friend of the family." I throw in this last bit of fantasy hoping Marvin will give me a pass.

He doesn't.

"Don't matter the reason. Attending the program until it's over is one of the requirements you must follow. So it'll go in your file, which the EAP will get, and adds one more day to your treatment."

I start to protest this last part but Marvin shakes his head at me. "Save it, Dana. Here's the deal. The only reasons for absence are if you're too sick to attend or there's a death in your own family—like mother, father. Right? And you got to call to let us know at least an hour before we start, so by five at the latest. Then there's the urine drops— they're random, and in your case, expect 'em often. Got it?"

My punishment for skipping out on the first drop. "What if I'm absent again and don't call?"

"We let you slide one time, so that's how we count yesterday, your one time. But if it happens again, I'll have to inform your EAP you're non-compliant, which means you will—"

I cut him off. "I know what it means."

"Do you? Do you know it means you're finished here and the EAP tells your boss you failed treatment?"

And that means I lose my job. "When did we get this explained? I don't remember anything about these rules."

"More like expectations. Jen went over them the first night of IOP. And it's also spelled out in the packet of information you got then."

The small print Hades told me about that I haven't followed up on. The real possibility of losing my job ignites the acid in my stomach and for a moment I appreciate Marvin's direct approach, even if I don't like what it portends. I'm reminded of Abandonato's covering for me last week, deflecting CiCi's mother's complaint to Koz.

I give silent thanks to whichever one of the three Fates watches out for me, excruciatingly aware that dodging the same bullet on these two separate occasions is more luck than most people are granted. Of course, neither Abandonato nor Marvin were looking for a quid pro quo in helping me—no, only Fabrizio is leveraging my DUI for his own gain and I haven't exactly dodged his bullet. Yet. But if I consider it objectively, any one of these three situations would cost me my job on the force. Father Mik would attribute it to divine intervention.

My phone shows there are two more hours of programming before I can get over to Flora's apartment to talk to her about her son. Not a problem. If I'm right about Jump being in Texas, he'll keep until IOP is finished for the night.

The doors next to us open and people spill into the hallway and head for the elevators. I hold up the unlit cigarette in my hand, tilt my head toward the crowd, asking mute permission from Marvin to take a break. He dismisses me with a flick of his hand.

Outside, it's dark and cold and I huddle near the building to light up before I call the station house where Flora originally reported her son missing. Hades approaches me and starts to talk but I wave him off and lean against the building. "Can't talk now." I give my badge number to the detective working in Missing Persons and explain my theory about Jump and my missing cell. Working with my cell provider they'll be able to triangulate location of the phone via satellite, which I'm hoping is still with Jump. I leave them to it, explaining I'm a friend of the mother and they can contact her through me since she doesn't own a phone.

Hades falls in step with me on the way back into IOP. "Marvin give you the slap on the wrist 'cause of missing yesterday?" The smokers pile into the elevator but I hang back, not wanting to push my way into the crowded, enclosed space. Not real eager to get back to IOP, either. Hades waits with me.

"Didn't read that fine print you warned me about," I say.

Hades holds up his hand for a high five and when I respond with a quizzical expression he tells me most people don't read the program material. "Shoot, you ain't alone there."

"Marvin's pretty strict, didn't cut me any slack even though I had a good excuse."

Hades nods. "Marvin's okay, considering."

Once again, I'm unsure of what Hades means. "Considering what?"

The elevator dings and the doors slide open. One person walks out and we enter, blessedly the only two. "Marvin, when he a shorty, life pretty hard for him."

"Chicago?"

"Mmm-hmm. Mama a drug addict. She lock him up in his bedroom, leave him there for days sometimes while she's out using. His auntie finally got custody but not before Marvin's mama OD'd, died in the street."

I cringe. "While he was locked up?"

"They didn't find him for a week."

We reach our floor and head back to our seats for the remainder of the session. By the time IOP is finished at nine Missing Persons contacts me with Jump's location. He's back in Texas, staying in the trailer Flora and the kids formerly shared with her cousin.

Flora is underwhelmed when I arrive at her place to tell her the news. "I ain't got no money to bring him back here," she says, a frown on her face.

"You want to call your cousin? At least find out how Jump's doing?" I hold out my cell to her. Again, I'm struck by the woman's inability to think about her children first. Her primary concern—and what seems to be her sole concern—is how their behavior affects her. She takes the phone and I show her again how to use it, then slip out of my jacket because I feel overheated. I realize this is the first time the apartment actually feels warm.

"So. Sharf came through and got your heat on," I say. My call to 311 apparently gave him a kick in the ass.

Flora stops studying the phone and regards me. "Today's the first time. He banged on the door at eight-thirty wanting the rent money —scared me. He did something to that gadget," she motions toward a lockbox surrounding the thermostat, "and I'm telling you, now my nose don't drip all day long 'cause I'm cold. It ain't Texas but it's a lot better'n it was."

"Were you able to make the rent?"

Flora nods. "Father Mik loaned me what we needed." Flora heads to the kitchen to make the call and I can hear the twins playing in her bedroom. I notice Porter isn't here but don't pursue his whereabouts; I've done what I can. I move into the living room where Emma, still awake at ten o'clock, plays with the headless doll on one of the mattresses. I plop down beside her and point to the empty space between the doll's plastic shoulders.

"What happened to that baby?"

Emma pokes her fingers into the hole left by the missing head. "Jump stole her. Broke her head."

"Jump shouldn't do that to your baby."

"He's a pig," Emma says in a matter-of-fact tone.

"I see. Did he take my cell phone, too?"

Emma hugs the baby doll for a long moment and then throws her on the floor. "No." She turns toward me and her face is open and honest.

"Did you take my cell phone to play with, Emma? From my jacket?"

"I liked the buttons making music."

I smile at the little girl. Although I'm peeved about my phone, her unaffected manner charms me. "So did you give Jump the phone?"

She shakes her head. "I wanted the keys so I traded with Porter."

For a minute I'm puzzled but then remember his neck chain strung with the apartment and skeleton keys. Okay, one additional step from Emma to Porter to Jump, but my guess is still right.

Flora comes into the room and hands me my phone. "Jump's gonna stay down there with Irene. She'll send your phone back in the mail."

~

HUNGRY, I stop in at the Brau Haus on my way home.

Rosie waves at me from behind the bar. "Hola, Dana."

The place is hopping, a Thursday night celebration of the coming weekend. Music blares from the jukebox and the tables are full. I push in at the end of the bar and a guy gives up his stool, waving me to it.

Rosie finishes mixing a cocktail and plunks it on a tray full of draft beers. The floor waitress grabs it and hurries to her tables.

"What can I get you?" Rosie leans forward, her lower arms against the bar, silver hoop bracelets thick on her right wrist. I smile at Rosie, large and fake. My embarrassment still burns bright over waking up at her apartment yesterday morning because I was too drunk to drive home the night before.

"How about a brat and a beer? I'm celebrating. I found a lost kid tonight." I aim for light and breezy but beneath Rosie's perfectly applied make-up it's easy to tell she's worried I'll repeat Tuesday night's boozy performance. I like this younger woman and her generous, thoughtful handling of my welfare. And I don't want to be responsible for jeopardizing her job—she already put herself on the line once for me.

I cover her bracelets with my left hand for a long moment. "Make it a brat and a Coke, Rosie. I'm driving myself home tonight."

She rewards me with a brilliant smile of perfect white teeth set against crimson lipstick.

30

F riday, 11/29, 9:30 a.m.

"Yeah, Moochy's cooling his heels in lock-up. Picked him up when his apartment manager gave us a ring." Pete Christakos chuckles as he relays the news while I finish a breakfast of coffee and cigarettes.

"Great. Father Mik wants to press charges, so let him know."

"But get this, Dana. I'm bringing Moochy in and he's denying every which way he stole the stuff. Says he hocked it for 'a friend.' But he won't spill with a name. I tell him he's gonna be booked for robbery and possible murder, and he spouts like a fountain with the kid's name." His voice trips lightly over this information. He's happy to catch another criminal.

I explain my theory about Flora's son needing money to go to Texas.

"You think this kid's involved with killing the old man?"

I consider his question and recall how Jump beat up his younger brother—he has a vicious streak. Could a thirteen-year-old boy murder an old man? Sure. It happens often enough in Chicago, though not routinely, so it is possible. "I don't know Jump very well, Pete. Right now he's in Texas. I—"

"The kid's name is Jump?"

"Yeah." I carry my cup to the sink. "His mother calls him that because he's always on the move. I can't remember his real name, but—"

"It's Porter."

I freeze for a second. "What did you say?" I rinse out my cup.

"The kid's real name is Porter, according to Moochy. Why the hell don't people go by normal names anymore?"

"Moochy told you *Porter* gave him the stuff to hock?"

"Yeah, right. The kid's got a paper route and Moochy's the van driver. Dishes out the papers to the kids. They deliver 'em. Porter's only ten. Guess he knew he couldn't pawn 'em himself, gave Moochy a cut. Hundred bucks."

And he wanted to make a big score so Flora would be proud of her little man. Ten on the creep-o-meter. "I'm talking about another kid, Pete. Jump is Porter's older brother. But this makes sense." Porter said Jump stole thirty dollars from him. More like two hundred and thirty. That little shit. No more feeling sorry for him, but at least I can find out if anything happened between him and Martin Nygaard.

I grab my jacket and backpack, ready to leave, when a vacuum cleaner starts up in the hall outside my studio. Sandor. I know it's him because he's the only one ever doing any work in and around the building. God only knows what his wife does all day. Judging from the size of the pink bathrobe he was wearing Thanksgiving night, my guess is she calls the shots and he follows orders. I start to cross the room to escape through the back door. Then I stop and reconsider Kendra's words from last night about how apologizing, admitting when she's wrong, helps her stay sober. I get a tiny kick in the pants to leave through the front and face Sandor.

In the hallway, Sandor's back is to me as he vacuums at the far end. I lock my door and approach him. He must feel the thump of my tread because he turns slightly and acknowledges me with a glance, then goes back to vacuuming. I feel foolish and unsure of what to say but I step forward and tap him on the shoulder. He shuts off the machine.

"Yes, Miss?"

"Good morning, Sandor."

"Good morning, Miss." His normally cheery face is solemn.

"Sandor, I—last week, on Thanksgiving, you know—"

He waves his hand at me, a gesture to mean I should go no further. "We do not talk of this anymore," he says.

I'm unprepared for him dismissing my apology. But now that I've started I want to finish. "Please?"

He waits a moment as if considering something and then nods.

"Thanks. Last week, Thanksgiving night? I really wasn't myself. It was late. You know I was in a car accident? Pretty banged up and sore." God, why did I say that? Now he'll know I was drinking and driving.

"This is no good, Miss. You are like the man from the alley, no? Drink too much and he's lying in my back street, garbage all over. Is no good." Sandor's reminding me of a guy he and I found several weeks ago who was passed out in the alley next to the building's dumpster. When the ambulance arrived and hauled the guy inside, the EMTs told me he was a recurring drunk they picked up frequently around the neighborhood and transported to detox.

"No, no, I'm not like that guy, Sandor." But I stop and consider what he's saying. Just this week I drank so much I passed out while Rosie tried to drive me home. I wasn't in an alley, but passed out is passed out. And all that other shit about it being late, about the accident, about being banged up, is placing the blame everywhere else except where it belongs: on me.

His face shows worry and distrust. I try again. "Last Thursday I did drink too much, you're right. And I was so noisy I woke you up. And on top of all that, I was mean to you, swore at you."

Sandor nods slowly at my recitation of our midnight conflict.

"I'm sorry I did that, Sandor. And I promise you I won't do it again."

His cheerful countenance returns and he pats my arm, setting to his work without another word. I head down the three flights and leave the building through the front door, surprised I could concede to this little man I barely know that I drink too much. Is that why the admission to him is easier than with Jimmy or Nuts? Whatever the reason, my apology to Sandor leaves me with a curiously light feeling.

I arrive at Flora's apartment at ten-thirty. She's still in her pajamas. After letting me in she sits on one of the mattresses abutting the wall, a half-empty cup of coffee at her feet. A game show is on TV. Emma slings herself up and down the hallway, kicking a ball back and forth from the kitchen to the living room. No one else is home. I perch next to Flora. "I need to talk to you about Porter."

No response.

"Turn off the TV, Flora."

Emma's ball shoots out of the hallway toward us. "Emma honey, shut off the TV for mama." The little girl runs to the TV, pokes the on-off button, grins at me, then kicks the ball back toward the hallway. "What's this about then?" Flora gazes at the silent TV.

I relay the information from Pete Christakos. "Porter wanted to earn a big wad of money for you so he stole the church chalices and candlesticks. But Jump stole the money from him. That's how he got to Texas. Where's Porter right now?"

"He walked the twins to school and he's out doing odd jobs. I can't get these boys to do what I want, you know? They got minds 'a their own." She pulls at her long braid, worries the end with her fingers.

Flora's reaction to the news Porter has committed a crime is so muted I'm no longer surprised or dismayed, just fed up with her. "I'm going to wait here for him and then we all go to the police station. They'll question him and the delivery guy about what happened that day."

Flora hugs her knees to her chest and rests her chin on top. "You think my boy did something to that man? That janitor dyin'?" Her gaze searches the wall opposite us. Finally. Some semblance of concern about her kids.

"I don't know. But something happened up there and maybe Porter can help us sort it out. Go get dressed while we wait for him."

She stands with what seems like great effort even though she's petite and probably weighs all of ninety pounds. "Porter'll likely be home by lunch. Now I got my Link Card he don't got to scrounge and beg outside like before." She trudges to her bedroom and shuts the door.

Emma comes running down the hallway again, kicking and controlling the ball with surprising agility. She calls my name and at the last second punts it to me. I catch it in mid-air. Squealing and laughing, she throws herself down on the mattress beside me. Strands of her white-blonde hair float upward from her head and because the air in the apartment is warm, Emma's hair registers some static electricity. I spit into my palms, rub them together and smooth them over her hair to tame it a bit. Emma stares intently at me while I perform this minor ministration. "Did you brung us some doughnuts?"

I clap my hands to my cheeks and pretend to be shocked. "Oh, no! I forgot!" And it's not an act because I really did forget. The last time I was here I told her I'd bring doughnuts the next time.

"'At's okay. Mama forgets a lot, too."

I cup her rosy cheeks with both my hands and smile at her. What a sweet child, so quick with forgiveness. I'm not pleased to be equated with Flora, though. "Tell you what. When we take Porter to the police station we'll stop and get doughnuts. How's that?"

"Yay!" Emma jumps up and grabs the ball. "I know! I'll go down by the kitchen and you stay here by the door. We can play catch!" When Emma scampers away Flora comes out of the bedroom and heads for the kitchen. I get up and stand by the door as instructed by Emma, who has made her way to other end of the hall, and she tosses me the ball. We play like this for a while. As I snatch the ball launched by a strong kick from Emma the front door opens and in walks Porter.

He gapes at me for a moment and quickly backs out but I catch his upper arm and escort him to the kitchen where Flora is making grilled cheese sandwiches. Emma runs to Flora and hangs onto her leg, watching me stiff-arm Porter into a chair at the table. "Let's eat lunch before we do any talking. I'm sure these kids is hungry. They're always hungry." She gives Emma some paper plates to distribute, so I grab a place next to Porter while Flora shovels out hot sandwiches for each of us. We eat in silence for a short while. Porter finishes first.

"You want any more, little man?" Flora asks. He shakes his head and starts to get up but I press a heavy hand on his shoulder and force him back into his seat. He begins to protest. Flora cuts him off. "No, Porter. You got to stay and listen to Miss Dana. She's gonna ask you some questions about some stolen things, things from the church where mama helps out."

I review the day Martin Nygaard died and the absent chalices and candlesticks. "On Wednesday you told me lots of people went in and out of the parish hall that day. But I think Moira was right. You were the only one there. Your mom was working and you snuck inside."

Porter fingers his empty paper plate and shakes his head. Flora smacks her hand on the table and it wobbles. "Porter! Tell the truth.

Did you take them cups?" Porter doesn't flinch at the sound of Flora's hand. He flips the edge of the paper plate between his fingers.

"We talked to Moochy," I say. Finally, a reaction from Porter. He stands, picks up the paper plate and flings it like a Frisbee into the trash. I go to him and guide him back to his seat at the table. I clamp my hand onto Porter's shoulder and continue. "Moochy says you stole the chalices and gave them to him to hock. Says you gave him a cut of the money. He got one hundred and you got two hundred."

Flora gasps. "Porter! You didn't give me no two hundred dollars."

The temptation to smack this woman right in the chops is so strong I mentally handcuff myself. "Flora, I want to find out what happened. Let's stick to that." She must get something from the expression I shoot her because at least her next question is more in keeping with what a real parent would want to know.

"Porter, did you steal them things from the church? Did you?"

Porter shakes his head but doggedly refuses to look at me. I lean heavily on his shoulder. "Listen to me, Porter. We *know* you did it." I squeeze his shoulder for added emphasis. "There's a security camera on Moochy's van, shows you giving him the candlesticks and chalices." It's a lie, but it sounds plausible enough.

The boy's thin shoulder trembles under my grip and he bursts out crying. "I did it 'cause we needed the money. We ain't got nothin' and my mama needs it for food. I'm her helper, is all." He jerks his shoulder from my grasp and sobs into his arms folded on the table.

I pat him on the back and wait for him to stop crying. "Okay, okay. Take it easy. Tell me what happened." Between hiccups Porter lays out how he saw the chalices previous times when Flora set up the altar. He knew they were expensive because of the jeweled surfaces. When Flora went upstairs to find out what made CiCi run screaming for her mother, he took the chalices and buried them in the sandbox outside. The candlesticks were a bit trickier. He only had time to grab two of the six and because they were on the altar, he had to climb on a step-stool the altar guild ladies used. He hid them behind the huge stone angel outside the parish hall entrance.

At five the next morning he got his papers from Moochy and the two of them went to the church in the newspaper van. In the pre-dawn darkness, he retrieved the stolen items and gave everything to the van driver for safekeeping until they could go to the pawnshop. "Did you ever go upstairs or do anything with Mr. Nygaard, like talk to him?"

Porter shakes his head. "I never seen him that day. We played outside and the girls went in once or twice but I stayed outside." I raise my eyebrows at him. He looks away. "Mostly."

"And what about all of the people you said went in and out of the church that day? Is that true? Or were you trying to make me think it could be someone else?" Porter takes his time answering but finally allows that he lied. No other people went in or out of the parish hall during the time he and his sisters played in the churchyard.

"Okay. We're all going to the police station where Moochy is in jail. You tell the police exactly what you told me. Understand?"

Porter starts whining to Flora but again she slams her hand on the table, harder this time. "Don't you even start! You can't steal stuff 'cause we need it. It's wrong, Porter."

I'm relieved and somewhat surprised Flora is actually concerned about her kids and their behavior instead of solely how it affects her.

Huge sigh from Flora. "Now I got to pay that money back, too."

Oops. There she goes.

When we're ready to leave for the station Porter starts in again with complaints about how Jump stole the money from him. Flora interrupts him with a scold, grips his upper arm and tugs him into the hallway. I hold Emma's small hand and we follow them. It's way too late for Flora to put on a show of tough parenting.

31

Friday, 11/29, 9:00 p.m.

Cisco Kid's bar is stuffed between two shuttered storefronts and located on the seamier side of Howard Street, which on this Friday night throngs with people done with a backbreaking work week and looking for a little relief. Inside, only one word comes to mind: *dive*. The entire room is painted in flat black that swallows the colored lights beaming from canned fixtures suspended from the ceiling. The "bar" is fashioned from long planks of plywood erected on sawhorses and is lined with bottles of hard liquor and wine. On the floor, a large washtub of beer on ice reflects the kaleidoscope colors from the ceiling lights—a sparkling invitation hard to ignore.

I balk at paying ten bucks for a can of beer but the bartender explains it's in lieu of a cover charge. I take the precious drink, unopened, and make my way to a small table in the back. Not more than twenty people pepper the thin rectangle of a room. Even though it's illegal, several people smoke cigarettes and I happily add my stream to the atmosphere.

Four young men emerge from a door behind me and continue past our tables to an area in front. There's no stage or even a raised platform, just a haphazard clearing for the band. Buddy Nygaard takes lead position at the mike. He appears younger than when I met him at his father's wake. His shoulder-length black hair, parted neatly down the middle, hangs straight and loose. Baggy jeans and a cream-colored sweater add to his college-boy demeanor. Buddy loops an acoustic guitar over his shoulder and does some minor tuning, taps his foot purposefully four times and then hits an opening chord and launches into a spirited version of "That's All Right."

I listen to Barely There, the name of Buddy Nygaard's group, for about an hour and a half before they break and I'm pleasantly surprised because their music is much better than the surroundings. They play lots of cover versions of songs I like and even some original stuff written by Buddy.

My ten-dollar can of beer stays on the table, unopened, during the first set. I didn't drink Wednesday, Thursday, or today, and I feel heartened. Maybe it's the lifting of the mental fog Marvin described. But I'm still bothered by my actions at Brau Haus on Tuesday—I went there not intending to drink any booze and yet ended up so drunk I passed out. No control.

At the break Buddy encourages the audience to buy the group's recently released CD. Copies are stacked on a table next to where they perform. I grab the unopened beer and make my way over to him. "Hi Buddy. I don't know if you remember me, Dana Demeter? I interpreted your father's wake on Wednesday." I stick out my hand, determined not to let this guy ignore me a second time. He stares at my hand as if considering whether or not to shake it, then becomes animated and pumps it up and down. Too much.

"Yeah. Yeah, I remember you. How're you doing? I'm a little spacey after playing this set. Takes a lot out of me, you know? Hard to come back to earth sometimes."

I tower over his slight frame. His hair is as black as the walls of the room and now hooks behind his ears. Sweat dots his forehead. The echo of his mother's face peers up at me. "I'm sorry about your father's death, Buddy. I didn't know him very well but I remember him from years ago as a kid. I went to St. Nick's with my parents."

"Uh-huh. Well, that's more than I ever remember. I never met him. My parents divorced when I was a baby. Hold on a sec." He turns to a young woman waiting behind me and sells her a CD.

"So, uh, Dana. I appreciate you coming here to pay your condolences about my father but I'm kind of busy." He gestures at the CDs. "I need to tap a kidney, get a beer before the next set." He fingers his throat. "Pipes need some rest." He scans the room, an irritated expression on his face. "Hard to sing with all this smoke."

I offer him my unopened can. "I'm driving. Had to buy it to get in."

"Sure." He takes the beer and cracks it open, takes a long drink and sighs. "Much better. Thanks."

"One more thing." I point to a CD and pull out some money.

"Fifteen bucks," he says. I give him twenty and wave off the five he proffers in return.

"I didn't tell you I'm also a private investigator checking into the possibility your father was murdered. Part of a robbery."

A deep frown covers his face. He bows his head and looks at the stack of plastic CD cases in front of him, avoiding eye contact with me. "Murder? My mother told me he died accidentally."

"That's what the police think." That's what I think too, especially now that I know who stole the chalices. But Buddy's evasiveness interests me. "Some valuable things were stolen from the church and it's unclear whether it happened at the same time your father died or if they were two separate incidents. I'm trying to talk with everyone who knew your father."

"Like I told you, I didn't know him. My mother kept it a secret from me. I didn't even know about him 'til a couple of months ago."

I raise my eyebrows at this information. Martin Nygaard died sometime in the twenty-four hours after twelve noon on November ninth. Three weeks ago. That's when Edna Nygaard said she told Buddy about his father. "A couple of *months* ago?" I watch Buddy closely and while he doesn't show much facial expression, is really pretty flat in his affect, he still doesn't meet my gaze—eyes darting all around. I press him. "Is that when your mother told you about your father?"

At last, he chooses to meet my gaze. "No. I mean, she told me when he died. But I already knew he lived in Chicago. A couple of months ago my grandmother was very sick, thought she was dying. She told me the truth about my father staying at St. Nick's, said she never approved of my mother lying to me." He attends to straightening an already straight stack of CDs, muttering something.

I touch his arm. "I didn't catch that."

He looks up, his eyes red with tears. "My bad luck—he died before I could meet him." He spits out this last sentence with heavy sarcasm.

"Sounds like you're pissed at your mom."

He squints and inhales sharply. I think he's going to unload his obvious anger but then he hesitates and his shoulders drop. "You know, well, we live with my grandparents in a small town in Indiana. Lots of religious people. Growing up there, divorced families were considered scum. I guess she wanted to protect me." One of the band members stops by to say they're starting again in five minutes.

"At the wake I thought I heard you apologizing to your father. But maybe I'm wrong."

Before Buddy responds, he lifts my beer, drains it and crushes the can with one hand. "Yeah. Well. I really am sorry I never got to know him."

32

Saturday, 11/30, 8:00 a.m.

SATURDAY MORNING. My old neighborhood is silent, people sleeping late. A light snow drifts down and gives our house a solid, warm appearance from the outside. Well, solid if you ignore the large blue plastic tarp covering the side being built out for the now-defunct nursery. Lynn Patner hasn't erected a For Sale sign yet, though I expect one as soon as I finish today's job. I lug a box of cleaning items inside. My mood darkens when I realize I forgot the CD player in the car, so I re-lace my boots and go out to retrieve it.

Before returning inside I stop and gaze at the edifice I once called home and feel defeated. I don't want to clean this house. I don't want to prepare it for whatever happy couple wants to buy it. I don't want to sell it to someone else so they can live my imagined life. But I can't afford the mortgage and bills for this house, plus rent on my studio, plus the added cost of the renovation on top of everything else. I'm left with no choice about what I want or don't want. Seems to be a repeated theme in my life these days.

I climb the porch stairs and enter the front hallway, close the door, and deposit the CD player on a nearby table that collects odds and ends. The house is cold. I keep the heat down while we're gone but the build-on of the nursery isn't completely insulated, either. After upping the heat I plug in the CD player, put on some music, and begin with the living room. It takes four hours to finish the first floor and I'm glad to be done more quickly than I estimated.

I break for lunch and eat at the local deli a couple of blocks away. If we weren't working, Jimmy and I would sleep in on Saturdays and then start the day with thick Italian subs from this place made by a nice Italian man named Mario. Today the guy behind the cold cuts case is unfamiliar, the sandwich he makes for me a lot thinner. The light snow left on the sidewalk from this morning scatters at my footsteps as I head back to finish the cleaning. Half a block away from home I become aware of an African-American couple standing arm-in-arm, checking out my house. When I approach and stop next to them they both regard me but say nothing.

I gesture at the house and try to sound upbeat. "Nice place."

The woman pulls at a red wool scarf that's wrapped around her mouth and tied in back like a little kid's. "It is. It's exactly what we've been hunting for." She says this gazing up at her partner and her broad smile plumps up her high cheekbones. He bestows on her the warmest smile any woman could wish for. When he turns to me the warmth dissolves and he's all business.

"Do you live in the neighborhood?"

"I did. For ten years." I gesture at our home. "My husband and I are the ones selling the house." He looks askance at my work clothes— brief but noticeable—and I explain I'm cleaning the house so it can be shown tomorrow.

"My wife and I are very interested," he says. "Our appointment is first thing tomorrow with Ms. Patner to view your place but we were too excited to wait. Thought today we could at least check the outside and then walk around the neighborhood a bit." The woman nods and steps closer to her husband, clutches his arm and brings it close to her body. The motion tightens her knee-length coat against her waist. She's pregnant.

I swallow hard a few times to keep my tears under wraps and bend to re-tie the lace on one of my boots that doesn't need re-tying. I speak to the ground. "My name's Dana. Dana Demeter." I straighten up and we shake hands. "I wish I could show you the inside right now, but I'm really in the middle of cleaning—"

The husband waves away my excuse. "No, please don't worry about it. We'll tour it tomorrow. By the way, I'm Sterling Johnson and this is my wife, Barbara." She nods at me and gestures at the blue tarp on the second floor. "I understand you are remodeling?"

"Were," I correct her. "We—our lives changed." That's the best spin I can put on my life as it now stands.

Sterling Johnson frowns at the sidewalk and then regards me directly. "Why are you selling the house?"

It takes me a long minute to sort through a variety of answers because I don't want to lie to these people. I also don't want to acknowledge or touch on any of my recent failings. "To be frank, Mr. Johnson, we need the money. And the house, it's too much for only the two of us." I palm a slight wave at Barbara's mid-section. "But I bet it will fit you all perfectly. When are you due?"

Mr. Johnson abruptly puts his arm in front of his wife, as if to cushion her from a sudden stop, and the effect stays her response. I squint at him, not understanding his interruption. "Is this neighborhood changing?" he asks.

I'm surprised at the hard edge to his voice. "I'm not sure what—"

"My wife and I aren't unaccustomed to Chicago ways, Ms. Demeter. This is the first property we've viewed where the owner is white. My question is simple—has this neighborhood turned and now the white people are leaving? Are you selling to black folk because the neighborhood's gone bad?" He slides off the ear-warmers surrounding his closely shaven head and his hands worry them.

I squint at him again, take a deep breath and blow it out. "I'm a Chicago cop. I get what you're saying." I gesture at the homes on the block. "In the ten years we lived here this block has been very stable. Still is. And it's not all white. Pretty cosmopolitan, really. Our summer block parties are a kind of festival of cultures—amazing food." I count down each house within sight, enumerate the family's nationality, the number of kids, how long they've lived here. "Red-lining is alive and well in Chicago, Mr. Johnson. But not on my street. You and your wife and baby will be welcome here." I'm not sure if this mollifies him but his wife smooths both gloved hands over her baby bump and leaves them there.

"I'm due in Mid-March. We're having a boy. Depending on how long it takes for the remodeling, we'll move in either before or after he makes his grand entrance." Her voice is cheery and ends with a chuckle. Mr. Johnson slips on his ear warmers and regards his wife with another silent, warm look. The same look I remember from Jimmy when I was pregnant not so long ago, a look that reinforces every ounce of my loneliness without him. I shake myself with phony cheerfulness.

"Brrr. Getting colder. Gotta get back to work so you can see the house tomorrow. The neighbors are great—on both sides. I'm sure you'll love it here. Nice meeting you both." I take the porch steps two at a time to get inside quickly, then covertly watch as they stroll up the block arm-in-arm and stop to point at homes and chat.

My coat still on, I sit on the stairs to the second floor and experience a strong recurrence of my earlier envy of some non-existent home buyer invading my home. Except now my envy is quite specific: I don't want this woman, this beautiful pregnant woman, to enjoy my life, in my house, with her baby boy and her doting husband.

Two cigarettes and half an hour of self-pity later, it's obvious even through my haze of envy that Mr. and Mrs. Sterling Johnson are the perfect people to inhabit our home and bring a new life into it.

I start working on the upstairs rooms, saving our bedroom for last because I know it will be empty of Jimmy's things. I risk a quick peek into the unfinished nursery and enter. I walk around, my arms crossed against the room's chill. The workers have completed everything save one wall's insulation and drywall plus a bit of the roof. The deep amber of the oak flooring projects warmth. Two southern facing windows will brighten Mrs. Johnson's decorating scheme.

From the hallway the music on the CD player ends, a signal to stop with the self-pity and procrastination. I debate whether to put on another CD or go into our bedroom accompanied by silence, no distractions. But I can't face the room alone so I sort through the stack of CDs, find the one I bought from Buddy Nygaard last night, and slip it into the player.

I enter our bedroom. Definitely eerie. Some parts are normal. The bed is made and an old quilt from my grandmother is folded over the lower half. A t-shirt I wear at night is hooked on the desk chair as if left there this morning. But some parts are disquieting, jarring. Jimmy's closet door gapes open. Inside, a barren pole holds a few empty hangers, no shoes on the floor. The bookshelf next to our bed shows selected volumes missing.

Two pictures of us in happier times, framed and topping his dresser, still remain. A check of his dresser yields some clothes he left behind, I assume for me to donate to charity. The rest of his arsenal went with him to L.A.

I quickly clear the remaining stuff but in the last drawer, underneath some worn t-shirts, are a small stack of cards I gave him over our ten years together. I sort through them, smiling at some of the gags, surprised and touched Jimmy has saved them. At the bottom of the batch is an anniversary card from February of this year, right after I found out I was pregnant, two months before I miscarried. Knowing what I'll find inside, I open the card anyway and read my handwriting, large and loopy.

Happy tenth (!) anniversary babe, looks like practice makes perfect...this time next year we'll be knee-deep in diapers—can't wait! I love you, D.

Here is what I lost.

That Jimmy saved many of the cards from our ten years together comforts me for a moment. But as with the photos on top of his dresser, he left them behind; like the house, like our marriage, like me. I close the card and slowly tear it in half, then halve it again, methodically continuing until the pieces are too small to manage another go at them.

I lower myself onto the bed and survey the room: No tears, only a feeling as empty as the hollow echo of the house. We were so happy our first night here. And so punchy we stayed up late and played gin rummy until almost—

Buddy Nygaard's music cuts through my thoughts, his plaintive song matching my melancholy. I strain to catch the words. The song sounds familiar and could be one from last night. I stick my head out the bedroom door to better hear the song.

"...but I love you all the same."

I rush over to the stack of CDs and pull the liner notes from Barely There's plastic case to find the song that just ended. In a black font staring back at me are the words to the mysterious poem I found in the kitchen at St. Nick's.

33

Sunday, 12/1, 4:00 p.m.

FOR ONCE MY lousy housekeeping has stood me in good stead. I wave the crumpled poem—retrieved from behind my wastebasket where I'd thrown it last Tuesday—in Buddy's face. "Found this in the kitchen of St. Nick's—where your father died! I actually believed your sob story." I mock him with his own words, my voice drips with sarcasm. "'My bad luck. He died before I could meet him.' Oh, *really*?" It took me twenty-four hours to track Buddy down and I'm livid. He surprises me by backing into his friend's apartment to make room for me and I enter. "Buddy, I need to know what really happened at St. Nick's that day. It's obvious you were there."

He drops onto one end of a faded corduroy couch. I sit at the other. Buddy's long black hair, worn loose, swings forward when he juts his head out and studies the floor. "I don't know how my father died, so quit asking me." His declaration sounds weak.

I try a different tack. "You've got it pretty good, you know, for a kid who's fatherless. You're a young guy who's doing what he wants, playing lead in a band, producing CDs of original music, whose mother lets him live at home even though he's twenty-two." I pause hoping for some kind of response but he doesn't speak, only shakes his head. "Okay," I say, "let me tell you about some kids who don't have it so good."

I recount Jump's running away to Texas to search for his phantom dad, relate Porter's brush with the law because he took on the role of the missing father in his life. "At least you're doing something positive, making music. You're not a victim like these other boys."

Buddy Nygaard inspects his left hand and runs his thumb along the fingertips rough with calluses from playing guitar. "You can't close the door on ghosts," he says. "You think what you don't know can't hurt you? You can't miss what you never had? Not me. I missed my father so much I felt physical pain."

He wraps his arms around his waist and hunches over. I wait for him to continue but he's done talking. I shake the paper with the lyrics trying to contain my frustration. "How'd this end up in the kitchen?"

He starts rocking slightly on the couch. "When I went to the church I brought that," he nods at the sheet, "to show my father I didn't need him. To show him I had talent and success, throw it in his face to show him what *he* missed. "But there he was, just this sad old man. I couldn't stay angry. Really, I wish I'd known years ago so I could've saved him from that pathetic place."

"What happened?"

"I didn't know he couldn't hear. My grandmother didn't tell me any of that, only about his depression and that he stayed in a mental institution because he tried to kill himself. Anyway, I stood in the kitchen doorway saying his name over and over. He had his back to me and kept washing that, that..." his voice cracks, "...fucking coffeepot."

Buddy shakes his head. "At first I thought he was ignoring me." A weak grin. "I can be kind of self-centered sometimes.

"Then I thought maybe the water, you know, him washing, made too much noise and he couldn't hear me because I was talking to his back. So I went up behind him and tapped him on the shoulder." The skin on his face is stark white and tears again form in his eyes. "I must've scared the shit out of him because he jerked upright. Then the pot slipped out of his hands. It started to fall and he tried to catch it." Buddy thrusts his arms out in vague mimicry.

"But he slipped and fell forward," I say.

Propping his elbows on his thighs, he covers his eyes with his hands. "His head hit the corner of the sink and he went down with a crash."

"What did you do then, Buddy?"

He lifts his head, his dark hair framing his oval face. Light beard stubble clings to his cheeks and chin though his upper lip is bare. He appears much younger than his twenty-two years.

"I—I didn't know what to do. I felt totally confused, frozen. I mean, I finally see him and it's great but at the same time I got so down about his appearance. He looked so *old*. And then before I could even talk to him he's knocked out cold and bleeding like crazy. I got scared and tore out of there. I guess that's when I dropped my lyrics."

The simplest explanation is usually the truth. In Buddy's case, I believe him. He asks me what's going to happen now, if I'm going to arrest him. "Arrest you for what? I'm not a cop and I can't arrest you. I don't know what happens in this case." And I really don't. He is distraught and I want to help. "How about this? I'll talk to some people I know who can advise you."

Buddy swipes his hands over his eyes and pulls out a handkerchief to blow his nose. Some color has returned to his face. "Okay."

"But the way I see it, Martin Nygaard had an accident. A lousy, unfortunate accident." I scoot closer to him on the couch, touch his arm, and try to hand him the poem. "I'm really sorry about your father."

He waves his hand at the paper, doesn't take it; I tuck it in my backpack. "Thanks. Me, too."

"Father Mik hired me to find out what happened but it might make more sense for you to tell him yourself. Would you do that?"

He thinks about it for a minute. "I guess so."

"Good. I'll let Father Mik know you'll be in touch." I get Buddy's cell phone number to follow up with some referrals. As I stand to leave he stays on the couch, eyes closed, so I let myself out. Of course, I want to call Father Mik immediately but only so I can tell him the news and allow some kind of closure with this whole mess. My nicotine addiction needs attention first, so I light up as I exit Buddy's building, get into my car and start the engine to run the heater. I get the old priest on the line.

"I'm so relieved an accident caused his death, Dana. That sounds odd, doesn't it? What I mean to say is I'm relieved Martin wasn't bullied or attacked by someone, which resulted in his death."

"I get what you mean, Father Mik."

"And I have to admit I was wrong and your professional instincts were correct from the outset. Martin's death and the theft of our liturgical items were indeed separate incidents. Well done."

I literally duck my head at Father Mik's praise. His admission pricks at me, though. "Well, if we're being honest here, I really didn't want to investigate this, thought it was a waste of time." Father Mik is quiet. I lower my window half-way and tap my ashes outside.

"Think of Buddy, Dana. He found his father. And Edna can now be more forthcoming with her son about the whole of Martin's life, the ups and downs. God bestows on us a life. He gives us a full array of experiences from which we grow and become more human. You had a direct hand in that."

I take a deep drag on the last inch of my cigarette and pitch the butt out the window. I'm overwhelmed at Father Mik's parsing of my work and his interpretation. I don't reject his Christian spin on it, he is a priest after all; I just don't think about God like that, if ever. What does impress me is that I don't credit others the way he has just done, and then share such insights. I'm more apt to criticize and complain.

"I am curious, Dana, whether there are any legal ramifications for Martin's son? If, in a sense, he is partially responsible for Martin's death."

"I'm not sure I follow."

"Well, I'm thinking that Martin hit his head but we don't know if he died instantly or if he was only rendered unconscious. If the latter, then Buddy needed to get some medical help for Martin that might have saved his life. You understand what I mean?"

"Buddy left Martin there to die," I say, trying on Father Mik's theory. "You're saying he acted with a depraved heart, purposely knowing if he did nothing it would result in Martin's death."

Father Mik hesitates, humming to himself. "When you put it that way, it sounds so cold, so premeditated."

"Right. If Buddy intended what you're implying, then yes, he would need to answer for his actions. But I don't think that's what happened at all, Father Mik. He's what, twenty-two? He's a kid who inadvertently caused an accident and I don't find any malice in his actions."

"Yes, yes. Of course you're right, Dana. And maybe it's better to leave it as it appears, an unfortunate accident. He and his mother will be able to collect the insurance this way."

"True." I add that I'm going to talk to some lawyer friends of mine to advise Buddy further. I'm struck again with how Father Mik is kind to people—certainly not my default position. No one will ever know for sure if Martin Nygaard died a long, slow death or if Buddy calling an ambulance would have made a difference. Let well enough alone. I'm sure there's a Bible story in there somewhere but damned if I know what it is.

"Listen, I asked Buddy to come tell you exactly how it happened because I'm hoping you can talk to him about his father a little bit."

"Of course, of course. Happy to do so. I'm indebted to you for your help in both matters, Dana."

"Sure, Father Mik."

I'm happy, too. Even though I'm on suspension my skills have been sharp enough to solve the conundrum of the missing chalices and Martin Nygaard's death. Too bad I can't brag about the win to my boss.

I picture the priceless chalices Father Mik showed me, now ensconced in the sacristy's safe. They embody the history of Saint Nick's and anchor the church's past to the present and for future generations. A parent might provide the same continuity when a child enters the world, which marks the moment in their personal histories. Without the parent the connection is lost. Buddy, as well as Jump and Porter, must keenly feel the missed link of their absent fathers, although they might be hard-pressed to say so, or why.

I consider my own father and how generously he provided for me growing up and even now. These past few weeks he loaned me money to replace my car after loaning me his car and then Evie's car. That last one might have been too generous. Even though JJ was clearly upset and worried about my drinking, he never busted my chops about it or withdrew his love for me. Not something I can say about my estranged husband, my disgruntled former partner in Homicide, or even my mother.

34

Monday, 12/2, 10:00 a.m.

THE NEXT MORNING, I drop off my bill for interpreting to Angeline and check my phone calendar before pulling away from the Deaf Catholic Office. Surprisingly, the house closing transpires today in Evanston at eleven-thirty. The realtor was able to perform this minor miracle telling me that the couple was making an all-cash offer, which I guess makes it a breeze compared to arranging a mortgage.

An inordinate thirst continues to dog me since waking up with a slight hangover. After the emotional roller-coaster of the weekend— the last cleaning of our home and finally putting to rest what happened to Martin Nygaard—I wanted nothing more than to drink and relax last night, which I did. A small voice nags at me about the drinking but I push it aside. I didn't drink for four days, five if you include yesterday during the day. I'm clearly not the 'going on a bender' type of alcoholic Jen likes to describe.

Even though I've chugged through two cans of Pepsi since leaving my studio, a stop at White Hen provides me with the largest to-go cup of pop available. I guzzle a third of it, never sure if it's the caffeine or the sugar responsible for clearing out the hangover headache. I nose my Camry east on Fullerton toward Lake Shore Drive to continue north, glad the morning's rush hour is done. The Drive ends at Edgewater Beach. I take Sheridan Road and follow it past Loyola University until I round the bend at the cemetery and enter Evanston.

Inside the realty company's large suite of offices I approach the front desk where a woman stands chatting with the receptionist. The woman rushes at me. "Can I get you some coffee, hon? You could use some, I think. Yes?" Even though I haven't met her, I recognize Lynn Patner's distinctive voice. We introduce ourselves and I approve the coffee offer. The Patner woman pulls me toward a set of double doors leading to a windowless conference room. "We're in here."

Still in their coats and at the far end of a large oval table sit the African-American couple I spoke with Saturday. Mr. and Mrs. Johnson appear overwhelmed. Next to them a young man, an open briefcase on the table in front of him, speed reads a thick packet of papers. Across from the trio stands a young woman sorting a stack of papers into three piles and talking out loud even though no one seems to be listening to her. The remaining plush armchairs at the table are empty. "Guess my lawyer's not here yet," I say.

"Ms. Crouch called. She's delayed in court but will join us by speaker-phone afterward. Should be about half an hour." Patner hands me a stack of papers. "Why don't you sit over there and read these while we wait for her to call?" She nudges me to a chair across from the Johnsons before leaving the room. A few beats later another woman enters carrying a large mug of steaming coffee that she places in front of me. I beam at her with genuine gratitude.

Mrs. Johnson and I make eye contact and I wiggle my fingers in a slight salute, raise my mug in a toast. The coffee is heaven and I position the mug under my nose so I can inhale the glorious scent. "Thank you for agreeing to our price," Mrs. Johnson says to me.

"Sure. Glad we didn't haggle back and forth." The couple came in only three thousand under my asking price and I gave it to them. Their all-cash offer made it easy to be nice. My sense of urgency to be rid of the house parallels my anger at Jimmy. The sooner the house is sold, the sooner he and I can sever communication with each other.

The coffee ignites my craving for a cigarette so I head outside. I can barely tolerate the escalating wind coming off the lake, my phone telling me the temp has dipped to single digits, which is not unusual for winter in Chicago but still makes me wish I didn't smoke. I take quick, heavy drags to hasten the nicotine into my body and hurry back inside. The realtor hands me a single sheet of paper. "This came in for you while you were outside."

The message on the fax is from Jimmy, terse and unremarkable. It authorizes me to sign the closing papers for him and holds the inked mark of a notary public. After what seems like hundreds of signatures later, the couple hands me a check, and we shake hands. "My husband is in California and his house keys are with him but I can get them to you within a week," I say.

Mr. Johnson makes a slight waving motion. "Not necessary if you have yours today. We'll change the locks," he looks at his wife, "tomorrow?" She nods.

I unzip my backpack and unhook my carabiner key ring from inside. Ten years ago, when Jimmy had the keys made for the new locks to our home he bought two carabiners as key rings, one for each of us, his clear symbol we would be climbing a lot of mountains—together —in our marriage. "We're a team, D. Don't ever forget that," he said.

Seems like I'm not the one who forgot.

From the metal ring I slip off the keys to the front and back doors. Some of the carabiner's green color is scratched away, a result of friction over the years, leaving exposed silver. I hesitate, but then slide the two keys back in place and hand the green metal ring to the husband. "I hope you'll be happy in your home," I say, and mean it.

I go to the bank and deposit the check in our joint account. After paying off the mortgage we'll realize a profit of somewhere around fifty thousand, half of it mine. Not a retirement plan by any standard, still, I feel relief at the hefty balance in the account, a nice cushion and enough to repay JJ his loan. At home I re-heat beef stew and sort through the closing papers to file them in some kind of order, then check the time on my cell. There's a message waiting. "Hi, it's me." Jimmy.

"You'll be getting papers in the mail. Divorce papers. You can keep all of the money from the house. There's one condition; you can't contest the divorce. You do that, you keep the money, and we're clear. Let me know, either way." Then he's gone, no goodbye.

I delete the message and carefully place the phone next to the closing papers. I slump in the chair at my little corner desk. Smoothed out for viewing and re-taped to the wall is Buddy Nygaard's ode to his lost father. The card from Dorothy, the woman from A.A., is propped up against a book on the desk. Next to it is the airplane Emma fashioned out of a piece of paper that we sailed back and forth to each other.

My hunger for lunch is gone. I snap off the stove burner, scrape the stew into a storage container and stick it in the fridge. The two most important things in my life—that define my life—are my marriage and my work. Jimmy severed our bond, neat and quick, I imagine much like his jet to L.A. that rocketed off the runway at O'Hare. He has not looked back.

What I understand most about his filing for divorce is this: I can't lose my job, my life as a detective, my partnership with Abandonato. It is the last thing left to me and all I possess. I need to watch my drinking during the next few weeks—maybe limit it to weekends—so I can make it through IOP, get a successful completion. Based on that last message from Nuts, I'm hopeful my relationship with him is salvage-able because I want what he wants, maybe even more: to get back to our partnership and our work in Homicide.

And, so. Fuck Jimmy. Fuck *him* and his *girlfriend* and his soft fucking *life* in L.A. I picture the green carabiner key ring I surrendered this morning. We are no longer a team—I'm climbing solo.

I file the closing papers in my file drawer. Emma's plane catches my eye again and I pick it up, remembering how she folded it with such serious attention. Such a simple toy made her happy. And the memory of tossing it back and forth with her ignites a ripple of joy in me in spite of how I feel from Jimmy's terse message. I'm going to ask Flora if I can take Emma downtown to see the Christmas decorations, and make this little girl happy—which makes me happy—instead of dwelling on what I've lost.

A closer examination of the paper plane shows some print. Curious, I unfold the plaything. It's a sheet of letterhead from the Department of Human Services with the logo for the food stamp program. Number of Adults served: one. Number of Children served: six. Monthly allotment: $300.00.

I ball up the paper and toss it in the trash. I'll buy Emma a real toy tomorrow, something she can pick out and play with that's not as disposable as a piece of paper. As soon as I think this, I mentally tally Flora's kids: Jump, Porter, the twins, and Emma. Five. My stomach drops like I'm descending too quickly in an elevator.

Small inconsistencies at Flora's apartment resolve themselves, lining up evenly like so many teeth in a comb: Flora's weird explanation for the six mattresses in the living room; a boy's purple sweater hanging on the closet doorknob and missing later but Porter not wearing it; Emma playing with the bubble gum, empty wrappers next to the closet; pull-up diapers that Emma doesn't need. I snatch the balled-up piece of paper from the trash, grab my coat, and hustle to my car.

35

_____

Monday, 12/2, 3:30 p.m.

No one answers when I bang on the door of Flora's apartment. I call out Flora's name but again no answer from inside. I listen and after a minute hear little feet skittering in the hallway toward the front door. I knock again, this time more softly. "Emma? Is that you? It's me, Dana. Open the door, honey."

Behind the door comes the sound of a chair dragging across the floor and then the chain lock scraping in its track, more chair noise and finally the deadbolt clanks open. I grab the doorknob and open the door slowly, mindful of Emma. Inside, the little girl sits on the chair she used to reach the lock. I kneel down in front of the winsome child. "Hi, Emma. Are you alone again? Where is everybody?" Emma shakes her head making her long blond braids that trail over her chest slide back and forth with the motion. "Where's your mom?"

"She took Porter to the church." Instruction about the Ten Commandments, no doubt, especially Thou Shalt Not Steal.

"And she left you here alone?"

Again, Emma shakes her head. "Mia and Moira were 'upposed to stay with me but they went outside to play and told me to stay here." The twins weren't outside the building when I arrived. Emma's grey eyes are sad and she looks tired. But then she brightens. She lifts her thin T-shirt and reveals a concave tummy, tiny chest, and prominent ribs. Porter's keys on a chain rest against her impossibly white skin. "Mama made Porter let me wear his keys until they come back," she says, sticking out her chest in a proud display.

"What a big girl you are. And you're not afraid to stay at home alone, are you?" Emma stares at me for a long minute, then gives an almost imperceptible shake of the head. I close my large hands over her small ones and rub them gently because they feel cold. Where is Emma's pink coat? She's wearing clothes proper for Texas, not Chicago in December. The apartment was warm a few days ago. Now Sharf is back to his original, illegal, stinginess. Playing games with the heat is the kind of mickey-mouse crap I loathe. Why is it so hard for some people to do the right thing? I'll have to deliver higher level of ultimatum here. I drape my coat over Emma's shoulders and lead her into the living room where we stop at the closet door. I kneel down in front of her and cradle her face between my hands. Our eyes meet. "You're not alone here, are you Emma?"

Her only response is to undrape the chain of keys from her neck and hand them to me. The skeleton key fits the lock on the closet door. I open the door and the room's natural light floods the dark interior of the tiny cloakroom. On the floor is a light-skinned African-American boy clad only in a pull-up diaper. He wears Emma's coat sparingly— the hood hooked on his head with the body of the jacket trailing down his back. The boy rocks back and forth, his limbs painfully thin, eyes squinting at the light. He sits on the purple sweater.

Emma points. "That's Mickey."

36

Monday, 12/2, 4:00 p.m.

WHEN I TRY to lead the little boy from the closet it becomes painfully clear his legs won't support his weight, even in his emaciated state. I lift him in my arms and onto one of the six mattresses in the living room. He folds into a fetal position. Emma covers him with one of the torn sheets, showing tenderness beyond her few years. I consider whether to call DHS, the cops, or wait until Flora returns before setting anything in motion. There's only two hours left before IOP.

Marvin is silent while I relate the entire scenario before me, explain why I won't be at the program tonight. "I know you told me I only get one pass and I've used it up already but this has to be more important than me missing one more night. You should see this boy," I say, pushing that button for all it's worth. I bend down over Mickey and pluck the sheet from him, take his picture—careful to leave his face hidden—and send the painful pile of bones to Marvin's phone. "I mean, it's possible I could make IOP if I call the cops now, they come and take over. But I hate to leave these kids with someone they don't know—they've been traumatized enough, you know?"

A sigh from Marvin. "This city's a sorry, sorry place. But it's been that way a long time and not gettin' much better any time soon."

I make a noise of agreement. "It can get a little bit better right now if we do this for these kids." I say nothing more, not wanting to interrupt his thoughts while he gazes at the photo and imagines how Mickey got into this sorry condition. Marvin doesn't know I'm manipulating him, big-time, by dredging up his past trauma at *his* mother's hands. For me though, IOP has to come in second after these kids, especially Mickey. God, I don't even want to know how long the little boy has been stuck in this closet like a forgotten shoe.

Marvin makes a strangled sound, a reaction to Mickey's picture no doubt, and I know I prevail for now, get a reprieve from IOP tonight. "You got to put yourself first, Dana. That means no work is more important, no emergency, no nothin' comes before you gettin' sober. The city can wait a few months while you get your head on right." Marvin's voice is stern.

I glance at Emma, now lying on the mattress next to Mickey, petting his hair in soothing strokes. She uses my jacket to cover both of them. Mickey's eyes are closed. I can't believe Marvin's *not* going to give me a pass tonight, but before I can ask for clarification, he capitulates. "This is between you and me, nobody else, got it? Stay with those kids and keep 'em safe—I'll mark you present for tonight, but no more. You know the consequences and I'll make sure they happen." He disconnects before I can thank him.

I make the call to DCFS and put in motion the process to investigate Flora's abuse and neglect of her children. I kick myself for my part in it, for waiting instead of acting, for not reporting Flora at the very first sign. I settle for calling the Department of Buildings to come inspect this stinking structure with the hope they'll ticket the numerous violations and take the owner to task. It is the least I can do.

37

———————

T uesday, 12/10, 9:00 a.m.

I PUSH AWAY my platter holding the remnants of a three-egg omelet and not much else. Hash browns, two pieces of rye toast and three sausages, all gone in a rush of eating. Comforting while I downed the food, now all that's left is a queasy feeling from overeating and the renewed promise to do better tomorrow. The waiter refills my coffee. Father Mik pushes his congealed oatmeal off to the side, half-eaten. "How's Mickey doing?" I ask.

"He's still at Shirley Ryan. He'll have to be there for quite a while, I'm afraid. We're fortunate to have their AbilityLab right here in Chicago where he'll get world class treatment. The boy is severely undernourished and of course can't walk because of the atrophy in his legs. Unfortunately, his arm is also broken."

I furrow my eyebrows at this news and posit a questioning expression on my face. When I watched the paramedics take Mickey from Flora's apartment and put the eight-year-old into the ambulance his arms were wire-thin but they weren't broken. Father Mik reads my non-verbal question and nods.

"When he first arrived at the hospital for observation and testing, they put him in a bed. I imagine the poor boy was scared to death. He tried to get up but his legs couldn't support his body and he fell."

"What's going to happen to him? Won't Flora lose custody because of the abuse and neglect?" The busboy arrives and Father Mik pauses while the young Latino guy clears our table. I realize he's the same kid I coerced into pouring the shot of ouzo for me. I think he recognizes me too, because he ducks his head and avoids any further eye contact before whisking away our dishes.

"I've been thinking about that. There's a new initiative in our Archdiocese calling for increased social action at individual parishes. It's administered by Catholic Charities and called One Church, One Child. Some churches are opting to support children in foreign countries, others are raising money for children's charities in Chicago. St. Nick's hasn't committed to any specific project yet but Mickey has given me an idea."

Father Mik tells me about a deaf couple at his church who foster children with disabilities. "I'm going to approach them about taking Mickey into their home, then ask if the congregation will become a group sponsor and raise money for his on-going care and rehabilitation." I love the idea and tell the old priest so.

"The world may conspire against the weak and helpless, Dana, but we can also push back with love and caring." I appreciate what he's trying to tell me. I'm horrified at the mess Flora has made in the lives of her six children. Hell, she'll be lucky to get any of her kids back.

"That reminds me," I say. "When Flora finally got home and knew I discovered her little secret, she tried to justify why she kept Mickey in the closet. She said he didn't listen to her and she couldn't make him behave. I'm thinking he might be deaf. I doubt she took him to the doctor to check his so-called 'hyperactivity.' The same with school, so

I'm pretty sure he never had a hearing test. And Mickey doesn't talk. If he could hear, he would've picked up some basic words from his brothers and sisters when they brought him out at night to sleep."

Father Mik nods. "I fear you are right, Dana. Of course, his hearing had to be screened as a newborn—all the states require it since the new millennium."

"Oh, right. The Feds. I forgot about that. Of course, that's assuming Flora had Mickey in a hospital. She's so poor it's likely she gave birth at home using a midwife."

Father Mik nods again at my assessment. "It appears Flora never sought out services for Mickey after his birth. The child will have many obstacles to overcome. I am going over to the hospital after this to visit him. Do you want to accompany me?"

I shake my head. I can't face the emaciated boy and his decimated body. I can't lose the image of little Emma hysterical when a DCFS worker lifted her into the emergency services van, her arms straining for her mother. I become furious at Flora all over again and I'm exhausted from being angry, at her, at Evie, at Jimmy. I want a break from people. Period. "Maybe another time," I tell the old priest.

Father Mik gazes at me. What I'm feeling must be reflected in my expression. "You know, I am struck with what I think of as God's hand in this, Dana. Your work uncovered an untenable situation for Mickey. You saved that boy's life. Certainly not a waste of time."

I am quiet. Father Mik's words are soft, comforting, and penetrate my sadness about Flora and her kids. This is the second time I hear from him I'm doing God's work; too bad it feels like hell. I drain the rest of the coffee in my cup and push away from the table. "I need to go pay a debt. Take care, Father Mik." He stands and we hug. I make my way to the front of the restaurant and find our waitress, give her a generous tip and ask her to split it with the busboy. I take a moment to adjust my backpack, the check to repay JJ's loan tucked inside.

As much as I need a break from most of the people in my life, when Marvin excused me from IOP last night to stay with Emma and Mickey, his understanding gave me a bump of hope. However, I am clear he won't excuse me again, phone call or no phone call, no matter what the extenuating circumstances might be. One more absence and I'll be kicked out of IOP, Koz will get the notice, and my career as a homicide detective in Chicago will be over—the last thing I want.

Lu Fabrizio's dirty 45K, now in five separate CD accounts bearing my name, lingers in my thoughts. I'll be forced to deal with him three months from now—but there's no way I'll help him launder that money. Exactly how I'm going to stop him from getting one over on me remains to be figured out.

Tonight is one-on-one counseling with Marvin and I'll be there—not going to count on any more luck. Hades told me once, "You make your own luck." I'm inclined to agree with him. I'm in the mood to unload all of the crap that's happened in the past few days. Sixty minutes with Marvin might not be enough time.

When I head outside, a homeless man sporting a large button displaying the name JIM stands on the sidewalk opposite the restaurant doors, making it hard for exiting customers to avoid him. His singsong voice is a gravelly bass.

"*Streetwise*, get your *Streetwise* paper here." He rattles a copy of the rag at me. "*Streetwise*, Miss?"

I pull my jacket close to me and glance at the bad news emblazoned on the paper. I look away.

"Not today."

IN CASE YOU MISSED IT!

Read *Signs of Murder,* the first Dana Demeter mystery!

Coming from an all-Deaf family, Dana Demeter assumed a position of authority at a young age: interpreting for her parents, alerting to sounds that meant trouble, and absorbing slights aimed at her deaf twin brother. A protector.

Now as a Chicago homicide cop, matters beyond Dana's control begin to pile up: her father's deaf friend is murdered and the lead investigator rejects her help, bungling the case; Dana's husband refuses to return home until she deals with her grief over a miscarriage; and her Lieutenant suspends her citing a claim she was drinking on the job. A bogus claim.

Can Dana bypass the lead detective and solve the murder on her own? Will she face her personal loss and save her marriage? Does she agree to alcoholism counseling to keep the job she loves? Dana struggles to conquer these challenges, unsure until the end whether to embrace defiance or submit to the status quo.

PRAISE FOR SIGNS OF MURDER: A DANA DEMETER MYSTERY #1

Best book I've read in a while, and I read a lot....a clever and complex plot....(and) an all-too human and flawed protagonist (who) feels like a friend. *Signs of Murder* is crime fiction with a heart.

KRIS CALVIN, AUTHOR, *ALL THAT FALL*

(A) satisfying mystery with an interesting, complex main character....all these threads work to build a satisfying story that was fun to read.

PAULA MIKRUT, AUTHOR

Great read! This suspenseful novel kept us coming back for more!

MARYBETH HUGHES, FAN

Buy now on Amazon: Signs of Murder

ACKNOWLEDGMENTS

My poetry prof Dirk Jellema once told me, "Whitehouse, all writing is re-writing." He was right.

In that spirit, my thanks to the following people who helped this novel evolve into a much finer effort:

Karen Burgess, my first beta reader, whose insight and honest critique changed the focus of the story.

Bob Carty, my husband, whose careful reading discovered, among other things, a major hole in the plot and helped me fill it.

Walter Whitehouse, my oldest brother, whose eye for detail provided much-needed amendments, especially regarding the Catholic Church.

I am deeply indebted to Mark Burgess for designing an outstanding book cover for this novel, as he did for my first Dana Demeter mystery. In this case, you *can* tell a book by its cover.

Thanks to Diane Piron-Gelman, Word Nerd Editorial Services (word nrd.com).

Finally, I want to acknowledge you, the reader, for taking precious time to read my work. Your support means a great deal to me.

ABOUT THE AUTHOR

A. F. (Addy) Whitehouse is a writer and a former Sign Language interpreter who hails from Chicago. She lives with her husband, Bob Carty, in a distant suburb.

Please visit my website: www.afwhitehouse.com

facebook.com/afwhitehouse

twitter.com/addyfran

amazon.com/author/afw